W9-APY-568

GAME OF STRENGTH AND STORM

RACHEL MENARD

Rachel Menard

flux
®
Mendota Heights, Minnesota

Game of Strength and Storm © 2022 by Rachel Menard. All rights reserved. No part of this book may be used or reproduced in any manner whatsoever, including internet usage, without written permission from Flux, except in the case of brief quotations embodied in critical articles and reviews.

First Edition
First Printing, 2022

Book design by Karli Kruse
Cover design by Jake Slavik
Cover illustration by S. Charlton (Beehive Illustration)

Flux, an imprint of North Star Editions, Inc.

This is a work of fiction. Names, characters, places, and incidents are either the product of the author's imagination or are used fictitiously, and any resemblance to actual persons living or dead, business establishments, events, or locales is entirely coincidental. Cover models used for illustrative purposes only and may not endorse or represent the book's subject.

Library of Congress Cataloging-in-Publication Data
Names: Menard, Rachel, 1979- author.
Title: Game of strength and storm / Rachel Menard.
Description: First edition. | Mendota Heights, Minnesota : Flux,
    [2022] | Audience: Grades 10-12. |
Summary: Seventeen-year-old Gen and eighteen-year-old Castor of Olympia race to
    be the first to complete six nearly impossible challenges to obtain their greatest
    desire, and only one will win while the other walks away with nothing--if she walks
    away at all.
Identifiers: LCCN 2021059182 (print) | LCCN 2021059183 (ebook) |
    ISBN 9781635830767 (paperback) | ISBN 9781635830774 (ebook)
Subjects: CYAC: Magic--Fiction. | Contests--Fiction. | Ability--
    Fiction. | Human-animal communication--Fiction. | Fantasy. |
    LCGFT: Fantasy fiction.
Classification: LCC PZ7.1.M4699 Gam 2022 (print) | LCC PZ7.1.M4699
    (ebook) | DDC [Fic]--dc23
LC record available at https://lccn.loc.gov/2021059182
LC ebook record available at https://lccn.loc.gov/2021059183

Flux
North Star Editions, Inc.
2297 Waters Drive
Mendota Heights, MN 55120
www.fluxnow.com

Printed in Canada

To my dear friend, Arleen. You were a true word artist.
Thank you for helping me to paint better with mine.

CHAPTER 1

GEN

Gen had grown accustomed to wearing soggy boots. A small price to pay for low cost, efficient sea travel. Crossing the ocean by whale truly was the best way to do it, and she normally didn't mind her cold, wet feet, or the salt stains on her pants, or the smell of fish that clung to her, or the bits of seaweed that tangled in her hair. Today, though, she would have preferred something a little drier.

Another glob of fish guts dropped from the roof of the infinity whale's mouth onto the shoulder of her jacket. Under the luminescent glow of his skin, the fish guts left a glimmering, blue smear on her sleeve. "Can you please swim more carefully?" she asked him.

Can you please swim more carefully? he snapped back, the retort ringing very clearly in her mind through their shared, mental connection, with just the right amount of petulance.

This was a new trick he'd learned, to mock her, and Gen couldn't completely blame him for it. Whales were whales. They did whale things. Every annoying human trait he had, he had learned from her. She would have to watch her mouth around him. And her thoughts, which was harder to do.

She brushed the fish scales from her sleeve. She didn't usually invest in new clothes for this reason. She'd spent two days uncovering a nest of slumber bees on the island of Hypnos to earn the coins for this jacket.

A tavern on the isle had been completely infested with the bugs, and anyone who tried to find the source of the hive quickly dropped off into insect-induced narcolepsy when they were inevitably stung. The tavern owner needed a MindWorker, someone like Gen, who could simply ask the bees why they were congregating in the bar. It turned out the queen bee had been trapped under the floorboards. Once Gen freed the queen, the bees left, and she collected her sack of coins. Then she went to the nearest tailor to find something nice to wear.

This jacket, which currently looked like it had been dredged from the inside of a fish barrel.

"Why do I even try?" she asked Chomp.

The squat, round, purple-haired mutt by her foot didn't stir. He had found a soft, warm patch of whale flesh to sleep in when they left Hypnos, and he hadn't moved since. She nudged Chomp in the ribs, and he flopped onto her pants. Some of his purple hair stuck to the salt water on her hem, adding to the mess.

She threw her arms in the air. "I give up."

"Play the part," her father had always said in their circus. "Show them the dream, not the reality."

Gen's life had never been perfect, but it had been much closer to it when her parents had been a part of it. In Alcmen's Amazing Animals, the most acclaimed circus in all of Olympia, they'd hidden the loose strings behind the curtains, covered the patches on their costumes with sequins, and hung banners across the tent walls to conceal the holes.

They'd had a ship then to travel from island to island, city to city, show to show. A beautiful ship with a carving of Gen's own mother on the prow. On the *Scylla*, whale slobber hadn't been an issue. Gen had slept in her own cabin with a closet full of fine jackets, boots, and dresses protected from the whale who swam alongside the ship. Their other creatures roamed the decks. Gen often awoke to chatter squirrels under her bed or chameleon monkeys scurrying across her ceiling.

Everything had been in perfect, chaotic order.

The whale gave a short whine, and Gen snapped her head upright. *We're here.* He sent the message through their mental connection.

Thank you, she sent back.

He flipped his tail and they rose upward. Gen could already feel the pressure release from inside the whale's mouth. His blowhole opened, and he sprayed rotten fish bones into the air. They lifted out of the water, and the whale wriggled his tail to push them into the shallows. He yawned his mouth wide, seawater flowing from the top of his jaw, and Gen blinked in the brilliant sun.

It had been a while since she'd been to the great isle of Athenia. The capital of all one hundred Olympian isles and the home of the Empresses sat in the southeast quadrant of the Empire. Gen usually took great care to avoid it and kept to the other isles, clinging to the outskirts like an unwanted pest.

As long as she didn't bother anyone, they usually didn't bother her, and she was tolerated when they needed something of her—like someone to clear out a hive of slumber bees.

It did not used to be that way.

Her father had once been the best MindWorker in the world. With a few drops of blood or some plucked hairs, he could control an entire ship full of creatures. Gen and her family had been as close to royalty as people with no lineage could be, revered for their skill.

Little had any of them known their downfall had been planned long before they'd been born.

A thousand years ago Hippolyta, Queen of the Mazons, scorned her Gargarean lover. The leader of the Gargareans declared war, and the silver-skinned women warriors and the golden brutes had been fighting for centuries. Four years ago, it all came to an end with the Gargareans annihilating the entire Mazon race . . . including Gen's mother.

Three months later, Gen's father had been arrested outside of a tavern, covered in blood, with a room full of dead Gargareans behind him. The tavern owner testified before the Empresses that Alcmen had been the one to kill them.

"He came into my bar and started spraying the Gargareans with his own blood. Once he did that, the Gargareans turned on themselves. But he made them do it . . . I saw it."

This was the piece that didn't quite fit because Gen had the same ability as her father—somewhat. She didn't have his level of control, but she had to adhere to the same rules.

"You never use mind magic on people."

It had been Alcmen's personal mantra, and he had instilled it in Gen repeatedly, not purely for the ethics behind it, but because it was difficult to control a sentient being. It became a game of will versus will, and if the subject had stronger will than the MindWorker, they could turn the connection.

Other factors also came into play: the skill of the MindWorker, the stubbornness of the subject, and the matter being influenced.

Gen's father possibly had the strength and skill, but the Gargareans were the most stubborn race in all of Olympia. They had fought a thousand-year war, and trying to convince someone to kill themselves or one of their friends would require mass amounts of blood and influence.

So, for things to have happened the way the tavern owner claimed they had, Alcmen's desire to kill the Gargareans would have had to outmatch their desire to live. He also would have had to feed each of them a cupful of his blood without fainting from weakness, and temporarily suspend all of his morals to do so.

If all of those conditions were met, he maybe, possibly, could have done it.

But he hadn't. Gen knew it with every piece of her soul. Not that it mattered what she thought. When Alcmen went down, he took all MindWorkers with him, and Gen fell the hardest. She was the daughter of a convicted murderer, one with the same ability. She might as well have been imprisoned with him.

At thirteen, she had become an orphan and an exile. And for the past four years, she had entered her name in the Olympian Empresses' annual lottery. The Empresses were the only ones who could overturn Alcmen's conviction, and they would only grant her the request if she won the lottery. Without them, she had no other options except to live forever in exile while her father rotted in prison.

This year, she had finally been chosen. She could make one wish of the esteemed rulers, and she would wish to free her father and clear their names. They would get their ship back, and their circus, and start rebuilding their lives together.

"Time to wake up." She nudged Chomp with her boot, and her purple chaeri yawned with a mouthful of pointed teeth.

She picked up her bag and pulled three black hairs from the top of her head. She felt a small patch of bare skin there. Whoops. She had to be more careful about varying her pulls. Thankfully, she'd gotten a new hat to go with the jacket.

She removed it from her bag, placed it on her head, and dropped the three hairs onto the whale's tongue. As soon as she did, the whale sent her a surge of emotion. Hunger, for one. Not a surprise. He couldn't eat while Gen and Chomp were in his mouth, not without drowning them.

"Go get yourself something to eat," she said to him. "I'll call when I need you."

She slung her bag over her shoulder and whistled to Chomp. They walked across the whale's spongy tongue. Ducking under the curtain of water running off the whale's mouth, she stepped into the shallows, seawater soaking into her boots.

A small crowd had gathered on the beach to admire the whale. Infinity whales didn't usually come into water this shallow. They kept to the deep where they could catch the most fish and stay hidden from whale hunters.

Even though it was illegal to kill the whales, poachers roamed the sea. It was said drinking the blood of an infinity whale could make you live forever.

Not true.

It might extend a few years, reduce a few wrinkles, but it couldn't make someone immortal. Still, people would pay quite a bit of coin for the promise of those extra years.

Most people, however, like the ones gathered on the beach, simply wanted to see an infinity whale. In the sunlight, Gen's whale glimmered blue and yellow, like the surface of the water at sunset. Gen and her family used to arrive in every town this way, emerging from inside the whale's mouth to an eager crowd. The people would cheer and clap, hoot and howl. For some, it was their first time seeing the circus. For others, it was their hundredth time.

But now, as Gen emerged from the whale, no one clapped, no one cheered. Some gasped, some shrieked, some glared. She sighed. It was a stupid thought, but she always held some infinitesimal bit of hope that she would show up somewhere and no one would recognize her, or hate her.

Since Alcmen's greatness had reached so far, when he dropped from his pedestal, he left a great dent behind. Gen and all MindWorkers had become something like a walking poison. The people expected her to start spraying them with blood and forcing them to murder one another. She couldn't even begin to discuss how vile or impossible that was.

"Come on, Chomp." She waved the chaeri forward, and the lingering crowd parted to let her pass.

"Disgusting," someone whispered. "They should all be jailed."

"Monster," someone else said, not as quietly.

Gen tugged her hat lower and sank into the collar of her jacket, yanking the sleeves over the silver bands on the backs of her hands. They made her too recognizable. The only race in all of Olympia with silver coloring had been the Mazons, who were all dead thanks to the Gargareans. The Mazon-ness she'd earned from her mother was the last piece of an entire race, and a beacon pointing out her existence.

"Don't look at her," a woman said, and dragged her child away by the wrist.

Gen raised her chin and walked faster, choking down her agony. She had shone in the circus, adored by all. Surrounded by all this hate, she dulled to an abysmal gray. After today, though, they would have to stop hating her. Once the Empresses recanted

Alcmen's sentence and set everything right, they would declare to all of Olympia that MindWorkers were safe.

And no one defied the Empresses. Not if they enjoyed breathing.

Gen marched quickly toward the palace through the colorful booths, performers, guests, and attendants all here in honor of the Empresses' birthday. In the center of it all sat a large, blue-and-white striped tent. Gen swallowed hard.

Her family used to perform inside that tent, every year on the Empresses' birthday as far back as she could remember. Except the past four years.

She kept walking, past the man swallowing fire and the dancers who swung from colorful vines, then to the food booths. She hesitated when she breathed in something sweet—small, frosted pink cakes on sticks. Grouseberry pops. Oh how she missed those!

The woman selling them tried to hide behind the counter when she saw Gen, but would she outright refuse to sell her one? If she wanted her to go away, the fastest way would be to give her a cake and send her off.

"He's so cute." A little girl with bright, pink skin and red pigtails knelt next to Chomp, hand outstretched.

"No!" Gen shouted as Chomp snapped at the girl with a mouthful of razor teeth.

The girl yanked her hand back and burst into sobs.

"Sorry," Gen called. "Sorry." Too late. The girl scampered up to two adults, one of them quite large and menacing, and not appearing to be at all afraid of Gen or her temperamental chaeri.

"Time to go." She grabbed Chomp by the scruff and dragged him toward the palace bridge. "If you don't behave yourself," she said through her teeth, "I'll feed you a cup of my blood and force you to cuddle every person here."

Blood was a more effective tool than hair; that part of the rumors about MindWorkers was true. With blood, she could control her unruly chaeri . . . not a roomful of Gargareans. She'd stopped influencing Chomp years ago. She thought they'd reached an understanding. She wouldn't feed him hair. He wouldn't bite children.

"That's her," someone else said as she passed. "The murderer's daughter."

Gen clutched Chomp under her arm and made her way to the palace.

She stopped at the edge of the bridge, taking in the entirety of the sleek, golden spire of the Empresses' tower. They called it the Beacon of Olympia. The four pillar stones at the entrance were each marked with a diamond shape to represent the four Oracles who had formed Olympia more than ten thousand years ago.

Hecate, Oracle of the Spirit; Tartarus, Oracle of the Sky; Ponos, Oracle of the Earth; and Keres, Oracle of the Mind. The four Oracles gave Gen and others their abilities. Even before Alcmen's downfall, people had been wary of MindWorkers.

Keres, the Oracle attributed to Gen's gift, had once taken a human lover. Her lover then fell in love with her sister, Hecate. Feeling betrayed, Keres sent a chimera to eat Hecate and the human. When Keres's brothers, Ponos and Tartarus, retaliated against her for killing Hecate, Keres invaded their minds and turned them against one another. Ponos and Tartarus murdered each other, and Keres, once she had seen what she had done, killed herself in grief.

Images of Keres were always depicted with sharp teeth and claws, and her story was told as a warning against wickedness.

Gen didn't want to be the villain. She wanted to be the star.

"Let's do this," she said to Chomp, and took her first step toward salvation when a boom of thunder shook the stones.

Gen gritted her teeth and slowly turned her eyes to the sky. A golden chariot looped through the clouds, pulled by two winged horses dressed in jeweled bridles and plumed headdresses. At the helm of the chariot stood a woman with pale white hair, snow-drop skin, and a glittering cape flowing behind her. Lightning crackled in the palm of her hand, the light of it glinting off her perfect smile.

"Of course," Gen whispered. The Storm Duke's daughter.

The StormMakers had played a part in Gen's downfall too. Gifted with the power of storms from the Oracle Tartarus, they'd always had a bit of an ego on their shoulders. At ten years old, Gen had performed a show for the Arcadian court, her first solo act with Chomp. She'd made him a special hat with bells to match her own. She'd practiced their act for hours, and it had gone flawlessly. He'd climbed the wire, leapt through the hoop of flames, and landed safely in her arms.

Everyone in the audience had cheered, except for one—Lady Castor. While people clapped and begged for more, the young Lady sat in her gilded chair and yawned.

As if that weren't enough, two years later, the Storm Duke sold a large supply of bottled lightning, rain, and thunder to the Gargareans. They used the bottles to destroy the island of Mazon, cooking the residents with lightning, and drowning them in floods and mudslides, which stole Gen's mother from her and put her father in prison for murder.

If she *could* control someone with her blood, she would feed it to the StormMakers and make them burn themselves with lightning to pay for what they'd done to her, to all of Mazon.

Castor's carriage landed in the center of the festivities, and a crowd quickly gathered. Castor pulled a small vial from the belt on her hip, opened the top, and a rainbow burst forth, spilling over the people in reds and yellows and blues.

They clapped and cheered, *oohed* and *aahed*, and Gen fought the urge to tear out her hair and scream. They clapped for the daughter of a man who sold genocide while they cursed at Gen. The hypocrisy stuck in her teeth like Aurelian taffy.

Besides, the StormMaker gifts weren't theirs alone. They'd found a way to bottle and sell their magic. Anyone could buy a jar of StormMaker rainbows and produce the same feat. But Gen's kind of magic couldn't be shared, and maybe that was why the people hated her for having it. Because they couldn't.

CHAPTER 2

CASTOR

Castor marched across the grounds toward the palace. The Empresses' guests smiled and waved as she passed, most of them StormMaker customers, and if not, they would be. To be certain, Castor pulled another rainbow vial from her belt and twisted it open. The colorful arc cut through the festivities, gaining more attention than the man swallowing fire.

Arcadia would be flooded with orders for rainbows after this.

Castor flashed her false smile to people as she passed. She was the face of the StormMaker family, and people would talk. After the lottery was done, and the booths taken down, people would be winging, sailing, or riding their way home, and undoubtedly, her father would get word of her.

She wanted him to hear she looked happy. This was, at least according to the tremendous lie she'd told him, to be her engagement day.

Entering the Empresses' lottery had not been easy. Castor owned most of what she wanted: money, an expansive wardrobe, a golden chariot, winged horses, and whatever else she needed, she could buy. All but one thing, the one thing she ached for and could never have—control of Arcadia.

To erase suspicions, she'd told the Storm Duke she'd entered her name in the Empresses' lottery to ask them for the betrothal of their godson, Drakos, on whom they'd bestowed the title of Baron. He was fourth in line for the Empire after various cousins and other relations.

As soon as she'd told him, her father's eyes had glistened with delight. The Olympian Empire spanned all the way from Lerna to Ceryneia, including all of the islands in between. Each island had its own government: a duchy like hers; a councilship like Psophis; or for the smaller, less important isles, it could be something as insignificant as a governor managing the day-to-day.

They also had their own way of choosing rulership. On Psophis, their councilmembers were selected through annual elections; on Leuctra, a competition of wits; and on many of the other isles, control was inherited.

Arcadia was one of those places, except unlike the others, they still adhered to the archaic laws set forth in a five-hundred-year-old piece of parchment.

Upon the death of the current Duke of Arcadia, the eldest born son will take control of the isle. If there is no son, then control will go to the eldest male relative.

Male relative.

Those two words gutted her every time she read them. If she could have, she would have destroyed the Arcadian Doctrine as soon as she touched her first jar of lightning. Not that it would have mattered. It was a decree so ingrained into her father, it couldn't be burned out with fire, and the *male relative* who would be inheriting *her* legacy would be her brother, Pollux. Pollux was unfit to rule anything. He could barely walk across a room without tripping over his own feet, and he was going to control one of the most esteemed isles in Olympia.

According to the Storm Duke, the best way Castor could serve her people was to make an alliance by marrying into something of value. She could marry a woman, which she would prefer, or a man, or a lizard, or a blade of grass. As long as her marriage offered Arcadia additional resources or gold, he didn't care. But marrying into the Empresses' family made the Storm Duke especially pleased.

With Castor embedded into the Empire, he would have a direct line of contact to the Empresses. No more petitioning for tax breaks or relaxed guidelines on lightning exports. He would be welcomed as a special guest. As family. Before she'd left, her father had patted Castor's arm, kissed the top of her head, and said, "I'm glad to see you're making a commitment to the family. Drakos is a fine choice."

It had taken everything in her power to smile and not vomit on his feet. Drakos was an *acceptable* choice if you liked sniveling sods who couldn't add any numbers past the count of their fingers. If you cared about marrying at all. Castor was here for much grander aspirations than a mate. She came here for all of Arcadia, she wanted the entire StormMaker legacy, and once she had it, no one on Arcadia would ever speak of giving away her island to some "male relative" ever again.

She stomped across the bridge to the palace and turned and waved to her fans before disappearing through the doors. No uninvited guests were permitted inside the palace on lottery day, the only reason her lie could survive. She would have some time before word of her true intentions reached her father.

"Lady Castor!" An exasperated and small, gray man scuttled toward her. "We've been waiting for you."

"My apologies," she said. "I ran into a windstorm near Lychos. I made a small stop to contain it." Another lie. Castor's well-meaning mother had tried to talk her out of the betrothal to Drakos. She knew Castor didn't love him, and thought she should reconsider. Her mother's good will was too little too late. Besides, Cas had no intention of marrying anyone. She had much better plans.

"Never mind. Right this way." The gray man waved her forward, into the grand entryway across the white polished floors and underneath the great, golden tower.

Castor had been here before, for parties and meetings and other events. The gilded palace dwarfed her own estate on Arcadia, but it lacked precision. The Empresses were collectors. They filled their home with eclectic pieces of art, painted vases, and various servants. All their things festered inside the halls and trod upon the tile, making the palace look more like a market than the home of the esteemed rulers of Olympia.

Not Castor's particular style.

"Right in here."

The small, gray man shoved her into the solarium, draped with hanging plants and vines, many of them poisonous. The Empresses were known to serve poisoned tea to anyone who displeased them, grinning at the victim while he forcibly drank it. A bit macabre, but effective. No one crossed the Empresses. No one.

"The Empresses will be here shortly," the man said, and closed the doors behind him.

Castor wandered toward the golden dais perched at the front of the room. The other lottery winners spoke in low voices and hovered near the spread of food.

When the list of this year's chosen had been announced, Castor had recognized a few of the names. And there was one of those names now, lingering near the diprocydus vines. Percy wore a crooked black hat and a threadbare jacket while he sipped on red wine that clung to his blue mustache.

If he stepped any closer to those hanging vines, the oil on them would give him a horrible rash. She should warn him, except she would rather have a diprocydus rash than start a conversation with Percy. He was a small-time inventor with no magic of his own, so he spent his time trying to profit off the magic of others. He had pitched her father on various containers for holding lightning and rainstorms, one of which was embedded in the heel of his boot. It had leaked all over their floors during his demonstration.

Behind him stood the MindWorker Thylox festering in the shadows. He leaned on his metal leg and picked something from his teeth. He'd lost the leg in an attempt to catch the flesh-eating Thracian Mares. Castor's father had planned to buy one of the horses if the MindWorker caught them. But he hadn't.

Then there was Genevieve, the other MindWorker, the half-Mazon circus girl stuffing her face at the buffet. She wore a sequined jacket and a hat that looked like it had been dredged up from the bottom of the Aegean Sea, complete with a strand of seaweed hanging off her shoulder.

"I heard she punched an old woman on Torinth," another woman in the room whispered, pointedly looking at Genevieve. Castor wouldn't be surprised. Gen's father was a murderer after all, and before that, he had been a performer. Castor had been forced to sit through the circus once. Nothing impressive, just a bunch of smelly animals turning in circles.

These were her fellow players—murderers' daughters and failed businessmen. She did not belong here. The Lady of Storms shouldn't have to grovel and beg, but this was what her father had reduced her to.

"Lady Castor!"

Oh no. Percy headed her way, likely to propose pants with rainstorms sewn inside that would wet themselves when they leaked.

"Lady Castor, how good to see you."

"You too, Mr. Pansy." She purposely mispronounced his name to express her annoyance.

"Uh, how is your father?" he stumbled. "I've been meaning to—"

"Thank you for your patience, everyone!"

Thank the Oracles. The gray man stood at the front of the room, arms raised, and silenced Percy's sales pitch.

"We are ready to get the lottery proceedings underway," the gray man continued. "Please rise for the presentation of their Royal Highnesses!"

The gray man yanked open the door behind the dais, and Castor respectfully lowered her head. The Mazon set down her plate of food and wiped grease on her pants. Her dog continued to gnaw on a pheasant bone, snarling and snorting. Castor rolled her eyes. None of these people were fit to stand in front of royalty.

Castor kept her chin down while the Empresses emerged, one small foot at a time. Their custom gown was made of two pieces, a design of blood red and soft white. It wrapped around the Empresses' slender waist and rose up to sharp collarbones. That was where it split, into a puffed red sleeve on the right and a long white sleeve on the left. From the center emerged two ivory necks, one with a black choker and ruby stone and the other a collar of diamonds.

The Red Empress pursed her lips under a crown of red hair, flowing over her head in waves of fire. The Crystal Empress wore a sweeter smile, glancing over the crowd with ice blue eyes. People called them fire and ice, sour and sweet, but they were both equally deadly and cruel. They had no magic. They didn't need it. What they had was unyielding power.

The Crystal Empress's smile faltered. She glared at a man in the back, one with numerous eyes. Castor could see the words hovering on the man's lips. *Two-Headed Empress.* The last person who dared say those words drank a mugful of poisoned tea that liquefied his insides. As much as Castor would enjoy a show, she preferred to get this moving and done before her father discovered her. Having to clean up after a poison killing would take hours.

"Welcome to Athenia," the Red Empress said, possibly showing him some mercy.

"We are delighted to meet you," the Crystal Empress added.

"We'd like to congratulate you all for being chosen for the lottery this year." The Red Empress gently clapped her hand on the side of her throne.

"We hope you've planned your requests well," the Crystal Empress said. "Because you only get one favor to ask, and once chosen for a lottery, you can never be chosen again."

Castor's lip curled at the reminder. This was her one chance. Nothing was guaranteed. All she had "won" was an invitation to the palace, a chance to ask the Empresses for her favor. Yes, they would likely grant her wish, but it wouldn't be a free exchange. They would want something from her in return.

It could be a year of her cleaning up the Empresses' stables, or using windstorms to chase birds off the palace spire. They could make the price as steep as they wanted, or they could outright refuse her. Then she would have to beg for a betrothal because her father would never forgive her.

"You shall approach us in the order you arrived," the Red Empress said. "Master Percy."

The blue-mustached inventor made his way toward the Empresses. Castor had arrived last, thanks to her mother, which meant she would be the last to make her request. She rolled her eyes. This would take far too long.

"Let's not waste everyone's time," the Red Empress said to Percy. "Please tell us what brought you here today."

He looked down at his fingernails, already nibbled to the bed. "Your Majesties." Percy knelt on one knee. "First, I would like to wish you a joyous birthday."

"Thank you, Master Percy," the Empresses said together, their voices different but complementary. Two snakes hissing at the same volume.

"Rise," the Red Empress said, "and tell us what brings you here today."

"I am a humble man." He stood up. "I ran into some trouble with the Lion on Nemea. I'd like to end that trouble."

Castor raised an eyebrow. Why was she not surprised? The Lion owned the most profitable casino in Olympia, the Lion's Den, and the Lion, unlike Percy, was an intelligent businesswoman. When people lost to her casino, she collected her debts, in blood if they couldn't be paid in coin.

"You wish for us to kill the Lion?" The Crystal Empress leaned closer to Percy.

"I will leave that to you to decide, Your Majesties," Percy said. "As long as I no longer have to look over my shoulder for her claws."

The two Empresses pushed their heads together and whispered in near silence. Castor knew they wouldn't kill the Lion. Her casino paid for this palace in taxes.

"We shall grant your request," the Red Empress finally said. "The Lion will be of no more trouble to you."

Percy exhaled. "Thank you, Your—"

The Crystal Empress held up a finger. "But as a birthday gift to your most beloved Empresses . . ."

". . . you shall give us your eldest son for the year, in our service," the Red Empress finished. "We hear he's quite handsome."

"And yet unmarried," the Crystal Empress added.

Percy twisted his mustache. "I cannot do that. He is betrothed, set to marry this spring. The alliance will mean much to our family."

Probably in monetary value, Castor thought, and a valueless point. His son couldn't marry anyone if the Lion slaughtered Percy and his entire family. Everyone knew the lottery didn't work out entirely in your favor.

The lottery was a way for the Empresses to make their own birthday gifts. They would ask for a year of service, or enough goods to last until the next birthday, and by the time that service ended, there was a new lottery, new victims. All told, it was genius.

"That is a shame." The Red Empress tapped her finger on her bottom lip. "There is nothing else of yours we desire, considering you are so deep in debt that you own nothing of real value."

The Crystal Empress giggled.

The Red Empress rolled her eyes and continued. "If you cannot lend us your son, then we cannot—"

"I accept," Percy sputtered. "I will send Cyrano on my fastest ship as soon as I return home. We can always postpone the wedding.

Thank you." He bowed his head and ducked back into the crowd. The fool had clearly come here unprepared for what the lottery would bring. Castor would not make the same mistake.

"Master Theus." The Empresses beckoned the next guest, a man with an earring and a pointed beard. He went through the bows and well wishes without groveling like Percy and asked the Empresses for a ship he called the *Hind*.

"It's the fastest in the sea," he said.

"How do you know this?" the Red Empress asked.

"Because it used to be mine. It was stolen, and I want it back."

"You can have your ship, Master Theus," the Crystal Empress said. "If you will use it in service to us for a year."

"I will," he said. "Thank you, Your Highnesses."

He returned to his place in the solarium.

"Welcome, Mistress Leona." The Empresses beckoned the next guest, a woman with dark brown skin and a single eye in the center of her forehead.

"Joyous birthday, Your Majesties," she said.

"Yes." The Crystal Empress dismissed her with a wave of her hand. "What else brings you here today?"

"On Psophis," she said, "there is a man they call the Boar. He's gained a following. He makes us pay for protection, and if we don't . . ." Her single eye glistened with tears. "We can't afford to pay him anymore. We barely have enough to eat."

The Crystal Empress leaned her ivory cheek on her palm, feigning pity.

"We shall take care of your Boar," the Red Empress said, "and you will send us ten able men for the year to work in our household."

"Yes, Your Majesties. Thank you, Your Majesties."

The next victim, the one with many eyes, stepped across the solarium and asked the Empresses to clean his stables. It cost him half of his herd of cattle. Castor shook her head. What a waste to use a lottery wish on mucking stables when a few servants could easily do the job.

The next guest asked the Empresses to chase away a flock of birds that had overrun the settlement on Stymphal, and once he agreed to part with ten women from the village, the following entrant stomped forward without being called.

The woman stood in front of the Empresses under a venomous lilac plant, snorting through her wide nostrils. Her skin shone bright red, and two short horns protruded from her forehead.

"I want Felonious Bull dead," she spat, dispensing with birthday greetings and begging. Castor appreciated her efficiency.

"Done," the Red Empress said. "In exchange—"

"I'll serve my year," the woman said. "As long as you bring me his head on a platter."

"We'd be delighted," the Crystal Empress said.

"Thank you, Your Highnesses," the woman said.

That was better. At the lottery, you could ask for anything, the Empresses' throne if you were brave enough. The Empresses could always refuse. Or make the price so high, the wisher wouldn't take it, but Castor didn't want the Empresses' throne. She wanted her own, control of Arcadia and the StormMakers, and she would do whatever was necessary to take it.

She would spend a year with her nose in the tiles, scrubbing them day after day. She would serve their meals morning, noon, and night with a smile on her face. She would sweep up leaves and debris in the gardens with her bottled wind, because if she didn't, she would be married off to some paunch lord, while her brother, Pollux, sank her beautiful Arcadia into debt and despair.

If she had been born on any other island, her sex wouldn't matter. Everything would be as it should be. She would take the helm, and her brother could worry about making married alliances.

Except Castor didn't want another island. She wanted Arcadia.

She didn't come here for an alliance. She wasn't here to settle a debt or gain vengeance. She came to take what should have been hers in the first place. She came for justice. She came here to ask the Empresses to name her the irrefutable heir of Arcadia so she could dredge her beloved home out of the past and carry it into the future.

That was the kind of request you saved for the lottery. Not these little chores. As soon as she had her turn, she would show them all how to ask for favors. How much you had to be willing to take. And sacrifice.

CHAPTER 3

GEN

The woman who had asked for someone to be killed returned to her place in the solarium wearing a satisfied smile. Gen tried not to make eye contact. A curved sword hung from the woman's tooth-studded belt along with what looked like someone's ear on the cord around her neck. She seemed fierce enough to kill her own enemies. If she needed help taking care of this Bull, he had to be dangerous.

Compared to that request, Gen's seemed so small. *I just want my father.*

So far, the lottery had gone as expected. The people asked for their most needed things, and the Empresses agreed to provide them for something in return, a year of service, some additional staff.

Except for Mr. Percy. His payment had seemed exceptionally steep, the cost of his son, and it was questionable if he even had the right to volunteer his grown son for fodder. But that was how the game was played. The Empresses offered a bad solution to a horrible problem, and once their word had been given, it couldn't be broken on either side. People didn't come to the lottery unless they were desperate, unless they had no other options.

"Master Thylox," the Red Empress called.

Gen took a step back as the grim-faced MindWorker pulled

from the shadows. This was another name she knew from the list of chosen entrants, another name that made her lip curl in distaste.

Thylox moved across the floor with a *thud-clink* as his metal leg pierced the tiles. His original leg had been digested long ago by the Thracian Mares in an attempt to capture them. She didn't know if she should pity Thylox or the Mares that had to eat a piece of him. He must have tasted terrible. If Thylox had a flavor, it would be sour milk mixed with the weeks-old fish guts she cleaned out of the whale's mouth.

"Haven't seen you in a while," he muttered as he passed. "You look well."

She didn't dignify that with a response. They were not on the same side, so to speak. He had met with her father once, and Alcmen had removed him from their ship. Thylox used his magic for the seedy underworld of illegal animal trade. If he got his hands on Gen's whale, he'd have it bled dry before lunch. Bottled and sold. When people thought of MindWorkers as filthy, conniving, criminals, they thought of Thylox.

The MindWorker stopped in front of the Empresses and bowed his head. "May you have a thousand more birthdays, Your Highnesses." He straightened up and smiled at them in something of a grimace. Anyone who met Thylox knew that was the best he could muster.

"What is it we can do for you?" the Red Empress asked.

"I want the Mares," he said.

Of course he did. And he couldn't do it on his own.

Not all MindWorkers were the same. Some could control simultaneous creatures without faltering, like Gen and her father, and some could only hold on to one or two animals, but they could be more possessive about it. A cupful of Thylox's blood could possibly drive someone to murder their best friend . . . if they could choke it down. Not that Gen would ever tell anyone that, and even Thylox could only control one. Not an entire horde of Gargareans.

"What are you going to do with them when you have them?" the Red Empress asked.

"Sell them to the highest bidder," he said unabashedly.

The Crystal Empress fluttered her eyelashes. "How very prospective of you."

Or cruel. Gen and her father always kept their creatures temporarily. They came and went. They performed a few acts and then Alcmen delivered them back to the wild. Except for the whale.

Alcmen had never even intended to keep the whale, either. It was why they'd never named it. The whale, despite his complaints, stayed because he wanted to stay. Gen only fed him pieces of her hair so they could communicate. Chomp, currently asleep next to a half-eaten pheasant leg, stayed for the food.

"You can have your Mares," the Red Empress said. "But we want to keep them for a year before you sell them, under your command, of course."

"Of course." Thylox bowed. "Happy to oblige."

When he step-*clinked* his way back to the shadows, he gave Gen another look, something along the lines of, "I knew I'd have them one day." Good for him. She hoped the Mares took his other leg when he got them.

"Mistress Geryon!"

The Crystal Empress waved her finger, and a small, frail woman with pale-blue hair approached the dais. Her hair floated back and forth over her head like smoke, yet clung to her when she made a slow, respectful bow.

She was the last request before Gen.

"Your Majesties," the woman said in a whisper. "A most felicitous of birthdays today."

Gen only paid partial attention to the conversation. She needed to prepare for her own request. *I want my father freed, cleared of his crimes, and our name restored. I want my father freed, cleared of his crimes, and our name restored.* That was all she had to say, agree to the payment the Empresses requested, and she would have her father. She would have her reputation.

"What can we grant you on this day?" the Crystal Empress asked the woman.

"My daughter." The woman's voice cracked. "Livia Kine. She's been missing for two years. She is my heart. My soul. If you have any power to return her to me, I will be eternally grateful."

The two Empresses looked to one another with a false show of pity. If they cared anything about their subjects, they would solve their problems without the pomp of the lottery. Without required servitude.

"What if your daughter is not alive?" the Crystal Empress finally said. "What would you have us do then?"

The woman took a breath. "I want her back . . . however she comes."

The Red Empress nodded. "Then you shall have her back. If we are unable to return her alive, you will be given her body, or at least her story."

"If we find her well," the Crystal Empress said, "then you will be happily reunited."

Gen held her breath, waiting for the price. It hung in the eerie silence like the poisonous vine on the wall.

"You may go," the Red Empress finally said, and shooed her away.

"Thank you, thank you, Your Highnesses. Bless you!" The woman scurried away and hid behind the tall man from Stymphal, likely afraid the Empresses would recant their offer.

On the surface, it looked like an unprecedented show of kindness. But it wasn't. This act of "kindness" was just a cloud of smoke meant to hide something else. Every other price paid now seemed higher in comparison. Those who had already signed away their lives or their people wondered if they had wept more, pleaded more, looked more wanting, could they have saved themselves the servitude? And Gen was next.

She stepped toward the dais, trying to convince herself no matter how hard she cried or begged, they would not give her Alcmen for nothing. She was not that pitiful or lucky.

"Mistress Genevieve," the Crystal Empress said. "So good to see you again."

"Your—"

"Gregor!" The Red Empress shouted over Gen's head.

The little gray attendant who had shown Gen to the room shuffled from the shadows, stepping quickly in front of Gen's toes. "Yes, Your Highness." He ducked his head.

"Go fetch that hideous statue of us from the drawing room."

"The statue?"

"Yes," the Crystal Empress said. "Bring it here."

"As quickly as I can." He spun on one foot and ran for the door. *What do they want with a statue? Why do they need it now?*

"Mistress Genevieve," the Red Empress said in a low, sultry voice.

"Yes, Your Highness. Joyous wishes on your birthday." Gen's tongue swelled in her mouth. Her hem was beginning to fray. She needed to stitch herself back together before she unraveled.

She folded her hands behind her back and bowed in a flourish, the way she did years ago in the circus . . . minus the thunderous applause.

"What brings you here on this special day, daughter of Zusma?" the Crystal Empress asked. Gen lifted from her bow at the mention of her mother's name.

The Empress smiled at her, pearl teeth in a long, venomous mouth.

"I, um, I've come to ask . . ."

Something crashed through the doors behind them, a giant marble statue of the two Empresses, carved in detailed likeness from their cruel, playful smiles to the Red Empress's ruby coif. And the statue walked into the room on the shoulders of four gold Gargareans.

Gen clenched her fists, and the silver bands on her arms surged with strength. Since the end of the Gargarean-Mazon war, the Gargareans had taken odd jobs on the islands, acting as general muscle and grunts, including serving on the Empresses' guard.

They dropped the statue to Gen's left, and one of the hulking, gold brutes cracked his knuckles. He looked at her like she was a loose thread, one he desperately wanted to pull—which she was. The last piece of an extinct race.

Most of the Mazons had been on their island when the Gargareans struck with their purchased lightning and storms.

Hippolyta kept her children close and didn't let anyone else onto the island, in part because of Gen's father.

Alcmen had played a show there years ago, met a strong and beautiful Mazon named Zusma, and fallen in love with her. He stole away with her in the night along with two of Zusma's sisters, Gryne and Elloine, who had wanted to leave the island for their own reasons.

Being away from the island, though, hadn't made them any less Mazon.

As of one thousand years ago, all Mazons were born only of Queen Hippolyta. When she learned she could make children on her own, Hippolyta dismissed the Gargareans, which incited the war.

The day Gen lost her mother, she and her parents had been eating sweet rolls on the deck of their ship, watching the sunfish leap out of the water. Midway through a bite of her breakfast, Zusma clutched her chest and fell twitching to the deck.

"My sisters. They're all dying."

She locked her hand around Gen's, and as the silver left Zusma's skin, it flowed onto Gen's. It rolled up her arms, down her shoulders, and across her chin. And with it came waves and waves of pain.

A billion voices, all dying, drowning, burning. That was the curse of the Mazons. Their strength came from the island itself, small particles of energy in the water and air, an element exclusive to Mazon called Amazonium.

The Amazonium could only attach to someone of Mazon blood. It could be called or sent from one Mazon to another, and it could connect across long distances. When Mazon was well, all Mazons were well. When Mazon was not well, every Mazon in Olympia felt the repercussions through their shared Amazonium link.

Gen survived it because she had another life, another parent. She was only half-Mazon, and now, the *only* Mazon.

The Gargarean narrowed his eyes, daring Gen to attack him. She curled her fist, tempted to use her ill-gotten strength to knock a hole in his teeth, but then she might be hauled out of here as a disturbance, and everyone would say, "See! She's just like her father."

She uncurled her fingers and flattened her palm to her leg.

"Thank you," the Crystal Empress finally said. "You may go." She dismissed the Gargareans with a wave of her fingers, and the gold brutes lumbered from the room.

"It's hideous," the Red Empress said as she turned her attention to the statue, which was, admittedly, hideous. The sculptor had tried to make the rulers appear jovial and kind and had failed. But in all fairness, that would be a difficult task. Even for a master sculptor.

"You look lovely," the Crystal Empress said. "I'm the one who looks awful. Like a piece of melted wax." She puffed out her lips. "Am I really that sour looking?"

"Not at all," the Red Empress said. "Which is why it needs to go. Can you break it?"

It took Gen a moment to realize they were talking to her. "Me?" She pressed her palm to her chest. "Is this my price for my favor?"

The Red Empress laughed. "Of course not. Consider it a gift."

Of course. How foolish.

"We would be much appreciative," the Crystal Empress said.

"Then I am more than happy to destroy it."

On with the show. If they wanted her to break the ugly statue, she would break the ugly statue. She would dance on this floor, rub poisonous plants on her skin, and even smile at a Gargarean if that was what it took to save Alcmen.

She circled the marble monstrosity, trying to decide how best to break it. When she'd been born, she'd only had a small amount of her mother's strength, passed to her at birth. She could easily open jars, throw a rock across the field, and run long distances without getting overtired.

Since the day her mother died, that strength had tripled, and it never felt right for Gen to use what wasn't hers. Zusma had been the strong act in the show. Not Gen. She only used her strength when she absolutely needed it, and this qualified. Keeping the Empresses happy was vital to her future.

"Dear Empresses." Gen raised her arms in the way Zusma had in their circus. "The problem with trying to copy beauty is that it must pass from the eyes to the hand of the artist." Gen grabbed one of the stone Empresses' hands, and her muscles surged. She snapped the stone arm free.

"And I think we can all see"—she swung the broken arm at the other—"that much is lost in translation." She shoved her foot into the knee of the right leg, crushing it in two. "Because it is impossible to make perfection in a piece of stone, when it already sits on a throne." She spun in a circle and caught the other leg of the statue with her foot.

Her boot cut through the stone, and as the last of the statue tipped forward, she stepped out of the way. The dismembered sculpture dropped at her feet. A plume of white dust rose into the air, coating the surrounding plants, and her jacket sleeve.

When the dust cleared, the former hideous statue sat in shambles on the floor. Gen bowed over the rubble, pleased. It hadn't been a bad performance considering she'd had no preparation or props.

The Crystal Empress clapped her hand on her side of the throne while someone else sighed. Gen peered under her elbow, and there was Lady Castor—yawning. Again.

"Quite a show," the Red Empress said.

"Thank you, Your Majesty."

"Now, what is it we can do for you?" the Crystal Empress asked.

Gen straightened her spine and cleared her throat. "I want my father. I want Alcmen released from prison and returned to me, with his name cleared of his supposed crime." It sounded like such a simple thing. *Give me my father. Don't keep an innocent man in prison.*

But she'd learned the simple things were never simple.

When she had last seen Alcmen, four years ago, he had kissed her on the forehead and told her he would be back soon. That had been a lie.

She had waited for him at his childhood home on the island of Creon for days, then weeks. He had taken the ship and the whale. She had nowhere else to go. Then the whale arrived on the beach six weeks later. Alone.

Gen dropped a few hairs in his mouth, and when they connected, he showed her what had happened, the small pieces he had seen: Alcmen being taken away by the Empresses' guard covered in blood, then their ship being torn apart and looted once he was gone.

The whale had followed Alcmen to Athenia and waited until their MindWorker connection withered away. Then he came to Gen. Shortly after he arrived, the Creon guard showed up at her door. She wasn't welcome on the island anymore.

She packed up her meager belongings, and Chomp, and set out with the whale for the nearest island of Thessaly, where she wrote her name down on a piece of paper and sent it via messenger to enter her name in the Empresses' lottery. She had done the same for the past four years, to be standing right where she was.

"Supposed?" the Crystal Empress said. "There were witnesses to his crime."

"One witness," Gen said. The tavern owner, who by his own admission had been hiding behind the counter throughout the ordeal.

"Because only one survived, apart from your father. Are you suggesting the Gargareans killed themselves by choice?"

Gen sucked air through her teeth. Yes, there were questions. Why had Alcmen been at the tavern, bathed in blood? Her father had told her she *shouldn't* use her magic on people. Not *couldn't*. She knew *she* wouldn't be able to convince a roomful of Gargareans to murder each other, but could Alcmen have done it? Had all the pieces been there?

After Zusma had exhaled her last breath, Alcmen had picked her up from the deck of their ship and sobbed over her lifeless body. He made sounds that had ripped into Gen's soul. They were the sounds of a man who had lost his only love. Who had watched her die while he stood aside, helpless. It had broken him. He had not been himself in the weeks that followed. Had he become the kind of person who could do the unthinkable?

No. She didn't believe that. He couldn't defy the limits of his own abilities, and he would never leave her like this on purpose.

"He's innocent," she said. "Mind magic doesn't work that way. You can't force someone to do something they are morally opposed to."

Behind her, Thylox snorted, as if he knew anything about morals.

"I must discuss this with my sister," the Red Empress said.

She turned her lips to the Crystal Empress's ear, and they whispered to one another in silent voices.

This was ridiculous. Even if her father *had* killed them, which he hadn't, the Gargareans slaughtered an entire race and went unpunished. Gen had stewed about that for months following Alcmen's arrest until she finally discovered the difference. It wasn't the killing that bothered people. It was how it had supposedly been done.

They might have shown Alcmen some leniency if he'd strolled into the bar and stabbed the Gargareans or struck them down with lightning. But what he had done, supposedly, had been much worse. He took away their free will. He made them into monsters.

That was exactly what the Oracle Keres had done. She had used her power to send a creature after her sister and then set her brothers against themselves. She had killed them all with grief and madness.

The Empresses parted, and Gen stood, arms behind her back, trying to read something from their expressions. Impossible. They were as immovable as they had been in stone.

"It's not lightly that we set a murderer loose on the people," the Red Empress said. "But we have taken into account Alcmen's state of mind at the time of the incident, his years served, and his prior record of no discernable crime."

Gen held her breath. This sounded promising.

"We will grant his release and clear his record," the Crystal Empress added. "But"—she raised her finger—"first you must prove you are capable of handling him should he go awry again."

"I can, I will." Whatever they needed her to do. She would tear down this entire palace with her bare hands if they asked. Kiss a Gargarean. She was so close.

"You will prove yourself by granting their requests." The Red Empress waved her jeweled hand across the room.

"I will what?" Gen's heart stopped.

"You will grant their requests," the Red Empress repeated. "If you can do that, then we'll know you are fully capable of keeping your father contained."

"If you can stop the Lion," the Crystal Empress said.

"Get the *Hind*," the Red Empress added.

"Take care of the Boar, the stables, the birds."

"The Mares, Mr. Bull, and find Ms. Kine as well."

"Oh, and we have our own requests." The Red Empress curled her hand around the edge of her throne. "I want you to kill the Hydra."

"And I want the belt of Hippolyta," the Crystal Empress added.

"You do these things for us, for *them*, then you shall have your father, name cleared, and anyone who dares speak of him having committed a crime shall be jailed in his place. Do we have a deal, Mistress Genevieve?"

Gen ran through the requests in her head. The Lion, the *Hind*, the stables, the Mares . . . the Mares? She didn't want Thylox to have them at all. She especially didn't want to *give* them to him, and she didn't dare think about the Hydra, the immortal nine-headed swamp monster. These were impossible tasks. That was why these people saved them for the lottery.

"You've made a mistake. I can't do those things."

The Red Empress sighed. "Then everyone will be quite disappointed. We already told them you could."

Gen shook her head. "No, you told them *you* would."

"Well, we changed our minds," the Crystal Empress said. "If

you refuse to do these things, then no one gets what they want . . . including you."

"Including us," the Red Empress added.

The woman from before, the one who lost her daughter, broke into a soft whimper. This was exceptionally cruel, even for the Empresses. They never passed the tasks onto someone else. Why now? Why her?

Gen turned to face the room. Mr. Percy, the man who needed to avoid the Lion, looked as if he might faint. The woman who wanted that man murdered clenched her fists into knots, ready to rage. If Gen refused, if she failed, everyone would despise her more than they already did. Her reputation would be more tarnished than before.

If she accepted, she wouldn't live long enough to see her father, let alone free him.

But what was that life without her father? Her reputation? It was a lifetime of being alone, of being feared, of being broken.

"What if I fail?" she asked.

"Then you fail," the Red Empress said. "But if you win"—her lips parted into a grin—"what better way to reclaim your reputation? Genevieve, the tamer of the Thracian Mares."

"Genevieve, who defeated the Hydra," the Crystal Empress added.

"Genevieve, the champion of Olympia," the Red Empress finished. "There will be so much praise for your name, there will be no room for insults."

Gen closed her eyes and imagined the crowds lined up outside her new circus tent with the criers outside. *Come see the Stupendous Gen and her Creature Spectacular*!

She had visions of herself holding one of the Hydra's heads, riding one of the murderous Mares with the Amazing Alcmen leaping out of the sea behind her. Like her, Alcmen had only thrived on center stage. Rotting in a dank prison cell would be killing him. They were both slowly dying, and it would take more than a word from the Empresses to save them.

She couldn't simply dredge her father out of prison. She needed to lift him up to the top, where they both belonged. To fix the damage, she needed to do something grand, something impossible. She needed to change the word "MindWorker" from something foul into something amazing, and no one would dare challenge the girl who slayed the Hydra. She would be invincible.

She opened her eyes. "I'll do it."

"Excellent." The Red Empress curled her tongue. "Be sure to send the Hydra our regards."

Gen stumbled back to her sleeping chaeri, dazed and delighted. When they rebuilt the circus, the lines for tickets would be unfathomable. She might even be able to keep one of the Hydra heads for exhibition. People would pay dearly for a close look at one of those.

Wait, what was she thinking?

A Hydra head?

To claim a Hydra head, she had to *kill* the Hydra. The thing was immortal! The Empresses, the all-powerful rulers of the Olympian Empire, who had an army of a hundred thousand at their fingertips, and the support of a hundred isles, had asked *her* to kill the Hydra because *they* couldn't with all of their power and resources.

She hadn't freed her father. She'd committed herself to die.

CHAPTER 4

CASTOR

Castor smiled as Gen returned to her place by the food. She wasn't stuffing her face now. She looked as if she might vomit. What a fool. It was obvious the Empresses didn't want to release the murderer Alcmen, and that was why they gave her the tasks to complete. They probably assumed she would refuse. Well, she would surely die trying to finish them.

Castor was glad now to be last. Her wish wouldn't be entrusted to the Mazon like the others. Maybe Genevieve could finish one or two tasks, depending on where she started, but if the Mares didn't tear her apart, the Hydra would.

Too bad for her.

"Finally, our last guest." The Red Empress beckoned Castor to the dais.

"You have much to aspire to, Lady Castor," the Crystal Empress said.

"Not that much." Castor crunched over the pieces of broken statue. Any brute could smash a rock.

She reached for one of the vials on her belt, a small, pocket-sized windstorm. She opened the vial, and the wind burst from the inside of the container, sweeping up the stone fragments the MindWorker had left behind. The gust of wind dropped them neatly in the corner before she called it back to the small metal vial.

"Happy birthday, Your Highnesses." Castor dropped into a low curtsy before the Empresses, head bowed on her forearm. Unlike the MindWorker, she knew how to behave in front of royalty. And clean up after herself.

"What brings you to us today?" the Crystal Empress asked.

Castor raised her head and kept her gaze respectfully on the Empresses' chins. "My brother," she said. "Our father is going to give the Arcadian throne to him."

She could barely say the words without snarling. The Arcadian family tree, painted on the great hall of their manor house, was a series of tangled branches filled with stern men and the supporting women beside them. Lording over the top sat her great-great-great-great-grandfather, Tyrus. He was the one who discovered they could bottle their power and sell it. He turned Arcadia from a desolate isle of dry rock and wilting trees into one of the most powerful isles in the Empire.

The StormMakers, contrary to the name, could not actually make storms; they could only capture and control them. Without the vials, Castor could hold a rainbow in her hand for ten or fifteen minutes before it faded away. She couldn't take it with her or show it to someone else. She could change its direction, turn it this way or that way, but she couldn't keep it. She couldn't use it.

Tyrus discovered the jars by accident. He had been given a vase by the Lord of Tegea as a gift, made from the metal mined solely in their country, Illumium. It had been a symbol of good faith, to make an alliance.

During a lightning storm, Tyrus needed something to draw the lightning down, to capture it. It had been common practice to use a piece of metal, generally a sword, but Tyrus grabbed the vase, and when the lightning crashed down into his hands, it went inside the vase and stayed.

No longer did the StormMakers need to wait for rain before they could send it over a drying field or a burning forest. They could capture the rain whenever they wanted and store it in an Illumium vial. They could have rain in drought. Sunny days in rain. Windstorms to send off their ships, and lightning to vanquish their enemies.

Even better—they could sell it. For enough coin, anyone could release the lightning, or the rains.

Tyrus became an icon, the face of Arcadia, and he took it upon himself to rewrite the future by creating the Arcadian Doctrine. He was revered by the people, which made his misogynistic rules difficult to eradicate. Castor foolishly thought, with enough dedication and hard work, she could convince her father to make a few edits to Tyrus's plans.

Her brother, Pollux, heir to Arcadia, spent much of his time ordering the MetalBenders in the manor to mold the Illumium into useless objects like violins and flutes to compose his sonatas and operas. Meanwhile, Castor clung to her father's side and learned everything she could about the StormMakers and their legacy. She attended his meetings and helped him devise new ways to bottle and sell wind and lightning. The weather exchange program had been her idea, a concept that brought millions of coins to Arcadia each year.

If a rainy island wanted sun, the StormMakers took their rainclouds from the sky, and once the island went dry, they sold their own rain back to them for a thousand coins.

When the Storm Duke had made the announcement about succession at dinner three months ago, Castor had nearly choked on her dessert.

"Pollux is to inherit Arcadia."

"Pollux is a fool," she snapped at her father later in his quarters.

Her brother was not entirely a fool. He had his skills, some reasonable ideas, and the people liked him. He had his uses but not in leadership.

"Pollux is misguided. He only needs some direction," the Storm Duke argued and, without pause, placed his signature on the bottom of the binding documents that made the decree official.

"He'll have Arcadia making violins and flutes!" She dug her nails into the soft wood of his desk, inlaid with a custom carving of Tyrus. In the image, her ancestor had his arms raised, releasing bolts of lightning from the vase in his hands. He had become a bloated image for the isle, and it was time for him to be deflated, to make room for someone else.

"That's why you'll need to advise him."

She slammed her hands on the desk. "Why can't he advise me?"

Her father's head finally lifted. "This is the way it's always been done, from father to son."

"Just because it's always been done that way, doesn't make it a good decision." She stormed from his office with no intention of giving up for the sake of tradition. Her father's words had been a challenge. Trying to infiltrate the legacy wasn't enough. If she wanted change, she had to smash the entire system. Only then could it be rebuilt.

"But the Arcadian rulership always goes from father to son," the Crystal Empress said, repeating the words that made Castor's nightmares.

"This time, I would prefer it didn't," Castor said through gritted teeth. "What if you had a brother, Your Highnesses? Would you give him the Empire simply because he'd been born a man?"

The Empresses were the only living children of the late Emperor Polycrates, and even so, when Polycrates had died, it had been a tumultuous change. Many of the island leaders fought against the Empresses rising to power because of their . . . togetherness.

In the end, though, those voices were silenced. Permanently. Of all people, the Empresses should empathize with Castor's plight. They knew how easily power could be granted and denied.

"Your point has been made," the Red Empress said, "but it won't be easy to convince your father to think differently."

"I hope you don't want us to kill Lord Pollux." The Crystal Empress pressed her fan to her chest in horror.

No, Castor didn't want that. She loved her brother in her own way, and even if Pollux met an untimely demise, without the Empresses' blessing, her stubborn father would just place the title on her cousin Ajax, the eldest male relative after Pollux. He would be a worse leader. Ajax was a womanizer and gambler. Arcadia would be broke in months.

"He's my brother," Castor said. "I love him, but Pollux is not competent to rule the StormMakers. He would be of more use as an advisor. If you command it of my father, he'll make the change. He won't defy your wise leadership."

Arcadia was loyal to Olympia. Castor's grandfather had been one who'd stood against the Empresses taking the throne, but he had wisely kept his mouth shut on the matter. In exchange, Arcadia had been granted a reduction in their export tariffs. In the deal Castor's father had made with the Gargareans, they'd saved a fortune. Her father wouldn't risk destroying that agreement for anything. Not even to protect Tyrus's ridiculous doctrine.

The Duke of Storms would do whatever the Empresses commanded, whatever his *pockets* demanded.

The Red Empress touched a finger to her lips. "We don't make a habit of meddling in the business affairs of the islands unless we have to. My sister and I will need a moment."

The Empresses leaned together and spoke in small whispers. Castor stood respectfully with her hands behind her back. No doubt they would decide in her favor. It was in their best interest for her to inherit Arcadia too. They stocked quite a bit of lightning here, and Pollux stood strongly against using weather as weaponry. With him in charge, they would see Arcadia slowly deteriorate, and the Empresses would lose a powerful supporter.

The Empresses parted, and Castor straightened her shoulders. Both women smiled brightly. This was it: she would finally gain her rightful title, the heiress to Arcadia. The future Duchess of Storms.

"Oh, let me tell it, please let me tell it. It's such a grand idea," the Crystal Empress begged.

"If you insist." The Red Empress held her hand, palm up, toward her sister.

"Lady Castor of Arcadia," the Crystal Empress began.

Castor lifted her chin. She was prepared to do whatever the Empresses asked. It couldn't be worse than the Mazon's price. It couldn't be worse than always being second tier, or losing Arcadia.

"You shall split the tasks with Genevieve," the Crystal Empress said. "You will both be responsible for completing the lottery this year."

Her stomach clenched. Split the tasks? No, this couldn't be.

They had made a mistake. She wasn't asking for a murderer to be freed. She was asking the Empresses for a title, a title that rightfully belonged to her.

She spun and glared at the Mazon. This was her fault. The Empresses knew she would never be able to complete the tasks on her own, and so Castor was burdened with them too.

"Isn't it wonderful?" the Crystal Empress said. "Creature and strength against wealth and power. Who will win?"

"Whoever completes more of the tasks before the other gets their request. The other will not," the Red Empress added.

Lightning coursed through Castor's veins. No. This was impossible. Unheard of. The Empresses never denied anyone.

"No!" Genevieve shouted, echoing Castor's sentiments. "No, that's not what we agreed to. You said I could have my father."

"We changed our minds," the Crystal Empress said coolly.

Castor took a breath. She had to be rational about this, calm. "What if we each complete five?" She quickly ran through the list in her head. The missing daughter, the ship, the Lion, the Boar, the Bull, the stables, the birds, the Mares, the belt, and the Hydra. She needed six to win. She could complete six of them before the Mazon.

"Then we will create a tiebreaker." The Crystal Empress turned to her sister, delighted. "Oh, Red, I think this is the most fun I've ever had on one of our birthdays."

"Me too," the Red Empress said. "Do you accept?" She leaned over her knees.

Castor chewed on the inside of her cheek, biting hard enough to taste blood. She didn't know if the Empresses wanted a game, or if they wanted her to keep the Mazon from winning. Either way, she had to play. Soon enough the truth would reach Arcadia and her father. He would know her lie. He would know what she had really asked. He would know she had betrayed him. The only path that led back to Arcadia was the one made by the Empresses.

If they wanted this game, she would win it.

"Of course, Your Highnesses. Your will is my command."

She spun on the heel of her boot, wrapping her cloak around her. Genevieve stood motionless as if she had swallowed her own tongue.

The last of the Mazons. The murderer's daughter. The estranged circus performer.

From here, in her soiled jacket, she didn't look like a threat. But Castor wouldn't underestimate her. She would have to be quick, efficient, and ruthless. She would pick the six simplest tasks and complete them before the Mazon moved from that spot.

She would not lose Arcadia. The StormMaker rule was hers to claim, and she would have it.

CHAPTER 5
GEN

Gen couldn't decide if it was better or worse that Lady Castor had been given half the tasks. *More* than half. For one of them to win, they had to claim six of the labors, otherwise it would be a tie.

Gen could win her father without facing the Hydra, but she could also lose him completely.

No, she could not do that. The only thing sustaining her these past years had been hope. One day she would be called to the lottery. One day she would have her life restored. Without that, she had nothing.

This was her one chance, and she had to claim it or lose it forever.

She grabbed a napkin from the table and a sharp pheasant bone from the empty platter. While the Empresses exited through their dais door, muttering their farewells, Gen surveyed the guests and dipped the bone in chutney. She scratched down their ten wishes on her soiled napkin.

Blue mustache – the Lion
young man – find the Hind ship
One-eyed woman – stop the Boar
Many-eyed figure – clean the stables
Tall man – Stymphal birds
Fierce woman – kill the Bull

Thylox - capture the Mares
weeping woman - find Livia Kine
Red Empress - kill the Hydra
Crystal Empress - retrieve the belt of Hippolyta

Gen held the list with both hands. Her eyes betrayed her by going straight for the Hydra. Her performer's heart wanted the glory from killing the beast, but she needed to focus on strategy. She wouldn't get far maimed or dead. She scratched a W next to it, for the "worry about later" list. She doubted Castor would chase the Hydra first, either.

She drew a faint W next to "kill the Bull" too. Murdering someone, even if he turned out to be a monster, would not help her or her father's reputation. Another W for the Mares. She would rather not hand them over to Thylox if possible. She starred the birds and the stables. Those would be the easiest to complete with her magic. She could politely ask the birds to leave and make the cattle clean their own stables.

Of course the state of the stables worried her. How bad were they if it required special favor from the Empresses to clean them? She put a question mark next to the star.

Beside the belt of Hippolyta, she drew another question mark. She had always wanted to go to her mother's home island, but as far as simplicity or glory went, this task ranked low. Hippolyta was dead, and her belt likely buried under rock and mudslides. It could take ages to find it.

"What are you planning to do?" Percy, the man with the blue mustache, eyed her list, focusing at the top—the Lion.

Her lip curled. Gen had no love for the Lion.

Alcmen's Amazing Animals had headlined at the Lion's Den casino at least a hundred times, to sold-out crowds. The Lion used to invite Gen and her family to dine with her at her private table in the casino restaurant, and she would slip Gen small gifts under the table. A doll, a pair of earrings, a bracelet.

After her exile, Gen had gone to the Lion, alone and hungry. She'd asked . . . no, begged to do a small show with Chomp. An opening act. A small exhibition between performances. Anything. She would have worked for a few scraps of food.

"You'll be bad for business," the Lion had said, and pointed her finger to the door without a second look.

The Lion's generosity only appeared when she could gain something from it. Gen would be happy to help loosen her clutches from Mr. Percy, and she could get supplies on Nemea too. But if she succeeded in stopping the Lion, Mr. Percy's son would pay the price, victim to whatever unusual fantasies the Empresses had planned.

"Do you really want to give them your son?" she asked him. Not that Percy could do much about it now. The Empresses clearly had their sights set on him. Even if his son refused the deal, it wouldn't matter. The Empresses always got what they wanted . . . eventually. Gen was more or less asking if there was a better option before she completed the task and sealed the bargain.

The man dropped his head. "I made some mistakes, I admit, but if he doesn't go to them, the Lion will have us all killed before the next full moon. Even Cyrano can't refute that. He is a good man. He will do what is needed, and in time, I hope he can forgive me." Percy wrung his hands. "At least he will be alive to forgive me."

Gen nodded. "Then it's settled."

She folded up her napkin and tucked it into her jacket pocket. She would start with the Lion, for Percy's sake and to get moving.

She hurried out of the palace and called to her whale on the way. *Come get me. Quickly.*

She felt a pull on their MindWorker ties and the whale's complaints rattled into her thoughts. He wasn't finished eating. He'd barely had any time to himself. Etcetera. Etcetera.

We're going to Nemea, she sent back, and his mood brightened. A large reef surrounded the southern side of the isle, packed with unusual and delicious fish.

On the beach, Gen waited for her whale to emerge from the water. Each second ticked off an eternity. Castor's golden chariot was nowhere to be seen. With those winged horses, she could be halfway to Delos by now.

The sea finally parted and the top of the whale appeared. He opened his mouth wide for her to step inside, and by the amount of fish scales on his tongue, he'd found plenty to eat. Gen slogged through the shallows to step onto his tongue and released Chomp to find a somewhat dry place to nap.

"To Nemea, please," she said to the whale. "Quickly."

His skin sparked gold and blue as he closed his mouth and sank into the sea. For as large as he was, the infinity whale swam quickly. He could get them to Nemea within hours, faster than any ship. Even Castor's flying chariot or the *Hind* on her list. If Gen could stay ahead of Castor for this competition, she would have a chance at it.

The whale burst into the water, and Gen sat down on his cushioned mouth near his right cheek, the driest place she could find. She slung her bag from her shoulder. Everything she owned lived in this bag, which wasn't much.

She reached an arm inside and pulled out a small pouch filled with slumber bees from her last job. She shook them gently. They were in an induced state of hibernation. Pursing her lips, she spat on the sleeping bees to keep them resting until she needed them. She didn't want the slumber bees getting loose on their own. Enough stings could put someone into an indefinite coma—the Lion possibly if she didn't agree to leave Percy alone.

She also removed three changes of clothes (her fourth set had been destroyed in an unfortunate incident with a fire-breathing crocodile), and at the bottom of her bag, she found a sack of dried apricots and a small tin.

She opened the tin with a tangle of hairs, *her* hairs, in case she didn't have time to pull them, and a wad of discarded cocoon from a whisper moth. She set those aside and dug out a jar of green slime—stink lizard pus. She opened the jar a crack, and her eyes burned with the odor of rotting corpse. It was still fresh and could heal most surface wounds instantly. It could keep her from bleeding to death from something more severe.

In the very bottom of her bag, among the dust and crumbs, sat her sack of coins. She had forty-two pieces of silver, the amount remaining after the purchase of her new hat and jacket.

She spread her wares across her lap. They looked so insignificant laid out across her legs in the faint glow of the whale's insides. Forty-two coins, a bag of bees, a wad of cocoon, and a jar of rotten pus. All this against Lady Castor and her endless funds, connections, jars of lightning, and winning smile.

Gen was going to lose.

She was a pale copy of Alcmen and an even paler shadow of

Zusma, and her parents, as wonderful as they were, would have had trouble with this list.

But Alcmen had not always been amazing. He had grown up on the east side of Creon as a goat herder, and he had used his magic for the simple task of tracking the goats. He'd never thought of using it for anything else until he saw his first infinity whale.

"All of a sudden, the water turned from gray to pink, and there he was, our whale," Alcmen had told her.

He hadn't wanted the whale for anything. He'd only wanted a closer look. Using a pocket crab, he had stuffed his hair in the crab's shell and sent it after the whale. After the crab dropped the hairs on the whale's back, Alcmen used his influence to coax the whale closer to shore.

"I'd never seen anything so incredible in my life," he'd said. "And that was when I came up with the idea for the circus. It didn't seem right that only MindWorkers should know these creatures. I wanted to share them with everyone."

He left goat herding behind and traveled the islands, collecting the most obscure and unusual creatures for his performances. As soon as word spread that for six coins, you could see a live infinity whale, he earned enough money to buy a great red-and-blue tent and became known throughout the isles as the Amazing Alcmen.

He had been nothing. Then something. The people had loved him, and then, at the first sign of failure, they'd discarded him. It had been so easy for him to rise, and even easier for him to fall. And if everything, success or failure, depended on one choice, one moment, how could Gen expect to complete this list without falling to pieces?

The whale whistled as he rose out of the water. He opened his mouth, and through the streams of water running off his teeth, the red sands of Nemea appeared before them. Gen stuffed her things back into her bag and smoothed her hair. Whether she was ready or not, whether she would lose or not, she had to begin.

She changed out of her black sequined jacket and put on the white one instead. She took off her hat and admired it once more before tucking it into the bag.

"Meet us on the western side of the isle," she said to the whale. "I'll call for you when we're ready."

She released another one of her hairs to the whale's tongue, and when it touched his skin, she felt his eagerness to get rid of her. He wanted to explore the reef.

"Come on, Chomp." She picked up the chaeri and carried him over the shallows to the sand. "Be careful," she called back to the whale.

He released a low moan in response. He knew these weren't safe waters for him.

Nemea wasn't safe for anything that could fetch a price. The island had nothing to offer in the way of resources. It was all infertile red sand. So the Nemean councilship loosened some of the laws on gambling and trade to have something to offer, with the Empresses' permission of course.

Thieves, murderers, and those in the illegal animal trade frequented here. Many set up shop. The saying on Nemea was, "Come with coins, leave with none," because visitors usually gambled them away, were robbed of them, or came specifically to spend them on things they shouldn't. It was the perfect place for a massive casino, and one of the few places Gen could show her face without being accosted. The people were used to undesirables in town.

She straightened her jacket and headed into the clustered

buildings near the northern shore. They rose up from the ground like sand-colored eggs. Ahead of her at the fountain, willowy green people gathered, filling cups and buckets with water.

"Qui S'toh," she said as she passed, the traditional Nemean greeting. She wanted to stay on the native islanders' good side if she could. Especially since she couldn't buy her way out of trouble if she found some.

Gen circled the fountain and stopped at a small shop set up on the south side. *Eris's Rare and Exotic Animals* was on the small hand-painted sign over the door and a chameleon monkey sat inside a cage below it.

Two Nemean children prodded at the monkey with sticks, and the poor creature's fur shifted from pink to red to yellow as he pinned himself to the bars to avoid them.

"Mishka," Gen said, "oku to dui."

The two children laughed and ran away. Her Nemean was limited but her message seemed to make its mark. "The monkey bites."

She ran the backs of her fingers over the monkey cage and spat through the bars onto the creature's fur. If Eris caught her using her magic on his animals, he would be furious, even if saliva connections had a limited effect.

As soon as her spit sank into the monkey's fur, she felt him. Scared, tired, restless, aching. Day after day after day children prodded fingers at him, and he couldn't escape them. Always the bars held him in place.

"It will be all right."

She reached for the price tag on his cage. Twenty-five pieces of silver? She released the tag before it tainted her hand with ridiculousness. The chameleon monkeys were common enough. They lived in the jungles of Lerna, coincidentally not far from the Hydra's lair, only far enough away they didn't get eaten. Any MindWorker could catch handfuls of them.

"I'm sorry, little monkey," she said. "I can't take you today." She had other creatures on her list and limited coin. Very limited.

The monkey's fur turned an ashen shade of gray, and along his stomach and back, little slits opened . . . eyes. A hundred black eyes. This changed things.

He wasn't just a chameleon monkey. He was an *Argosian* monkey. A rare offshoot of the chameleon monkey. This one had been born with a hundred eyes, all blinking in a dewy-eyed stare. Twenty-five was still more than she wanted to spend, but the monkey was of far more value now. She could always use an extra fifty sets of eyes.

She carried the monkey into Eris's shop and choked on the horrific odor beyond the door. Animal waste, terror, and embalming fluid, the particular perfume of Eris's shop. She swore she'd never come again, but that had been before she'd unwittingly entered into a deadly contest to save her father.

On the way to the counter, she passed by a cage of chatter squirrels. They scrambled over one another, fighting for space in the small cage, and her stomach clenched.

After she had been tossed out of the Lion's Den, she'd been desperate. Two days without food, she'd caught a few chatter squirrels and brought them here to sell. The tall, sallow, green Eris had barely looked at the squirrels, instead eyeing the whale outside.

"I'll give you ten thousand for the whale," he'd said.

Ten thousand. For a long moment, longer than she'd ever admit, she'd considered it. Ten thousand would have been enough to buy herself a new ship, to start a new life, to not worry about where she'd find her next meal or what would happen when her clothes turned to rags.

It was also robbery. The whale was worth at least twenty or thirty thousand, but she had been thirteen years old, alone, destitute, and hungry.

"I can't," she'd finally said. Chomp and the whale were the last threads of her tattered life. "I'm just selling the squirrels."

"One piece." He slammed one grubby coin on the counter. It had bought her food for a day, and she had vowed never to send another creature to this foul shop. She found odd jobs in creature control instead, what she had been doing for survival up until today.

One of the chatter squirrels in the shop rattled the bars of the cage.

"I'm sorry," she said to these squirrels. Even though they weren't the same ones she'd sold, she felt the need to apologize to someone.

"I'm sorry. I'm sorry." The squirrels all repeated in succession. They could mimic any sound, and did so, repeatedly.

"Well, well, well."

She snapped to the front of the shop, where Eris emerged from behind a stained curtain, wiping something from his hands. Blood, maybe. Over his head, the taxidermied bust of a five-legged deer stared back. Eris and Thylox were great friends. Thylox caught the creatures, and Eris slaughtered them and mounted them for show.

"Haven't seen you in a while." Eris leaned a green elbow on the counter. "What have you come to sell today?"

"Nothing." Gen held up the monkey cage. "I came to buy." Or liberate.

"Good, take the monkey. He doesn't draw in enough people

anyway." He waved eight fingers at the cage, and the monkey's fur turned the same shade of green.

"I'm not done," she said. "I also need a smoke rat and a pocket crab."

His thin nostrils flared. "What do you need those for? You going into business for yourself?"

"No." As if she would ever keep creatures caged like this. "I just want the rat and the crab if you have them."

"All right."

Eris scratched his back, digging long fingers into his thick skin. He made his way through the stacks of cages and bowls and crates and picked up a small cage with a black rodent inside. While the rat slept, small tendrils of smoke curled from his nostrils. Excellent for distractions or creating an atmosphere.

The second cage Eris dragged from the stacks contained a small blue crab—the pocket crab. Like her father, she planned to stuff the crab's shell with her hairs and have him pitch a few onto the deadly Mares. She could feed the horses some hair without having to get too close to their snapping teeth, and the crab would be protected from hooves and teeth by its shell.

"Fifty-three silver for the lot." Eris set the cage on the counter.

She reached into her bag for her coin sack and the measly forty-two coins inside. If she hadn't splurged on the new jacket and top hat, she would have the money. But she had never expected to be out here, scrambling to grant lottery wishes. She had expected to be mopping the Empresses' floors or cleaning up after their horses for the next year while Alcmen lived free and rebuilt their lives.

She cleared her throat. "The crab is so small and the rat barely smokes. I'll give you forty for the lot."

Eris rubbed his chin. "Forty and a vial of your whale's blood." He removed an empty jar and set it on the table, like a dare.

"I assume you're joking." She wasn't a child anymore. She knew the value of her things, and Eris insulted her. Greatly. "Forty-two. Final offer." That was all the coin she had.

Eris shook his head. "Fifty-three or the whale blood."

"You're not getting the whale blood or fifty-three from me."

"Then I guess you have some choices to make."

He crossed his arms over his chest. Eris wouldn't budge on this point, and she couldn't. She would never drain the whale. Not a drop. Especially not for Eris. Curse him. Whatever creature she didn't choose would be stuck here forever in Eris's shop of terrors.

"I'll just take the monkey and the rat then."

"Thirty-five."

Gen mouthed her apologies to the crab as Eris placed it behind the counter. The rat held more opportunity to be useful, and since she had already connected with the monkey and could feel how much he despised it here, she couldn't let him go.

She pulled her coins from her pocket and gave thirty-five of them to Eris. Once he closed them in his fist, her purse was much lighter and her soul much heavier.

"Come back," he said. "When you decide to sell the whale."

"Then we're both decided on never."

It had been a mistake to come here this time. If she spat on all these trapped animals, her head would be filled with misery and terror.

"I'm sorry. I'm sorry. I'm sorry." The chatter squirrels whispered at her as she passed.

Gen hurried outside and opened the monkey's cage to set him

free. Once she spat on the rat, she let him go too. Along the thin strings of their connection, sensations of relief and gratitude prickled her thoughts.

"You're welcome," she said and tucked the rat into her bag. The monkey she set on her shoulder.

She looked back at the shop once more. One day, when this was done, and she had her name and fortune, she would buy every creature in that shop and set them loose. With her father in prison, she understood too well how awful it was to keep things unnecessarily caged.

CHAPTER 6

CASTOR

Castor stepped into the back of her chariot and waved to the crowd before she snapped the reins to launch the two winged horses into the air. They reared their heads, flapped their wings, and lifted skyward. She sat down on the cushioned seat of her chariot and let the smile fall from her lips.

She hated performing, walking through crowds, flashing rainbows and smiling as if she cared what they thought of her. But she had to keep up the pretense that the lottery proceedings had gone well. It would take time for the truth about the lottery to leave the palace walls and seep across the sea to her father, and Castor needed more time to secure the win before that happened. She wanted the first news he received of this day to be that she looked overjoyed.

Her lie was never meant to survive for this long. She had planned to tell her father the truth immediately after the Empresses granted her request. *I lied, Father. The Empresses have seen it fit in their wisdom for me to inherit Arcadia, and I think, when you consider it, you will too.*

He would have shouted and cursed, and then after a period of reflection, would have realized it was best for everyone. He was limited by that doctrine as much as everyone else, possibly more. He needed a reason to change, and an irrefutable order from the Empresses could be that reason.

However, her father had varying levels of anger. There was the type of anger that came from Castor borrowing a few pieces of gold and confessing to it (that had resulted in a profuse apology and a vow to never do it again), and then there was the type of anger that came from her stealing a vial of highly charged lightning from her father's office, blasting a hole in the manor, and lying about how it happened (that had resulted in home confinement for two months).

He had grounded her for two months for a little hole in the wall, and now she was attempting to steal all of Arcadia, shatter their traditions, and destroy her ancestor's revered doctrine.

If the Duke of Storms discovered her before she gained the Empresses' blessing, he would be furious, and she wouldn't have the backing of the Empire leaders to protect her. News would spread soon enough from the mouths of servants or one of the lottery participants. She would have to be faster than the gossip *and* the Mazon if she wanted to succeed.

Castor reached for the wooden box under her seat and set it on her knee. The inside of it pulsed with a faint heartbeat. It had been a birthday gift from her father for her most recent birthday, her eighteenth, the night of the fateful decree that Pollux would be inheriting the throne.

Her brother had gotten a new suit, to prep him for his role as heir to Arcadia. Castor unquestionably received the better gift, but it was a bribe meant to keep her quiet about losing the island.

She creaked the hinge on the box to reveal the glowing orb inside.

"Delia," Castor snapped, "I need you."

"How can I serve you, Lady Castor?" The glowing orb blinked with each word.

She was a ghost, a spirit forever anchored to this box. She had been caught and captured by a SpiritWatcher, one of the children of the Oracle Hecate. Castor's father must have paid a fortune for it. Most SpiritWatchers could only lure the ghosts back from the dead for a brief conversation at most. Very few could make them tangible enough to keep. As long as Castor owned the box, she owned the ghost.

"I have a list of things to do, and I need your help." Castor said. "One, I need to convince the Lion to leave a man named Percy alone." That should be easy enough. The Lion spoke Castor's language— money. She would pay off Percy's debts and cross it off her list.

However, her brother was playing a show there tonight. She'd have to wait until he was gone. Nuisance. If they ran into one another at the casino, he would want to know why she wasn't with her future intended. Or back at home. Too many questions with answers that could find their way to their father.

"Two, I need to find a ship called the *Hind*," Castor continued. "Three, I need to take care of someone called the Boar on Psophis, and I want you to get details on the stables on Elis . . . size, number of cattle."

If she could pick and choose, she'd ignore the stables altogether and let the Mazon deal with the piles of manure. But there weren't enough tasks to ignore anything, even mountains of waste.

"Next, tell me about the birds on Stymphal and retrieve any details you can on a man named Felonious Bull."

He might be a hard man to kill if it required the Empresses to intervene.

"I also need the last known whereabouts of Livia Kine and the belt of Hippolyta." She would look into the Thracian Mares and the Lernean Hydra later.

Much later. Those would be her last tasks to complete, if she even needed to complete them. First, she would eliminate as many of the simpler tasks as possible and let the MindWorker deal with the more difficult, dangerous ones. If Genevieve were to be trampled by Mares or devoured by the Hydra . . . oh, well. As long as Castor was ahead when the Mazon took her last breaths, she didn't really care.

And if an opportunity arose to help facilitate the Mazon's exit from the competition, Castor would take it. There were no awards for following the rules, only awards for winning. The Empire would probably thank her for keeping Genevieve's father in prison and eliminating his vicious spawn.

Their blood magic was dangerous. Everyone knew it. Even the Oracle who made them had turned against her own siblings. If they could make a horde of Gargareans kill themselves, they could make anyone bow to their will. Castor would have to be careful.

"I will let you know what I find," Delia said.

"Come back quickly."

The light inside the box flickered and went dim as the spirit left to gather information. Cas closed the lid. Open or closed, Delia would have to return to the box the moment Castor called for her. It was part of the spell that bound her. Delia could also send messages, gather information unseen, and cross long distances quickly.

Castor leaned over the edge of her chariot and watched the waters of the Aegean Sea crest white below her. Somewhere down there, the Mazon was inside her smelly whale, off to one of the labors. Castor couldn't let her get ahead. Her entire strategy depended on completing the labors before Genevieve.

The box in Castor's hand shook. She flipped open the lid to the glowing white light.

"I have some information," Delia said.

"Go." This was the benefit of having an assistant not hindered by a body.

"The last known location of Livia Kine was her home island of Eurythia."

"Not helpful." Castor rolled her eyes. "What else do you have?"

"The stables of Elis are twenty-three thousand square feet in diameter and are currently filled with seventeen tons of excrement."

That decided that, the Mazon could have it. "What about the Stymphal birds?"

"The island of Stymphal is home to almost forty thousand rock crows."

"That is a lot of birds." Castor hated birds, flying vermin. "What is a rock crow?"

"They're indigenous to the island. They call them rock crows because they are hard as rock. They bear sharp, bronze beaks and metallic feathers. The people have been trapped in their homes by the birds, slowly starving."

Castor could see now why the man needed help from the Empresses. However, if they had metallic feathers, they would be extremely susceptible to lightning. Not to mention, her horses were already headed west, toward Stymphal.

"We'll start with the birds then."

They would likely be a high task on the MindWorker's list, too, with her talent for controlling beasts. Castor would either beat Genevieve there, or they would meet on the battlefield. Luckily, the Mazon would be susceptible to lightning too. If Castor disposed of Gen today, she could claim her title before nightfall.

She pulled the drawer out from under her seat to restock her weather vials. Her insides warmed at the sight of them, a hundred silver vials with every type of weather imaginable, from lightning storms to rainbows, gentle breezes to hurricanes. Even though they sold their weather to other islands, they always kept the best storms for themselves . . . unless someone was willing to pay. Everything could be sold for enough gold.

Like the storms they'd sold to the Gargareans.

Castor attached her vials to her belt and stood up. The wind pulled at her hair and dragged her cape behind her. She searched the sky for any other flying chariots, like her father's. Apart from a few clouds and a flock of birds to her left, the sky was clear. She leaned over the side of the chariot and checked the water again, for the Mazon and her whale.

"Delia, would it be possible to locate Genevieve, the Mazon?"

"Yes, if you tell me where to look."

"She'll be on her way to one of our labors. She travels by whale . . . underwater." Whales had to surface eventually though, didn't they?

"I can try, but it could take some time."

"How much time?"

"Hours, days, weeks. I'm not certain. It's a large sea."

Castor made a difficult decision. "I would rather have you here then." As much as she wanted to keep track of Genevieve, it was more important to stay on task before her father discovered the truth.

If her father caught her in her lie before she had the Empresses' backing, he might keep her imprisoned at the manor for all eternity. Or marry her off to the first wealthy imbecile he found. Or he could exile her to the Tegean mines, and Pollux would take her place at the helm of Arcadia.

Her fist curled. The thought of Pollux sitting behind the desk in her father's office made her blood boil, in part because Pollux was so unsuitable to rule.

He was, for lack of a better word, a fool. He missed meetings because he was playing his violin or wandering an art exhibit, and back when Genevieve's circus existed, he would steal away with their father's chariot and go see it again and again—until Alcmen was arrested.

Their father wrongly thought he could change Pollux. With enough nagging and opportunity, he thought he could turn Pollux into a capable leader, even though he had never succeeded in changing their mother. The Duke of Storms was so stubborn and arrogant, he couldn't see that Castor was exactly like him, made to take his place.

She had spent her entire life preparing to be an Arcadian ruler. It was all she had ever wanted. If she lost this, it wouldn't matter what her father did to her. She would have nothing left to lose.

Up ahead, something rose out of the mist-covered water, the top of the Stymphal Mountains, a sharp and jagged cut of black rock. Most of the island was made up of this black rock. It was useless. Too porous to build with. Too ugly to admire.

Stymphal didn't have anything of value to offer Olympia. Castor knew this because she didn't sell them storms. They weren't wealthy enough or numerous enough to be of notice. The only thing they did have was location. They were the westernmost isle in Olympia, only two leagues from the border of the Elysium Empire. The Empresses kept and protected the isle to keep it from Elysium.

Castor tied her hair into a knot at the back of her head and grabbed the reins for her horses. "Hah," she called and pulled them into the mist surrounding the isle. It quickly filled in around her, turning everything gray.

Holding the reins in one hand, she grabbed an empty vial with her other to collect some of this haze. She untwisted the cap to the vial and held out her palm. The surface of her skin tingled as the mist swirled around her arm, inexplicably drawn to her. She poured the mist she captured into the vial and reached for the cap to close it in.

Something struck her hand. "Ow." The vial and its contents went over the side of the chariot, lost to the mist.

"What was that?"

"Over forty thousand rock crows have taken over the island," Delia said from within her box.

A long red welt cut across Castor's hand. She grabbed the reins as another bird slammed into the side of the chariot, and another. *Ping! Ping!* One left a dent.

"We need to get underneath them." She yanked on the reins, and the horses bucked against her. She pulled harder. Thundercloud, the gray mare on her right, violently shook her head. Castor gave the reins a sharp yank, cutting the bridle into her neck, and the mare did as commanded, diving for the isle.

Ping! Ping! More birds hit the side of the chariot. Wind pulled tears from Castor's eyes and tugged on her cape. The sky turned dark, almost black below them. It looked like a low-lying storm. Too low.

Those were the damn birds!

Castor drew back on the reins, too late. *Ping! Ping! Ping!* Birds slammed against both sides of the chariot. One got itself tangled in the horse tack. Another one struck Dewdrop, the other mare, and she bucked, knocking Castor to the back of her chariot.

"Is there a problem, Lady Castor?" Delia asked.

"Quiet!" She hissed.

She needed to get control of this situation. She reached for a vial on her belt and uncapped it. A tunnel of wind exploded from inside, sending metal-winged birds soaring off in all directions.

Castor cracked the reins. "Go! Now! Before they come back." The crows were already starting to fill in the empty space. Below, she made out the clearing in the center of the mountain range, a low-lying valley with a lake.

She jerked the horses that way, slamming into some of the crows. Castor uncapped a vial of thunder. It burst from the jar and exploded with a *boom!* It rattled through her ribs, down her legs, around her bones. She welcomed the sound. It terrified the birds. They scattered.

The horses came down wild, bucking and kicking, trying to keep the crows off their backs. Castor leapt out of the chariot and grabbed a handful of storm vials. She would hit these disgusting birds with everything she had.

The birds came in around her, and she uncapped another vial of thunder. It sounded across the valley, shaking rocks loose from the mountains. Birds that had been nesting in the trees dropped to the ground. Some of them fell into the lake and didn't come up again.

The stupid crows couldn't swim.

She reached for her hurricane and ripped open the top. A gray cloud spilled from the jar, spewing rain and wind. Castor raised her arms to the sky, and the rain soaked through her clothes. She was the storm. She was the rain. She was the wind.

She used her magic to direct the wind and clouds to the largest flock of birds. The wind swept them up and dumped them into the lake. The pouring rain kept them from escaping.

"More rain!"

Castor closed her fist and squeezed what she could from the storm. Rain pattered off her chariot and plinked off the birds' metal wings. Crows tumbled from the sky and stuck in the mud puddles. Castor shifted the rain to drown them where they sat. When they choked on the water, they stopped making so much noise.

That was better, but not good enough. There were still too many crows in the sky.

Castor pulled another vial of lightning. She opened the jar, and lines of fire poured from the sky. The birds scattered to the trees, and she waved her hand to the woods to send the lightning after them. The crows dropped from the branches in flames. Once she was sure they were dead, she moved her hurricane to douse the blaze.

The lightning lit up the sky, and the rain came down to put it out. Like a dance. Everyone thought Pollux was so talented for making music with his storms. Castor made her own music. Rain to pull the birds from the sky, lightning to strike them dead, and wind to shake them from the trees.

She pushed her wet hair from her face and blew a group of birds out of the air and dropped them beside the lake. She struck them with lightning. Their metal wings melted together until they became one smoldering pile.

The birds circled over her head in a panic, and she smiled. She wanted them dead, and not only for the sake of the lottery. She despised birds, always leaving behind feathers and droppings.

From up on the rocky mountainside, she heard cawing. The little winged beasts mocked her from up there. She struck the rock with a blast of lightning. It crumbled down the side of the hill, and the birds took flight.

They circled her once, and instead of cowering in the trees like the others, they came for her. Castor pulled on the hurricane winds, and they answered her with little more than a breeze. Her hurricane was fading. She'd squeezed all the strength out of it.

"Lightning!" She sent a bolt of it straight through the flock and only two birds burst into sparks. Castor grabbed for another vial. Before she could remove the top, one of the birds struck her in the side.

Sharp claws cut into her arm. She tumbled three times, kicking and punching to get the filthy bird off her. She heard her horses crying and kicking. The birds were on them too. She sent whatever wind she could draw from her hurricane to shake them off. She wouldn't make it to her next labor if the birds ripped apart her horses.

One of the birds snatched at her hair, pulling out a clump. It would pay for that. She tried to grab another vial and couldn't get her hands on one. The bird screamed in her face. She held up her bleeding arm, and it pecked at her flesh.

Then the bird was gone, hit with a solid whack.

Where it had been stood one of the island natives, brandishing a large axe.

He towered over her, tall and spindly with large, black eyes. "You've come to save us." He held out a hand. "We'll help you."

Over his shoulder, Castor found more of the villagers emerging from their wooden huts.

"No!" Castor got to her feet. "I have to do this. Alone."

Two years ago, a man named Apollo had hired someone to perform his servitude to the Empresses for his lottery wish. He thought he'd outwitted the rulers, but no one did that. The Empresses considered his promise moot and reclaimed his lottery prize.

Castor could not have her prize reclaimed, and she didn't know what the Empresses would consider a trespass. *She* needed to kill these birds.

"Get back into your houses. Wait there until they're gone." She ran her fingers over her remaining storm vials and grabbed the one marked "tornado." She hated to use it so soon in the game, but she had no choice.

She opened the vial and the tunnel of wind burst out of the jar. It ripped branches from the trees, roots from the ground, and pulled the birds from every place they hid. They screeched while they spun around and around. Castor raised her hands to try and keep the twister from ravaging the houses or her chariot. She couldn't start her reign as Storm Duchess with a reputation for trashing villages. She needed to show control. Perfection.

The wind drew up the last of the birds, keeping them trapped but very much alive. That wasn't good enough. Castor grabbed a new vial of lightning, unscrewed the top, and pitched the entire thing into the twister.

Sparks of light chased the birds inside the windstorm, and as the birds were struck, they dropped to the ground, half-melted piles of flesh and feathers. The faster the tornado spun, the brighter the light became. She could see the shadows of the remaining birds inside, only a handful of them now.

On the next turn, the rest of them dropped. Castor opened her jars and tried to recapture the tornado and the lightning that remained. She called them back to their vials and sealed them inside. Unfortunately, reused storms were never as strong as the originals. Fresh weather was best.

Castor stood in the mud and took a breath. With the birds gone, the weather recaptured, and the air cleared, she heard the sound of raindrops running off what was left of the trees. The glow of dead birds melting in her lightning fire shone against the puddles. The villagers emerged from their homes and looked immediately to the sky. They probably hadn't seen it in a while.

That was what Castor had always loved about storms. They appeared to be disorderly and devastating, and they were. But some things needed to be destroyed to make way for something else. Sometimes the filth needed to be washed away so something better could be built in its place.

Like the Arcadian Doctrine.

"She did it," one of the villagers exclaimed. "We're free." He raised his axe and the others joined him in his cheers.

"We've been saved by the StormMakers," a woman cried.

Castor smiled. She had taken darkness and turned it to light. She had saved these people from starvation and misery. She had done exactly what a commanding ruler should do, and the people loved her for it.

Her father couldn't see it, but he would. He would come to understand that she was the true heir of Arcadia. He'd have no choice once she won this game and the Empresses forced him to look in the right direction.

CHAPTER 7

GEN

The Lion's Den casino was on the far side of the isle. Rather than interrupt the whale's dinner to call him back, Gen decided to find other transport to the Lion, even though it cost two of her precious remaining coins to take the caravan there.

Before she climbed into the back of the wagon, she stopped to admire the two drakons pulling the carriages. The massive, blue lizards each bore six legs and a row of spines on their back. One turned to her, blinked a yellow eye, and flicked its forked tongue at her.

She was tempted to spit on him, just for a sense of what he was thinking. Did he enjoy pulling these carriages?

"You comin' or not?" the driver barked at her.

"Coming," she said, and backed away. Now was not the time to go spitting on other people's animals.

She climbed into the open wagon at the end of the train. She found a seat alone, after the women she sat next to moved abruptly to the back of the cart.

"You know who that is?" one woman said to the other.

"Yes, I know."

They both clutched their bags a little tighter. Gen remembered when people would whisper, "You know who that is?" and then clamber over themselves for her father's autograph. That memory was so tarnished, it was almost gone. But not all the way gone. If she finished this game, and defeated these labors, she could make it real again.

She pulled Chomp into her lap as the carriage set into motion over the red sands. He curled into a ball and fell asleep. The monkey clung to her shoulder and chattered in her ear. Their saliva connection had already waned. She plucked two hairs from her head and wrapped them around some of the dried apricots from her bag. She fed one to the monkey and the other to the rat.

The instant a piece of her touched their tongues, they connected. The monkey was curious about the wagon and the people inside. The rat wanted more fruit. Gen fed him a second piece without the hair.

"Keep watch for Lady Castor," she said to the monkey.

She sent him a mental image of the fierce Lady Castor with her alabaster skin and white hair. The monkey's tiny lip curled in disgust. She might have fed him some of her more personal feelings with the image. It was always hard to separate the two. MindWorker communication wasn't one-sided. If she could read their thoughts, they could read hers.

Gen leaned against the seat and ate one of her dried apricots. She watched the sky for a sign of Lady Castor and her winged chariot. There were other winged chariots sailing through the air, just not Castor's. Gen used to love watching the string of golden chariots soaring toward the casino. The people inside would all be crowding into the theater to see Alcmen and his Amazing Animals. Now they would be spending those coins on something else.

The wagon train crossed another dune, and from the sand, the great pyramid of the Lion's Den casino rose up from the ground. Lanterns burned in front of the entrance, lighting the way up the grand, red carpet and through the pearl-inlaid doors. The carving featured a lion, of course, standing on a rock, roaring with pearl-carved teeth.

This wasn't *the* Lion. Just a lion.

Gen nudged Chomp awake and carried him out of the carriage. She stood to the side and stretched her arms and legs to give the crowd some time to disperse.

"Stay two nights for the price of one at the Lion's Den with the purchase of a meal plan," one of the criers shouted while he waved a hand-painted sign of a plate of food with a turkey leg and roasted greens on top of a pile of golden potatoes.

Gen's stomach growled in response.

"One night only—Lux!"

Another crier waved a banner in her face painted with the image of a thin man with pale skin and hollow cheeks. His scraggly, white hair hung around his shoulders, brushing the top of a violin pinned under his chin. From the end of it, a burst of lightning cut across the fabric.

He looked familiar. "Is that Pollux?" Gen asked the crier.

"I believe you mean the great and talented Lux," he said, and wandered away to shout at the patrons in the carriages.

No. Gen shook her head. That was impossible. Great and talented Lux? That was most certainly Lord Pollux, Lady Castor's brother.

Gen had met him once, at the same show where she'd encountered Castor for the first time. She would never forget his face, especially since it had barely changed. It was still gaunt and dreary, with that sharp nose and wistful eyes. He always looked like he had just been crying or was about to start.

Castor had mentioned his violin playing to the Empresses. But when did the Lord of Storms start headlining shows at the casino?

She thought back to that boy in the Arcadian court, slumped in his gilded chair carved with bolts of lightning shooting from the headrest. While his sister had yawned, he'd sat up straight, hands coming together in raucous applause.

"Are you Gen?" A man approached her. His skin had a faint blue tinge to it. His hair, a darker hue. He came from Leuctra, the same island where Chomp was born. The island dipped in the middle like a bowl and collected water, about ankle deep. A blue algae grew there that made everything, well . . . a little blue.

Gen took a step back, debating how to answer the man's question. He stood taller than she did, by at least ten inches. He also carried a plain box in his hands and wore a sword on his belt along with a wrinkled black jacket and boots with loose laces. He could be approaching her for a number of reasons.

It was unlikely that news of the lottery would be widespread at this point, but the Empresses could have spies planted throughout the game to keep an eye on her. Gen was certain they had known how the lottery proceedings would go long before they made their official decree. They left very little up to chance. It was possible this man worked for them.

Or he could simply need some help with a wayward creature.

Or he could be here to shout at her for being a MindWorker.

She supposed, though, if he wanted a fight, she could always outrun him and he would trip over his untied boots.

"I am," she said. "What do you want? If you're looking for creature help, I'm currently unavailable." As much as she could use some more coin, she didn't have the time to chase slumber bees or save crops from invisible vermin.

He laughed. "I don't want anything from you. Despite much

protesting, I've come against my will. To give you this." He shoved the box at her.

The side of it bent inward, and the man wandered off, grumbling as he walked.

Gen held the box, debating whether or not she should open it. In her position, accepting odd boxes from strange men seemed like a bad idea. She took a quick look around to see if the man or anyone else was watching her. Everyone seemed to be focused on themselves, not on her.

She carefully lifted one corner of the box and held her breath. When nothing exploded or burst out of it, she took off the entire lid.

On top of a piece of yellow tissue paper sat an envelope, sealed with a wax seal. Gen removed the letter and sliced open the top.

Dear Genevieve,

I hope this letter finds you well. I have been informed of your arrangement with the Empresses, and I would like to help you. I think it's in both our best interests. Come to my show this evening, and we can speak in more detail afterward.

– Pollux

Gen raised her head and took another look at the sign the crier carried in front of her for Lux, Lord of Storms. Lux, Lord Pollux, the Storm Duke's son and Castor's twin brother. In the same envelope as the letter, she found a ticket for his show this evening, front row, balcony, seat A, the best seat in the casino.

She tapped her finger on the ticket. This was odd. How had Lord Pollux found out about the lottery so quickly and how had he known she would be here? Had Castor told him?

That didn't seem likely. Castor wouldn't announce her plans to steal the throne to the person she was trying to steal it from. In that regard Gen and Pollux were on the same side—defeat Castor. This gift could be an olive branch.

Gen went back to the box and tore open the tissue paper below the envelope. A shimmering blue cloth appeared—water silk. She yanked the garment from the box, and it unfurled into a beautiful off-the-shoulder silk gown.

As the skirt cascaded to her feet, the color of the fabric changed from light blue to deep blue, to white-crested waves. It kissed her fingers with a whisper. The water silk came from the water worms on Oyges, who only spun in the flood months and produced less than a hundred yards of this a year. And Gen held an entire gown made of it.

She clutched the dress in her fingers. She'd dreamed of one day having her own piece of water silk, and here it was, hanging from her fingers. But it would be a mistake to accept an extravagant gift from an almost stranger, especially the brother of the girl she was currently racing to defeat, right?

On the other hand, it wouldn't be accepting the dress to just hold on to it for the moment. What else could she do with it? Leave it here in the sand? She discarded the wrappings and gently folded the dress inside her bag. She would decide what to do about Lord Pollux later.

"Let's go inside."

She led Chomp and the monkey through the pearl doors onto the casino floor. Loud music blared from a stage set up in the center of the floor, surrounded by gaming tables of all kinds. People placed stacks of coins on green felt, kissed stones, and blew on cards, all hoping for that one big win that would change their life.

One patron got his win. A funnel under a spinning wheel opened wide and spat coins in his hands, and almost immediately, two girls in feathered skirts curled up to either side of him. He would be lucky to walk out of here with a single one of those coins in his pocket. Most likely, he would gamble those coins away and get himself into more trouble than he came in with.

If he lost too much, he'd never leave. He'd become a slave to the Lion to pay off his debts and, like Percy, have to run for his life or be made a painful example.

Years ago, Gen and Alcmen and Zusma had walked through here like royalty. Then, after her fall from grace, Gen had been shoved from the doors like a common thief. This place held no promises, no guarantees except that the Lion ruled the Den and everyone inside it was subject to her rule. It was a lesson Gen wished she had learned sooner.

She stopped in the center of the floor and scratched the monkey behind the ear. "Keep watch for Castor," she whispered before she set him loose. He scurried up the curtains, turning red to match the audacious hue. Their MindWorker strings lengthened, pulling taut like a length of rubber. The monkey's voice became a whisper in her thoughts, but it was still there. She would hear him if he called to her, and he could hear her too.

She left him to his spying and wove through the spinning wheels, musicians, gamblers, and card tables, keeping a wary eye on anyone she passed. No one here was her friend, proven as she approached the doors that would take her to the Lion's private quarters. Her insides knotted when the hulking, gold Gargarean standing there crossed his muscled arms. *Of course.* It was as if the Gargareans' new task, now that the war had ended, was to ruin her life.

Well, she had to face him. This was the only way to the Lion.

"Excuse me," she said through clenched teeth, and her Mazon strength came to life. The silver bands on her arms swelled, filling her with enough hate-inspired muscle to make her dizzy.

The Gargarean dropped his gold chin and smiled, as if she were something he could pick from his crooked teeth. "What do you want?"

"Gen the MindWorker to see the Lion."

"The Lion isn't seeing anyone."

"You can tell her I bring word from the Empresses." She dragged out the *esses* in *Empresses* to make her mission sound more important.

"Doesn't matter. She told me not to let anyone up. Try again later, little Mazon." He picked something from his nose and wiped it on his sleeve. The Gargareans weren't known for their manners, or hygiene. Gen couldn't blame Hippolyta for finding a way to breed without them.

"Trust me, I will."

She spun on her heel and stomped away. This was an unexpected setback, and one she couldn't bear. Peering at the doors from behind one of the casino games, she watched the Gargarean guard continue to pick his massive nose. Disgusting.

She needed to get him away from the doors. If she tried to drag him away herself, she would unquestionably be removed from the casino, which wouldn't get her any closer. What she needed was a distraction.

Monkey, I could use your help.

The threads connecting them vibrated as he made his way

toward her. His fur changed to a gold color to match the casino railings, then to a mix of blue and yellow when he dropped onto someone's back, and finally to her own olive tone when he landed on her arm.

"You see that disgusting gold brute there?" she whispered to him.

The monkey chattered in confirmation.

"I need you to get him away from that elevator. Go over there and break some things, make noise, make a mess, whatever you need to do, but stay hidden and run if he gets close. He won't be forgiving."

The monkey blinked a series of eyes in understanding. He would be careful. He also liked the idea of wreaking havoc in the casino. So many shiny things to break.

"Go ahead," she said to the monkey. "Break whatever you like."

The monkey leapt from her shoulder to the top of one of the spinning wheels. He shifted to a mix of yellow and red, to match the bold colors. He blended in perfectly. The woman below didn't bat an eyelash.

"I've won! I've won!" She threw all four of her arms up in celebration as coins slid down the tube and then suddenly stopped when the monkey turned the wheel.

"What happened?" The woman frowned. "I was winning. Those coins were mine!" Her shouts drew the attention of the Gargarean guard, but didn't move him.

I need more, Gen sent to the monkey.

"I need to speak to someone! I was robbed!" the woman shouted as the table beside her collapsed.

Glasses shattered, coins tumbled to the floor, and people scrambled to grab them. A man spilled his drink onto another woman's shirt, and when she started screaming, the monkey changed to red to match her wig and ripped it from her head.

"How dare you!" The woman slapped the man, who stumbled into a cocktail waitress, causing her to fling her tray onto another Gargarean security guard.

That did the trick.

The door guard rushed in to inspect the chaos, and Gen made her move.

"Stay close," she said to Chomp. The monkey dropped the stolen wig onto the guard, giving Gen a chance to leap over the broken table and spilled drinks. She reached the door and pulled.

The door didn't budge. She leaned back and flexed her muscles, and Chomp snarled at her feet. A second later, a meaty hand clamped onto her shoulder.

"Where do you think you're going?" She recognized the Gargarean's dimwitted voice.

She pried his fingers from her skin and spun to face him. "It's later, isn't it?"

"You cause all this?" He thumbed over his shoulder to the maids already sweeping up broken glass, and the casino official taking a statement from the woman who had lost her winnings.

"I have no idea what you're talking about." She tried to smile, but it was an impossible expression to muster in the face of a Gargarean.

"All right, that's it, little Mazon. Time for you to go." He reached for her arm, and Gen snatched it back. She couldn't be removed from the casino. This was her only way to the Lion, and while she grappled with this Gargarean beast, Castor was out there, checking labors off their list.

"Wait," Gen pleaded, trying to think of a way to fix this when she saw another sign for Lux's show hanging from the wall. "I'm a special guest of Lux," she said, and reached into her bag for the ticket. "I thought while I was here, I would see the Lion. We are old acquaintances." She shoved the gold ticket in the Gargarean's face, and he squinted at it, cocking his head to the side. She wondered if he could read it.

"Lux will be very disappointed if I'm not at his show," she added. "He might refuse to play here ever again if I were mistreated." With that, the Gargarean's face changed. He must have been given the instruction to "keep Lux happy," the only thing saving her from being tossed out of this casino. Again.

"Stay out of trouble," he grunted. "I see you again, and you're out of here."

"Of course." She stepped away before he changed his mind.

Come on, she called to the monkey. *We're done here.*

He scurried down from the wall and landed on her shoulder. Gen took the gold ticket and examined it herself. After her failed attempt at sneaking through the doors, this could be her only chance to get to the Lion. Lux, the star of the performance, Lord of Storms, would have more clout to get past the guard than she did, but was it worth the risk?

The only people she despised more than the Gargareans were the gold-grabbing Arcadians and their deadly storms. Stronger than her hate for either of them, though, was her need to save her father, and she had promised herself she would do anything for him. Even if it meant temporarily allying with an Arcadian.

"Come on," Gen said to her creatures. "We'll graze the buffet before the show begins."

She reached into her bag for her few remaining coins and her fingers brushed the soft water silk dress. She couldn't go to a show dressed in her dusty pants and jacket, could she?

"Wait here," she said to Chomp and the monkey. "I'm going to the washroom to change first."

CHAPTER 8

GEN

The casino buffet wasn't nearly as grand or mouthwatering as the sign outside had depicted, but what did Gen expect for one piece of silver? She picked at her soggy seaweed salad while the monkey stole pieces of fried nectarine off her plate, the rat munched on a dried crust of bread, and Chomp gnawed on a turkey leg under the table.

The sign over the buffet stated *Strictly No Sharing*, and the woman at the counter glared at Gen when she went up for a second turkey leg for Chomp. Gen smiled at her in response, and the woman stepped back in horror.

This was when being feared and hated became useful. The woman wouldn't dare confront Gen about being in the casino with her menagerie or feeding them under the table. It wasn't worth the risk of being "blood poisoned."

Gen sat down and unfolded her napkin list of tasks. Even though she hadn't finished labor number one, she needed to think ahead, plan her next steps. She looked too long at the Mares and the Hydra. Her mother's strategy had always been to do the hardest thing first, to get it out of the way. It was why she always did her greatest feats of strength at the beginning of the performance before she got tired.

It made sense, except in this case, Gen might not survive the hardest things.

She went further down the list and stopped at the birds. Her magic would be useful for controlling the birds, and Castor would likely pick that as a top task too. Gen would head to Stymphal as soon as she had Percy's debts settled.

"Lux's performance begins in thirty minutes," a wandering crier called. "If you have tickets, please come for priority seating. No one is admitted after the performance begins, per Lux's request."

Across the dining room, a handful of young women squealed with delight. Other people abandoned their trays of food, half-eaten, nearly knocking over one another to get to the door as if the crier had said the building was on fire. Could the Lord of Storms really be that impressive? Gen wanted to find out for herself.

She finished her salad and made her way to the theater, halted by a mass of bodies clogging the doors. She stood at the end of a long line of patrons, many of them young women around her age, shrieking in excitement.

"You know last time I saw him, he winked at me!"

"He did not. He winked at me!"

"You're both wrong. He had something in his eye."

Were they talking about the same Lord Pollux? The pale, skinny boy with the sunken cheeks? That didn't seem right. Granted, Pollux had money, and power, and apparently some musical talent, but still . . . that didn't seem like enough to send women into fits.

At the front of the line, tickets were checked and double-checked. The Gargarean guards dragged away two people by the collars of their shirts for having counterfeits. Gen pinched the skirt of the soft water silk gown while she waited her turn. By the large clock on the wall, she only had five minutes before the doors closed.

Finally she reached the front and held out her ticket to the attendant, a man in a black suit who saw the silver stripes on her arms and suddenly had somewhere else to go.

"I can help you."

A young woman snatched Gen's ticket and held it to the light. She swept her coif of pink hair from her face and squinted at the seat assignment while the lanterns caught the little gemstones adhered to her eyebrows. They matched the short, silver-sequined dress she wore.

"Right this way." The girl waved Gen into the hall with long, pale arms marked with fine blue lines.

Gen thought of the weeping woman at the lottery. *That* woman and *this* woman must come from the same island. Gen opened her mouth to ask this girl if she knew Livia Kine and stopped herself when she realized how ridiculous that would be. Just because two people were of the same island, the same race, didn't mean they knew one another. That was the mistake people always made about her, that her being a MindWorker made her dangerous or unscrupulous.

She and the girl walked the length of the theater, down the thin red runner that stretched between the rows of plush, gold seats. The auditorium reached almost to the top of the pyramid and nearly every seat on every tier held a vying patron.

A sold-out show. Before Lux, the only shows to fill the casino were Alcmen's Amazing Animals and Tykara, a singer from Molorchus who sang in three different harmonies at once.

"You're right here," the woman said. "Special guest of Lux himself." She winked at Gen, returned her ticket to her, and closed the curtain to the small balcony behind her.

Gen heaved Chomp onto the second seat and leaned over the balcony. The monkey climbed up the curtain for a better view, and the rat remained in her bag, eating bread crumbs. Below her, and slightly to her left, the stage stretched across the room, a smooth, empty glass floor. No preset props or sets. Curious.

"Doors close in two minutes. No exceptions," another crier called. A woman picked up her skirt and raced to her seat, practically climbing over others to get there, and four people squeezed through the doors before they sealed shut. Then the lanterns went dim and what looked like bottled sunlight hit the stage.

The light illuminated a lone figure holding a violin—Pollux. He looked even less impressive onstage than he had in the ad. Pale white hair hung long and thin down either side of his face as he hunched over his instrument. He was stiff and cold. He looked like he had been carved from ice.

The crowd exploded into applause, shrieking, "I love you, Lux!" until he raised his bow. As the tip of it caught the light, the crowd went silent, some of them gasping in mid-scream. What was the fuss about? What could he possibly do without sets or costumes that sent people into fits?

Pollux lifted his violin, a sleek, purple instrument with a bolt of lightning crossing under the strings. His gaze flicked to her for the barest moment, probably to make sure she'd come, and then his bow pulled on the violin strings.

The first note sounded long and low, like a sigh, and while it played, a wisp of cloud rose from the center of the violin. Another light flashed down from the ceiling, pink this time, and illuminated the cloud as it took shape into the silhouette of a girl with another high-pitched note. From the crack in the curtain, she spotted the man who had given her the dress and invitation. He opened jars of sunlight while Pollux made the music and the cloud figure.

She understood now. The violin was some custom StormMaker instrument. It must have been made from that metal, the Illumium. Pollux somehow released the storms and recaptured them with the pull of his bow. It was clever, she supposed, but if he pulled the wrong string, he could blast everyone dead with lightning, and no one here seemed to care.

Lower notes played, and another puff of cloud emerged. A gust of wind shaped it into a larger figure, a boy, and then with a series of twittering sounds, the two clouds spun around each other, followed by the lights. When the two clouds parted, the music changed, and the pink cloud raced around the stage in a circle while the blue cloud followed in pursuit.

The blue cloud had almost caught the pink when the violin trilled, and the little pink cloud danced across the crowd to gasps of *oohs* and *ahhs*.

"It's not that impressive," Gen muttered under her breath.

It was a cheap trick, making the audience feel more engaged by bringing the show closer to their seats. Alcmen had been doing it long before Pollux and his violin, and others long before that.

Pollux bent his chin over his violin and dug deeper into the strings. The sounds went from lilting and playful to hard and quick. A dark cloud swirled overhead, drawing another gasp from the crowd as rain poured down onto the stage, each droplet poking a new hole in the smoke figures while simultaneously plastering Pollux's thin hair to his cheeks.

The two smoke figures reached for one another with quickly fading arms. Then a gust of wind and a new series of notes swept the rain droplets into a towering figure with the uncanny resemblance to a Gargarean.

It raised a watery fist and slammed it hard to the stage. When it hit the glass, it shattered into droplets that splattered the guests in the first few rows. The two wisp figures rose out of the violin again, clasping hands. They tried to escape the water villain and couldn't. High shrill notes sounded like screams, then lower ones became sobs when the rain Gargarean crushed the pink wisps of cloud in thick fingers.

The blue cloud grew larger, more threatening, and raised a wisp arm to strike the Gargarean when a bolt of lightning came from the ceiling and pierced him in half. He disappeared into mist, a fog that flowed over the crowd.

The water Gargarean clutched his stomach and laughed in bouncing, deep tones, accompanied by thunder and blasts of lightning. He was so caught up in his own revelry, he didn't notice the fog re-forming into a shape behind him.

Gen dug her nails into the balcony railing while the blue cloud grew larger. It grabbed one of the bolts of lightning before it touched the stage. The figure wrapped the lightning around his hand, a crackling ball of fire, and when the rain Gargarean finally noticed, it was too late.

The blue cloud struck at the rain villain, and loud, piercing sounds came from the violin as the water Gargarean shattered into a flood that ran from the stage onto the red carpet below. The blue cloud fell to his knees, chest heaving in somber notes. He pawed at the stage looking for remnants of the pink cloud that was no more. He buried his face into hands and wept, shaking as the music changed, high and quiet . . . and then a small, almost infinitesimal wisp of pink rose from the strings.

The room went dark again briefly, and the theater exploded

into applause and cheers, a sound that rivaled the false thunder. Gen kept one hand on the balcony, the other hand on her chest. She was speechless. Breathless. Somehow he had managed to make her ache for cloud and rain.

She hated clouds, she hated thunder, she hated everything StormMaker except for this.

The house lights brightened, and the cheers and applause turned to groans. Gen dropped her hand to her lap. She had to admit he created quite a show. Unique. Of course, it would have been better with more substance: other musicians, sets, props, an opening act. No doubt he had talent, and an amazing choreographer; he just needed more.

This had been helpful, though. She knew what she would be up against once she reclaimed her circus.

Someone cleared their throat behind her.

Gen turned, wiping the budding tears from her eyes. The Leuctran man from before stood behind her. He leaned against the balcony wall. How long had he been there?

"Enjoy the show?" He picked something from his fingernail and reached for Chomp.

Before she could warn him away from the temperamental chaeri, his blue fingers tangled in purple fur. Oh well. If Chomp bit him, it would be his own fault.

Chomp, however, only glared at him before closing his eyes. That was odd. Chomp usually bit everyone who wasn't Gen. Maybe some part of him recognized the man from his brief stay on their shared home island. Or he was too tired to bite him.

"Come with me," he said.

"Why?"

He pinched the bridge of his nose. "You're here, aren't you? If you want to talk to Pollux, I'd suggest you get up and start walking."

He turned and stumbled through the curtain, and Gen stood up to follow, depositing Chomp onto the rug beside her.

She kept her distance, following the strange man down a set of dimly lit stairs that led to the catacomb of tunnels. The monkey followed behind, picking at costumes and dress wigs, and swinging from pulley ropes. Gen let him play as she made her way to the dressing area.

Like in the theater, squealing boys and girls surrounded the door. They pushed at one another to get closer to the room, begging for autographs and kisses while two Gargarean guards held them back.

"Move," the Leuctran man said, and swatted Pollux's fans away like flies to get to the door. Gen followed in his wake, underneath the glare of one of the Gargarean guards.

"She's with me," the Leuctran man added, and the Gargarean begrudgingly made space for them to pass.

She smiled at him as she did, the silver bands of skin tightening around her neck, begging her to slap him. She refrained, slipping into the open crack of a door while the fans outside craned for a view into Pollux's chamber.

Various gifts filled his dressing room. Tables piled with exotic flowers and snacks, an entire three-tiered tray of various sweets that Gen recognized as delicacies from at least five different islands, including her coveted Grouseberry pops. She and her family had played sold-out shows, too, and had never been given a sweet tower.

Pollux was in the process of changing from his rain-soaked clothes. He dropped a new shirt over his thin frame, and his head emerged, pale hair still wet and stringy, his blue, almost colorless eyes hauntingly large when framed by such dark lashes.

"Genevieve," he said. "You came." He sounded surprised. Even he thought it was a mistake for her to be here.

"Pollux," she said, specifically omitting the "Lord." He wasn't *her* lord. She had been born on her father's sailing ship. She had no island and paid fealty only to the Empresses. "Thank you for the dress. It's lovely."

"You're welcome. It was Bale's idea." He gestured to the Leuctran who was currently picking through Pollux's tables of treats. He smiled when he picked up a bottle of wine.

"We hadn't been formally introduced," Gen said. "The dress was your idea?"

He shrugged as he opened up the wine. "Simple pleasures for simple people." He held up the wine, and she wasn't sure who he was calling "simple." Her or him.

Pollux took a step, caught his foot on the side of his chair, and stumbled. He steadied himself on the dressing room table before he planted to the floor, and Gen winced. How could someone who made such lovely music be so unfortunately awkward, and how could so many people be enrapt with . . . this?

She cleared her throat. "I got your note. How did you know about the lottery?"

"I had someone monitoring the events," Pollux said.

"And how did you know I would come here first?"

"I didn't. I had this performance booked long before the lottery. Had we not met here, I would have found you elsewhere."

"Must be fate," Bale muttered before he tipped back the wine.

"I don't believe in fate." If she started believing in it, she would have to admit that this was where she was meant to be, and no amount of struggling would lift her back up. "How do I know you're not trying to sabotage me?"

"My sister can't be ruler of Arcadia," Pollux said.

"She says the same about you."

"She's probably right." He picked at the violin string with his fingernail. *Ping, ping, ping.* "Our people will be left with bad or worse when my father dies, but bad is better than worse."

"Do you even want the throne?"

"It doesn't matter. I don't want Castor to have it. She would sell lightning to anyone and everyone who could pay for it, like the Gargareans."

Gen flinched. He knew exactly where to strike her. She would never wish the Mazons' fate, *her* fate, on anyone. "I don't want that, but what would *you* do with the storms?"

"The same as we have been doing." He turned another peg. *Ping, ping, ping.* "Weather management for growth, protection."

"Music?" She nodded to his violin.

"It's performance art." He lowered the violin. "And, yes, there's a small market for storm instruments." He stood up, chin down, eyes somewhere on her shoulder. "I want to help you to help my sister. If she wins her game, she'll get her throne, but not until our father is gone. He won't be happy she defied him. I don't think she realizes the consequences of what she's doing."

Gen understood. This had nothing to do with her, and everything to do with his sordid family drama. She wanted no part of that. She had her own family drama.

"I hope you're not suggesting an alliance."

Pollux and Bale looked to one another, Bale with a knowing look on his unshaven face. "That was . . . sort of the plan," Pollux said.

Gen shook her head. "I will defeat your sister, but I don't want you tagging along with me."

"It isn't—"

Gen stopped him. "I could, however, use some help getting to the Lion. She's under tight security."

"I can do that," Pollux said.

"Good," Gen exhaled.

"I guess we're going out then." Bale drank the rest of the wine and wiped the residue from his chin.

Looking between the two of them, the half-drunken Bale and the fair-haired Pollux, did she really have reason to worry? Even if they tried to cross her, they wouldn't get far. She was part Mazon, after all. But you could never fully trust an Arcadian. They always had a bolt of lightning hiding in their sleeve, and they would strike you with it when you least expected it.

CHAPTER 9

GEN

We're going to see the Lion," Bale said to the same Gargarean guard who had turned Gen away earlier.

"Right away," the Gargarean grunted as he pushed open the doors.

Gen batted her eyelashes, trying not to look smug about getting past his defenses. She couldn't seem to manage it. The smugness crept to her face against her will.

Come on, she called to the monkey. *We're going upstairs.*

The monkey climbed down the curtains and landed on Gen's shoulder, temporarily revealing himself when he changed from blue to golden brown to match her.

"You have some interesting friends," Bale said.

The monkey plucked a bug from his fur and held it out to Bale as an offering.

Bale looked to Gen. "Am I supposed to take this?"

"I suppose you are."

Bale plucked the bug from the monkey's fingers and dropped it to the rug when the monkey's attention was diverted. He ground it into the fibers with the toe of his boot.

"What is his name?" Pollux asked.

"Monkey," Gen said.

"You're not going to name him?"

"No. Giving something a name declares ownership. I don't own him. He stays because he is grateful."

"Grateful of what?"

"That I rescued him from a cage."

"Let's move," Bale said.

Gen, Pollux, Bale, Chomp, and the monkey stepped through the doors onto a wooden platform. The Gargarean grabbed the handle on a large crank and grunted as he spun it, his golden arms flexing. With each turn, their platform lifted, inching toward the top of the pyramid.

When the crank clicked into place, they had reached the top.

The Gargarean pushed open the doors, and Gen smiled at him. "You could have saved us both a lot of time and effort if you'd simply let me pass the first time."

"Tinshe," the Gargarean muttered, and Gen's smug grin faded. Loosely translated, it meant "whore." What the Gargareans had called the Mazons when they'd been breeding.

"Corchek," she snapped back. The insult meant "kept one," "slave," which was what he was working as the Lion's elevator guard.

He raised his fist, and Pollux shook his head. The Gargarean lowered his arm.

"What did you say to him?" Bale asked.

"You don't speak Gargarean?"

"No," Bale said.

"Well then." Gen smiled. "It's a form of gratitude. You should be sure to say it to every Gargarean you meet."

"That didn't look like a greeting," Bale said.

"It wasn't," Pollux said. "She called him a slave."

"That sounds like a dangerous thing to call a Gargarean," Bale said.

"Only if you're afraid of them." She was not. Gen had too much anger for the Gargareans to fear them.

They stepped up to a set of silver doors, and Pollux tightened his grip on his violin case. This was the door to the Lion's rooms. Gen wished she could get a better read on Pollux. He said so little of consequence. Was he white-knuckling his violin case because he was angry or afraid?

It was always hard to read the intentions of quiet people. Pollux could be worried either for her or because of her. He could be leading her into an elaborately crafted plot to take her out of this contest. Or he could just be afraid to be seen with her in front of the Lion. She supposed she would find out soon enough.

Gen pushed open the doors to the Lion's rooms and nudged Chomp inside. When his paw touched the tile, the floor beneath him turned purple. The Aphrodite tiles were made from the white stone mined on Cythera. They reacted to pressure and, supposedly, could read people's emotions. Heavy, angry footsteps turned red. Light, lilting, happy steps shone yellow. It was completely inaccurate, though, because it didn't account for things like weight, or a limp, or that one person everyone knew who moved through a room like air.

Even so, Gen paid attention to her toes when she stepped forward. The floor illuminated red. No surprise. She certainly wasn't pleased to be here. Bale, yellow, which seemed odd. He didn't seem to be in a good mood at all, and Pollux, pale blue. Slightly worried.

About what? Facing the Lion? Or something much deeper?

Above them, the ceiling reached to a point, the top of the pyramid made completely from glass. Night sky spread from end to end, dotted with pinpricks of stars and the sliver of their yellow moon hanging on the black.

More guards lined the wall, some Gargareans, some other large figures with equally threatening grimaces and rippling muscles. Attendants, chairs, potted plants, and plush sofas occupied the rest of the room along with the Lion, curled up in the center on a white settee.

She stretched her legs like a cat and stood to greet them. Her red-and-orange-striped hair fell long on browned shoulders, and she blinked with yellow eyes marked with slitted pupils. As she walked across the floor, the stones turned gold underneath her feet and her long tail swished back and forth behind her. She waltzed through the room in a trail of confidence. Or conceit, Gen thought.

No one knew where the Lion came from, if she'd had a name before the Lion, if she had been born with the gold, catlike eyes and sharp cheekbones, and the tail, or if she had made a bargain with a mage to become more lionlike.

"Lord Pollux," she purred while she ran a sharp fingernail down his arm.

She didn't acknowledge Gen standing right beside him. It was as if she were simply another potted plant or errant chairs. After years and years of sold-out shows, this was what she had become—as unnoticeable as a piece of furniture.

"Wonderful show." The Lion kissed Pollux on the cheek. "I was watching from the upper deck. Breathtaking. When can you play again?"

"I'm not sure. I'm working on something else right now." He turned to Gen, luring the Lion's gaze.

When the Lion's eyes finally found hers, they soaked in every inch of the water silk gown. "It looks like you've improved *your* standings."

Gen ignored the implication. "I'm here on behalf of the Empresses. They've asked——"

The Lion waved her hand. "I know all about the lottery, so you can stop right there. As much as I'd like to see you scratch your way out of poverty, I can't go forgiving Percy's debt. It will set a bad example."

Did everyone in Olympia know about the lottery? News must be spreading like wildfire on the backs of winged horses. "Then can you give him more time to pay it?"

The Lion laughed. "Percy owes me almost eighty thousand coins, and he hasn't paid one. I could give him a thousand years, and I'd never see it."

The nice man with the blue mustache had not looked like a deadbeat gambler, but they never did.

"You can tell your friend Percy," the Lion continued, "he has three days to show his face here, and if he doesn't, he can become proof of what happens when you cross the Lion. Now if you'll excuse me . . ."

Before she could finish, the silver doors opened behind them, and in came two Gargarean guards, dragging the woman who had led Gen to her seat behind them. The floor tiles turned green as the woman's knees scraped over them, revealing her fear. On either side of her, the Gargareans walked with heavy, red footsteps.

They dumped the girl at the Lion's feet, and the floor turned purple with worry.

"Ah, see." The Lion pointed at the woman with a gold fingernail, sharpened to a knife point. "This is what comes of lax rules. This young lady decided she had served enough of her time and was free to go."

"That's not what I thought." The woman shivered as blood ran from her split lip. "I was helping a customer to his ship."

"By crawling into the cargo hold?" The Lion grabbed the woman by the hair and yanked her head upright. Gen winced. The monkey on her shoulder trembled. "I can't have liars and thieves working for me, Miss Livia Kine."

Gen's heart stopped. This was Livia Kine? *The* Livia Kine?

It made perfect sense. Livia would not be the first to disappear under the Lion's thumb. Her entire business ran on the blood of those indebted to her. Livia hadn't been lost, she'd been here for the past two years, working off a debt, which meant Gen had two tasks right here in front of her. And she couldn't touch either one.

"Bring the orthus!" The Lion shouted.

Two of the Gargareans marched to a door at the back of the room and cranked it open. When the door rose, a two-headed canine emerged with two sets of snapping teeth, frothing jaws, and fierce red eyes.

Gen tugged on Pollux's sleeve. "Livia is one of my tasks," she whispered to him. "I need to get her home."

His spine straightened. He hadn't made the connection, and obviously the Lion hadn't received the full lottery list, either, or she wouldn't be threatening Livia with a two-headed dog. Not when she was so valuable.

The poor dog pulled against its leash, snapping and struggling. Red, raw skin peered out from under the collar. Even though the beast was about to devour Livia, Gen couldn't help pitying it. Animals only acted as they had been treated.

Alcmen had asked on several occasions to see the orthus. The Lion always refused, afraid Alcmen would spit in the cage and take it. But controlling a beast like this with spittle would be impossible, even for the Amazing Alcmen. Animals like this shouldn't be controlled at all.

"This girl thinks she can choose her own payment terms." The Lion held Livia in place with the point of her heel. "I decide the payment terms, and for attempted escape, it will be a date with my orthus."

"Don't do this!" Pollux shouted. "I'll pay her debt."

"Too late for that." The Lion waved her hand, and the Gargarean guard released the snapping orthus. It lunged for the easiest and safest prey, the one pinned under the Lion's shoe.

Bale jumped and grabbed Livia by the shoulders, yanking her aside, and Gen lunged for the beast. Her fingers caught the edge of the collar, and the dog's right head spun on her arm, teeth sinking in deep.

She snapped her hand back as excruciating pain rolled up to her shoulder. Blood ran from two puncture wounds in her flesh, and her head filled with foreign feelings. Hunger, anger, need, fear, disgust, and mild affection.

The orthus's emotions seeped into her own. The right half of the dog held back, blood dripping from its jaw—her blood. He must have felt new things too, like her desperation to keep him away from Livia.

"Stop him!" Gen shouted.

She pointed to the left half of the dog, and the right head turned and snapped, jaws frothing. He had consumed enough of her blood that he was under her veritable control. At least, half of him was.

The other half reeled back in surprise as its brother nipped at it. The orthus scrambled across the floor, knocking over plants and people, one half snarling and snapping, the other trying to escape.

Blood ran down Gen's arm and dropped onto her leg. Where it soaked into the water silk, the pale blue skirt turned rusty red. The most beautiful and expensive dress she had ever owned—ruined.

"Let Livia go," Gen snapped at the Lion, "and release Percy from his debt, or I'll send the orthus after you." If she was leaving here with a bloodied dress, she would also be leaving with the two labors marked off her list.

"I don't take orders from you." The Lion snapped her fingers and retreated to the same door the orthus came from.

Gen moved to follow. The Gargarean guards shifted to block her way. Pollux flipped the latch on his violin case and drew it out. He pulled on the strings, and a wall of rushing air and music struck the guards in the chest. They slid across the floor, leaving red footsteps in their wake.

"Go!" Pollux shouted, and played a series of quick notes. At the top of the pyramid, a black cloud emerged, crackling with lightning.

"Stay with him," she said to the monkey. "Chomp, you come with me."

Gen ducked under the storm and slid across the floor in time to reach the door before it sealed closed. She grasped the bottom, and her Mazon strength surged. More blood poured from her bite wound. Beside her, Chomp scratched at the floor.

She shifted her legs underneath her for more leverage and pulled, burying the agony from her injured arm under the desperation to mark these two things off her list. The door creaked. Her thigh muscles expanded and something ripped—the skirt of the water silk dress split at the seam.

Gen had nothing left to lose. She pulled harder, drawing on the inherited Mazon strength she'd never fully used before. She'd never had the need. Or the desire. This strength never felt like it belonged to her. It had been her mother's. Gen had only been the closest vessel to receive it when she'd died. But it was a gift, this strength, and Gen needed it now.

She sank her fingers into the door, gritted her teeth, and pulled. The gears of the closing mechanism whined in defeat. The door slid up to her knees and stopped there with an exhale. She shimmied underneath, and Chomp crawled in beside her.

Behind her, lightning flashed and rain beat against the walls from Pollux's violin. The orthus chased itself in circles. The monkey pitched broken pots at the heads of the Gargareans, and Bale tossed him more things to throw, laughing to himself each time the monkey hit his mark.

Chaos.

But in the back room, things remained quiet. Gen stood in the Lion's bedroom, and behind the four-poster bed with the golden sheets, the Lion crouched like a cornered cat.

"There's nowhere for you to go," Gen said while blood pattered off the ends of her fingers.

"Then come and get me," the Lion purred, luring Gen with a pointed claw.

"Fine."

She wasn't going to be tossed out by the Lion again.

Gen lunged. The Lion raised a crossbow. The bolt snapped and whipped by Gen's ear. Chomp pulled back his lip and bared his sharp teeth. He scrambled across the floor toward the Lion. She aimed the bow at him.

"No!" Gen shouted. Fool chaeri. She couldn't lose him. She yanked the rat from her bag and nudged him awake. "Smoke, smoke! We need smoke!"

The rat opened his jaw in a wide yawn and smoke poured from his lungs. It engulfed the room in a haze that smelled like wilted lettuce. The bow released. Gen held her breath, waiting for Chomp's yelp of pain.

It didn't come.

The Lion must have missed. Gen hoped she missed. It was impossible to tell. The entire room had clouded over in gray. She couldn't see anything. Not even her hand somewhere in front of her. The rat smoke hung more thickly than real fog. It draped everything in an impenetrable curtain of haze.

Gen strained to hear something in the room, a breath, a whisper, a snarl, anything. If she called out, the Lion would hear her and likely shoot her. If she released her slumber bees, they wouldn't know where to go.

Gen called to the rat, *Where is she?*

He was the only one who could navigate his own smoke.

A tiny tail curled around her finger and pulled her forward. Gen crawled on hands and knees as quietly as possible, letting the rat lead her around the bed. She held her breath and shuffled forward. She would have one chance at this. As soon as she made a move, the Lion would hear her and shoot.

They rounded the bed, and Gen's shoulder slammed into the side. She heard the click of the bow and lunged, waiting for the bolt to pierce her somewhere. Her fingers tangled in the Lion's hair. Claws raked across her injured arm. She screamed and grabbed whatever she could find.

By chance, she caught the Lion by the neck. The Lion continued to claw at Gen's arm until she squeezed harder, closing off the Lion's air supply.

"No more smoke, please," Gen called to the rat. She needed to see what she was doing.

The Lion twisted and kicked, trying to wriggle free. "You're crushing me," she choked.

"Then give up. Let Livia go and release Percy from his debts," Gen said. With Mazon strength flooding her body, she felt powerful, invincible. Was this how her mother had felt all the time?

"Let *me* go," the Lion choked.

"I will as soon as you agree to give me Percy and Livia."

"Never."

They were at a standstill. Gen didn't want to kill the Lion. She also couldn't leave here without her two labors complete.

"Can't you just accept Pollux's offer to pay?" she asked.

"No," the Lion rasped. "I had no idea Livia was so valuable to you."

If the Lion hadn't pieced together that Livia was on the list, she did now, and she would want to be properly compensated for her.

Gen sighed. She could think of only one thing that might tempt the Lion. "What if Pollux performed a second time, a charity show of sorts?"

A sold-out show like Pollux's brought the casino much more than Mr. Percy or Livia could possibly owe. In addition to the ticket cost, the Lion sold rooms and food, and collected coins as every one of Lux's fans gambled away their savings. In the end, she would profit on the exchange.

The Lion ceased squirming. "He would do it completely free? No charge?"

"If I can get him to agree to it—yes." He had already offered to pay, and what did the Lord of Storms need with show money?

"Then you can have them," the Lion said.

"Thank you." Gen released the Lion from her grip. The Lion dropped to all fours and gasped for air, heaving and choking. The smoke in the room had cleared to a thin haze. Gen searched desperately for Chomp and found him cowering under the bed.

"You can come out now." She coaxed him to her lap.

Shivering, Chomp made his way to her. He appeared to be unharmed, apart from his nerves. He was too old for this kind of excitement.

The Lion rose to her elbows. "I might offer you a job on my guard staff if I didn't despise you so much." She revealed the points of her canines as she snarled.

"I might accept it if I didn't feel the same." Gen held a hand out to the Lion. The woman ignored it and used her bed to stand instead.

"Remember, I didn't do this out of the goodness of my heart." The Lion clawed through her tangled hair. "I didn't want to be strangled to death. But no show. No Percy."

"You'll get it." She hoped. Pollux still had to agree to this.

Blood ran down Gen's arm and splattered on the skirt of her dress. When she'd first put it on, it had been perfect, flawless. Now it was bloodied and torn like a common rag. Maybe she could find some superior tailor who could mend it . . . for coin she didn't have.

At least the dress's death had not been in vain. Its sacrifice had gained her two tasks, two on her way to six. Four more, and she would have everything.

In the main room, Pollux's violin storm continued to rage. Gen's stained and ripped dress soaked through with rain, and wind plastered it to her legs. Pollux stood in the center of the storm with his violin while Livia hid behind him, and Bale watched the show with a smirk on his face.

Pollux played fiercely and quickly. The muscles in his forearm turned taut while he whipped the guards with rain and music. He was a different person when he played. Almost attractive. Interesting to say the least. She was beginning to see why girls shrieked when he entered the room. They didn't see wan Lord Pollux. They saw violin-wielding Lux.

The monkey had a different battle approach. He was playing a game of hide-and-seek with a Gargarean, crawling all over the guard's body. The Gargarean slapped and pinched himself trying to catch the beast. Gen laughed to herself. Stupid Gargarean was being bested by a monkey.

The Lion crawled under the broken door and raised her arms. "Stop!" she cried. "Gen and I have struck a bargain. Everyone can stop."

No one stopped.

"I said stop," the Lion shouted at the Gargareans. "Can you not hear?"

The Gargareans lowered their fists and only then did Pollux lay down his bow. The wind fell flat at their feet, and the dark cloud at the top of the pyramid disappeared.

"You can stop too," Gen said to her half of the orthus.

As soon as she released the right head from the bond, the two heads uncurled their lips and panted with exhaustion. Along her MindWorker strings she sensed relief. She let the monkey torment the Gargarean for a few more turns before she called him away. The

Gargarean gave himself one final slap before the monkey scurried across the floor and vaulted onto Gen's shoulder.

She tiptoed across the puddles on the floor, around the broken pots, and over the cracks in the tiles. The Lion's settee had been struck with a blast of lightning and leaked smoking mounds of fluff into the air. Scorch marks lined the walls.

Pollux lowered his violin as he took in the blood running down Gen's arm and the red marks on the Lion's neck.

"What agreement did you make?" He raised an eyebrow.

"You'll be playing a charity show at the casino in exchange for Livia's and Percy's debts. I hope that's all right?" She fluttered her eyes for effect. Without him, she would have to return to strangling the Lion to get her way because she had less than five coins to her name.

He nodded. "I'll do it."

"Thank you."

"How very generous of you," the Lion said. "I'll schedule it with Bale, but right now, I'd like you all to leave." She pointed a claw to the door, a familiar gesture, except this time, Gen happily obliged.

"Come with me." She grabbed Livia by the wrist and dragged her through the doors.

"I'm free?" Livia said through her split lip. Her eyes sparkled with impending tears.

She probably thought she'd never leave, which was highly likely. If she had worked up a debt as large as Percy's, she could have been working for centuries. The Lion forced her indentured servants to stay in the casino, then charged them for room and board so they only earned a few coins a day. Never enough to buy their freedom.

Gen couldn't wait for the Gargarean guard to lower the platform for them and, more importantly, didn't want to. She pried open the lift doors herself and pulled Livia inside.

"Where are you going?" Pollux called as he replaced his violin in the case.

"None of your business," she said. "Although I do appreciate your help, and the charity show, I will be completing the rest of the tasks alone."

She slammed the lift doors and grabbed the crank, wheeling her and Livia back down to the lower level. She needed to get out of this casino before the Lion changed her mind, or Castor showed up, or one of the Gargarean guards tore her to pieces.

As much of a help as Pollux had been for this task, he was a liability. He was in this for his family's welfare, which meant they weren't on the same side, not exactly. If it ever came time to choose between *her* win and *his* family, he could easily become her enemy. Best to leave before that happened.

"I still can't believe I'm free." Livia clutched her elbows to her chest.

"We're not free yet."

They still had to get through the casino floor.

The lift hit the ground and Gen pulled the doors open. The Gargarean guard turned and snarled. Gen took Livia by the arm and pulled her toward the doors without breaking stride. Outside in the cool, night air, Gen called to the whale.

Come get me.

He would be able to find her by their connection. He could simply follow it like a rope.

I'm not done eating, he replied.

Gen sighed. "Where is it you live?" she asked Livia.

"Eurythia," she said. "You have a ship?"

"Not exactly, but I can get you there."

We're going to Eurythia, she told the whale, and his mood brightened. He remembered a particularly delicious school of fish he had devoured off the coast of the Eurythia isle some one hundred and fifteen years ago.

How wonderful. Come quickly then.

With Livia and Percy marked off her napkin, Stymphal would be next, and once she chased away the birds, she would be halfway to Alcmen, halfway to salvation.

She pulled Livia to the beach behind the casino where lawn chairs and umbrellas were set in the sand for casino patrons to enjoy the seashore. From the depths of these waters, the whale rose, covered in seaweed and a half-eaten fish carcass hanging from his lower jaw.

"It's an infinity whale," Livia gasped.

"This is our ride. I hope you don't mind fish guts."

CHAPTER 10

POLLUX

Pollux stared at the closed doors. Three minutes ago, Gen had emerged from the back room covered in blood, and a breath later, she was gone. Usually girls ran toward him, not away from him, and not that he wanted them to run toward him . . . but Gen, well, he would have preferred for her to stay.

"We need to go."

Pollux waved Bale to the lift. They rang the bell and waited for the Gargarean guard to crank it back up to the top. Behind them, the Lion shouted at her staff to clean up her room while sweat beaded up on the back of Pollux's neck.

"Sweep up that mess! Get me a new sofa!"

Pollux probably could have kept the Gargareans back without destroying the room if he'd had more time to plan. He rarely used his violin for defense. It wasn't made for that. It was made to bring joy, not cause chaos, but everything he did for the sake of this contest, for Gen, would be improvised.

The lift finally arrived. He stepped inside, followed close behind by Bale. His faithful assistant shadowed him wherever he went, even into this half-hearted plan of inserting themselves into the lottery games. Pollux never understood why Bale stayed with him. He assumed it was only temporary, that the man would one day wander off the same way he had wandered into Arcadia, like a passing cloud. But Pollux appreciated the company, however long it lasted.

Droplets of blood spotted the elevator floor, most likely Gen's blood from the orthus bite.

"Why do you think she took off so fast?" Bale asked as the Gargarean cranked them back down.

"I don't know." Pollux smeared his boot across a blood droplet and spread it into a red line.

Bale wrinkled his nose. "That lie smells worse than this Gargarean here."

The Gargarean turned, curling his lip. Pollux offered him a wan, apologetic smile.

"Gen has history with our family. Not good history," Pollux said under his breath.

"That sounds like most of Olympia," Bale said, which was true. Arcadia wasn't one of the wealthy islands because they were kind or generous. The bottled storms they sold to the Gargareans had killed Gen's mother, and Castor was currently working to keep Gen's father in prison.

He couldn't blame Gen for despising him on sight. He despised most of his family on sight, which was why he was the best person to help her. He knew exactly how ruthless they could be, and how to avoid their fury.

Unconsciously, he rubbed the scar on his arm, a gift from Castor when they'd been children. She'd burned him because he'd accidentally broken one of her dolls. Their father was a fool for believing his sister had entered the lottery for a husband. She would rather cut out her tongue than marry the Empresses' godson. But their father assumed everyone would blindly follow his rule and Cas would respect the long-held traditions of Arcadia and dutifully accept her fate as he'd instructed.

Pollux shook his head.

His father didn't know Cas at all, and Cas didn't know their father well enough. Truthfully, Pollux had thought the Duke would choose Cas to rule despite the doctrine. That law was sorely outdated. No other island in the Empire discriminated in the way that Arcadia did. Pollux was in favor of it being changed, and he thought if anyone could do it, it would be Cas.

His sister was smart, ruthless. She loved the business of Arcadia and had the passion to make it grow. That was why Pollux *didn't* want her to have unfettered control. With Castor it was always one step too far, like this lottery. This would push their father to the brink, and his pride would force him to retaliate. Pollux had been on the dark side of their father's wrath, and he wouldn't wish it on anyone, not even his troublesome sister.

The lift reached the bottom, and the doors swung open on the casino floor.

"Where did she go?" Pollux asked the guard. The Gargarean would have tracked Gen's movement. Before, he had looked at her like something to eat. Pollux had wanted to say something, to remind the guard that Gen was his guest. But he couldn't find the words, or couldn't make them emerge from his mouth.

Of course Gen had no problem finding her own words with enough courage to call the guard a "slave." She was fearless. Pollux envied that.

"She went that way, with another girl," the guard said.

"Thank you."

The Gargarean pointed toward the front doors. Pollux hurried through the casino. A group of young women gathered near the fountain, talking about him and his show. He ducked into his collar, hoping they wouldn't see him.

Ironic that he should be hiding from his fans while simultaneously chasing after his own idol.

"Maybe we should let her go," Bale said, and Pollux shot him a dark glare before he ducked behind a card table and made for the doors.

Bale didn't understand. Pollux didn't completely understand it himself. His relationship with Gen wasn't even a relationship . . . at least to her. In Pollux's mind, Gen was everything. He had been a fan of hers ever since the circus had performed at the manor.

Amusement and pleasure were curse words to the Storm Duke. You did not maintain a thriving empire watching shows and playing music, as Pollux's father had told him numerous times. But somehow, Pollux's mother had convinced the Duke to invite the circus.

When his parents came to tell him, they found Pollux in his room, tinkering with his violin. He had the violin open, the inner workings exposed while he attached vials of wind and rain to the inside. He needed to find a way to keep the vials open, to recapture the weather as soon as it was spent in order to make the displays he wanted.

"What are you doing with that?"

At the sound of his father's voice, Pollux moved to shield his violin. He'd already lost two to the Duke's rage.

"Tinkering," Pollux said. "This could be a new market for us."

He had rehearsed the line a thousand times, trying to make his violin sound profitable and worthy; however, in his shaking voice, he sounded desperate and afraid.

The Duke rushed toward Pollux and snatched the violin from

his fingers. "There will never be a market for these. Music is for children, and children can't afford to purchase weather. I never should have let Giselda teach you to play."

The Duke threw the violin to the floor. Pollux bit into his lip to keep from crying out. The violin strings whined as the Storm Duke's boot came down on them.

Pollux balled his fists and sucked sharp breaths through his nose to keep the tears contained. He managed to hold them back until his father left.

His mother knelt before him and took his arms.

"Shh. Shh. Don't cry. The circus is coming today. You'll enjoy that."

"No, I won't."

At that moment, he had vowed to be a better son. To abandon music, and art, and everything he enjoyed. He was resolute to despise the circus for being immature and worthless, just like his father wanted, and when the show began, he sat between his parents, arms crossed, lips pressed together. The lights came down and a hush fell over the crowd. Gen and her family burst onto the stage, riding on the backs of massive wolves. They circled the inside of the tent, leapt off the wolves' backs, and Gen landed right in front of him and smiled.

She danced across the stage in a silver suit that sparkled like stars. Her grin stretched across her face, infallible. Pollux sat upright, his jaw dropping. The girl was the most beautiful creature he had ever seen. She coaxed her chaeri through various obstacles and hoops, and Pollux forgot everything else. He whooped and clapped and felt alive for the first time in his young life.

Later that night, he started work on a new violin, number four, the one he carried now. He also composed his first piece: "The Girl in the Circus."

Gen saved him. She saved his music.

Then Pollux failed her when his father sold the storms to the Gargareans. Not that he could have stopped it. He did try. Perhaps he should have tried harder. If he had known it would kill Gen's mother off the island, he would have.

This time, though, he could not fail her. He would take this all the way to the end, even if he had to chase Gen across every island in the Empire.

"Do you see her?" Pollux stretched his neck and searched the crowd for signs of Gen's silver skin.

"No." Bale pulled a glass box from his pocket.

Inside, a blue stone tapped against the right side. A matching stone was sewn inside Gen's dress. Asymilyte. It could only be dredged from the bottom of the Aegean Sea, and as far as Pollux knew, there were only half a dozen in existence. Thankfully, his father had one of the stones, and once it was split in two, it would always point to its other half—the one they'd sewn into Gen's dress.

"Which way?"

"North."

Pollux and Bale raced through the sand to follow the stone.

He had lied to Gen. The water silk dress had been his idea, a peace offering. Planting the tracker inside the hem had been Bale's. So overall, it had been a team effort.

Pollux pushed some casino patrons out of the way to follow the tapping stone. "Sorry," he shouted behind him.

He couldn't risk losing her again. He'd lost her once when the circus closed, and only heard her name again when the lottery had been announced. Hopeful, he'd sent one of his guards, Cristos, to watch the proceedings. Cristos came here as soon as things ended to tell Pollux about the competition. He arrived with the news only an hour before Gen. It seemed like fate drawing them together. Pollux could finally right the wrong that his family had done to her and stop Castor from destroying the precarious balance of their family where their father controlled everything unquestionably.

Pollux barreled through people to reach the seashore. He skidded across the sand as Gen's infinity whale disappeared under the water.

He pounded his fist in the air. Next to him, Bale held the glass with the clinking stone. It gave Pollux hope that this wasn't quite over yet.

"Are you sure you want to do this?" Bale asked. "It seems like a lot of effort to keep your sister out of trouble. Especially since she's apt to find it again."

"I told you, you didn't have to help." As soon as Cristos had shown up with the message about the strange lottery proceedings, Pollux had made the split-second decision that he would do anything to help Gen win, and very little of that decision had to do with Cas.

Staring at the rippling sea, Pollux thought only of the girl in the silver suit with her dancing chaeri. He wanted to bring the circus back, he wanted to see her smile again, and he wanted her to possibly share that smile with him.

"I don't trust MindWorkers," Bale said, "and if you're going to do this, I'm going to stick with you, to make sure she doesn't try any tricks."

"Gen isn't like that," Pollux said.

Bale gave him a half grin. "They're all like that. If you don't want to lose her trail, we should get moving. I'll get the chariot." He handed Pollux the glass with the blue stone.

As it tapped against the glass in a persistent, tinkling tune, notes and melodies swirled through his head. It was the story of a girl who forgave the boy and his awful family for ruining her life. He would call it "The Girl in the Circus Rises Again."

CHAPTER 11

GEN

Gen was being followed.

After she delivered Livia to her family on Eurythia, Gen spat on an obliging gull and politely asked him to check the skies for her. He reported back that a winged chariot was soaring their way, fast.

Gen stepped inside her whale and headed immediately to their next destination—Stymphal. It bothered her that the gull hadn't known who was behind her, though, because now she had to guess, and she had three viable possibilities.

One, and the most likely, Castor sent someone after her, either to watch her or potentially destroy her. She wouldn't put it past Castor to have her killed to win this. The thought had crept into Gen's head once or twice too . . . not that she would follow through.

The second potential—Pollux. Maybe he was so desperate to help, he followed her. He knew she would be taking Livia home, so he would have known where to find her.

Three, the Empresses had one of their servants trailing her. Despite promising she could have her father if she defeated more labors than Castor, they had made no promises about not meddling in the competition.

Since some had been averse to them taking the throne, the Empresses created the lottery to prove they could command anyone and everyone. If you wished for favor from the Empresses, you had to grant them a favor in return.

Gen held no presumptions that this competition would be fair. The only thing she could count on was the Empresses' word. If she won her six labors, she would win her father. If she didn't, she'd never see him again. If she and Castor tied, the Empresses would string them on a while longer.

Gen reached into her bag for something to eat. She took out her sack of dried fruit and bread she had pocketed from the casino buffet. She fed the monkey and the rat fresh pieces of hair with their snack. The MindWorker strings tying them together tightened.

She chewed on a dried piece of apricot and took the water silk dress from her bag. The sight of it made her stomach turn. Even the faint blue light in the whale's mouth couldn't hide the brown splatters on the skirt and the long tear down the side. Thousands of coin, destroyed in minutes. She doubted anyone would be able to fix it, but she couldn't bring herself to throw it away. Maybe she could pluck apart enough usable pieces to make a skirt or a scarf or a headband.

She buried the dress back in the bag and took out her jar of stink lizard pus. The orthus bite on her arm was mostly healed from the first application. Only two pink divots sat in her skin. She could clear those up with another smear of lizard pus, but the unpleasant odor of the first dose still hung in the whale's mouth. Combined with the remnants of fish guts, her ride was on the verge of becoming uninhabitable.

She could live with the scars.

Gen took out her napkin list of remaining labors and spread it across her lap. The monkey stared at it from her shoulder. Chomp slept, undeterred, and the rat wandered around the whale's mouth, picking at leftover fish bones.

Gen went down her list.

Blue mustache - the Lion
young man - find the Hind ship
One-eyed woman - stop the Boar
Many-eyed figure - clean the stables
Tall man - Stymphal birds
Fierce woman - kill the Bull
Thylop - capture the Mares
Weeping woman - find Livia Kine
Red Empress - kill the Hydra
Crystal Empress - retrieve the belt of Hippolyta

Livia was home and Percy's debts had been cleared. She needed four more to win. If she could choose the four quickest and easiest, they would be the birds, the Boar, the belt and, unfortunately, the stables. None of those tasks involved murdering someone or fighting impossible beasts. The ship and the belt would both require searching, and of the two, she felt she'd have a better chance at finding the belt. Maybe something in her Mazon heritage could lead her to it.

Castor was not a fool though. She would seek the easiest, fastest tasks as well. They would undoubtedly cross paths. Gen would worry about that when it happened.

"What do you think?" she asked the monkey.

He scrunched his nose before scurrying across her shoulders. The monkey had no opinion on her labors; he was just delighted to be out of that cage.

We're here, the whale said.

Gen folded up her napkin list, replaced it in her bag, and called the rat back to her. She brushed fish bones off her pants and stood up. *All right, Gen, you can do this.* The birds would be her third labor, halfway there.

The whale rose out of the water, opening his mouth as soon as he reached the surface. Gen nudged Chomp awake and stepped under the curtain of seaweed hanging from the whale's mouth onto the very small stretch of beach.

"Don't go too far," she told the whale. "I'm hoping this won't take too long."

He snorted through his blowhole in response and ducked back under the water. Gen looked up to the high peaks of the black mountain in front of her. The entire island of Stymphal was encircled by these rocks; the people lived in the center.

"I guess we should get started." Gen lifted Chomp into her bag and strapped it to her shoulders. The monkey started the climb on his own, bouncing from rock to rock. Gen followed in his footsteps. He had the innate ability for finding the best footholds.

The Mazon strength surged through her, fueling her muscles to pull her body up each step, each ledge of the mountainside. She had come here once with her father to collect a few stone wolves for their act. Back then, they'd had a pair of giant cormorants with the circus that had carried them up this mountainside. Once Alcmen had connected to the stone wolves, they rode down the rocks on their backs.

Gen had clung to their fur while they bounded down the mountain almost vertical, and she hadn't for a second thought to be scared. Because her father was in control. He would never let her fall.

That had been Alcmen's gift, to everyone. He could make vicious wolves seem tame. He could bring infinity whales up from the depths of the sea and put them inches from your face. He brought creatures from all the isles . . . from the sea, the sky, the desert, and the forest and gathered them together inside one, small circus tent. He made people without magic feel magical.

That had been the hardest thing about losing him. Everything turned a little dimmer, a little dirtier, a little more melancholy without Alcmen's shine. She knew she could never go back to how things were, but she wanted some of the sparkle back, just a piece of it, to wake up and know something good *could* happen, even if it never did.

She grabbed another rock and pulled her body up until her boot found a ledge. The monkey was a few steps ahead of her, and a breeze wafted down the mountainside. It smelled like smoke.

Up in the sky, a thin wisp of cloud cut through the air like a jagged slash.

"Oh no," Gen whispered.

She reached for the next rock and scrambled up the mountain. The monkey stayed by her side. At the top, the smoke came up in a plume from near the lake. Gen skidded down the rocks on the other side until she hit the ground.

Her boots sank deep into the mud. She picked up her foot, and in addition to the grime, blackened feathers clung to her treads. The charred corpse of one of the crows stuck out of the mud.

It looked as if it had been cooked, or struck by a bolt of lightning, and it wasn't alone. Little bird corpses littered the ground, all frozen in a state of shock and horror as they were cooked, drowned, or buried in mud.

Gen pressed her hand to her mouth. She was going to be sick.

Up ahead, smoke poured from a giant bonfire.

"Come on." Gen waved the monkey forward, and he leapt from burned tree to burned tree toward the village.

The closer they got, the more the smoke smelled like charred bird. She stopped several feet away from it, and her jaw dropped. A mountain of dead birds sat in front of her, all in various stages of burning. Their metal feathers melted to reveal blistered flesh and bone. The bottom of the pyre had already been reduced to ash and coal.

The long-limbed residents swept up more little bodies with brooms, shovels, and pie plates and dumped them onto the fire.

Gen closed her arms around her stomach.

Thousands of little lives lost to this game, and it didn't have to be this way. Gen could have stopped the birds without killing them. *Castor* could have too. But that would have taken too much time. It had been easier for her to slaughter them than chase them away with wind.

A woman kicked another bird onto the coals.

"Was Lady Castor here?" Gen asked, even though she knew the answer. These birds hadn't killed themselves.

"Yes, she was." The woman's birds crackled and glowed as the fire took hold. "She saved us all. This is the first time I've been outside in months."

Of course. Not only had Castor killed the birds, she was being praised for it. Her family could kill an entire species, twice, and always be adored. How nice to be one of the StormMakers.

"When did she come? When did she leave?"

"Yesterday. We've been burning birds all night, and I suppose we'll be doing it all day too." The woman wandered away to collect more.

When Gen squinted her eyes, the small feathered bodies became silver ones, long and lean. Strong and sharp. The Mazons died the same way, burned and drowned and charred until there was nothing left.

Gen's stomach lurched. The smell of burning flesh and feathers choked her lungs. She couldn't stay here. She had to move on, find another task, and finish this before Castor caused more damage.

"Come get me," she whispered to the whale.

Along their connected strings, he argued he wasn't done with breakfast.

"I don't care!" she shouted.

While she stood here, Castor was out there with her jars of lightning, plowing ahead, killing everything in her path.

Gen turned back for the mountains to get to the beach. From above the clouds and smoke, a golden chariot appeared, pulled by two magnificent winged horses. This was the chariot the gull had seen.

Damn the Empresses. Gen's silver skin prickled with terror. If this was Castor, she would unquestionably cook Gen like one of the crows and drop her charred body on the fire.

The chariot circled over the lake, and Gen ran for the mountains. She scrambled up the rock and lost her footing. She slid back down. Tears burned her eyes. Her mother never would have been so clumsy. Her father wouldn't have run. He would have turned around, called a horde of creatures to him, and stopped Castor right here.

But Gen was not her father, and she certainly wasn't her mother. She reached up to try the climb again and stopped when she heard violin music. Thank the Oracles. The chariot was Pollux's, not Castor's, the *least* menacing of her possible stalkers.

She dusted off her pants and faced him. Pollux and Bale stood at the edge of the lake, surveying the scene. With each pass, the violin in Pollux's fingers dropped lower and lower.

"Castor was here," he said. Not a question. Clearly Castor had a history of destruction.

"Why are *you* here?" This was a bit much, following her across Olympia. No one was *that* determined to be helpful, at least no one she knew. There had to be another reason, and she wanted to know what it was.

"We want to help you," Pollux said.

"I don't need your help. I can handle this on my own."

"Can you?" Bale asked.

"Yes," she said, even though she wouldn't have defeated the Lion without Pollux and his free show. "I'm not incompetent."

"No one is saying you're incompetent, but these tasks are difficult. My sister, even more so," Pollux said.

"I can see that." The crackling tower of birds was a clear sign that Castor would kill, burn, and electrify anything that stood in her way. "Which is why I don't want to be a part of your family feud."

"You're already a part of it. The moment you agreed to this game, you became part of it."

"Well, I don't want to be any more a part of it."

She sensed the whale had finally come to retrieve her and was upset she wasn't on the beach after calling to him so urgently.

I'll be there in a minute.

"My whale is waiting for me. I have to go." She moved to climb the mountain once more.

"Wait!" Pollux rushed after her, stomping through the mud with a beautiful pair of black, oilskin boots. Did the Arcadians have respect for nothing? Those boots cost more than everything she owned.

"I can't," she said. "I have a long list of things to do."

"Which is why we want to help."

She shook her head. "You'll have to find another way to sort out your family business."

"There is no other way. You don't know my father. When he learns about this lottery, he'll be furious. If he catches Castor in the act, he'll disown her. If she wins, he'll make her suffer for it until his last breath. Her only hope is to lose. She does that, and he'll be satisfied that she learned her lesson. Everything can go back to the way it's supposed to be. You can have your father, and I'll be the future Storm Duke." He said the last part in a sigh.

"Interesting." She twined her finger in the monkey's tail. She could win this easily by contacting the current Storm Duke and letting him know where to find his wayward daughter.

"Don't," Pollux said, as if he had read her mind. "Please don't, for yourself as much as her. Castor will lash back if you lash at her, and she strikes hard. If you win the competition fairly, she'll let this go. She won't defy the Empresses."

He made a valid point. Gen didn't want to walk away from this with new enemies. She wanted to be loved again. She wanted her name on posters. She wanted smiles instead of shrieks.

"Fine, but I can still do it on my own."

"You want my advice?" Bale said.

"No, not particularly."

He smiled. "Well, you're going to get it anyway. What you're trying to do, make your father seem respectable again? It won't work. You can win this game. You can strangle the Hydra with your bare hands, and no one will ever forget what Alcmen did, what he's capable of."

Gen sucked in a breath. A part of her knew that was true. Even if she did win this game, and the Empresses made their decree, people would still believe what they wanted to believe. They would still think the worst of all of them.

"That's not true," Pollux said. "The people have been tainted by the Empresses. Prove them wrong. Take your prize and remind them how great you can be."

Something stirred inside her chest, a flash of what it used to be like when people cheered for her in the circus.

Bale clapped his hand on Pollux's shoulder. "There," he said in his gruff voice. "That's why you should let us help you. Because even I think this is a terrible idea. But I'm here because *Lord* Pollux has inspired me to believe that you are a worthy cause."

"I don't need your charity."

"Don't you? We're already searching for the *Hind*. Are you?"

Gen squinted at Pollux's servant, if you could call him that. He seemed to follow Pollux around without providing any real assistance. Beside him stood the fragile Storm Lord with his weather-making violin. Were these really her best allies? Could she trust them?

No. She needed something more.

"Tell me how you found me here. I thought I lost you at Psophis."

"We put an Asymilyte stone in the dress," Pollux said.

She shot him a murderous look as she reached inside her bag for the shreds of the dress. She knew she shouldn't have accepted the gift. He had tricked her in the simplest way possible.

"You know it's creepy to chase a girl across the Empire." She snatched the dress from her bag.

"We know," Bale said, completely unashamed.

"At least we all agree on something." She found the piece of stone buried in the hem, ripped it out, and tossed it back to Pollux. "Stay away from me."

"I can't do that," Pollux said.

"Why not?"

"Because I can't let my sister win this. Please, just let us help you."

Gen considered this. She had little in the way of resources, and here was Lord Pollux, offering her his coin and bottled storms.

"Do you know where Castor is going next?" she asked.

"No." Pollux shook his head, and a length of white hair fell across his cheek. "When my sister doesn't want to be found, she won't be found."

"You should consider that good luck." Bale kicked one of the dead birds.

Gen made a face.

"We're looking for her," Pollux said. "Just like we're looking for the *Hind*. I have one of my guards searching the skies for any sign of them."

"Where do you *think* Castor will go next?" she asked.

Pollux tucked the loose hair behind his ear. "I'm sure she's keeping track of you. She'll know you've taken care of Livia and the Lion. From the remaining tasks, the Boar or the Bull will be her top picks. She's good at threatening people, and she knows she needs to be quick. She doesn't just have to beat you, she also has to stay ahead of our father."

This was very useful information. "Would she go after the belt?"

"It wouldn't be her first choice, but she'd try to get the belt before she would face the Hydra or the Mares."

Pollux had one other use. He would be the best source for

calculating Castor's moves, and if Gen could keep in front of Castor, she might win this and avoid another tragic slaughter of innocent creatures.

But she couldn't trust him. Even if he didn't have any ill intent for her now, he was and would always be a StormMaker. However, if he was going to stalk her, she'd rather have him where she could see him and take whatever information he had to give along the way.

"I'm going to Mazon," she said. "I'm going to find the belt. You can come if you want."

"We do. We will," Pollux said, a little too eagerly.

Gen turned back to the mountain and took a breath. She had to make it this time or lose all credibility with Pollux and Bale watching. She grabbed the first rock she could reach and tugged on it to make sure it would hold her. When it didn't budge, she pulled herself higher, and higher, one foothold at a time.

The winged chariot lifted into the skies behind her. Gen moved faster, trying to race it to the top. Her foot slipped once, and she caught herself before she tumbled down the mountain. Her heart beat against her ribs. The monkey waited for her a few rocks ahead. Chomp poked his head out of her bag and licked her ear.

I can do this.

She kicked a foothold into the rock and pulled herself to the top. Below, the whale waited for her in the shallows.

Catch me.

It had been years since she and the whale had performed this act, and honestly, she'd been much smaller and lighter then, and her mother had been with her. She'd also never done it from this high before. She clung to the rock, regretting her choice. Ahead, Pollux's carriage winged its way to the sunset. Castor had the same carriage, and while Gen stood here, clinging to the mountain, Castor was in her chariot, soaring off to more labors.

Gen closed her eyes and took a breath. "Hold on," she said to Chomp, and held her bag tight before she leapt from the mountain toward the water.

Her mother had taught her this trick. Zusma and her sisters used to leap from the white cliffs into the waters of Mazon when they were children without the benefit of an infinity whale there to catch them. "It feels like flying," her fearless mother had said.

To Gen, it felt like falling. The wind whipped violently through her hair and across her cheeks. She heard the spout of the whale and tucked her knees to her chest, cradling Chomp and the rat in her arms. The monkey scurried down the mountain on his own.

The whale's spout rushed up to meet her, hitting her hard. She pinched her eyes tight while the water closed around her and gently set her loose. She rolled down the whale's side and collapsed into the tides.

Well, that had been less glamorous than their circus performance, but at least she hadn't been smashed to a thousand pieces.

While the monkey climbed the rest of the way down, Gen gazed at the mountaintop, an unfathomable distance away. She had flung herself off that.

"Excellent catch," she said to the whale, and patted his side.

You're late, he said.

I know, and I'm sorry.

I'm still hungry.

We're going to Mazon.

The whale whistled and opened his jaw. This seemed to appease him. He hadn't been to Mazon in over twenty years. The last time he'd gone to the island had been with Alcmen, when he'd brought him there with the circus, when Zusma had left home to run away with the most handsome MindWorker in all of Olympia.

The whale didn't give her all that, of course. Gen embellished a little. She had to. She, and the whale, and Alcmen were the only three creatures who knew their story—for now. When Gen had her life back, she would make sure more people remembered. Their story wasn't over yet, not while she had breath in her lungs to tell it.

CHAPTER 12

CASTOR

astor received word that Pollux had finished his little performance at the Lion's Den. Before Nemea, she made a slight detour to Plutos to get more coin from one of their vaults and find something to eat.

While she was dining on a lamb wrap with mint jelly, she heard some of Pollux's fans already returning from his performance.

"Isn't he splendid?" one of the girls said.

"I still have chills," another one replied.

Castor had trouble digesting the rest of her lunch. All her brother did was pluck a few strings on his violin and everyone in Olympia swooned. Meanwhile, she worked day and night to bring more revenue to the StormMakers and no one cared. Well, they would once she became Duchess of all Arcadia.

She tossed the rest of her lunch on the ground and made her way to her chariot with a sack full of coins. Relieving Percy of his ill-gotten debts stood next on her list.

She climbed into the chariot and opened Delia's box.

"Any news to report?" Castor asked. While she ate, she had sent Delia off to gather information on the status of the lottery. It had been three days since she and Genevieve had set off on their tasks. Word about the lottery had begun to spread, which was good and bad for Castor. Gossip gave her a better chance at tracking Gen and also a greater risk of her father discovering her.

"I have a location update on Genevieve the MindWorker," Delia said.

"Finally." This was excellent news. "Where is she?"

"She stopped on Stymphal. A merchant ship saw her whale headed toward Mazon after she left."

Castor smiled. So Genevieve had been to Stymphal? Oh, how she wished she could have been there to see the look on Genevieve's face when she found the birds all dead and burning. Gen was welcome to the belt too. She could spend years trying to rescue it from the rubble of the ruined isle while Castor finished up the remaining labors and claimed her prize. Winning this could prove to be much easier than she'd thought.

"Has she completed any other tasks?"

"Yes. Two."

"What?" Castor slammed her fist on the side of her chariot. "Two? Which ones?"

Impossible! Castor had been so efficient with the birds, and this stop had only taken her a few hours out of her way. How had Gen already doubled her tasks?

"Mr. Percy is free of his debts and Livia Kine has been returned home," Delia said.

Castor closed her fist hard, digging her nails into her palm. How had Gen beat her to the Lion?

She stood up and grabbed the reins, whipping them hard across the horses' backs. They reared up and lifted into the sky. Castor yanked them east, toward Psophis and the Boar.

The Mazon had two, and what if she found the belt? That would be three, three to Castor's one. She could lose this, and if she lost this, her father would never forgive her. It would add embarrassment, shame, and failure to her existing crimes of lying and betraying him.

But Castor didn't lose. She had never lost anything, from foot races, to storm battles, sewing, island languages, and dance. If she didn't excel at something, she practiced until she did.

Her toes held calluses the size of rocks from the hours she spent in the dance studio. She could strike a mosquito on a wall fifty feet away with a well-aimed blast of lightning. She could fluently speak five island languages and muddle her way through five more. She spent a summer tearing apart her clothes, simply to learn to sew them together again.

The only thing she had ever lost was her mother's approval. It had happened years ago, when Castor had burned Pollux with lightning for breaking one of her dolls. When their mother heard Pollux shrieking, she came to the room and cradled him, and she looked at Castor like she had murdered him.

"Why would you do something like that?" she asked as she kissed away Pollux's tears. She always coddled him. Too much.

"He broke my doll," Castor said matter-of-factly, which hadn't improved things.

Her mother, like Pollux, was an idealist. A dreamer. She didn't take command of anything. She rarely raised her voice. She waltzed around the manor in airy dresses and smiles, made music and arranged flowers.

Castor did not lament losing her favor to Pollux. He could have it.

This contest, though, she couldn't lose. She also couldn't practice. But she could play harder, smarter. The coins she had for Percy's debts could also work as a bribe for the Boar. Everyone could be bought, and if they couldn't be bought, they could be intimidated.

Thankfully, Psophis wasn't far from Plutos, only a few hours by chariot. As she neared the island, the sun beat down on her relentlessly from above. It was as if the clouds avoided Psophis on purpose, which was why the island council bought a steady supply of Arcadian cloud cover each month.

Her father came here on the first of each month with new clouds, thicker clouds, clouds that would last longer, spread wider. The city council would watch him give his presentation, salivating while he spoke, and agree to the new price, handing him sacks of gold for these precious new clouds.

They were not thicker, though, or wider spreading, or long lasting. They were the same clouds they had always been. The Psophis council paid them extra coins for a lie and her father's way of making it sound truthful.

Castor could see why the Boar chose this island for his operations. The council had their heads so far lodged in their back ends, they would never notice a crook working under their noses.

She tugged the reins and brought her horses down from the sky. Foam formed at the corners of their mouths. They couldn't take this heat either. Their hooves clattered to the cobblestone road where fifty other carriages and chariots had settled. Castor wiped the sweat from her brow and opened Delia's box.

"Delia, go find out where this Boar is hiding. I don't want to search the entire isle."

"Yes, Lady Castor." Delia's light exited the box and soared off into the sunlight.

Castor stepped out of her chariot onto the stone road, shielding her face from the bright light with the back of her hand. Open-air carriages bounced by her, weaving through tall, gray stone buildings that did little to block the sunlight and did much more for echoing the noise from the mass of people here.

Castor unhitched the horses and tied them up near a trough of water. They drank greedily. Castor fanned herself and considered leaping into that trough to cool down. She might have if the water weren't such a murky gray color.

Castor's box rattled. Delia had returned quickly.

"I've found him," she said.

"Where?"

"A restaurant called Chews Better."

"Really?" Castor rolled her eyes. She hated bad puns even more than filthy birds. "Where is it?"

"To the east."

"Then let's go there before I melt." She tucked Delia's box into her pocket and opened a vial of low cloud cover, releasing a small wisp of it, enough to give herself some shade. To conserve their purchased clouds, the people of Psophis only used the cloud cover on even numbered days. She happened to arrive on an odd day.

"Where is this place?" Castor craned her neck around the crowd for a sign of the restaurant.

"A few buildings ahead. It's the short one with the green awning in front."

Castor plowed ahead, using her own ability to keep her cloud wisp directly overhead. Carriages whipped by her, and elbows brushed her side. The residents all had a sun-darkened complexion and a single eye in the middle of their foreheads, half-covered with thick lashes as their own sun protection. As they passed fair-skinned Castor and her personal cloud, they stared.

She ducked into her collarbones and pulled her cloud back into the jar. She was too exposed. If her father knew about the lottery, he would be looking for her, and reports would soon be rolling in that she had been spotted on Psophis. The Empresses likely also had spies all over this contest, monitoring her every move. She would do the same if she were running things.

She would have to finish this quickly. Discreetly. Damn the Mazon for putting her in this panic. She'd never had to watch her back so closely before.

Castor reached the restaurant and gratefully stepped through the blackened doors into a dimly lit, somewhat cool building. She blinked several times to adjust her eyes to the change in light. A few scattered tables clustered on the stained rug. Over half of them were filled with dingy patrons speaking in hushed voices.

Castor wrinkled her nose and walked up to the girl behind the bar. Her thick orange hair fell over her shoulder as she wiped the counter. The blue vest she wore hugged tight to her waist, fitted snugly in a way that accentuated her curves. Not that she needed to advertise. Castor noticed her. *Everyone* in the room noticed her.

"Can I get you something?" the girl asked. She leaned over the counter and twirled her hair on her finger.

"I need to speak to the Boar."

The girl hesitated on her next breath. "He's not here."

"You're lying. Tell him Lady Castor of Arcadia is here to see him. He will want to talk to me."

"I'll let him know."

She flicked her single eye to the back of the room and someone new approached. A heavyset man who was not a local. He looked at Castor with two eyes over the top of an upturned nose. His reddish skin fell in shiny folds and wrinkles down his cheeks and neck.

"Who are you?" he grunted.

"Lady Castor for the Boar."

"He's not seeing anyone."

"Bring her back," another voice called. "Don't leave our lady waiting."

Castor knew that voice belonged to the Boar. It carried the over-confident, smug air of a bully.

She stepped around the Boar's henchman and made her way to a separate room protected by a moth-eaten curtain. When she ducked under the folds, she found another red-faced figure, larger, with a wider nose and two rounded teeth protruding from his lower jaw.

She could see why they called him the Boar. He looked like an overgrown pig.

"Have a seat." He gestured to the chair across from him, a plush armchair with gold trim. He had built himself a shabby kingdom in this discount restaurant. *How cute.*

She sat down and crossed her legs. "You've got quite the business here."

"I do all right." He blinked beady eyes at her and pushed aside the half-eaten bowl of food in front of him, chunks of unrecognizable meat and bone in a red sauce that smelled like rotten fish. "What brings you here, Lady Castor of Arcadia?"

"I've come to ask you to leave Psophis and find another island to bully."

He snorted in something like a laugh and slammed his hand on the table. "That's a pretty lofty request for such a little girl."

"Maybe." She ran her finger over one of the lightning jars on her hip. "But it's what I'm asking, and I don't have much time. What will it cost?" She pulled her bag of coins from her belt and set it on the table.

He snorted at the sack. "I make more than that in a week here. Try again."

That was a shame. She thought she could handle this the easy way. She snatched a jar of lightning, and as her fingers made contact, four large figures emerged from the shadows. The Boar held them back and tossed something on the table between them.

A small, black stone. No bigger than her thumb.

Castor went still. This explained why he had such a strong hold on Psophis. The stone was a seed from a Semele tree, long banned by the Empresses because the wood was highly combustible, as were the seeds.

If he tossed that seed at her with enough force, she would go up in flames before she could scream. The entire restaurant would probably burn with her. Maybe the neighboring shops too.

"You might want to rethink that," the Boar said.

Castor released her lightning vial and folded her hands in her lap.

"Good choice." He scooped up the seed and returned it to his pocket. "It seems like our business is done here."

"No, it isn't," she said. "If you haven't heard . . ."

"We've heard. We know what you're doing for the Empresses."

"Then you know if you don't leave Psophis, the MindWorker will be coming for you next. One drop of her blood, and she'll have you killing yourselves, like her father did with the Gargareans."

The Boar's beady eyes flared, her threat almost as effective as a blast of lightning. "I can handle the MindWorker," he lied.

"I'm sure you can. However, if you leave at my request, you will get a prize."

"It better be more than what's in that bag."

"It is. If you know about the lottery and the competition, then you know what I get when I win: Arcadia. As Duchess, I'll need a team to manage shipments. You'll have a fleet of Arcadian ships, all equipped with the best storms, and if you know Arcadia, you know we always keep the best things for ourselves and those most loyal to us."

He grunted. "The way I understand it, you won't be getting the title right away. Just a claim to it."

"That doesn't mean I can't feed my friends a few extras in the meantime."

As a show of faith, she reached for her lightning again. The overgrown pigs at the back of the room moved in until she put the jar on the table and slid it toward the Boar.

The Boar held up the lightning vial, *her* lightning vial, and pushed his upturned nose toward it. He was no fool. He knew the Arcadians kept the best and purest storms for themselves. What they sold to everyone else was hardly a spark compared to what she held. Her weapons could destroy islands. His could only terrify a group of already gullible people.

Hers were also replenishable. The skies would never run out of lightning. His seeds were much harder to acquire.

"What happens if you lose to the MindWorker?" he asked.

"Make sure I don't lose. Help me."

"Now you want me to win your prize for you?" He broke into a series of snorts.

"No . . . just take the MindWorker out of the game. She has an infinity whale. It's circling Mazon right now. Kill the whale and sell the parts, leave her stranded on the island, and then you can set up operations on whatever island you like and wait for your delivery of goods." Castor stood up. "Do we have a deal, Mr. Boar, or should I take my lightning back?" She held her hand out for the vial.

In three seconds, she would walk away. It was one of her father's favorite sales tactics. Make the deal urgent, irrefutable. One, two . . .

"We have a deal." The Boar snatched up the lightning with one hand and took her fingers with the other. The deal was made. Castor reclaimed her hand and wiped the Boar's sweat on her thigh.

"How soon will you leave?" she asked. "You won't have much time to catch that infinity whale."

"We'll be out by tonight. I'll just leave a few men behind to close up shop."

"Perfect." She smiled. "I'll be in touch soon."

The task was complete. She made for the doors, letting her eyes linger on the beautiful bartender's sculptured waist once more.

After Castor shattered Arcadian tradition, she could shatter everything else with it. Like her father's expectations. She wouldn't have to make married alliances. She could be like the Empresses, toying with lovers until she tired of them.

She could date a penniless bartender. Or a no-name store clerk. She could do whatever or *whomever* she wanted. No deposit required. Once she broke Old Arcadia, she could rebuild New Arcadia exactly as she wanted, with her own doctrine.

Castor stepped into the broiling heat and made her way back to the horses. She had two tasks. Two to two, and soon, Gen would be without transportation. Even if she found the belt, she'd never leave Mazon. She would die there with the rest of her forgotten race, leaving the win to Castor.

CHAPTER 13

GEN

Zusma had rarely spoken of her home island. The few times she'd told Gen stories of Mazon, they'd come blended with fondness and sorrow. Zusma would sit on the edge of Gen's cot on their ship and stare through the porthole window while she dredged up some memory of her youth, like the first time she had used a spear (because all Mazons trained as warriors), or how she and her sisters used to climb bare-handed to the top of the white, rocky cliffs and then dive from the tops to the ocean below.

"When you're in the air," Zusma would say, "it feels like you're falling forever, and when you hit the water and sink so deep below, you think you'll never find the surface again." Then she'd smile. "But you always do."

Gen stood on the edge of her whale's tongue now, hesitant to take that first step onto the white sands of Mazon. The isle had been outlawed. If Zusma had ever dared to go back, she would have been torn to pieces for defying her queen. Gen had been raised to fear this island, but the stain on the white shores had been its queen, Hippolyta. Since she was dead, Gen had nothing to fear, in theory.

She slung her bag over her shoulder. "I might be gone for a while," she said to her whale. "More than a day, maybe."

She ran her fingers down his soft side, and he responded with glee. Not from her touch, but from the prospect of having hours to eat undisturbed.

"It's nice to know I'll be missed. Don't go too far, keep moving, and avoid ships."

The whale moaned, in a vocal version of an eye roll.

"Take care of yourself, all right?"

Along their threads, he sent her a "you too," so to speak. Despite all of his complaining, she meant as much to him as he did to her.

She patted the inside of his cheek one more time and called Chomp to her side. The little monkey clung to her shoulder, tail wrapped around her neck, and the rat slept soundly in her bag. Together, she and her furry crew embarked on the shores of Mazon.

She couldn't stay more than a day or two here. The whale wouldn't be safe lingering in one place too long, and she couldn't waste all her time on one labor while Castor checked off the rest. If Gen didn't find the belt by end of day tomorrow, she would have to leave it and move on.

A wave cascaded to the shore. Salt spray rolled off the water and clung to her hair. The bold, yellow sun glinted off the shimmering ocean. The white cliffs her mother used to leap from surrounded her on all sides. If it weren't for the debris littering the beach, it would have been a dream.

She nudged aside a broken shield half-buried in the sand and revealed something underneath, something round and white. She quickly covered it again. *That is not a skull. It is not the remnant of a dead Mazon.*

A bitter taste filled her throat as a shadow crossed over the clifftops—Pollux's chariot. Wonderful. As it circled over her head, the bitterness grew. The Gargareans and Mazons had been at war for centuries. It wasn't until *someone's* family sold them a handful of bottled storms that the Gargareans finally conquered the Mazon race and killed her mother.

Had it been a mistake to invite Pollux along? If it was, it was too late to go back. The chariot had already lowered to the ground. The horses pulling it kicked up bits of shell and bone.

Gen covered her face with her arm so she didn't inadvertently get a tiny piece of skeleton in her mouth. The monkey skittered to her back to use her shoulders as protection. Chomp slept undisturbed while bits of sand clung to his lashes. The horses came to a rest, and Pollux appeared in his mud-splattered boots with Bale behind him, dressed in a loose cotton tunic.

They looked like two tourists about to embark on a beach vacation. Clearly, neither of them had been reduced to stealing crackers for their next meal, or renting a room for an hour to have a place to wash.

Bale gave her a long, hard look before he pulled a small paper bag from his pocket. The monkey dropped from Gen's shoulder, skittered across the sand, and climbed up Bale's pant leg. The monkey grabbed the paper bag, leapt to Bale's shoulder, and removed a handful of sugared lolo berries. The sweets came from Leuctra, Chomp and Bale's home island.

"Does it normally do this?" Bale snatched the bag of berries back from the monkey and tucked it into his pocket.

"I don't know. I haven't known him for long."

She did know, however, that for a creature that had been poked and prodded through the bars of a cage, he should be more wary of strangers. Chomp had also neglected to bite the man. Did Bale have a touch of mind magic? Creatures could sometimes sense these things.

The monkey skittered down Bale's shoulder and tried to get the paper bag from his pocket. Again.

"Quit that." Bale tried to push the monkey out of his pockets, and the monkey opened all one-hundred eyes on his body and sharpened them into a glare.

"That's a lot of eyes," he said.

"It's incredible," Pollux argued. "Did he have all those before? I didn't notice in the casino."

The monkey returned to her shoulders with his prize, two fistfuls of sugar berries. "He doesn't keep them all open all the time." She scratched the monkey, and he offered her one of the berries. "He's an Argosian monkey, a rare breed of chameleon monkey."

"He really should have a name," Pollux said. "How about Argos?"

"Fine, if you insist." She told Pollux he could come along, not name her creatures. He was proving to be an exceptional nuisance.

"Where are we headed?" Bale asked.

Pollux nudged a piece of a spear with the toe of his boot. Gen pictured the spear whole, clutched in strong, silver fingers, the Mazon battling to her last breath against the monstrous Gargareans and their weather vials.

"Themiscyra." Gen cleared her throat. "Hippolyta would have been there when . . ." *When her children were destroyed by storms.*

Themiscyra was, or had been, the capital of Mazon. Hippolyta would have stood there to watch her island crumble and burn.

"We can take the chariot," Pollux offered.

Gen looked to the two beautiful winged stallions harnessed to the gilded chariot, etched with a design of wind and cloud. Sweat beaded up on their white hides and foam clung to their mouths. They were exhausted.

Gen spat on her hand and pressed her palm to one of their shoulders. The horse was warm to the touch, and when her thoughts connected to his through the spittle strings, she sensed his tiredness.

"You've been overworking your horses. They need water and grass."

"I was going to do that as soon as we got here," Pollux said.

"Then why aren't they resting? Unhook the harness. We'll walk them up the cliffs."

"What are we going to do with the chariot?"

Gen eyed the golden monstrosity. It was no bigger or heavier than that ugly statue of the Empresses. "I'll pull it." If only to give the horses a rest. If only to prove she could.

"You don't need to do that. We can pull it," Pollux offered.

Bale laughed. "Speak for yourself, *Lord* Pollux."

"As much as I'd like to see you try," Gen said. "If we want to get anywhere today, I should do it."

She unhooked the bridle from the first horse and reached for the second as Pollux met her there. Their hands brushed. She felt the calluses on his fingers from his violin playing, then snatched her hand back. She shook off his touch and released the horses. They happily wandered off to graze the tall grasses that grew from the rocks.

The poor horses. Such fine creatures and so rare. They were difficult to catch and deserved better than being worked to the bone by Pollux and his servant. You could tell much about a person by how they treated their creatures, and this tale was not working out in Pollux's favor.

Gen grabbed a piece of driftwood from the beach, tied the reins to either end of it, and gripped it in her fingers. She took a breath and flexed her muscles before she pushed it forward. A silver line crawled up her knuckle like a river, and she released the driftwood.

"Is everything all right?" Pollux asked.

Gen ran a finger over the new line. She should have expected this. They were on Mazon, the home of the Mazon warriors. The Amazonium was everywhere: in the sand, the air, the water, the grass . . . it had been waiting for her, and now that she was here, it attached itself to her, building up her muscles, strengthening her skin, turning it silver, and making her more like Zusma.

"It's fine." She picked up the reins.

This change wasn't necessarily a bad thing. She could use some additional strength to win the game, but she could never forget the downside of the Mazon magic. When Mazon suffered, so did its people. Gen didn't want to make herself vulnerable if something else were to happen to this isle.

She pulled the chariot to the top of the cliffs. Pollux, Bale, and the horses followed. At the summit, the horses picked at the lush grass. Pollux took out his violin and played a quiet, somber song. A small rain cloud formed in front of them, filling a divot in the dirt with clean water. The horses lapped it up.

Pollux patted each one on the neck, and through her gentle connection to them, Gen sensed the horses didn't hate him. Their feelings were more of respect and appreciation. He had never beaten them or treated them roughly, just ridden them too hard.

She had worked the whale pretty hard for this competition too.

So he didn't abuse his horses, and he could make rain with pretty little songs. That didn't make him innocent. He was still an Arcadian. He could still betray her, and he was likely to do so. Everyone knew the StormMakers favored those with the most coin and influence, and since she had neither, she could be easily discarded.

"This is a nice island," Bale said.

"I'm sure it was lovelier before the Gargareans tore it apart and murdered everyone," Gen snapped. "We should keep moving." She put Chomp in the back of the chariot and picked up the reins. She broke into a jog toward the ruins of Themiscyra in the distance.

It was farther than she thought it would be. Gen's mother talked as if they lived right next to the beach. But they were Mazon, stronger and faster than most. Gen was too, mostly. She broke into a run, cutting through the tall grass. The horses, freshly fed and watered, kept up beside her, their manes blowing in the wind.

Pollux and Bale fell far behind.

As the chariot bounced up and down, it ran over broken shields and things Gen tried to convince herself weren't sun-bleached bones. Each skull and femur was a piece of one of her aunts who'd fallen in war. She'd never met any of them, but they were still family. Every Mazon for the past thousand years had come from Hippolyta, Gen's late grandmother. They were all part of her and part of this island, even if Gen was a little less than others.

When Zusma and her two sisters, Gryne and Elloine, escaped with Alcmen, they all went their separate ways, each finding their own corner of the Empire to settle in. Over the years, Zusma had lost touch.

Eight months after her exile, Gen had searched for them. Zusma's sister Gryne had set up home on Paphos. She'd opened a bakery, and her assistant said she had died on the same day as Zusma. No children. Gen never found Elloine, but she probably died with her sisters too.

It was then that Gen knew she was the last of the Mazons.

She glanced over her shoulder. Pollux and Bale were barely shadows in the distance, stumbling over their own feet. Good, she thought. Let them trip over every skull and rusted sword. They should see what the StormMakers leave behind.

She didn't stop until she reached the main gates of Themiscyra, reduced to rubble now. Beside the broken arches stood the headless statue of a woman dressed in a layer of moss and algae. Thick lines of muscle twined the statue's arms and legs. The headless warrior held a long sword aloft, bringing it down on some invisible foe. A Gargarean presumably.

Gen bent down and cleared the dirt from the base, revealing the words. *Sál er maeld med hulum hennar.* "A soul is measured by its strength."

"Gen . . ." Pollux called.

Behind her, she heard Pollux and Bale stumbling their last few steps to the city, wheezing and panting while they did. She smiled. She wanted Pollux to suffer.

Across the plains, a heavy gust of wind pulled at Gen's hair. In it, she heard a voice.

Forgive.

"Did you hear that?" She searched the tall stalks of grass for someone else here, someone hiding in the weeds.

"Hear what?" Bale asked between gasps.

"Nothing." It must have been a trick of the wind. Or one of the ghosts of her dead aunts. If a soul was measured by its strength, then the Gargareans *and* the StormMakers had reduced her soul to ash by destroying all the other parts of it: her father and mother.

It had been a mistake to let Pollux join her. She thought having him close might give her insight into Castor's plans, or keep him in view. Really, though, he was only a distraction, a dangerous one.

"I've changed my mind about accepting your help. I think you should go."

"Couldn't you have said this before we ran all this way?" Bale panted.

Pollux waved him away. "Don't do this, Gen. I'm sorry. What happened to this island, to the Mazons, shouldn't have happened. Our storms weren't meant for this, and if I could take it back, I would."

"Not meant for this . . . what did you think the Gargareans would do with the lightning you sold them? Make a charming light display?" Her lip quivered. She bit the inside of her cheek to make it stop. She would not let him see her cry.

"I'm not denying it. We all knew what would happen, and I'm sorry."

"I think she makes a good point," Bale said.

"What?" Pollux turned on him.

Bale shrugged. "She can't trust you because your family burned up hers. You can't trust her because she's a MindWorker."

"That's not true. I trust her."

Gen's skin tingled. No one had ever said they trusted her with that much conviction, and it was a StormMaker who had said it, of all people. But she couldn't return the sentiment.

"I can't," Gen said.

Pollux leaned toward her, his pale hair falling over his cheekbones. "I don't want something like this to happen again," he said. "Our storms . . . they can do great things. They can also do terrible things. That is why we have to stop my sister from winning this game. Castor and my father can't see the difference between great and terrible. It's all the same to them."

"You would do that? You would turn against your family?"

"Yes. My family is already divided, and it will be worse if Castor wins this. I don't know what else I can do to convince you that we are on the same side."

"I don't either." Words and promises would never be enough, not from an Arcadian.

"Then there's only one thing we can do." Pollux reached his hand out toward Bale, palm side up. "Give them to me."

"No," Bale said.

"Please," Pollux said even though he was the *lord* and Bale was supposed to be the servant.

"Fine. But remember, I warned you." Bale reached into his pack and removed two thin circlets of silver. The monkey, Argos now, she supposed, leaned off her shoulder to smell them. Gen already knew what they were . . . bonding bracelets.

The MetalBenders, the earth children of Ponos, made them. The MetalBenders could bend ore with their minds and attach thoughts and feelings to it, in a similar way she could attach herself to creatures. Their magic was more of a one application per object, though. MetalBenders often attached their magic to coins, to make them double or disappear from one person's pocket into another. They were also frequently asked to make these bonding bracelets.

Pollux handed them both to her. "Will it with your command, and I will wear it."

Gen gently took both bracelets and clutched them in her fingers. This was a measure beyond trust. Whatever desire she whispered into the bracelets, Pollux would be held to it. Or the bracelet would tighten to the point of severing his hand.

They had used one of the bonding bracelets on Alcmen before his trial. Gen didn't know what promise Alcmen had been forced to make; she only learned at the trial that the results of using it had been "inconclusive."

In front of her, Pollux held out his length of violin-playing arm. If he defied her and lost his hand, he would never play again. He was giving her control of his music, his soul. She had seen him play. It was everything to him, and he was handing it to her freely.

That was a promise she could trust.

Looking him in the eye, she slid one bracelet onto his wrist and the other onto hers. "You will promise to do whatever is in your power to help me defeat these six labors and win this contest, or you will answer to this bracelet."

"I swear it," he agreed without hesitation.

The silver bracelets sparked red before they cooled to gray. The promise was made; the magic sealed.

"Are you satisfied?" He held her gaze.

Gen touched the circlet on her arm. "I'm satisfied. Now let's find the belt."

They left the horses untied outside the gates along with the chariot and ventured into the ruins on foot. Walking through shells of buildings, over broken stones covered in moss, rusted shields, and bone shards, Gen felt sick. She could only imagine how this city must have looked before the Gargareans struck it down. Streets filled with silver-skinned warriors surrounded by white stone towers.

The Empresses had purposely left the island vacant. The Gargareans wanted it. So did others. It offered sandy beaches, healthy soil, and a plentiful water supply. No one could set up residence without the Empresses' approval, and they hadn't bestowed it on anyone. Not yet. Either they were waiting for someone to offer them an irrefutable price, or they enjoyed keeping things that other people wanted. Most likely the latter.

The three of them passed by what looked like a market with broken pots and moldy pillows leaking rotted wool. The waterline marked halfway up the wall, far over Gen's neck, high enough to drown everyone inside. She imagined the silver women fighting to break free, to take one last gasp of air. She wondered if they knew, even if they took that breath, that they'd die anyway.

As the Amazonium in their bodies perished with the dying Mazons, it sent out stabs of agony across the Empire. The loss of one or two Mazons, even ten, would have gone unnoticed. But thousands of them? It had been too much agony for the Mazons to suffer, for anyone to suffer. They died because they couldn't take the pain of losing their sisters. That was what had killed Zusma . . . the heartbreak.

Gen crawled through a broken window and stopped at the base of a mountain made of rusted armor and broken shields. Chomp nosed at a piece of bone and Gen pushed him away with her foot.

"We need to get to the top if we want to see anything," she said.

Her boots crunched on dented armor and more bones, and she winced with each step. This was where the battle had been fought and lost. This was where Mazon had fallen.

"This is the biggest graveyard I've ever seen," Bale said.

"Our storms were never intended for this." Pollux eyed the carnage, shaking. "They were made for weather control, for growing crops."

"But they did do this."

Even if she temporarily set aside her suspicions of Pollux, she couldn't forget what he could do. His shiny little violin could cook or drown them all, and Castor had hundreds of these storms at her fingertips. She wouldn't hesitate to use them.

They reached the top of the mound, and the rest of Themiscyra stretched into miles of rubble and ruin. Somewhere in all this mess was one golden belt. Gen's shoulders sagged. Where would she start? It would take centuries to search everything. As the last of the sunlight drifted from the sky, she knew whatever she decided to do would have to wait until morning.

"We should go back to the gates. We can search tomorrow." They could divide and conquer, each take a section of the city and pick through the rubble, and if they didn't find it by the end of the day . . . well, she would worry about that then.

"We can go a little farther." Pollux removed his violin and ran his bow across the strings. A small wisp of fog rose from the instrument. The stream twisted and turned until it made the shape of an elk, and when Pollux's long fingers stretched up the strings, and the notes shortened, small sparks of lightning illuminated the elk cloud, making it sort of a cloud torch.

Gen sucked in a breath. It was beautiful. Whenever she was determined to hate everything the StormMakers did, Pollux made something infuriatingly wonderful like this.

His mist elk danced ahead of them, lighting a small path through the rubble. They followed it until they reached a wall. Shattered buildings and crumbling rock surrounded them on all sides. Gen could climb the wall easily, but Bale and Pollux could not, and Gen needed Pollux's light elk to find her way on the other side. Chomp yawned, and Argos picked through Gen's hair for something to eat. They were all overdue for a rest.

"We'll find a way around in the morning," she said, as a gust blew across the remains, coating her in dust and bone fragments.

Leave, Daughter of Zusma. There's danger for you here.

The silver bands on her arm tightened. The voice again. "Did you hear it that time?"

"What? The music?" Bale nodded to Pollux.

"No, a voice. A woman's voice."

"Someone's here?" Pollux asked.

He sent his illuminated elk frolicking across the wall. In the shadows it cast from broken stone, Gen saw the images of Mazon warriors, spears raised. Illusions. Then the elk flitted past something real, a small figure crouched on the very edge of the stones.

"There!"

Gen dropped her bag and pulled her body up the wall. The girl disappeared, but not before Gen glimpsed her silver hair and skin. A Mazon. One had survived.

"Gen!" Pollux called.

The Mazon girl darted across the wall and leapt to another building.

"Wait!" Gen shouted after her.

The girl kept running.

Gen closed her eyes and clenched her fists. She let the Mazon strength flow through her limbs before she leapt from the wall, arms scrambling. She grasped the edge of the pillar and pulled herself up. The girl was already leaping to another building. Gen ran carefully along the length of a wall, trying to keep the girl in view. Thankfully the moonlight highlighted her silver skin.

The girl dropped down from her wall and disappeared in the darkness. Gen took another leap. She caught the edge of a crumbling roof and dove to the end. Down below, a small cloud of dust emerged from under a moonlit slab of rock.

She jumped down and made her way toward it. Without Pollux's elk, the ghost city had gone dark. She knelt beside the slab and felt cool air rising up from the ground. There was a hole under the rock that led . . . somewhere.

It looked dark down there, and cold. She turned over her shoulder. The ruined city stretched out in a sea of broken stone and blackness. No sign of Pollux, Bale, or Chomp, and the girl, moving at her speed, could be a half mile ahead already.

What if there were others? They might know where to find the belt, and they were, technically, her family.

She had to follow.

She sat at the edge of the hole and let her legs dangle into nothingness. The wind blew across the ruins, and she heard the phantom whisper one last time.

Be careful.

"I will," she answered, and dropped.

CHAPTER 14
GEN

Gen hit the ground, tumbling to her knees. Her palms scraped on loose gravel, and a sharp rock ripped through her pants. She picked at the ragged hole and frowned. First the dress, now her pants. These labors would be the death of her wardrobe if they didn't become the death of her.

She stood up and brushed the dust from her skin. Behind her, something else scrambled down the hole. Argos leapt from the dirt wall to her shoulder. The little monkey changed color to match the dusky interior of the cave.

"I'm glad you made it." She scratched his chin, and he chattered in her ear. She was glad not to make this journey alone.

A flickering torch clung to the wall. Gen grabbed it from the sconce and waved it in front of her, finding more blackness ahead. She had two choices: go back up to the surface or down the tunnel, and chasing the girl all the way down here would have been pointless if she didn't keep going.

Gen moved into the tunnel where another torch burned on the wall, and another, and another. They hung about six to eight feet apart. The girl couldn't have lit all of these herself, not while racing by, which meant the girl wasn't alone.

Thank the Oracles.

Of all the things Gen hated about her current station, one of the worst, after being an assumed menace, was being the last of the

Mazons. She wasn't Mazon. She was *half*-Mazon, only a portion of her mother's grace and strength and fearlessness. She'd never deserved the title or wanted it, and regardless of what happened down here, at least she could stop being "the last Mazon."

Argos tugged on her hair and pointed ahead. He heard voices. Another few steps, and Gen heard them too. Many of them, all speaking in Mazon.

Gen pressed to the wall and listened.

I'm hungry. I'm tired. Stop hitting me. Give that back.

They sounded young, like children.

There's a strange girl outside, one voice said.

Gen held her breath. They knew she was here.

"You may enter, Daughter of Zusma."

The deep and raspy voice called to her in the universal Olympian instead of Mazon.

"Don't be afraid. Come closer," the voice spoke again, and each word rang down Gen's spine in warning.

The voices outside had advised her to be careful, but who were they? The ghosts of her dead aunts? On the other side of this stone entrance, there were real, live Mazons, and possibly the belt too.

Gen took a step toward the light, carefully, and at the end of the tunnel, a wide, brightly lit cavern appeared, filled with silver-skinned girls. White marble pillars held the ceiling aloft, a dome painted with a mural of the Mazon Queen surrounded by a handful of her daughters, all brandishing swords and spears with armor and sleek, silver skin. Cracks raced along the edges where dirt spilled through along with a trickle of water that formed a pool in the corner. The Mazon girls splashed each other and laughed.

One girl shrieked when her sister threw water at her. The

shrieking girl shuffled away on stunted legs. The other girl blinked her single, crooked eye in response. Gen scanned the room and found more with missing limbs and curved spines. Had these girls been injured in the war?

"Welcome, Daughter of Zusma."

The lone adult in the room stepped toward Gen, bare feet on the dusty floor. Even in her simple state, the Mazon Queen was breathtaking.

"Hippolyta," Gen whispered, too stunned to say anything else.

Zusma had once said to stand before Hippolyta was to stand before a mountain. In the shadow of the great Mazon warrior, Gen understood. She felt small and insignificant. Worthless and weak. What right did she have to stand here? To look at this woman? To breathe her same air?

"You finally found me." In Hippolyta's muscular arms, two babies clung to her breasts. By the way her gown fell, she was expecting another one soon, and right below that, the links of a golden belt gleamed.

"I thought you were dead, Your Highness." Gen made a quick bow, her gaze never leaving the golden links of the belt. "How are you here . . . I mean, how are you alive?" She had always told herself there was nothing they could have done for Zusma. There was no way for her to survive, and somehow, Hippolyta had.

"You can't kill me," the Queen crooned. "I *am* Mazon. I am made of this rock and stone, every blade of grass, every drop of water. As long as there is one speck of Mazon dust in the Empire, I will live."

Gen bit into her cheek. As happy as she was to see the Mazon Queen alive and breathing, this did complicate things. This was no longer a recovery mission for the belt. To get it now, Gen would have to wrestle it from Hippolyta's iron grasp. She would never willingly let it go. It had belonged to Hippolyta's former lover, the first Gargarean she killed, which started the war and caused the eventual downfall of Mazon. It was a trophy, a meaningful trophy.

"I will admit," Hippolyta said as she passed the two babies to an older girl, the one Gen had followed here, "it caused indescribable pain to watch all of my daughters die. I felt each loss." She pressed her fist to her chest. "I wanted to die too, except I knew I had to avenge my babies. I had to keep going."

Speaking of babies, the ones in the girl's arms broke into cries. She bobbed them up and down in her small limbs. She was shy a few fingers on each hand, three on one, two on the other.

She looked to be about ten. She must have survived the war too, along with half of the other girls. How? Gen understood how Hippolyta survived. She was the first, the eldest, the strongest, but what about these girls? And how had it affected the younger ones? Of the two babies the girl held, one had no feet, the other, two very small hands with nubbed fingers. Had the Gargareans damaged the island so much, even new Mazons were affected?

"How did your older daughters survive?" Gen asked. As young as they were, they should have had less resistance to the shared Amazonium pain. Gen had only felt a portion of that agony, a hundred leagues away, and it had been enough to bring her to her knees.

"They didn't," Hippolyta said. "These girls are new, all of them. I needed to rebuild. I can produce a new girl in three weeks." She patted one of her daughters on the head. "But the results aren't very good."

The eldest of the girls stuck out her tongue at Hippolyta's back. She must have understood more of the Olympian language than Hippolyta thought, and clearly she didn't like being referred to as "not very good," or knowing she was being bred as a soldier. Gen didn't appreciate it either. After trying to chase the girl here, Gen knew these children were quite good and would be something to fear once they came of age . . . if they stayed with Hippolyta. Gen's mother had run from being a soldier as fast and as far as she could.

"Four months is the closest to perfection," Hippolyta continued, speaking more to herself than Gen. "The problem is once they're born, I need to constantly feed them to make them grow more quickly. It's exhausting." Another Mazon baby broke into tears, and milk leaked through Hippolyta's gown. "See?"

"I do." Gen saw why Zusma had left when she'd had the chance, why she never regretted not being able to come back. A life here meant a life being Hippolyta's puppet, her soldier, of never being good enough, fast enough, or strong enough.

"You look like her." Hippolyta ran the backs of her fingers across Gen's cheek, sending cold shivers across her skin. "I have borne more than a million babies, and I remember them all." She drew her hand back. "It's also very hard to forget the ones who betrayed you."

"She didn't betray you. She loved my father."

Hippolyta laughed. "I loved once too and look where it left me." She raised her hands to the ceiling. "Living underground like a rat with all of my dead children buried around me."

The golden disks swayed back and forth on Hippolyta's waist while she wandered the dirt floor in tight circles, muttering to herself. Gen's mother had warned her once never to come here. *"She only likes those she can control, and once she controls you, you cease to be yourself. You can't win with her. All you can do is stay far away."* Gen wouldn't have come if she'd known Hippolyta was here.

Gen needed to get the belt and leave.

She reached for her bag, and the slumber bees inside, and felt nothing . . . because she'd dropped the bag before chasing after the Mazon girl.

"How are the Gargareans?" Hippolyta spun on her. "We don't get much news down here. Are they gloating? Attacking some other island?"

"No." Gen laced her fingers together. "They mostly work low-paying security jobs."

Hippolyta grinned. "How quickly they fall from grace. When my army is ready, I will crawl from this hole and erase the Gargareans from the world like they tried to erase me." Hippolyta snatched Gen's arm and examined the silver stripes crawling up to her elbow, twice what they had been when she first set foot on the beach. The Amazonium continued to cling to her.

"You have more of our strength than I thought you would," the Queen said. "People think our strength is endless, that the island will continually feed it to us no matter what." Hippolyta dropped Gen's arm, leaving behind crescent-shaped nail marks. "But that is wrong. We feed each other. We tend to the island, and in turn, it tends to us. We took quite a hit when the Gargareans came for us. It takes everything I have to rebuild, and it's exhausting."

"Why don't you take a rest?" Gen suggested, and backed to the tunnel exit. She needed her bag. She could never match Hippolyta's strength.

"Why don't I take a rest? Do you hear yourself?" Hippolyta spat through her teeth. "We were nearly destroyed. If the Gargareans were to return today, we most certainly would be. I am the one thread holding this entire island, this entire race together. I have to protect my children, this island. That is why I hide in this pit and make babies day after day. It is my duty."

The Mazon Queen paced. Another baby broke into tears, grabbing for Hippolyta's arms. "If only Zusma had understood that. She stole from me. She stole my strength, and she took two of my children with her. I have to take it back. It's the only way."

In a blur of silver, she launched at Gen and closed a tight hand on her neck. Gen slammed into the wall. Argos screeched and scurried up the stones. Gen clawed at the Mazon Queen's hand, like twigs scratching at iron, fighting for a breath.

"You can't escape me. No one can escape me. I was born of sand and stone. I *am* Mazon. You are nothing more than a weed growing on my surface, and the only way to stop a weed is to rip it from the ground."

Nails dug into Gen's windpipe. She kicked and writhed uselessly, feeling how the Lion must have felt in Gen's hold. The bold, silver marks on her skin faded to gray, like they had when Zusma died. If Hippolyta had been vengeful before, she was now unhinged *and* vengeful.

This was not how Gen had pictured her death, murdered by the Mazon Queen. She assumed she would be beaten by an angry mob, or that she would simply curl up and die of loneliness one day. Not now. Not when she was so close to getting her life back.

"You know the real reason I stopped breeding with the Gargareans?" Hippolyta whispered in her ear. "They were weak. By mixing blood, my children were only a shadow of what they could be. Like you."

She was right. Gen wasn't good enough. She wasn't as strong as her mother, or as clever as her father. She was only part of them, and not the best parts.

"Goodbye, little half-blood," Hippolyta whispered. "Good riddance."

Gen's limbs went limp. Her vision darkened at the corners. She gave one last kick for freedom and heard a small whisper in the back of her thoughts.

Sugar berries.

Argos smelled sugar berries, like the ones in Bale's pocket. With a trill of violin, the room lit up white.

"StormMaker," Hippolyta hissed, and opened her hand.

Gen dropped to the ground and gasped for air, drawing it in through her bruised throat. She sucked it in as if she might never get a taste of it again. Blessed, blessed air. Through blurred vision, she saw Pollux in the opening of the tunnel with the violin to his chin. He moved the bow across the strings in sharp strokes and quick blasts of lightning struck at Hippolyta in high staccato.

"Watch the girls," Gen tried to say. Her voice came out in a rasp, but Pollux nodded. Bale leaned against the wall beside him, watching the show in some bored fascination.

The silver-skinned girls cowered against the walls, clinging to one another. Gen sensed their fear. They never asked to be made. They never asked to be soldiers.

"You brought one of the lightning keepers here?" Hippolyta shrieked. Sharp lines cut through her forehead, shattering her smooth, silver complexion.

Pollux played a series of notes, and a black cloud formed at the top of the room. Lightning crackled across the ceiling and struck the ground at Hippolyta's feet. The Queen bared her teeth and leapt backward.

"Come on, Gen." Pollux waved her to him.

She crawled to her knees with one glance back at Hippolyta and her belt. This task would bring her to three, half of her labors, and it was so close.

"Gen!" Pollux shouted.

She looked back at him and saw her bag sitting next to Bale's boots.

"Bale, my bag!"

Bale bent down and grabbed it by the straps. "You want this?"

"Yes, throw it to me."

He flung it at her while Pollux played another blast of lightning. Hippolyta picked up a piece of the shattered ceiling and lobbed it over her head. Pollux drove it away with a gust of wind. The rock smashed against the wall. The girls scattered in shrieks. Argos picked up the smaller bits of rock with his tail and flung them back at Hippolyta.

Gen caught her bag and ripped into it looking for the bees. Where were they?

Hippolyta threw another piece of stone at Pollux. This time, it struck him in the shoulder.

His violin slipped from his chin as he whirled back. The Queen grabbed another piece of rock. Chomp lunged from the shadows with his teeth bared, and Gen grabbed the sack of bees and spat inside.

Wake up! Wake up!

Slowly the little yellow and white bees fluttered to life. She scooped them out of the bag and threw them at Hippolyta.

"What is this?" Hippolyta screeched, as the bees circled her.

"Get her," Gen said, and the first bee embedded in the Queen's silver leg.

"How dare you?" Hippolyta plucked the bee from her thigh and flicked it across the room. The little bee splattered on the stones, and Gen felt the MindWorker string rip free, like pulling out a strand of hair.

The poor little bee. She sensed the rest of the hive's sorrow at his loss, and their resulting fury at his murderer. Slumber bees were known for two things: carrying a venom that put most creatures into immediate sleep and unfailing loyalty to their hive.

The remaining bees flew at Hippolyta, sinking into her neck, her arms, her side.

"Stop that!"

The Queen flailed at them with weakening arms, her knees buckled, her shoulders sagged, and with her drooping eyes, she gave Gen one last venomous glare before collapsing into a silver heap.

Gen exhaled a long sigh. The bees continued to circle the Queen, taking turns to draw her blood. When Hippolyta woke, she would have a few bumps and bruises and some lingering drowsiness. Nothing exceedingly painful, which was more than Gen could say. She touched her swollen neck and winced. She felt like she had been struck with a hammer. Or strangled by a ruthless, Mazon Queen.

"Are you all right?" Pollux reached his hand down toward her. White dust from the crushed stone clung to his cheeks and shoulder. The bonding bracelet winked at her from his wrist.

He had unquestionably saved her. If he hadn't arrived at that exact moment, she would be dead, and she still couldn't bring herself to take his hand.

She brushed off her knees and stood by herself. "I'm fine."

Slowly, she made her way to the sleeping Queen, waiting for her to leap to her feet and grab her by the neck again. Leaning over her, Gen found lines of her mother in Hippolyta's face, along her jawline and the curve of her brow. Gen couldn't count how many nights she'd lain awake inside the whale's mouth wishing for family, and here it was. How fitting that the last of her family would want her dead.

"I hope you get your vengeance," Gen whispered, "but not from me."

She unhooked the belt from Hippolyta's waist and dropped it in her bag. This was her third task, complete, but Gen didn't feel like celebrating.

The little silver girls in the room whispered and moaned, shivering and clinging to one another for safety.

"She will be all right," Gen assured them. "Kala." *She will be well.*

They cried louder and waved to the tunnel entrance. "Anka shah, loka ta." *Go away, LightningMaker.*

Hippolyta must have raised the girls on stories of the foul Gargareans and their StormMaker friends, and Gen had brought their worst nightmare here.

"We should go," she said to Pollux, and called Argos down from the ceiling. She patted Chomp on the back, his hackles still raised, and cradled him in the crook of her elbow.

Pollux sealed his violin in his case and pushed his hair from his face. The muscle in his jaw pulsed. She wondered if he regretted making his vow to help her.

"I didn't know she was still alive," Gen said. "Or that she would be so terrible."

Except she had been warned by the bodiless voices in the air.

Maybe they could have been more specific. *Don't go down there. Hippolyta is alive and slightly unhinged.*

"You shouldn't have run from us. You should have waited." His voice cut with an edge she hadn't heard before, and Gen didn't think it was deserved.

"I wasn't running from you," she snapped back. "I was running *toward* the Mazon girl. I didn't want to lose her."

"You almost . . ." He didn't finish his sentence, but she knew how it ended.

She didn't want to admit that without Pollux and his well-timed lightning, she would be a husk on the floor of this filthy cave. She didn't want to admit that she couldn't do this on her own, that she needed him. She couldn't possibly accept that while her own Mazon blood had tried to strangle the life from her, it had been an Arcadian to step in for the rescue.

"I would have figured something out if you hadn't shown up," she said.

"How about a thank-you," Bale finally spoke.

"Fine. Thank you," Gen mumbled.

"You're welcome," Pollux replied in an equally sullen voice.

They reached the end of the tunnel. Where the moonlight spilled down, Gen held out her hand. Her skin had returned to its bright, silver color, even more than it had been minutes ago. The platinum bled across the backs of her hands and into the grooves of her knuckles.

Hippolyta had been right about one thing: Gen was "stealing" Mazon strength, a little more every second she stayed here. Maybe with fewer Mazons on the island, she was more of a lure to the Amazonium. She didn't know all the rules. Her mother had died before she could explain it all.

"How are we supposed to get up?" Bale craned his neck into the dark tunnel.

"Grow wings," Gen said, and smiled. "Or I can give you a boost." She laced her fingers together and held them in front of him. Bale stepped into her hands, and she lifted upward. Bale launched up through the hole and called down from the top.

"I'm up."

Pollux handed Bale his violin and Gen pushed Chomp up to him. Argos scrambled up on his own.

"I suppose it's my turn," Pollux said, tapping his fingers on his palm in the shapes of violin notes.

"You could always blast yourself up with some wind."

"That's very unreliable," he said. "I could end up half a mile in the sky."

Gen hadn't been serious. Maybe he wasn't being serious either.

"It's probably easier this way." She held her laced fingers in front of him and he placed his beautiful mud-splattered boot in her palms. "I'll go easy on you."

She lifted him upward. He grasped at the walls of the cave, slipped, and fell against her.

He caught himself on her shoulders, his chest pressed to hers. Red swooped across his cheeks, and his pale blue eyes went wide. Gen didn't know whether to laugh or scold him. He was so clumsy.

"Sorry." He pulled his hands from her shoulders and stepped back.

"Should we try again? And maybe you go up this time."

"I'll do my best."

They tried again, and the second attempt was more successful even though it involved a lot of scrambling and falling dust. Bale reached his hand down the hole and helped Pollux the last few inches to the top.

Using the previously made handholds, Gen pulled herself up last. She collapsed on a pile of broken stone, and Chomp nuzzled up beside her. She rumpled his fur and looked out at the moonlit ruins.

Themiscyra felt less ominous than before. The city wasn't dead. It was sleeping. Waiting. Growing.

"Is it strange that I'm glad she's alive?" Gen asked.

"Yes," Bale said as he shooed Argos away from his pockets. The monkey wanted more berries. "The woman almost killed you."

"No," Pollux said. "It's not strange. I'm glad she's here too. Castor and my father might not have cared, but I never wanted to be a part of destroying something."

One day Hippolyta would crawl from her hole, rebuild, and reap her vengeance on the Gargareans, and Gen wouldn't warn them. She wanted the Gargareans to pay for what they'd done, and Hippolyta deserved her chance to collect.

"How long will she sleep?" Bale asked.

"An hour or two." Slumber bee venom didn't have quite the same effect on those with Mazon blood. She knew that from experience. "And we do not want to be here when she wakes up. Bee hangover makes you irritable."

"Then let's get moving," Bale said. "I don't want to see that woman when she's in a bad mood."

They picked up their things and hiked through the ruins by the light of Pollux's lighted elk. Gen's neck throbbed with every step. Only halfway through her challenge, and she already felt broken. These were supposed to be the easier tasks, the least deadly, and already she had been chewed on by an orthus and strangled by a Mazon Queen.

The point being, she had made a mistake. There were no easy tasks on this list. Only those that appeared to be easy, and those that didn't even bother pretending. She would be more prepared for the next one, and as she looked to Pollux, playing his violin while his glowing elk danced in front of them, she decided she would try not to leave him behind again.

They reached the outskirts of the ruins where Pollux's chariot and horses waited.

"We can take you on our chariot." Pollux rubbed his injured shoulder, the one Hippolyta had hit with stone.

"No," Gen said. "I won't leave my whale."

"Where are we headed next?" Bale asked. "Hopefully somewhere with something decent to drink."

"I don't know." She hadn't planned beyond Mazon. "For now, let's leave this island." She reached out to her whale. *Come get me, please. I'll meet you at the beach.*

"Are you going to leave us again?" Pollux asked.

She didn't answer him. Something was wrong. The whale didn't respond. She should have heard his droning thread of disappointment, his complaints about being hungry, about not having enough time to eat his fill.

Where are you?

She tugged harder on their connected strings. They hadn't broken, but they'd gone dormant. Did he go too far?

"Gen, what's wrong?" Pollux asked.

"Shh." She held up a finger and stretched herself as thin as possible to reach her whale.

She received a sharp stab of fear, a tug of helplessness in response. *I'm surrounded. No way out.* The whale sent her an image of ten wooden ships, circling around him like sharks on a hunt.

Poachers.

"Run!" She screamed as loud as she could, burning holes in her swollen throat.

"What's wrong?" Pollux grabbed her arm.

A harpoon fired from one of the ships. The whale turned to the side and collided with another ship. Pain spiraled across Gen's cheek. She pressed her fingers to her face as a piercing stab struck her thigh.

The whale moaned. The harpoon stuck to his side. Droplets of shimmering blood floated across the surface of the water.

Gen fell to her knees. "No, no, no."

"Gen!" Pollux grabbed her shoulders and shook her. She barely saw him. She only saw the whale.

The whale used the last of his breath to emit one high-pitched shriek. The cry for help. The blood in Gen's veins went cold. He was dying, and there was nothing she could do to stop it.

A crank turned on one of the ships, reeling the whale in for the catch. Her whale didn't struggle. He knew the end neared and used his time to think of all the fish he would never eat, of all the places he would never see. Then he thought of Alcmen and her.

Family.

"I'm with you," she said. "I'm here."

His last thought was of the circus, when he would come out of the water to a crowd of smiling faces, all cheering for him. He would miss them. He would miss being loved. He let out his final gasp, and the strings connecting them snapped like a coiled spring.

Untethered, unconnected, broken, and torn, Gen had nothing to hold on to. She crashed.

CHAPTER 15

POLLUX

Gen!"

Pollux dropped to the ground beside Gen, cupped the back of her neck with one hand, and pressed his other to her cheek. Her skin was warm and feverish, slick with sweat.

An illness couldn't strike this quickly. Before she had collapsed, it was as if she'd been in the throes of a nightmare. She'd been wild, terrified. Of what? Bright red marks stood out against the skin on her neck. The Mazon Queen's fingerprints. Pollux thought he'd arrived just in time. What if Hippolyta left a more damaging mark? What if there was no saving Gen?

"What happened?"

Bale knelt beside him. Gen's chaeri nosed at her limp leg and made a sound between a snarl and a whimper. Her chest rose and fell with breath. Whatever had happened, it hadn't killed her yet.

"We need to get her out of here," Pollux said.

"Do you need help getting her into the chariot?" Bale asked.

"No, I don't think so. I can carry her if you carry the violin."

Bale scooped up the violin and Gen's bag, and Pollux shifted himself to slide one hand under Gen's shoulders and the other behind her legs. As he did, the chaeri snarled.

It was as if he knew more selfish thoughts lingered in Pollux's head.

He stood up, and Gen lay limp in his arms. Her head lolled to the side. The band of silver on her neck seemed larger than before. Or maybe he was only noticing it because he had an unobstructed view. Underneath her shirt, her chest rose and fell softly with breath. He watched it rise three times before turning away. He didn't want to leer.

Crushes were supposed to fade, especially these types of crushes. The types his fans carried for him. They only saw his music and performance, his money, his title. If they had to spend more than an hour with him, the glimmer would peel away and they would be sorely disappointed.

When he lost Gen in the ruins and found her in the crushing grip of the Mazon Queen, Pollux realized then the crush he held for Gen wasn't one of those kinds of crushes.

It was real.

The more time he spent with her, near her, the deeper she dug into him. She cared so fiercely for her father and her creatures, so much that she would kill herself to save them. He knew he didn't deserve an ounce of that fierce affection, but he wanted it. He wanted it more than he had ever wanted anything. He would have sold his soul for a smile.

He climbed into the chariot and set her on the bench. He straightened her arms and legs and swept the silver hair from her cheek, letting his fingers linger a second longer than necessary. In his thoughts, ominous music droned. Minor chords, long, low, groaning notes. "The Sonata of Gen's Collapse."

"Where is the whale?" Bale asked.

"I don't know. I assume she can call him later."

That was a wild assumption. Pollux had no idea how Gen's magic worked. From the outside, it looked effortless. It wasn't showy like their storm magic. The animals just did as she willed.

But the whale could wait. They needed to get Gen to a healer.

"Get us out of here," Pollux said. "To the nearest island with a capable healer."

Bale hitched the horses to the chariot and took the reins.

The horses lurched forward. Even they seemed to understand the urgency. The monkey, Argos, climbed to Bale's shoulder to pick through his pockets, and they lifted into the sky. Pollux fumbled for a spare vial of wind and let it loose. He picked up his violin and played a soft melody to help the wind speed them on their journey.

The chaeri jumped onto Gen's legs and pawed at her shins. He whimpered and growled.

Gen stirred. "I'm so sorry. I'm so sorry."

"You have nothing to be sorry about," Pollux said, and continued to play. For her. Always for her.

He cursed himself. There was only one way this could end: him with his heart shattered. Why couldn't he like someone else? One of the squealing fans, or the debutants his father brought to the manor? Why did it have to be the one girl in the Empire who despised his existence?

"Pollux?"

He set down his bow. Even in her roughened voice, the sound of his name from her lips made his pulse race, proof he was too far gone to turn back now.

The chaeri jumped onto Gen's chest and licked her arms with his mouthful of pointed teeth. Gen hugged him to her neck. She buried her nose in his fur and kissed his ears. Pollux envied the purple beast.

"He's gone, Chomp. They got him," she whispered.

"Who?" Pollux lowered his violin.

Her dark eyes pooled with tears, and the song in Pollux's head turned angry, low and quick with dark clouds and raging storms.

"Poachers," she said. "They killed my whale, and it was my fault. He was here because of me."

One of the tears escaped and rolled down her cheek. Pollux held his violin tight to keep himself from doing something ridiculous like wiping it from her skin.

"It's not your fault."

"Yes, it is. I know you're trying to make me feel better, but you don't need to lie. It *is* my fault."

Pollux didn't know what else to say. That was all he had.

"His last thoughts were of me, and my father, and our circus. In his dying breaths, he thought of us."

"You meant a lot to him."

"He meant a lot to me." She wrung her fingers through the chaeri's fur. "I have to win this. For him. For us." She hugged the chaeri closer.

"You will," Pollux said. "I'll make sure of it."

He touched the bracelet on his wrist. He had no choice. He would lose his hand if he didn't do his best. Not that he'd had much of a choice before, either.

The survival of Queen Hippolyta only proved how dangerous the StormMakers could be. They made enemies, and if Castor took control, she would sell more lightning, make more enemies. Hurt more people like Gen. He didn't like the Arcadian Doctrine, either, or complying with his father's wishes, but worse would be setting Cas loose on the Empire with the power of Arcadia behind her and no tether to keep her contained.

"Are we still going to a healer?" Bale called.

"No," Gen said.

"Then where are we going?"

"I don't know." She smeared the tear across her cheek and pulled something from her pocket, a stained napkin.

He still would have liked for Gen to go to a healer, but he wouldn't force her. Cas wouldn't stop for a healer. She would limp to victory on broken legs if that was what it took. His sister thrived on competition. To beat her, they couldn't stop.

"So should I keep flying east?" Bale asked. "Or go around in circles until you decide?"

"Give her a moment," Pollux said, sometimes regretting his arrangement with Bale.

Bale had appeared on the island of Arcadia two years ago with no story and no explanation. He had found work delivering messages in the manor, messages he frequently lost or forgot to deliver. When he lost one of the Storm Duke's messages, he was swiftly fired.

The Duke raged at him, and while he raged, Bale sat back with a disinterested smile on his face, completely unbothered by the Storm Duke or his temper. The Duke had been bothering Pollux for a while about hiring some staff, and at that moment, Bale became the perfect person to keep by his side—someone impervious to the Duke's fits of outrage.

Pollux told Bale he would give him a raise and not expect too much, just some help with his performances, a few simple tasks, and to not report any of his movements to the Storm Duke. Bale seemed to like that request, and for the most part, their relationship worked. But it had its rough patches. Sometimes Pollux wished Bale would at least pretend to care.

Gen looked over her napkin, bleary-eyed and solemn. He dared a glance at her, catching the small lines around her mouth and the shadows on her cheeks, the places where she carried the death of her whale.

He wished he could tell her he hurt for the whale too. He'd seen the circus fourteen times, and at each performance, his mouth dropped the moment the whale emerged from the water. Even if it returned, the circus would never be the same.

Pollux leaned over Gen's shoulder and saw the napkin held her list of tasks. The ones completed had been smudged.

> ~~Blue mustache - the Lion~~
> young man - find the Hind ship
> One-eyed woman - stop the Boar
> Many-eyed figure - clean the stables
> ~~Tall man - Stymphal birds~~
> Fierce woman - kill the Bull
> Thylop - capture the Mares
> ~~weeping woman - find Livia King~~
> Red Empress - kill the Hydra
> Crystal Empress - retrieve the belt of Hippolyta

Gen smeared her finger across "retrieve the belt of Hippolyta" as she read it. There were probably more finished. Castor would have done something while they were on Mazon. Not the Hydra, though. Cas would only face it if it was necessary. She would fear the beast, and not for the right reasons, not because it would eat her, but because she could fail in killing it, and losing terrified his sister more than anything.

"The stables," Gen said. "Can you take me to Elis?" She turned to Pollux. "I hope you and Bale are up to shoveling manure."

"I'm not sure that we can," Pollux said, and he was not saying that purely because he had no desire to clean stables. "The tasks are yours . . . yours and Castor's. If Bale and I help with the actual labors, you could be disqualified."

"I'd also like to add that I will not be cleaning any stables," Bale said. "For any reason."

Gen bit into her lower lip, that beautiful, plush lower lip. As much as he hated the idea of shoveling manure, he would for her. But he had given this a lot of thought.

He knew the Empresses and how they worked. His father did business with the rulers, and whenever he did, he required a detailed contract to be signed by all parties. Even so, if ever there was a loophole, the Empresses found it and exploited it. These labors were a test of wit as much as anything else. Make the wrong choices, and Gen could lose.

His free concert for the release of Livia Kine, he decided, would pass the test. Gen had been the one to make the negotiation and secure the deal. He was only acting as payment. But scooping up manure would give him direct contact with the labor.

"You are probably right," she agreed. "I still choose the stables. I'm not ready to fight anyone again." Her fingers crept up to her swollen neck and lingered there.

No, Pollux didn't want to see her nearly killed again, either.

"To Elis then." Bale pulled the horses to the south.

"There's another rider," Gen whispered, sitting upright.

Pollux squinted at the night sky, finding nothing but stars. "I don't see one."

"Neither do I. Argos does."

Pollux looked to the odd little monkey on Gen's shoulder. He stared off to their left. Pollux stood at the side of the chariot and gazed in the same direction.

A few minutes later, a single horse came into view. "It's not Castor," he said, and exhaled a tight breath. He did not want to run into his sister while he was with Gen. Cas would be furious he had sided against her and might shoot them both with lightning out of spite.

"It looks like an Arcadian rider though," Bale said.

Pollux drew his mouth tight as he faced Gen. "You should hide yourself under the bench."

Gen gave him a look that said, "I knew it," before she tucked herself and her creatures under the bench. She wasn't wrong. He had promised her help, and here was trouble, chasing after them. He touched the metal bracelet on his wrist. Whoever this was, whatever they did, he couldn't break his promise to Gen. Not that he had planned to, anyway.

The rider swept through the sky, and Pollux recognized the horse before the man. Soter always chose Tempest.

"Lord Pollux!" Soter saluted him from the back of his steed.

Pollux rolled his eyes and held up his hand in response. He and Soter used to be friends. Their mothers were friends, and when they'd been children, they'd run around the manor halls with Castor and Soter's sister, Ariete, scampering behind them, wreaking havoc on the floors.

That had been fine when they'd been children. But as they got older, expectations changed. No more running up and down the halls, enjoying themselves. Pollux had to become the Storm Duke, and Soter had to serve him.

Soter was a true Arcadian loyalist. If the Duke told Soter to drown himself in rainwater, he would do it without question, which didn't make him an ally to Pollux at the moment. The Storm Duke knew Pollux had gone to Nemea for a couple of days. He should have been home by now, but Pollux was prone to wander. It was rare the Duke sent someone after him. Pollux always ended up back home eventually. Sending Soter to fetch him sent a clear message: his father wanted him home. Now.

Soter brought his horse alongside them, as close as he could get without his mount's wings knocking into the chariot.

"I bring word from your father." He held out a folded piece of parchment, sealed with the wax lightning bolt of their family. Pollux's lip curled. Official messages from his father were never good news. Did he know about the lottery? If so, that would shorten the reins on Pollux's time to save Cas.

"I'll take that." Bale snatched the letter from Soter on his behalf.

"Where are you headed?" Soter asked.

"Home," Pollux lied, eyeing the bracelet on his wrist. Was it getting tighter? How much did he have to do to keep his promise to Gen? Kill Soter or just make him leave?

"You're headed in the wrong direction then, my lord."

Pollux took a breath. He needed more time, and to get more time, he needed to lose Soter. With a loyalist like him, there was only one thing Pollux could do . . . pull rank. He drew his brow and swallowed.

"Did you come here to deliver a message or to interrogate me?" he snapped in his best imitation of the Storm Duke. It bothered him how much he sounded like his father when he spoke like this.

"Your father wants you home," Soter said.

"I heard you, and your message has been delivered. I don't need an escort."

"Pollux . . ." Soter appealed to him as if they were still friends, and they couldn't be friends, not as long as Soter served his father.

"That is Lord Pollux to you. If you recall, I stand to inherit."

"Of course, my lord." Soter bowed his head like a cowed child. Pollux's palms sweated. He wasn't sure how long he could keep this impression going before he broke.

"You can tell my father," Pollux continued, "I will be home as soon as I can, and I suggest you leave directly to alert him. The Duke of Storms hates to be kept waiting."

Soter raised his head and gave Pollux an ice-cold stare that cut to his bones. Honestly, if it came down to a fight, Soter would win. He was twice Pollux's girth and could handle a vial of lightning as well as Cas. Pollux, on the other hand, could pelt him with an airy sonata. The only advantage Pollux had over him was a birthright and an old piece of parchment that declared him more powerful.

"As you wish, my lord," Soter said as he pulled his horse away from them.

This time, the piece of old parchment won.

Pollux let out a long breath as Gen crawled out from under the bench. He rubbed the back of his neck where two tight knots had formed on either side of his spine. He felt sick with himself, and all he had gained was a temporary reprieve. The Duke would keep coming for him. They would have to be more discreet.

"Very well handled," Bale said.

"Yes, very well handled," Gen said without the same enthusiasm. "You sounded just like your bully of a father."

The knots in Pollux's neck tightened. "Because I've been bullied by him enough to have it memorized." He snatched the letter from Bale, and a wave of compassion crossed Gen's face.

He tore open the envelope and removed the letter. At the sight of his father's sharp letters and heavy pen, Pollux's stomach twisted.

His father was angry. Not that it was unusual for him to be angry. Even in his wedding portrait, he'd looked annoyed, like he was calculating the costs of every meal, every drink wasted on the guests. *"Why do we have to spend so much gold on one day of festivities?"*

His letter began,

Pollux,

I know what Castor is doing, and I assume you do too. I need you home immediately so we can deal with this. Don't make me come after you with force.

Duke Tyndareus of Arcadia

Pollux crumped up the letter. He knew this would happen eventually. He'd hoped they'd be further ahead in the game when it did.

"My father knows about the lottery," he said. "We need to hurry." He nodded to the bench. "We should get some rest. It's going to be a long day tomorrow."

CHAPTER 16

GEN

Sleep eluded Gen. Her burning throat, aching bones, and broken heart kept it away. Her mind replayed the images of her whale, her beautiful whale, speared and bleeding. He had died afraid, alone. He had trusted her, and she'd failed him. Her small family kept shrinking, slipping through her fingers. She sat in the corner of the chariot and hugged Chomp to her chest while Pollux and Bale slept side by side on the bench with Argos curled between them.

Gen kept the horses on their trek to Elis with her ability. She'd spat on both of them to keep them focused on their destination. They were harder to control than the whale had been. She'd only had to tell him once where to go and he went there. These horses needed constant reminders.

Oh how she missed her whale.

This was useless. She would never sleep.

On the floor of the chariot, Gen picked up the crumpled letter from the Storm Duke. *Duke Tyndareus of Arcadia.* Is that how he signed a letter to his son? Gen's father had always signed his *your proud father.*

The entire time Gen had hid underneath the bench from the Duke's messenger, she'd fought to keep from leaping out to tell the rider what Castor was doing and where he might find her.

The man who gave the Gargareans the power to kill Gen's mother was coincidentally the man who could pull Castor out of this contest.

If the Storm Duke took care of Castor, Gen wouldn't have to. It would have been so easy to tattle on her, apart from Pollux, who stood in her way, figuratively and literally.

He had saved her twice, once from the Lion and then from Hippolyta. She owed him something. Maybe that something was to keep his father out of this.

Gen took the crumpled letter and pitched it over the side of the chariot. The wind ripped it away.

Her stomach rumbled. She poked around the chariot for something to eat and found a latch in the floor. When she lifted it up, she discovered where Pollux and Bale stored their things. In a single row along the side sat fifteen neatly labeled storm vials: "lightning," "thunder," "rain," "wind," "fog" . . . all the tools a StormMaker needed to destroy something.

Or make something, she thought, looking at Pollux's violin and remembering the little cloud elk that danced on the rocks.

Enough of that. She shook the dream from her thoughts. Pollux might be the odd one in his family, but she had heard him talk to that rider. He was only a few steps away from becoming just like them, and she couldn't forget that.

She dug deeper into the compartment, still hunting for food when her fingers brushed something soft. She yanked whatever it was out of the hole and gasped. Bless the Oracles, Pollux had a golden wool sweater.

Gen pressed the silken threads to her cheek. The golden wool caressed her skin like kisses. It was the softest material in the Empire and, consequently, the most expensive. More expensive than water silk. Golden sheep took twenty years to grow a coat of wool and only grew it once, and Pollux had it buried in this chariot like a common rag.

"You're awake."

Gen dropped the sweater at the sound of Pollux's voice.

"I was looking for . . . food." She picked up the sweater and shoved it back in the compartment, then pulled it out and neatly folded it. This sweater didn't deserve such abuse. "This is a beautiful sweater."

"You can have it," he said without pause.

Gen frowned. "Because I need your charity?"

"No. You want the sweater, you can have the sweater."

Gen tucked it back into the compartment. "I'd rather have my rags that I earned than your cast-offs." If she had sunk low enough to need StormMaker hand-me-downs, then there was no hope for her.

Pollux sighed. "How about something to eat?" He pushed the sweater aside and pulled out a small box of food, rosemary bread and goat cheese, dried meats and fig spread. It made her paltry food supplies look like dirt.

She took a slice of bread with cheese and fig spread because she had no other choice, and it was insultingly delicious. Why wouldn't a StormMaker have the best of everything? She truly hadn't been this bitter about other people's wealth and fortune until she'd lost all of her own.

No. She hadn't lost it; it had been stolen from her.

"You look different than before," Pollux said.

"I'm sure I'm a mess."

"No, you look perfect, I mean great, I mean . . . you're more silver than before."

Gen looked at the back of her hand, and the fat silver band

running across her skin. "I think I absorbed more Amazonium while I was there."

"Does it make you stronger?"

"I guess we'll see, won't we?"

The more she looked at herself, the more silver she found hiding in unexpected places. She'd collected quite a bit of the Amazonium on her short visit to the isle of Mazon. She wondered how much strength she had gained. Enough to tame the Mares? To vanquish the Hydra?

Doubtful. Her best bet would be to claim six labors without including the Hydra. Last she'd checked, *immortal* meant something could never die.

Pollux wiped the crumbs from his snack onto his linen pants. "You should try to sleep. I can watch the horses."

"I wish I could." Gen looked longingly at Chomp, who could sleep anywhere. "I keep thinking about the whale."

"I'm so sorry," he said, and he truly did sound sorry. "Let me play you something. Maybe that will help you sleep." He took his violin from the case and held it under his chin.

"Something quiet," Gen said. "You don't want to wake Bale."

Pollux smiled. "That is not easy to do. Have you ever been to Arcadia?" He turned the top peg of his violin.

"Once."

"Of course. You came with the circus. Well, it can be loud, especially in the manor. Someone is always opening a vial of thunder or rain. You either learn to become a heavy sleeper, or you take sleep where you can find it."

"What do you do?" she asked.

"I leave as much as I'm allowed and find peace elsewhere." He gave her an anxious smile and stretched the bow across the strings.

Long and low notes filled the chariot along with a thin wisp of cloud. Pollux moved the bow up the neck, and a light breeze blew the cloud into the loose shape of a whale, *her* whale. At least she assumed it was her whale because where else would Pollux have seen an infinity whale?

The notes climbed higher, and the little cloud whale flew in a circle around Pollux's head. Pollux plucked short, quick notes for a low rumble of thunder that sounded like the spray from the whale's blowhole complete with a spout of fine mist. The little cloud whale swam through it in a loop before he took a sharp dive.

Pollux's cloud version of her whale was perfect, right down to the bend in his tail and the shape of his fins. How had Pollux remembered so much? He played one last note, and the cloud whale disappeared into vapor. Pollux lowered his violin, and Gen clutched her chest, trying to breathe.

She thought everyone had forgotten her and her whale. Or no longer cared.

"That was my whale," she whispered.

"I know."

"How did you remember him so clearly?"

"You always remember your first infinity whale. Your circus was important to me. I wouldn't be playing my music if not for you . . . for it. For the circus."

She used to hear that a thousand times a day. People would stop Alcmen in the street, in the market.

Your circus changed me. It showed me magic. It gave me hope.

It had meant something to people, but the moment Alcmen's

purity had been questioned, they threw it away. When she rebuilt it, she would make it impossible to discard.

"I have great ideas for improvements," she said. "New acts and costumes."

"It was perfect the way it was."

"Well, I have more competition now. The circus needs to be at its best." She gestured to his violin.

"I don't play to compete."

"I know that, but the entertainment market is always changing. You need to stay ahead of the game. If you added some more musicians, sets, props—"

"I don't want to *add* anything else." He snapped the case shut.

"Oh, I see." Clearly he thought he was too good for constructive criticism.

He picked up his violin and played another song, a quieter one with no cloud whales or dancing elks. Gen leaned against the back of the chariot and closed her eyes. Arrogant StormMaker. They were all the same.

CHAPTER 17

GEN

Gen awoke to a bump and the most horrific smell she had ever encountered in her life.

"What in the Oracles' name is that?" She sat up, choking, and held her hand over her mouth to find Pollux and Bale had already covered their faces with tied pieces of cloth.

"We've reached Elis," Bale choked.

Gen moved to stand, and Pollux pushed her back down. "There's a problem."

"I know. I can smell it." She gagged after she spoke. Opening her mouth had let some of the putrid smell onto her tongue. She reached into her bag and rifled through her things for something to stanch the odor. All she had was the damaged water silk dress. Without hesitation, she ripped off a strip of it and tied it over her nose and mouth. She would have torn apart an entire clothier's shop if it would save her from this horrific stench.

"There's another problem," Pollux said. "Castor is here."

At the mention of her name, thunder rumbled through the sky. Gen stood up cautiously and peered over the side of the chariot.

There, in the center of the most incredible mass of cow manure Gen had ever seen, stood Castor under a swirl of black rain clouds. Her rain poured down on her and the muck, barely cutting through the mess. Feces stretched in all directions, and Castor stood in it up to her thighs. It was like throwing a cupful of water on a raging fire.

Gen sat back down in the chariot.

"She can't do it. It's too much," she said.

"Castor doesn't quit," Pollux said. "She'll stay here and find a way to finish it."

"I say let her clean it up," Bale said, "and we can move on to something else."

"Three something elses," Gen said. "I need three more tasks to win."

She took her napkin list from her bag. They only had the Boar, the murder of Mr. Bull, the *Hind*, the Mares, and the Hydra left, and Castor had to have completed one or more of those tasks by now.

Gen doubted Castor had slain the Hydra or captured the Mares. She didn't look beat-up enough for those. But Castor could have killed Mr. Bull, stopped the Boar, or found the *Hind*. If she'd done all three plus the birds, then this could be her fifth task.

"We should go," Pollux said.

"Where?" Gen shoved her napkin list into her bag. "To the Hydra? We don't know what else she's done. I need this task."

If Gen had to choose between facing Castor and facing the Hydra, she would choose Castor. The Storm Lady had only one head.

"She'll fight you for the task," Pollux warned.

That was the whole point of making this a contest. "I don't plan on fighting her. I'm simply going to walk out there and send the cows down the hill to clean their own mess. Castor can leave or be trampled."

"It's not that simple with Cas." He rolled up his sleeve and exposed a round scar on his forearm. "We were six. I was playing with one of her dolls, and I snapped the arm. She struck me with lightning."

Gen shuddered, imagining the young, yawning Lady Castor armed with vials of lightning. She'd only gotten more dangerous and brutal with age. The murdered Stymphal crows could attest to that, and if Castor would zap her own brother for playing with a doll, why would she spare her competitor?

Gen shook her head. No, she couldn't scare herself out of this one. If she did, she might as well hand Castor the win. Three more tasks and Gen had this. She'd free her father, make sure Castor never took control of the StormMakers, and get her life back.

"I'm going. If you want me to win to help your sister, this is how I can do it. I can finish six tasks and keep us both from the Hydra."

Pollux's jaw flexed. "Bale and I can't help you out there. Cas can't know we're with you."

"You said it yourself. I have to face these tasks alone. I'll be all right. I am Mazon after all." She offered him a weak smile.

Mazon strength couldn't help her here. The entire race of silver warriors had fallen in the face of the Arcadian's bottled weather. Her plan was to stay as far from Castor and her lightning as possible and let the cows do the dirty work.

"Come on, Argos. We have work to do." Gen beckoned the small monkey onto her shoulder before she stood up. Chomp moved to follow, and she froze.

"Not you, Chomp. You stay here."

He gave her an indignant look at being told to "stay." Gen kept her finger pointed at the chariot. Her loyal chaeri was too old and too impetuous to face off against Castor. The rat would be safe in Gen's bag and the monkey could hide himself, but Chomp didn't have the same vigor he had as a pup. She couldn't lose another member of her family.

"I'll be back soon," she said. "You two stay here with Chomp and the horses."

"Sounds good to me." Bale kicked his feet up on the side of the chariot.

"Be careful. Cas always goes straight for the lightning." Pollux gave her one last warning before Gen stepped into the mud.

Her eyes burned. The odor seeped into her pores, her hair, her mouth, her lungs . . . everywhere. The snack she'd eaten earlier came forcefully back up. She spat it on the ground and blinked away tears.

She'd never thought she would smell anything worse than stink lizard pus and was sorry to be wrong. She could see why the man had used his lottery wish on this. How was Castor able to suffer it? Gen hadn't even reached the mass of manure and already her stomach churned.

Keep going.

She forced herself to step forward, taking short breaths. The azure cattle lingered on the hill above the manure-covered stables. Castor stood to Gen's left with her arms raised to the sky under a thunderous rain cloud.

"Come on," Gen said to the monkey, and ducked slightly lower, trying not to vomit on her boots.

It wasn't as if she had never been around animal waste. She had worked in a circus. But she and Alcmen had been able to communicate to the animals that their business could be done in certain places, and they'd removed it in a timely manner. This had to be years of neglected waste, left here to fester and grow and become something unnatural.

At the base of the hill, she stopped. An angry crack of thunder boomed, and Castor shouted at the sky before she bent over and clutched her stomach, retching into her puddles.

At least Gen wasn't the only one suffering.

Before Gen climbed the hill, she took the rat from her bag and held him in her palm.

"I need smoke cover. Just a little."

The rat wrinkled his nose and a thin wisp of steam curled out from her pocket, enough to blur the air around her and make her less easy to spot as she moved toward the cattle. She placed the rat back into her bag.

The nearest cow stood fifteen feet in front of her, chewing grass and dropping more manure to the already soiled ground. Gen only needed a few cows under her control to create a stampede. They were herd animals. They followed the leader, and Gen would send them down the hill in a trampling mass to chase Castor out of her way. Simple . . . as long as everyone played their part.

She reached into her bag and removed her tin of spare hairs. The cow raised her head. Gen gagged once more and crawled toward the beast.

"Come a little closer, Brown Eyes. I won't hurt you."

The cow blinked her aforementioned brown eyes and continued to chew on her grass.

Gen plucked a handful of grass, twisted the hair around it, and reached toward the creature.

"Come on," she whispered, stretching her hand a little farther. She choked down the latest round of bile threatening to rise up, and the cow moved to her. Her mouth brushed Gen's hand before the cow froze and snapped her head up. She backed away.

"Wait," Gen said, and tasted something new in the air, something sharp—lightning!

Argos leapt from her shoulder as Gen dove for safety. The blast struck the ground where she'd been, leaving behind a large, black mark in the grass. The cow rose up on two legs and raced for the safety of her herd. The other cattle scattered, running in all directions, slamming into one another to escape the storm. Her stampede was going in the wrong direction.

The black cloud overhead crackled with lines of lightning. Castor stood underneath and offered Gen a silent challenge. *"Try it. I dare you."*

Lightning seared through the sky. Gen dove a second time and tumbled down the hill. Her legs flipped over her head. Her elbow smashed into a rock. She flipped three more times and flopped at the edge of the excrement pile, knocking the air from her lungs.

She sucked in a breath and a mouthful of manure-stained air. She had lost the water silk scarf. Not that it mattered. She spat feces from her mouth and climbed to her knees. Castor moved toward her, clumping through manure step by step.

Even covered in dung, she looked as striking as she had on the day of the lottery. This time, though, she didn't carry rainbows. She tossed a crackling ball of lightning from hand to hand as Pollux warned she would.

"You picked the wrong labor," Castor said before she tossed fire at Gen's face.

Gen twisted and scrambled to her feet, aided by the new Mazon strength in her legs. She took three long strides, crossing yards in each one, before a blast of lightning struck the grass in front of her. Argos took off running for the nearest tree.

Gen skidded backward and turned to her right. White light struck there too, close enough to singe the hairs on her arms.

She was being herded. Castor wanted her to fight.

"Going somewhere?" Castor flung one more ball of lightning aimed for the space between Gen's eyes.

She dropped and landed with her chest in the muck. Her stomach lurched, and Castor already had a new ball of lightning bouncing on her palm. Gen glanced toward the chariot partially hidden in the trees. She should have listened to Pollux. She should have let Castor clean the stables.

Castor flung her next ball of lightning, and Gen flipped to her side. The fire sizzled in the manure with a puff of smoke. As Castor pulled another bolt of lightning from the sky and curled it in her fingers, Gen grabbed at the manure and flung it back at Castor.

It flew with shockingly accurate aim and strength, striking her on the cheek. It splattered across her white skin and knocked her into the muck.

Gen crawled to her feet while Castor clawed at manure to free herself.

"You are dead, Mazon." Castor raised her arm to snatch more lightning.

Gen launched herself at Castor and hit her in the chest. They both skidded through the muck.

"Get off me!" Castor snarled.

"Stop trying to cook me."

"You shouldn't be here," Castor said, and hit Gen with a gust of wind.

She rolled off her into the mud. Castor tried to scramble away.

Gen grabbed her by the ankle and yanked her back. She had to keep her from drawing off her lightning. "You can't finish the task."

"Yes I can." Castor fumbled for her belt, and Gen tugged her leg until Castor went face-first in the muck. She came back up gagging and spitting. "What are you going to do? Kill me like your father killed all those people?"

The silver bands on Gen's arms pulsed with heat. She had heard her father called *murderer* a thousand times, but coming from Castor, the insult struck harder.

"*Your* father's the murderer. He slaughtered the Mazons." Gen had walked through their remains only hours ago.

"It was business. If the Mazons had come to us with the coin and the request, we would have sold it to them. That ridiculous war had to end." Castor sat back on the muck. "This is pointless. If we keep battling each other, we will both lose. What will it take to make you go away? You want your circus back? Your reputation? I'll pay you fifty thousand to go away now. You can buy reputations for less than that."

Gen hesitated, her head swimming with the possibility of fifty thousand in gold, no more tasks, no fighting Castor, no Mares, no Hydra. She could hire a mercenary to wrench Alcmen from prison. Or pay his guards to turn a blind eye while she yanked him free.

Except they would have to go into hiding. Alcmen would be a fugitive. They would both be in exile. Forever.

"I can't do that."

Castor flung a handful of manure at Gen's face. She swatted it aside. "You won't win this," Castor hissed. "I will take everything you have. I already took your whale. What next, Genevieve? That little beast that follows you around? Will it be worth it?"

"The whale?" The words stuck in Gen's throat, and her ears rang with his last cries. Of course it hadn't been coincidence. How foolish of her to think random hunters had slaughtered him. "You killed him." Gen curled her fingers into a fist. "He wasn't a ship. He was a living thing!"

Castor shrugged, uncaring, unfeeling. If she had a heart underneath that expensive shirt, then it was so small and shriveled, it ceased to beat.

"You're the monster," Gen continued. "You're the murderer."

She pressed her nails into her palms and pulled her arm back. Castor opened her mouth to scream and lunged to the side. Gen dove and caught Castor by the ankle. She dropped Castor in the muck. Castor would crush anything and everything that stood in her path. The only way Gen could win this was to do the same.

"Let me go." Castor spat manure in Gen's face.

"Why? So you can slaughter more whales?" She pinned Castor under her knees and pushed on her chest.

The horrific odor of this manure pile twined around her. She wanted out of here. She wanted to be done with these tasks. It wasn't fair. She pushed on Castor, and the Lady of Storms sank deeper into the mud. In her thoughts, Gen heard the whale's dying moans. If she buried Castor under the manure, she could silence it. She could win this contest. She could go home like the whale wanted.

Castor clawed at Gen's fingers, helpless. She had everything: money, security, family, fame, and she had asked the Empresses for more. More money. More power. But what she didn't have was strength. Without her money and lightning, she was just a girl.

The manure dropped onto Castor's cheeks and tumbled into her mouth. It swallowed her shoulders and her neck. Castor pulled at Gen's arms, and Gen pushed harder.

"I knew you'd do it," Castor choked. "You're a murderer, exactly like him."

Gen yanked her hands back. No. No. This wasn't her. She wasn't a killer. Neither was Alcmen.

Castor twisted her way free and rolled to her side, coughing and sputtering. Gen sat back on her heels and looked at her hands. Silver stretched down the center of her palms, covering more than half. The Amazonium was still growing. How? She wasn't on Mazon anymore.

Gen closed her fists, burying the silver inside. She thought of Hippolyta's hands on her neck, the same way she had tried to kill Castor. Gen couldn't win this way. She couldn't make everyone's fears come true.

She stood up and swept some of the muck from her arm. Her stomach clenched, and she retched again, as much for the odor as the shame.

"You touch me again, and I'll kill you." Castor reached up to draw more of her lightning from the clouds.

"I won't touch you."

Castor could have the task. It would take her days to clean this. Her rainstorms weren't enough. She'd need a flood to wash this away, a river . . .

A river.

Prickles rolled over Gen's shoulders as she turned to the east, where a dam sat between two hillcrests. She'd barely noticed it before. Just part of the scenery. But the dam stood directly above this field, made of wood posts and mounds of rock, not impenetrable.

If someone were to break the dam, the water would rush down

here and wash away this mess, and whoever did that would claim this task without having to kill anyone.

Gen stepped over Castor and ran toward the dam as fast as her silver legs would carry her. Castor would figure out her plan soon enough, and if she snatched a bolt of lightning before Gen could shatter the dam, Castor could strike her with lightning and then break the dam herself.

Gen leapt from the edge of the manure onto grass. She skidded several feet and stumbled over her own boots before regaining control. Her legs moved faster than she could keep up. Her body was changing with each step, for good or bad or both.

Argos came out of hiding and ran along beside her. Gen launched over a boulder set in the path and turned over her shoulder. Castor pulled another vial from her belt. No doubt it would be something explosive and fiery. Gen skidded to a stop in front of the dam and caught herself on the pilings.

The dam loomed over her, twenty or thirty feet high, held in place by wooden posts she could barely wrap her arms around. From below, it hadn't seemed this impressive.

She grabbed the middle post and dug her heels into the ground. Impressive or not, she had to find a way to break it. She pulled back on the post. Her arms tingled, her legs surged, and her muscles pushed against her jacket as she wrenched back on the piling. Something shifted, and a trickle of water leaked from the stones. Not enough.

Above her, Argos skittered across the top of the dam, pulling small stones out of the cracks. Behind her, Castor stood in the mud, gathering a massive ball of lightning. Gen crushed the pole against her chest and put both boots against the rocks.

"Come on," she growled.

The electricity in the air lifted the hairs on her neck. She tightened her shoulders and gave the dam one more pull. If it didn't break, she'd have to run.

Something cracked.

The post she held split in the middle, quickly bending outward. Water spilled from the rocks, and the first one rolled free, cracking another post. Gen leapt to the side to avoid being crushed. Argos climbed down to her shoulder.

Water pushed the rest of the rocks aside and swept down the hill. She slipped on wet grass trying to escape the bulk of it. The river crested in a massive wave and crashed into the mud. Down below, Castor lowered her arm and moved to higher ground. Her lightning storm dissipated.

Gen pressed herself against the rise of another hill.

In the manure field, Castor stopped in the middle and faced the oncoming flood.

She wasn't running.

Why wasn't she running?

The water reached the edge of the manure, ripping it away, and still, Castor stood solid.

Gen had to pull Castor out of the way, didn't she? Or would it be so terrible if she left her there? *What is the difference between killing someone and simply letting them die?*

The difference, if there was one, was so small, she couldn't find it.

Gen charged down the hill, racing against the water. Her legs again moved faster than she could manage. She skidded in the wet grass as the wave crested over Castor's head. Even with extra Mazonness, she couldn't reach her.

Castor raised her arms and lifted her chin, as if she welcomed the flood. The wave came down, and all Gen could think was how devastated Pollux would be that he lost his sister. Or maybe he would be angry with her for not being faster, or better, or for causing the flood that killed her. Thoughts she should have had earlier, when she'd had Castor pressed into the manure.

A boom sounded, and the wave ripped in two, parting on either side of Lady Castor. She held up her hands and parted the water with a gust of wind.

Gen leaned over her knees, breathing heavily. Castor would live to cook harmless animals another day, and she might still win the game, but she wouldn't be able to mark this task off her list. Gen had claimed it with her flood. Number four. Only two more to go.

CHAPTER 18

CASTOR

The Mazon could actually win this, Castor thought as Genevieve scrambled up the hill. She headed straight for the dam, and if she managed to break it, the water would cut right through this valley, washing away the manure and Castor's hope at keeping this task.

It had been a last-minute decision to come here. With no lead on the *Hind*, and assuming Genevieve was stuck on Mazon, Cas thought she could wash away the mess and be on her way.

She had made several incorrect assumptions.

She crawled out of the muck and reached up to steal some lightning from the sky. Already her storm faded. She inhaled another acrid mouthful of shit and gagged. She retched to the side and lost the hold on her lightning. The crap was everywhere. Embedded in her skin, tangled in her hair, smearing her eyes.

That bitch had tried to drown her in it. Castor would never forget that.

Genevieve wouldn't take money. She wouldn't accept reason. She was a menace, like her father, a public hazard. She needed to be disposed of. Castor yanked some lightning from the sky and balled it in her hand. She smiled, imagining the circus girl ignited in yellow flames. The only downside would be the odor. Trash smelled horrible when it burned. Worse than this festering pit.

She took aim at Gen and pulled her hand back to pitch the

lightning at her when the dam split apart. The water rushed toward her, and she let her lightning go. If she threw it now, she'd hit the water, and they'd both cook.

Castor climbed to the highest mound she could find and tugged another vial from her belt—wind. She moved to unscrew the cap, and it slipped from her hand. She lost it in the muck.

The water thundered toward her. It would crush her, drown her, if she didn't do something. She fumbled for another vial. It was the remainder of her tornado. She hoped it was enough.

The flood hit the manure. It crashed into the mud, turning brown, then it crested over her head. Castor ripped open the jar and pushed with everything she had. What remained of her tornado sliced through the water like a knife, parting the waves. Water rose up on either side of her, twenty or thirty feet high. Behind her, the river reconnected and carried away the manure and her chance at this labor.

Castor screamed. She'd lost the task. No, not lost. It had been stolen from her. Genevieve had stopped the Lion and found Livia Kine; she likely had the Mazon belt too if she found her way off the island, even without her precious whale. Gen had four tasks to Castor's two—the Boar and the birds. She could truly lose this. To a washed-up circus girl.

No, she couldn't lose. *Wouldn't* lose. Leading Arcadia was her destiny, and she would grab it by any means possible.

The rush of water finally stopped and settled in a pool around Castor. The last of her wind petered out. Her storm above had dissipated. She had only what remained on her belt, the half-used jars from her visit to Stymphal. She had a few strikes of lightning and a touch of hurricane. She should have restocked before she left the chariot. She hadn't known she would be battling the Mazon. Gen was supposed to be stranded.

It didn't matter. She only needed one sharp blast of lightning to take care of Genevieve. She could electrify the water now that she stood safely out of it.

The Mazon came down the hill, smeared in manure, drenched in rainwater, and *smiling.* That bitch stole Castor's task and had the nerve to be smug about it. Castor loosened the top on her lightning jar.

The Mazon stopped at the edge of the manure pool as if she knew what Castor planned. *A little closer, a few more steps.*

"Nice work with the dam," Castor said, trying to sound genuine.

The Mazon admired the cleared field while Castor held her jar.

"Let's part here," Genevieve said. "Best of luck to you on the rest of your journey. Hopefully we won't see each other again."

"I can guarantee it."

Castor clenched her fist. She needed Genevieve to take one more step. When she had been a girl, she used to kill the rats in the basement this way. She would leave bread crumbs in puddles and when the rats padded to the center of the water, she would—

"Don't do it, Cas."

Castor spun around and found her brother standing safely at the edge of the water, the toes of his boots out of harm's way. Pollux had been there to see her sweep away the charred bodies of her rat experiments. He knew her tricks.

"What are you doing here?" She'd lost track of her brother after his show on Nemea, or more reasonably, she'd stopped caring where he was. Maybe that had been a mistake. "Did Father send you?" It would be just like him to enlist Pollux to track her down, as if Lux could stop her with songs and cloud wisps.

"I came on my own. Get out of the water, Gen."

The Mazon leapt away from the water as if it were already on fire. How easily she followed his command, the word of a StormMaker. Castor looked between her brother and Gen, their shared glances and secret nods, and a pain struck her in the stomach.

That was how she'd escaped Mazon with no whale. Pollux had helped her! Lux was obsessed with the circus and its star. He used to sneak out of the house to go see her show and then he would come home and play his weepy violin all night.

He had betrayed his own family for *her*. Although Castor and Pollux rarely agreed on anything, they had one unspoken commitment—they stayed out of each other's way.

"You're helping her," Castor growled. Had he witnessed his precious circus girl trying to kill her?

"I'm trying to help *you*. Give this up before it gets worse." He perched his bow on the edge of his violin.

"Are you upset I'm trying to take the throne? Or that I want to defy the doctrine? Stand there and tell me you want Arcadia. Tell me you care, that you've dreamed about it your entire life, and I'll end this."

He paused, like she knew he would. She did this for him as much as for herself and her people. That foul doctrine cursed him too. He didn't want Arcadia. He wanted his music. If he helped her win this, they could both have everything they wanted.

"I want to help our people," he said quietly, with no conviction, one of his greater flaws. He never showed the strength to fight for anything, which made him easy to defeat.

"Selling violins won't help them. I will."

"Even if you win this, you won't get what you want. Father isn't going to hand over Arcadia without a fight."

"You think I don't know that?"

Their father would be angry, possibly furious. But he would have to follow the Empresses' command, and in time, he would come to accept and likely approve the situation. And if not . . . well, he couldn't live forever.

"Cas, come home with me. We can talk to Father. I never intended to leave you out of Arcadia. It was never going to be mine. It was always going to be *ours*."

"It's not the same."

If it was theirs, it would be theirs because Pollux shared it with her. He could always draw it back. He could always choose how much to share or when to close the door on her. If she wanted a guaranteed place, she needed to take it for herself, and she needed to make sure no one could take it from her.

"It's better than dying in this game," Pollux said. "Or what Father will do if you lose."

"I don't lose," Castor said, wincing at the possibility. The Mazon was ahead, no doubt due to Pollux's help, but her lead wouldn't last.

"Why don't you help me?" Castor said. "When I'm Duchess, you can do whatever you want. You can travel the Empire playing your shows and leave Arcadia to me." She could also win faster without Pollux helping the competition.

"How many shows will I play when you've sold death to everyone? When it comes back to reap its revenge?"

She rolled her eyes. "Is that what this is about? Other islands sell weapons. It's only a matter of time until someone makes something stronger than our lightning. We need to stay ahead. That's how we protect our legacy. By being better, stronger."

Her brother would never understand having to fight to maintain position. His had been granted to him, and he assumed that he and Arcadia would always thrive. He didn't see the work and innovation it took behind the scenes to make it possible.

She could stand here all day trying to argue it, and he would never see it. You had to live it to know it.

She loosened the cap to her lightning a little more. She would send a blast close enough to his boots to drive him back, and aim her second strike for Genevieve. She wouldn't be able to get much more from this vial than that.

She took aim when something moved to her right. Genevieve rushed at her, a blur of tan and silver. Castor's lungs tightened at the memory of being nearly drowned in manure. She struck at Genevieve and missed, hitting the mud behind her. Her lightning cracked with a hiss and a puff of smoke, and then her brother's violin sounded.

A gust of wind pushed against her other side. Castor spun again and took her second strike at Pollux, and this time, she didn't miss.

Sparks flew. He cried out, dropped his violin, and collapsed to the ground. Smoke curled upward from his chest. Charred flesh wafted on the air. Castor dropped her empty vial. She hadn't meant to hit him. Only scare him. It was Gen's fault. She had distracted her.

"Lux." Castor stepped toward her brother, brushed aside by the Mazon. Genevieve skidded to Pollux's side and cradled his head in her arm.

Castor narrowed her eyes. What else would this beast take from her? She grabbed at her near-empty belt and hesitated. Without a full charge of lightning or a massive windstorm, she wouldn't go anywhere *near* the MindWorker.

Gen scooped Pollux and his violin from the ground and cradled him in her arms like a child. He hung limp, long arms nearly brushing the ground.

"How could you?" Genevieve said, as if this were her fault. "He's your brother."

"He's a traitor," Castor spat. "Take him and hope we don't meet again."

"Same to you."

The Mazon broke into a run. As she and Pollux bounded away from her, Castor's shoulders dropped. Why had she said that? She had meant to apologize, to ask how badly he was injured. But how could she apologize? Her brother had betrayed her. The Mazon had tried to kill her. Why couldn't Pollux have stayed home, or played another performance? Why had he teamed up with the circus girl to defeat her?

Damn! Castor kicked at manure and stomped back to her chariot. The parameters of this contest kept changing, twisting into tighter knots and complications. With Pollux, Genevieve had more resources: access to Pollux's money, his storms, his connections. That had to be why she was so far ahead. What had once been a match in Castor's favor now skewed heavily toward Genevieve.

Castor had to change that, and she had two choices: either eliminate Genevieve's advantages or find her own.

"Delia!" she shouted.

"I see Lord Pollux's chariot here." The glowing spirit blinked as she spoke.

"Yes, I'm well aware." She could have used that information

earlier. "I need you to speak to the Boar for me. Ask him what happened. How did he let the Mazon get away from him? How did she end up with my brother?"

"Right away." Delia disappeared from the box and streaked across the sky.

Castor pushed her crap-stained hair from her face and opened her panel of storm vials. First, she took out a rainstorm and poured it over her head, washing off as much of the manure as she could. Then she selected her strongest, most violent storms and loaded them into her belt. No more mistakes.

Delia's light returned to the box. "The Boar says if the Mazon is here, it's your fault, not his. He took care of the whale. They're draining it right now."

"You can tell him . . ."

"There's more," Delia interrupted. "He also says if you can't protect his investment, he will."

"How does he intend to do that?"

"He said he'll take care of her his way."

Castor knew what his way would be, one of the Semele seeds, which Castor wholly approved except . . . Gen was with her brother. What if the Boar killed Pollux too?

She should send Delia back and make it clear, Pollux was not to be harmed. She never wanted him dead, not even if his death would guarantee her Arcadia, which it wouldn't.

She loved her brother. Sometimes. Maybe love wasn't the right word. They belonged to each other. They had been born together. They lived together. They understood one another, even if they didn't always agree.

Except he had chosen Genevieve. Not her.

Everyone loved Pollux. Their mother, the servants, their class-mates, his adoring fans. Castor had only had their father's approval, and as of their birthday, he'd bestowed that on Pollux too. She had nothing. No one. Not even Pollux.

Fine. He wanted the Mazon? Then he could have her. He could fall with her too.

Castor pushed back her wet hair and grabbed the reins for her chariot. She snapped them once to wake up the horses. They spread their wings and stamped their hooves. "Get moving," she yelled. "We're going to Crete."

She'd kill the Bull and then find the *Hind* by any means necessary. And her brother? He had made his choice. The wrong one.

CHAPTER 19

GEN

G en cradled Pollux to her chest and ran to the chariot, trying not to jostle him. She worried if she shook him too hard, his burned and blistered skin would slide from his sharp cheekbones. His formerly ivory complexion glistened red and raw, bleeding. The lightning had burned all the way from his cheek to his shoulder, tearing through his shirt, cooking his skin. Castor had roasted him like a Stymphal crow. Her own brother.

"How bad is it?" Pollux moaned.

"Barely noticeable," she lied in an unconvincing, shaky voice. It was awful. Worse than awful. His face would never be the same.

Argos chattered in her ear anxiously. Even he recognized the signs of a gravely injured man. Pollux had saved her again, and what she would never know was why he had done it. Because he wanted to, or because of the band on his wrist?

"Bale! Help me!" Gen called.

Bale stepped out of the gilded chariot, eyes wide, lips drawn.

"Give him to me." He reached out his arms. Gen passed Pollux to Bale, who laid him gently on the chariot bench. "What happened to him?"

"Castor."

Bale grunted as if he already knew. "We'll go to Arcadia. They have one of the best healers in Olympia."

"No," Pollux said. The single word split his lip down the middle. A drop of red blood pooled on his skin.

"Don't be ridiculous." Gen set his violin down on the chariot floor. "You *need* a healer." She had never seen anyone else in as desperate need of medical attention as Pollux. These injuries were the reason healers trained.

"I can't go home. I can't see my father," Pollux said. "If he knows where I am, he'll never let me out of his sight."

She couldn't blame him for that. If his father was anything like Castor, she would avoid him too. "I know a healer on Panacaea. It's not far from here. She's the healer we would visit when we were sick."

Panacaea needed gifted healers. A poisonous serpent called a fanus lived there among the colorful blooms. One bite from the snake caused the victim to swell to enormous size with pus-filled blisters. Untreated, they would slowly lose their ability to breathe.

Gen considered how one of those serpents might affect Castor. It was no less than she deserved after what she had done to Pollux, and she would be able to find a healer in time with her resources. Gen unfurled her hands, eyeing the thick stripe of silver on her palm.

No. She'd already tried to kill Castor once, and she didn't want to win that way.

"No, no healers, no detours. Go to Thracia. Get the Mares," Pollux said.

"The contest can wait. I give you a respite from your promise." She reached to take the bracelet off his wrist.

Pollux snatched it away. "Leave it. I think it's fairly obvious my sister is determined. We can't let her win."

"We can still win. A stop to Panacaea won't take that long."

"Long enough."

"I won't leave you like this." Something knotted in the pit of her stomach, something more than guilt. She didn't like seeing him in pain, or thinking of him forever scarred from her labors.

"Panacaea," she mouthed to Bale, and he nodded in agreement.

They could get Pollux to Panacaea, heal him, and be back in the game within a day, and considering this was her decision, not his, the bonding bracelet shouldn't be affected. She hoped.

"She didn't blind me," Pollux said. "I can see you two making deals. Winning this is more important than my face. You have to finish. There's medicine in the storage compartment. Use it and go to Thracia. That's an order."

It was the first time Gen had ever heard Pollux give "an order," and it sounded strange coming from his lips, unnatural.

Bale laughed. "No offense, *sir*, but I don't take orders."

"This is also my burden," Gen said. "These are *my* tasks, and I say we stop for a healer."

"She is *my* sister, after *my* title, and I say we don't."

Bale crossed his arms over his chest. "The only place these horses are going is to a healer."

"There. Two against one."

"Fine, then I'll take the horses." Pollux tried to stand, and Gen gently pushed him back down. He was as stubborn as his sister.

"You're going to kill yourself."

"Maybe." A smug smile crossed his burned lips.

Gen reached for her manure-stained bag. "You are going to regret this the next time they paint one of your show posters. I might be able to fix some of the burns, not all of them. You need proper medicine and stitches."

"Do what you can. My face was never my best asset, anyway."

She frowned as she fished for the stink lizard pus in her bag. She might have agreed with him once. No, he wasn't the kind of person you would gawk at for his unfathomable good looks, but he'd had an interesting face, something worth looking at, admiring. Gen caught herself roving down the angles of his cheeks more than once, exploring the shadows and dips.

Pollux's best asset would be his violin-playing hands, which he could also lose because of his insistence to wear that bracelet. She sat on the bench beside him and took out the half-used jar of lizard pus.

"What's that?" Bale asked.

"Stink lizard pus. It's regenerative." She opened the jar, and Bale gagged.

"It smells worse than you do."

"I find that hard to believe."

The remaining odor roiling off her clothes and hair made her stomach convulse. As soon as Pollux's injuries were taken care of, she planned to take one of Pollux's bottled rainstorms to blast the manure off her.

Bale took up the reins and set the horses in motion. They spread their wings wide and bounced across the terrain until they lifted in the air. Gen didn't start on Pollux's face until they settled into a comfortable glide.

"Try to stay still." She patted his shoulder, and Pollux gently nodded before he closed his eyes.

Gen dabbed the green goo on his face, smearing pus over the blisters on his cheekbones and the peeled and blackened skin along his forehead. "Why would she do this to you?" Gen had no siblings, so she wasn't sure how they were supposed to act, but she liked to think if she did have one, she wouldn't try to kill them.

"It is partly my fault," Pollux mumbled. "I let her bully me. If I had stood up to her before, she might not be this way now."

"You can't blame yourself for her."

"She's not as bad as you think. She likely assumed I would deflect her strike, and I would have if the string hadn't broken on my violin."

"She shouldn't have been firing at you with lightning at all."

"You mean other families don't try to kill one another?" He cracked another smile, and Gen applied some ointment on the bleeding corners of his mouth. "I guess I'll always make excuses for her. She's my sister."

Gen wondered if she was doing the same with Alcmen. Everyone had seen Alcmen covered in blood. The tavern owner said he had done it. What if he had killed those Gargareans, and she simply refused to see it?

No. She had to believe in the Alcmen she knew. That Alcmen would never kill anyone. He would never leave her to fend for herself, parentless and alone. She had to trust that.

Gen worked the ointment down the side of Pollux's face, dabbing the goo on the worst of the blisters around his jawline. Some of the blackened skin peeled away like ash in her fingers. She wiped her fingers on her pants and kept going to the bottom of his chin. She applied a thinner layer of pus here. Only a small glob sat in the bottom of her jar. She wouldn't be able to fully repair his neck and shoulder. Barely enough to heal the wound. They would scar. The lizard pus also couldn't regrow the missing hunk of his ear, or his burned hair.

Only time could grow that back. The missing ear could be permanent. Healers preferred to work with fresh injuries, not already healed ones. He would forever be marked with this day.

She sealed the empty jar, and Pollux lay back on the pillow, breathing easier. At least the pus eased the pain.

"It's not going to be perfect," she said.

"It never was."

Her eyes dropped to the silver loop on his wrist. She had wanted him to make a vow she could trust, and he had. Now she worried he would go too far to keep it.

"You don't have to wear the bracelet anymore. I trust you."

"You don't," he argued. "You feel bad for me. If you trusted me, the bracelet wouldn't be a problem. It only harms me if I break that trust."

Speaking of breaking trust, she thought of his trust for her, and how she almost broke it when she attacked his sister.

"Were you watching me the entire time on Elis?" she asked. For some reason, she didn't want him to think less of her, even though she shouldn't give two hairs about what a StormMaker thought of her.

"You mean did we see you tumble down the hill into the manure?" Bale asked. "That was one of my favorite parts."

"It wasn't one of mine," Gen said.

"There was another reason I didn't want you to face Castor," Pollux said. "She has a way of pushing people to their worst."

"She does," Gen agreed.

"What did she do?"

"She killed the whale."

Pollux winced. "I'm sorry."

"It's not your fault."

"It is, in a way. I'm always going to feel partly responsible for what she does. It's part of being a twin."

"She is not you," Gen said, and meant it. The more time she spent with Pollux, the more obvious it became that he and Castor were two very different people, and Pollux had as little control over his sister as anyone. "Get some rest. The more you move your face around, the less effective the pus will be."

"All right."

He closed his eyes, and Gen remained beside him. Chomp curled up next to her feet and the rat ate the remaining crackers out of her bag. Argos climbed onto Bale's shoulder, and after Bale unsuccessfully tried to shoo him away, he let the monkey stay.

Here, in this gilded chariot with her creatures, Pollux, and Bale, Gen had this undeniable feeling of rightness, like she had when she'd sailed on her father's ship with their sparse crew and menagerie of animals. Her whale was gone, but she wasn't alone. She felt like she belonged somewhere, to someone.

Don't get too attached.

None of this was real. Pollux and Bale were here only because they needed her. As soon as they defeated the labors, Pollux would be gone too, off to claim his title on Arcadia.

Once Pollux was asleep, Gen took one of his rain vials and opened it over the side of the chariot.

"Careful with that," Bale said too late. The rain shot out of the jar, up her nose and into her eyes.

She sputtered and slapped the cover on the vial. "Is it supposed to do that?" She had never touched StormMaker products.

"Only if you don't know what you're doing. You're not a StormMaker. You can't control it like they do. You can just use it. Poorly," he added.

Gen opened the jar a small amount, enough to pour some

rainwater on her hands, and used that to wash off her face and arms. She could clean up more once they reached Thracia.

She replaced the vial in the compartment and found a box filled with plums. "Hungry?" she asked Bale.

"Starving."

She handed him one of the plums. Argos tried to snatch it from him so Gen tossed the monkey one of his own.

She pointed to the sword on Bale's belt. "Why do you carry that if you never use it?"

"I do use it. When I need to. If I had known Castor was going to char him, you can guarantee I would have used it today."

"But you serve the Arcadian family."

He spat his plum pit over the side of the carriage. "I don't serve anyone. I work for Pollux because I choose to."

"How did you find your way to Arcadia from Leuctra?"

"A ship."

"Fine, you don't want to talk, we don't have to talk." Gen was used to not talking to humans. She had the rat and Argos in her head for enough company, and animals were far more forthcoming.

"It was one of you," Bale eventually said. "A MindWorker."

"What?"

He turned from the horses to look her in the eye, his blue skin flushed purple. "It was a MindWorker. That's why I left Leuctra."

Gen tossed her plum pit over the side of the chariot and sat very still.

"What happened?" she asked, cautiously. This wouldn't be the first time someone blamed her for other trouble with a MindWorker. Even before Alcmen's arrest, MindWorkers hadn't been perfect. Thylox was a testament to that. But nobody was perfect. MetalBenders made bracelets that could cut off people's hands, SpiritWatchers could send a ghost to haunt someone to their own untimely death, and the StormMakers, well . . . everyone knew what they could do.

"I had a girl." He set his hand on his belt, near the unused sword. "Andromeda. She was beautiful. Shy. Her little skiff had come loose from the docks after she'd tied it up, and it drifted out to sea. She knew it was high tide, a bad time to go past the reef. A MindWorker pushed her into swimming after it. She never made it to the boat. She never made it back."

"I am so sorry," Gen said. "But—"

"I know. It's what you all say. If she didn't want to do it, the MindWorker wouldn't have been able to push her into it. But, if the MindWorker had left her alone, she would be alive today." He shook his head. "You have too much power. It should be checked. You're dangerous."

Gen crossed her arms over her chest. She had heard this a thousand times before. "What about their power?" She nodded to Pollux. "Why doesn't it deserve to be checked?"

"It does. Why do you think I'm here? Why do you think I agreed to help him help you? Because he is the only decent person you'll find in that family. Trust me when I say the entire Empire should want Pollux to sit at the helm of the StormMakers. Because the alternatives are worse."

A fair point. Gen certainly didn't want Castor there. "I don't use my ability on people. I want you to know that."

"I almost believe you. I also wonder if we put the bonding bracelets on in the right order." He pointed to her wrist. "Be certain, though, if you ever try to hurt him"—his fingers brushed the top of the sword—"you will see me use this sword. You will see it very closely."

"I won't hurt him," she whispered softly, shocked at this protective older brother role Bale had assumed when he seemed so disinterested in everything else. Or maybe he had only been disinterested in her.

This was what she would stand against, even when she freed Alcmen. So many people had a story like Bale's to perpetuate their hatred for MindWorkers. The Empresses had been right in saying she would need to do more to win the hearts of the people. Bale could be her first experiment. If she could win him, she could win the others.

CHAPTER 20
POLLUX

Pollux sat upright, dredged out of a nightmare. Sweat coated his skin. His heart pounded. In his dream, Castor had burned him with lightning. It was so real, he'd felt the burns on his shoulder. He touched his cheek, and his fingers ran over smooth skin. Then his fingers wandered farther and trailed across bald patches where he used to have hair.

"Are you all right?"

Pollux snapped his head to Bale at the reins and Gen asleep on the floor of his chariot, and everything came back to him: the manure, the pool of water, and Castor about to boil Gen alive. The string on his violin had snapped. He hadn't been able to push the lightning away. At least it hadn't killed him.

"I've been better," he said. "I used to have more hair."

He ran his fingers down the side of his face and felt puffed scars on his neck and a piece of his ear missing from the top, as if something, or some*one* had chewed it off.

He breathed in and out. Gen and Bale had wanted to take him to a healer. He had refused. Gen had promised only to do her best. But Gen . . . with the scars, would she, could she, did he still have some farfetched hope that she might like him?

Yes, he did.

Maybe he'd imagined it. Maybe he hadn't. When she had healed his injuries, she'd looked at him like he was worth something. Like he wasn't responsible for murdering her mother's family. It made him almost glad Cas had charred him. Again.

He wanted this to be real with Gen and knew it wouldn't be. As soon as she had her fame and reputation back in her hands, she wouldn't think twice about him, burn scars or no burn scars. Maybe they'd pass here and there in the entertainment circles; they'd smile at one another. She'd ask how he was doing, and he'd tell her he was "fine," while wishing he could say more, do more, be closer to her. Always.

The music in his head sounded scattered and raw, two different songs trying to play at once. He missed his curtain of hair. He'd grown it long to hide his face, his hollow cheeks and narrow chin. Castor used to tell him he looked like a skeleton. With his hair burned away, he had nowhere to hide.

"Your face looks better than I thought it would," Bale said. "That gunk worked."

"How is she?" Pollux gazed again at the silver-and-tan girl curled up at his feet. Her purple chaeri had folded into her side with a rat wedged in between them.

"She's fine," Bale said.

"How can she be fine? My sister tried to kill her."

"If I recall, Gen tried to kill her too."

"No, she didn't."

He had been watching them fight with great interest. At one point, when Gen had Cas in the muck, he'd reached for his violin and set it down as soon as Gen released his sister.

That was the difference between them: Gen knew when to stop. Cas didn't.

When Cas felt threatened, she lashed out with fire and anger. He was sure she had expected him to defend himself, which he would have, if the string hadn't snapped.

Except he never could be sure, could he? Before she hit him, she'd looked at him with malice he'd never seen. Even worse than when he broke her doll. Or the night their father officially declared he would be the next Storm Duke. She hadn't blamed him for that, but she blamed him for this.

He had entered this contest to save his sister from their father. He never thought he could lose her, that he could push her so far out of reach.

Of course—he touched the scars again—she was the one who did the pushing.

Pollux picked up his violin and removed a new string from the inside of the case to replace the broken one. He also needed to replace some of the storm vials inside. His lightning was spent, something that had never happened to him before. He always knew exactly how much lightning he needed for a show, and he always replenished it before it ran out. He removed the empty jar and replaced it with a new one, his very last lightning vial aboard the chariot. He never carried much. He would have to use this vial sparingly.

He wouldn't be able to use lightning to help Gen on her next task, anyway. If he struck down the Mares, that would go against catching them. The other MindWorker wanted them alive for the task to be done. Pollux inserted a new vial of wind and thunder beside the lightning.

"Bale? Do you think I'm making a mistake, trying to help Cas?" He twisted the new vials into place.

"Yes," Bale said, bluntly. One of the reasons Pollux liked having him around. He didn't try to kiss his boots because he was Lux, Lord of Storms. "She charred your face. If she were my sister, I'd let her sink herself, and I wouldn't bother throwing her a float."

Pollux laughed. "Funny enough, Cas would probably agree with you."

"Because we're both out for ourselves. You're not. It's probably going to get you killed one day. You have as much power as she does, all you have to do is use it."

Pollux turned his gaze to his violin. As Bale had pointed out, it was packed with as many storm vials as Cas kept on her belt. It was no secret he was the softer sibling in the family. The one people approached when they needed leniency. He loved the power of storms with the same passion as his father and Cas. He loved being able to coax clouds into shapes and stories with a note and a breath. But he took after his mother, who did not have the StormMaker abilities. He had the power and her temperament, her love of music. Could he blast his sister with lightning? Physically, yes . . . did he want to? No.

"I do use it. For my music." He twisted another gust of wind to the inside of the violin and brought it back into tune.

If Gen won this contest, he would have to take his rightful place as Duke. He hoped, in time, Cas would forgive him and join him at the helm. Arcadia needed her strength *and* his leniency. He believed there was a place for both of them there, if only Cas would make some room.

He wished she had talked to him before going to the Empresses. He would have given her half of everything. He would have let her run the business. But Castor needed boundaries. If she had free reign of the StormMaker operations, the Empire would be at war in months, blasting each other with lightning and hurricanes. There would be more desolate islands like Mazon. More vengeful queens. He hated that doctrine too. It needed updating, and he'd always thought that he and Cas would do it together.

Unfortunately his sister had other plans.

"What are you going to do about Gen?" Bale asked him.

Pollux refocused his gaze on Gen's silver-striped cheek. "See her through it to the end."

"I don't trust her," Bale said.

"Why not?"

"She's a MindWorker."

"I never took you as one to buy into gossip. It's not true, what they say about her father." Pollux believed that with his entire soul.

"When did you become an expert on MindWorkers? You don't know what they're capable of." He fingered the sword at his belt. Bale rarely used it. Pollux's mother only insisted that if Bale was going to act as his personal guard, he carry it.

"I'm not an expert on them. But I am an expert on malicious people." Pollux plucked one of the violin strings. "I could tell you didn't like Gen. Is it only because she's a MindWorker?"

"No, I also don't like how much *you* like her."

Pollux's finger slipped. He swallowed and looked to Gen, making sure she couldn't hear. "Do you think she knows?" he whispered.

"I think she's suspicious."

Pollux exhaled. "I've never known anyone like her before."

"You're quick to trust, Pollux, and not likely to stand up for yourself. She will crush you. Did you see her pull this chariot?"

Yes, he had. Without breaking a sweat. And Bale had a point. If Gen had him buried in the mud, ready to strangle him, he would let her.

"When did you get so protective?"

"When you started acting so recklessly." Bale twisted the reins in his fingers. "You know I only agreed to work for you because I thought I'd just be flashing lights on clouds for your shows. Not chasing across the islands for a MindWorker."

"Do you want another raise?" Pollux ran his fingers across the violin strings.

"No. I want you to be careful. I want you to show the Storm Duke and your sister that you are the right person to rule Arcadia."

"I'm not sure if that's true."

"It can be. If you don't let yourself get distracted." Another pointed look at Gen.

"I like being distracted."

Pollux turned away from Bale and picked up the bow to play a quiet concerto. Music always helped him think. He looked to Gen while he played, curled up with her creatures. She was more than his muse. Perhaps she always had been, even when he'd only once seen her those years ago. She was a door to another life, a magical one with applause and laughter far from the rest of his family. He'd wanted to run away with the circus then, and now, he wanted to help her rebuild it. He wanted that life. With her.

Sadly, he would never have it.

He pulled his bow across the strings, long and low, when something small and round landed inside the chariot.

"What is—" Before Bale could finish, the thing burst into green flames, spreading fast.

Gen lifted her head and let out a scream. Pollux pulled back on his violin and released the fresh vial of wind. The gust wrapped around them, lifting himself, Gen, Bale, and her creatures into a tunnel of air.

They swept upward. Below, the chariot and everything else blasted into green flame. As soon as the horses were free, they soared in different directions, away from the fire. Pollux pulled his bow across the strings, playing quickly to keep everyone aloft with whatever remained of the wind. Thankfully, it was a fresh vial.

"What happened?" Gen screamed.

"What do you think?" he shouted back. This bore the mark of his sister, fire and anger.

"Castor," Gen said with the bitterness usually saved for people who had known his sister longer than a few days.

But Gen had seen the worst of her. Pollux was seeing Castor's worst too. She really meant to kill them.

"I think it was a Semele seed," Bale shouted as the strength of Pollux's wind waned, the vial nearly spent. He wouldn't be able to hold them much longer. With a pull of his strings, he brought them closer to the water. Quickly. Sweat beaded on his cheeks as he played higher and higher notes to keep the wind from dissipating.

The wind broke several yards above the water. They dropped. He hit the surface and sank into the sea. He kicked frantically to push his way back up, away from the salt water that stung his freshly scarred face. He took a breath and looked for Gen and Bale. He found them bobbing on the sea along with what remained of their things.

Thank the Oracles.

Pollux held his violin in one hand and reached for the floating violin case. Bale swam to meet him. Gen scooped up her creatures and the golden wool sweater sinking into the sea. Argos sat on Gen's head, trying not to get wet.

"Is everyone all right? Can you swim, Gen?" Pollux asked.

"Of course I can swim," Gen snapped. "There's a ship over there. We can wave them down."

"No," Bale said. "They are probably the ones who hit us with the seed."

Pollux squinted at the ship. He didn't recognize it. It was too broad to be one of theirs. The Arcadian ships were thin, sleek, made to cut through water, not plow through it. Even though it wasn't Arcadian, he knew Castor was involved. Somehow.

"If I had my whale, this wouldn't be a problem," Gen said.

Pollux winced. His sister had taken that from Gen too. If only they could end this contest, they could stop her. "We need to find land."

"There's an island there." Bale pointed east to a low beach spotted with bright yellow trees.

Gen leaned over Pollux's arm to examine it. As she kicked her legs to tread water, her thigh grazed against his and his breath caught.

"I know that island," she said. "It's called Quisces."

"Isn't that a restricted island?" Bale said.

"Yes, but it's fine."

"Why is it restricted?" Pollux asked.

Typhon was restricted because of explosive volcanoes and fiery ash. Deimos was restricted because of a native plant that leaked poisonous gas into the air. Was Quisces better or worse than that? Better or worse than drowning?

"Caterpillars," Gen said.

"Caterpillars?" Pollux repeated. He must not have heard her correctly.

"Yes. Trust me. It will be fine. I've been here before. I can take care of it." She looped her arm through her bag, put her whining chaeri on her back, and broke into a broad stroke with the monkey riding on her head.

"What do you think?" Pollux turned to Bale.

"I think we have to go. We can't float here all day."

"I'm thinking the same thing."

They followed in Gen's wake, kicking and scrambling to keep her in sight. It reminded him of when they had chased her on Mazon. Either she didn't know how fast she was, or she didn't care if she left them behind.

The glance over her shoulder to make sure they were still there reassured him she wasn't trying to escape again.

The waves pushed them closer to shore. As Pollux stumbled onto the sand with his wet violin, a ringing sound echoed in his ears.

"Do you hear that?" Bale shouted.

"What?" Pollux shouted back. He saw Bale's mouth moving but heard no sound. Only the high-pitched hum.

Ahead, on the beach, Gen plucked something from her bag and stuffed it into the chaeri's ears. Then she stuffed something into her own. The humming sound ripped through Pollux's skull, tearing away everything else. He couldn't hear the water lapping around him or the sound of his own breath.

His head throbbed with it. Gen said something to him. Her mouth moved in silent commands. She handed him a wad of cotton and gestured for him to put it in his ears. As soon as he did, everything went blissfully silent.

She gave some to Bale and Argos, tucked two tiny pieces into the rat's ears, and picked up a loose branch from the beach. She wrote in the sand.

They're called shrieking caterpillars. I gave you a piece of the cocoon, the only thing that silences them. Don't take out the cocoon or you will go deaf, then DIE.

She wrote the last part in capital letters to make her point. It was received. She had him terrified at the first part. His face he could lose; his ears he could not. His music depended on his hearing.

I know someone in the village. Let's go see if he can help us, Gen wrote before waving them into the trees.

Pollux shook the water from his violin and opened the soggy case. He plucked a vial of wind from the inner compartment and used it to dry off himself and his violin. Then he checked the cocoon husks one more time to make sure they were secure before he followed her into the trees. At least his father wouldn't be able to find him here. Or Castor. As long as the caterpillars didn't kill them, they had a few hours to breathe.

CHAPTER 21
CASTOR

Castor held tight to the reins as they flew toward Crete. Crete did not buy bottled weather from the Arcadians. They simply submitted to the will of nature. Fools, Castor thought as her horses struggled to cut through the fierce wind surrounding the island.

Castor couldn't do anything about it. To capture the wind, she'd have to release the reins and they'd all blow away before she could seal the vial.

"Stay focused," she shouted at the horses, and jerked them to her left. Some of the gilded edging on her chariot pulled free and disappeared behind her. Her hair escaped from its tie and whipped her across the cheeks. They needed to get below the wind or they would be ripped apart.

She whipped the horses. They dove and hit the beach running. The chariot shook. The wheels rattled. Castor fell backward on the bench and reached for one of the Illumium vials. When she stood up, she held out her hand and pulled on the wind as if it were the rope to a kite.

She wound it around her fingers and drew it into the jar. Her hair stopped beating against her cheeks and the sand settled where it lay. When she sealed the bottle closed, she heard the birds in the nearby trees and the dockworkers on the pier, cursing at one another.

"That's better." Castor tucked the vial into her belt and smoothed down her hair.

She picked up Delia's box and flipped the lid. The little white orb pulsed in response.

"How can I help you, Lady Castor?"

"I want you to check in with the Boar. See if he has any updates."

"I'll be as quick as I can."

Delia's light shot out of the wooden box and disappeared into the sky. Castor didn't know what she hoped to hear. Did she want Delia to tell her that Gen and possibly Pollux were destroyed? Or did she want Delia to come back and say the Boar had been unable to find them, and Gen was still checking labors off their list?

Definitely not that one.

Whatever Pollux suffered in this game, it would be his own unmaking. She didn't need to feel so much guilt.

Castor stepped out of the chariot and made her way across the sand toward the dockworkers. The people of Crete all had reddish skin, ranging from bright orange to deep rose, and some sort of horns on the top of their head, thin and curly or stout and sharp. If she and her fellow Arcadians looked to be carved from ice, then the Cretians looked to be molded from fire.

"Excuse me." Castor approached a man on the beach who was pulling up shellfish traps from the water. "I'm looking for someone named Felonious Bull. Do you know where I might find him?"

The man's head snapped up, and his eyes went wild. "What do you want with him?" he stammered.

"That's my business. Do you know where he is?" Castor tapped the vials on her belt.

"You'll find him by the docks. Don't tell him I sent you."

"I don't even know who you are."

"Keep it that way." He went back to his traps, and Castor continued up the beach.

The Cretians had fleets of wooden ships, all carved from the cypress trees that grew on the island. They sold fish and shellfish to the other isles, and since they were going back and forth between the islands, they carried other goods for a fee.

The Arcadians shipped some of their weather vials on Cretian ships, usually the ones they wanted to send quietly, without the pomp of her father's ships, like the storm vials they sold to the Gargareans. Once Castor won this contest and brought the Boar and his men in as their secret shippers, they wouldn't need to rely on the Cretian ships anymore.

Twelve of these boats were lined up by the docks, sitting perfectly still since she'd captured the wind. Workers scurried across the planks, loading one of the ships with heavy crates.

"Move faster, you worthless worms!" a man shouted at the workers, and cracked a whip at their heels. He was twice their size with rolls of muscles on his blood-red arms and legs. Two massive black horns curled up from the top of his head, longer than Castor's legs and sharper than a knifepoint.

"Put that down over there!" he yelled, and the two women carrying the crate under his nose scurried onto the ship, terrified.

He had full command over his team. They obeyed his every word. He was probably why the Cretians operated such a successful shipping operation. It would be a shame to kill him—finding good management was never easy—but she needed him dead to claim the task.

"Mr. Bull!" Castor grabbed a vial of lightning as she shouted his name. He ignored her and cracked his whip at the shoulders of one of his workers. "Felonious Bull!" She opened the vial of lightning and sent a single spark to his cheek.

It singed his skin, and he turned. "Yeah, what do you want?" he grunted.

Castor held up the lightning vial. "I bring word from the Empresses. Your services are no longer needed." She opened the jar of lightning completely and grasped it like a spear. She pulled her arm back and flung the bolt of crackling fire directly into his chest.

It exploded in a spray of sparks. The dockworkers shrieked and scattered. Castor grinned and put the empty vial back onto her belt. That was easy.

She turned to leave and deep, mocking laughter echoed behind her.

"That tickled."

The smoke cleared, and the Bull emerged from the haze, completely unharmed apart from a burned tunic and a small black mark in the center of his chest. Impossible. That had been a fresh vial of lightning.

"Now it's my turn." The Bull stretched to his full height, fifteen or twenty feet above her. He pulled back a massive fist, and Castor grabbed one of her jars.

His fist came down, and she ripped open the jar. She had no idea what it was until the gust of wind struck at the Bull. His fist plowed through it and hit her in the ribs. She heard something crack as she rolled off the docks into the sand. She couldn't breathe.

She got to her knees and spat sand from her teeth. The Bull came at her, still grinning. She snatched another jar. More lightning. The first jar must have been stale, or partly used. She ripped it open and the beach lit up white with fire. The lightning cracked when it hit the Bull. Castor took a shallow breath, and the Bull emerged again, missing more of his tunic and nothing else.

He was fireproof. Lightning proof. Wind proof. How could she kill him?

"You're becoming quite the nuisance." He raised his fist for another strike. Castor looked back at her chariot. Should she run? If the Boar did his job, Gen was dead and couldn't win.

But if he didn't . . .

Genevieve had the Lion, Livia Kine, and the Mazon belt, and she stole the stables. If she was still breathing, she could be claiming her fifth task. Castor had to find a way to kill this man.

She stood up, wincing at the ache in her side. Fire couldn't kill him. Wind clearly had no effect on him. What else did she have?

Water.

Behind the Bull, the sea sat fairly calm. But it hadn't been. Not when the wind had been raging.

Castor reached for another vial of wind and backed toward the water.

"I'm going to crush you when I get my hands on you." With each step he made, the ground underneath them quivered.

"You're never going to get your hands on me."

"I wouldn't be so sure about that."

Castor took another step back and felt the ocean waves lapping at her heels. "Tell me, Mr. Bull, what did you do to the woman who wants you dead?"

He laughed. "Hard to say. A lot of people want me dead."

"I can imagine."

"The problem is, I'm not an easy man to kill."

"I've noticed." She loosened the top of her second wind vial.

"There is nothing inside your little storm jars that can hurt me."

"I agree with you," she said, and the Bull hesitated. "But a storm isn't self-contained. It controls everything. It can level cities, tear up trees, burn down houses, and sink ships."

"I prefer to do my killing the old-fashioned way." He lunged at her, and before Castor could open her vial, he closed his fingers around her throat.

She instinctively kicked at him, trying to break free. Her head pulsed, and her lungs ached.

He grinned at her with disgusting, yellow teeth. "It was Helene who sent you after me, wasn't it?" he growled.

She hung in front of him, struggling for one gasp of air. "I don't know her name."

"You know this is her third attempt to kill me, and the most pathetic. She should have let it go. Her brother was a lazy worker. He serves more purpose as fish bait than anything else. Any last words?"

"Yes," Castor croaked. "I hope you can swim."

She flicked open the jar with her thumb and focused the wind into one long tunnel. It grabbed at the ocean beside them and pulled it over their heads, high enough to block out the sun.

The Bull loosened his grip, and Castor sucked in a breath before she brought the water down on both of their heads. It slammed into her sore ribs. It wrapped around her and took her from the light. She sank deep into a swirling tunnel of water with no idea of which direction led upward.

She pulled her thumb from the top of her wind vial and aimed it toward her feet. The bubbles pushed her hard and fast through the water. The space above her became lighter and lighter until she shot from the water and tumbled to the beach.

She coughed and sputtered, spitting up seawater. The act of it crushed her chest. If this didn't work, and the Bull came crawling out of the waves to strike her again, she would die. She could barely stand.

But he didn't come. The water went back out to sea. The surf returned to its gentle wave, and no Bull rose up from the depths.

She exhaled.

Someone stepped up beside her. "You killed him." It was the old man who'd been pulling up crab traps before.

Castor stood up and brushed the salt and sand from her clothes. "You're welcome."

The dockworkers put down their crates and wandered to the shore to stare at the water. They must have been afraid the Bull would rise out of it too.

"He's really dead," a woman said. "You don't know how awful he was. I've been working here ten years and never had a day off. Once I showed up late and he held me under the water until I nearly drowned."

Castor squeezed the water from her hair. "Maybe you could have handled him yourselves if you'd had a few storm vials." She shook her empty wind vial at the woman and made for her chariot.

Not that it was entirely the woman's fault. The Cretian lord made her father look like a mewling kitten. He gave the Bull his reign of terror, and had this contest not been blessed by the Empresses, Castor could face some repercussions for killing his dockmaster.

She did have some repercussions, though: a set of bruised ribs, possibly broken.

Seawater dropped from her clothes, and every breath she took put a stitch in her side. This was only her third task, still behind the

Mazon. If Gen wasn't dead, then Castor was still a breath away from losing everything.

She climbed into the chariot and found a vial of snow. She released enough of it to freeze her wet clothing to stick to her injured ribs. She didn't have time to stop for a healer. She needed to do the best with what she had and keep moving.

"Delia, are you here?"

She opened the small box and sighed at the little white light inside. Without Delia's insight, she would be further behind than this.

"I have returned with word from the Boar."

"What did he say?" Castor bit into her lip.

"Ship taken care of. Went down on Quisces."

This was what she had wanted, wasn't it? Then why did she have this feeling like she wanted to take it back? "Where is Quisces? Is the Mazon dead? What about Pollux?"

Her head filled with fond memories of her brother, of sending kites into the air on gusts of bottled wind. Of making little wooden boats and sailing them around puddles.

"Quisces is a restricted island. There was no sign of the Mazon or your brother."

"Restricted? Why is it restricted?"

"Quisces is home to a species called the whisper moth. During its larva stage, the caterpillar produces a shrill sound that causes loss of hearing and eventually death."

A caterpillar seemed like a tolerable nuisance, especially with the MindWorker around. If they survived and made it to the island, both Gen and Pollux could be alive.

Castor clutched her chest and felt for something, relief or pain. When she and Pollux were younger, and closer, she could sense him.

She knew when he was upset or injured. Now she felt . . . nothing. If he was alive or dead, she couldn't tell.

Her brother, the eternal fool.

He risked his life for an idle crush, a dream. He had always been that way, choosing the things he could create instead of grabbing the sensible things right in front of him. It was why he had no place running Arcadia, and for some reason, she was the only person who saw that. Their father was so obsessed with tradition, he would sacrifice their entire livelihood to keep it.

Without the Mazon's body as proof, Castor had to unfortunately assume they had survived. All Castor had gained was time while they found their way back into the game.

"I have some other news," Delia added.

"Yes?" Castor pulled a piece of seaweed from her hair and tossed it into the sand.

"I may have found the *Hind*."

"Where?" Castor shouted, and set off her injured ribs.

"Some merchants saw a ship moving at unfathomable speeds. It was headed to Ceryneia."

"Then that's where we're going." It made sense. Ceryneia was a market island. The man at the lottery had said his ship had been stolen. The thief who took the ship probably stole other things that he needed to sell.

Castor cracked the reins. Her horses flapped their wings and lifted from the island, an easier take-off without the wind knocking them around. If she got the *Hind*, it would be her fourth task, putting her on equal footing with Gen. And then there would only be the Mares and the Hydra left, the two deadliest tasks.

Ahead, a cloud of black smoke hovered over a mostly hidden

land mass, another restricted island, Typhon. It had been formed by the cooled volcanic rock that constantly spewed from the volcano in the center. Ash clouded the air above it and floated on the water for miles around it. Ceryneia sat only ten miles on the other side.

Travelers always went around the isle, by air or sea. From here, though, it would extend her trip by half a day. She could lose the *Hind*. Castor kept the horses on a direct path. They could sweep right through it. Everything would be fine.

"You're headed for Typhon," Delia said.

"I know."

"There is an active volcano there."

"I know."

"Then why are you going that way?"

Delia, who never sounded anxious, sounded anxious. If Castor were to die, Delia would still be bound to the box, and whoever owned the box next. That would be Pollux. Prior to this game, he had been named the recipient of all her worldly possessions in case of her death. She would have to change that later.

If the box were destroyed, then Delia would be a lost soul. She wouldn't be able to move on. She wouldn't have anything to connect her here.

"It will be fine," Castor said.

The horses tried to veer away from the smoke and ash. Castor opened a small vial of lightning and sent a spark to their hind quarters to keep them on their path.

The air stung her eyes and tasted sour on her tongue. She could barely see the horses. She cracked the reins again to get them through this quicker. When she coughed, it burned her lungs.

Red ash floated in the air. Castor reached for a vial of rainwater as the fog lit up red. A ball of fiery ash flew toward them. The horses cried out and tried to fly in both directions. Thundercloud went right. Dewdrop went left. One of her hooves connected with the chariot. Castor gripped the edge to keep from tumbling to her death.

"Keep it together!"

Another ball of fire hurtled toward them. This one ripped through the harness. Fire leapt into the air, and the horses broke free. They took off into the smoke and the chariot dropped. Castor fumbled through vials. Thunder, lightning, rain . . . she needed wind. She dropped an ice storm and snatched at another jar.

"We're going to crash!" Delia shouted.

"I know!" Castor grabbed one more vial. She couldn't read it. She ripped open the top and a rush of wind and rain filled the chariot.

Castor moved the storm underneath them. It pushed them upward and pelted them with rain. The air cleared, and the ocean rushed up to meet them. They hit it with a splash, and Castor used the rest of the storm to push away from the island.

She dropped the empty vial and slid down to the bench. Ash and storm vials rolled across the floor as they bobbed on the waves. Her gilded chariot was blackened with soot and warped along the top. Her horses were gone.

It can all be fixed.

When she became future Duchess, she would have endless funds, staff, and chariots at her disposal.

"Delia," Castor breathed. "Search the area for a ship that can take us to Ceryneia. Offer them five hundred coins if they get here before sunset."

"Yes, Lady Castor."

Delia's blinking orb took off into the clouds, and Castor picked up her storm vials, lining them up along her belt.

She had no one to blame for this except herself. No, she did have someone else to blame—Pollux. If he had helped her instead of Genevieve, then she wouldn't be so far behind. She wouldn't have been making foolish choices in her haste.

CHAPTER 22

POLLUX

Pollux stuffed the cocoon husks deeper into his ear and kept close to Gen's heels. The little caterpillars crawling all over the trees, shrubs, and grass didn't look like they could steal his hearing or burst his brain, but what he had heard from the beach had been enough to convince him. He'd already lost half of his face to this contest and could potentially lose his hand. He didn't want to lose anything else.

Gen shook her finger at her chaeri as he tried to claw the cocoon pieces from his ears. She was taking them to a friend of hers named Flek who could hopefully sail them to the nearest island of Dion, a vacationer's isle with sandy beaches and plentiful taverns. They purchased plenty of sunny days from Arcadia. He could easily hire a ship from there.

It's not far, Gen wrote with her stick in the dirt. The monkey sat on her shoulder, picking up the caterpillars that landed on her shirt to eat them.

How do the people live here? Pollux scrawled.

The Croecians are deaf, she wrote, and plucked more of the cocoon husks from an obliging bush, shoving them into her bag.

She did that everywhere they went, he'd noticed. If she found something useful, she picked it up and tucked it in her bag. She had done the same with his golden wool sweater. He'd taken a quick peek inside her bag while she'd slept, and it looked like the inside of a rat's nest, complete with a rat.

Why did you come here before? Pollux wrote.

The caterpillars were dying. Flek asked if I could help.

They wanted to save them? Bale wrote.

Yes, they protect the island. It's restricted because of them.

Pollux took a moment to admire the scenery. When he stopped worrying about losing his hearing, Quisces reminded him of Arcadia. Lush fields spread out in front of them under a cloudless sky. Rolling hills rose up beyond. A pristine lake shimmered like glass to the east, and all of this was managed without altering the environment with bottled rain and sunshine. It was all natural.

Gen led them up another hill. At the top, he looked down to rows of stone houses with thatched roofs. Each one had a small yard with goats and chickens pecking around them. As soon as he saw it, he heard the music piecing together inside his head, something lively but soothing. He would have to work it out once he had these cocoon husks out of his ears.

Are the goats deaf too? Bale wrote.

Yes.

Gen waved them down the hill where the first of the residents came into view, a woman with pale pink skin and bright white hair tied in braids around her head. She was tall, and thin, admittedly beautiful. Her presence added to the concerto coming together in his head, and he understood the value of the caterpillars.

Without them, people like his father would come down here, trying to sell cloud cover and rainbows. Prospectors would see what natural resources they could mine or harvest, inns and taverns would set up near the lake to attract tourists for a "peaceful week away," and eventually this island would be like all of the others—another coin purse for the Empresses to draw from.

Gen approached the woman and waved. The woman raised her head and smiled with bright white teeth. She lifted her entire right hand in greeting and waved all ten fingers. Gen returned the gesture with two hands, and the woman set aside her broom.

She pointed to Bale and made another hand gesture, two fingers along her chin to her eyes where she swiped them across her forehead. Then she held her hand out to Pollux and raised four fingers, dropping them in front of her like rain.

She was speaking with her hands, calling him rain-something and Bale eye-something as far as he could tell. It might take him a while to figure out the language.

Gen made another sign, a crown of eight fingers, and the woman led them deeper into the village. As they walked, people stared, and not in the way his fans stared at him, with excited awe. It was more of a curious wonder. Not that it mattered. He didn't like being stared at in any way, and he'd lost half of his curtain of hair to hide behind. He pulled up the collar of his shirt and kept close to Gen. If there was anyone who should be stared at, it was her.

She, admittedly, didn't look her best after tromping through a field of manure and being dumped into the ocean, but that was the point. She held her head high even with salt-crusted clothes and tangled hair. It had never been the glamour that attracted him to her. It had been her. All of her.

They stopped in front a stone building with open doors and strange, metal sculptures hanging from the ceiling. Another Croecian was inside, hunched over his worktable, sparks rising up from the piece of metal he burned with his fingers.

They glowed bright red, and when he touched the metal, it bent to his will, turning into something that looked like a bird . . . no, a moth. This had to be the next stage of the caterpillars.

The woman banged her fist on the wall, and the Croecian stepped back. When he did, his fingers cooled to pale blue. Flek was a MetalBender. He took Gen's hands and mouthed something to her that Pollux couldn't see. What he could see, though, was Gen grinning back at him.

The song in his head took a dark turn.

Flek released her and wrote something in the dirt.

Welcome. My name is Flek.

Pollux, Pollux wrote in stark, stiff letters. If the woman who brought them here could be called "pretty," Pollux didn't know what words he would use to describe Flek. Handsome didn't feel like enough. Pollux pressed a hand to his scarred neck knowing he would never come close to the realm of "handsome." Tolerable seemed more like it.

Please, come inside.

Flek waved them into the house, another stone building with no door, just an open archway draped with plants and more caterpillars. Gen walked around them, tiptoeing between the bugs to not crush them. Pollux tried to do the same and slipped, crushing four under his boot. He froze, making sure Gen hadn't noticed. She seemed distracted. By Flek.

Flek's house opened to a tall-ceilinged single room with tiled floors and a large sculpture of swinging metal moths. Admittedly, it was impressive. Each moth hung from an almost invisible line, so when a breeze blew through the open windows, their wings fluttered, making it look like they were really flying.

Flek is an artist, Gen wrote. *He sells these sculptures at market.*

No surprise this good-looking Croecian was talented too.

Flek swept some of the caterpillars from the table and invited them to sit before he went to the kitchen. He returned with a tray of tea and plate of cookies, some paper and charcoal. Bale took three of the cookies and shoved them in his mouth. Argos reached down from Gen's shoulder and snatched four, tucking them in his little paws.

What brings you here? Flek wrote.

Pollux picked up a paper and charcoal. *Our chariot has been destroyed. We need help.* He didn't want to stay here any longer than necessary, in part because he didn't trust the cocoon in his ears to protect him indefinitely and because he also had some sad, pathetic notion that being here with Flek could damage things with Gen. Not that there were any "things" to destroy.

I'm sorry, Flek wrote.

Can you give us a ride to Dion? Gen wrote.

Flek shook his head. *I wish I could. Gronk has the ship. He won't be back until tomorrow.*

Gen's face fell. Tomorrow wasn't soon enough for her, for any of them. Cas could have this buttoned up and won by then.

What is the rush? Flek wrote.

I have a chance to help my father, but I am in a race to do it, Gen wrote. *If I lose, he stays in jail. My whale is gone. We have no other way.*

You and your friends are welcome to stay the night. I will give you a lift wherever you want to go tomorrow. It's the best I can do.

Is there another ship on this island? Pollux wrote.

No. Not many of us choose to leave.

Gen sighed. *Then thank you for the offer, Flek. We'll be happy to stay and take that ride in the morning.*

Flek smiled with the whitest, warmest grin Pollux had ever seen. Pollux was this close to piecing together a raft and sailing them off this island himself.

CHAPTER 23

GEN

After tea, Flek made them a vegetable stew with wild grains. He set the bowl in front of Gen, and she inhaled the warm scent of broth and spices. She tried to remember the last time she'd eaten a meal this good, and she couldn't. Stolen pieces of fruit and dried husks of bread made up most of her food memories. It had been a long time since someone had cooked for her.

They'd had a galley on their ship, and her parents had cooked most of the meals together, arguing about how much salt the rice needed or how long to cook the vegetables. Gen could always taste when her mother had won the salt argument and her father had won the cooking time battle. It had added to the flavor in a way tavern food couldn't.

While they ate, Flek told them about the argument he'd had with the Croecian council. He wanted Quisces to be more involved in Olympia; the council wanted to keep the island secluded, as it was. While Flek animatedly scribbled the story on his parchment, Gen took another helping of stew and tried to nod appropriately.

It would be rude to say she sided with the council. She loved this island because it wasn't in the Empresses' skirt pocket. Even now, she could sit here and enjoy her soup without worrying about Castor trying to murder her again or the Empresses spying on their game.

The Croecians didn't know her history. Flek didn't know that she had been someone famous and then not, that mothers fled with their children when she came into a room and called her "monster" behind her back. All he knew was that someone at the Cerynian market had told him to find her for help with his caterpillar problems and whatever else she did or didn't tell him.

Here, she could see how she looked without the rumors painting her another color.

Are you enjoying the food? Flek wrote to Pollux, who had barely picked at his stew.

It's wonderful, thank you, Pollux wrote in stark letters.

Pollux, on the other hand, had been uncomfortable since they got here. Maybe because his sister had tried to kill him. Twice. Or he was upset with how his injuries had healed.

As she'd thought, the pus took care of the worst of his burns, healed the blisters and cuts on his face, but left scars on his neck. His long hair only hung down the left side of his face, exposing his pale blue eye and sharp cheekbone.

Honestly, the injuries made him more interesting. More to see. More to ask. He had his own story now: the tale of the Lord of Storms versus the cunning Lightning Witch.

His fans would probably love the change in appearance.

Gen scraped up the last of her stew and wondered how often Pollux personally invited fans to his private box. As she recalled the screaming crowd outside his room, many of them beautiful young women, her jaw clenched.

How could she compete with that? She meant for the fans, of course. Not a seat in Pollux's private box. He'd only offered that to her because of this contest. He had no interest in her. Not that she wanted him to be interested in her, but she did want him to like her, and right now he looked as if he hated everything. Had this contest gone too far for him? Would he eventually abandon her like everyone else?

Why don't I take you to your rooms? Flek wrote.

Yes, please. Gen welcomed the distraction.

He waved them upstairs, underneath the flapping wings of his largest moth sculpture. Flek lived alone; she had learned this on her last visit. His parents were on the council and forbade him to leave the island, go to the markets, sell his art, and bring attention to Quisces, so he moved out.

At the top of the stairs, Flek gestured to a room littered with hunks of unburned metal, curls of wire, and various tools, an extension to his studio.

I'm sorry it's not roomier, he wrote to Pollux and Bale. *I don't usually have company.*

We'll be fine, thank you, Pollux wrote, and if letters could have spite, his did.

Gen will be right next door, Flek wrote.

Gen scratched the monkey under the chin and followed Flek to the next room with Chomp's nails clicking on the floor behind her. Flek opened the doors to a bright and airy room, much too large to be a guest room. A plush bed sat in the center underneath a curtain of Flek's metal moths.

Windows covered every inch of the far wall with a balcony that led to a deck overlooking a pond. Chomp climbed uninvited onto the bed and circled three times before settling into the center.

This is your room, she wrote.

Flek shrugged. *I have only one spare room.*

I can't stay here.

He touched her arm. *Yes, you can.*

Her skin prickled where he touched her. Gen pulled her arm back. She liked Flek, but she didn't want to send any mixed messages. Dating was something other people did, people with stable lives, who slept in the same bed every night and didn't create a mob when they stepped into a crowd.

Even when she did have those things, would she date someone like Flek?

She didn't know. It was hard to think about that right now. She needed to save all of her focus for the Empresses' list.

She made her way to the balcony, where the setting sun cast orange light across the green fields and pond below. Flek stood silently beside her. One of the whisper moths landed on the railing. Gen licked her finger and touched the wing. Thin MindWorker strings branched between them. She asked the moth to flutter in a swirl down to the pond, and it was happy to comply.

The little moth flew in a spiraling circle before it touched the water and returned.

"Wonderful," Flek mouthed. He leaned against the railings with both arms. *What happened to your whale?* He wrote.

She swallowed the rock in her throat. *He was killed.*

By whom?

A girl named Castor. She's in this competition with me. I have to defeat the better half of ten labors before she does if I want to save my father. She didn't mention that Castor and Pollux were related. Pollux shouldn't have to pay for the crimes of his sister, like she shouldn't have to pay for the *supposed* crimes of her father.

And how do your companions play into the contest? He pointed to the neighboring room.

Pollux wants Castor to lose. He's helping me. Bale is his assistant.

Flek hesitated before he wrote his next words. *Do you trust them?*

Her skin tightened as she stared at the page. Before he had asked that, she would have said yes. Pollux had saved her several times, once at the cost of his face, and when she had offered to remove the bracelet, he'd insisted on keeping it.

Why do you ask? she wrote.

He touched a finger to the bottom of his eye. *I watch people when I'm at the markets. I've learned to tell when someone is hiding something. Your friend Pollux looks suspicious, like he has secrets.*

She twisted her charcoal in her fingers. This she didn't want to hear. Not now. If he had told her this at the casino, she would have heartily agreed. But not now.

He's wearing a bonding bracelet. If he betrays me, it will cut off his hand. She pointed to the matching one on her wrist.

I didn't say he was staging a coup. I said he looks suspicious.

That was a good point. She hadn't thought of all the other ways Pollux could turn against her, all the lies he could have told her. The only thing he had vowed on the bracelet was to help her win the contest.

Flek tapped her arm. *I didn't mean to worry you.*

I'm already worried. But she hadn't been. Not about Pollux.

If you need help, I can help you, he wrote. *You don't have to depend on strangers.*

It was a kind offer, and she rarely refused those few instances of kindness she'd been given. Not many offered to help the murderer's daughter. Pollux had been the first, but he had an ulterior motive, to defend his title, his family. Flek had no motives. He sincerely wanted to help her.

She found that more unsettling than someone trying to sabotage her.

I'm fine, really, and this contest is dangerous.

Flek was too kind to go against Castor, and Gen didn't want to see him cooked or drowned. At least Pollux had a family obligation to this.

I can be dangerous, Flek wrote.

I'm sure you can.

He reached for her hand and ran one of his fingers down the backs of her knuckles. *You seem more silver than last time,* he wrote.

She drew her hand back. *We went to Mazon.* She didn't elaborate about the Queen and her new brood of children, or the continued increase of Mazon-ness.

We should get some rest, he wrote. *The ship will be here in the morning and I'll get you on your way.*

Thank you.

He left her on the balcony, and she stood outside a while longer, watching the sunset. In the next room, the light flickered to life, and Flek's warning flashed behind her eyes. She shook her head. It had to be nothing. True, Pollux did have a secretive look about him. She took that as a sign of his anxiety, not his faithlessness. But what if she was wrong?

Up until Flek had planted his doubts, she had been beginning to think that maybe all Arcadians weren't raised from the fires of Hades, and maybe some of them could be nice and caring and incredibly talented, and maybe, after all of this was done, she and Pollux would still see each other and possibly remain friends.

But how could that happen with someone she couldn't trust?

CHAPTER 24

CASTOR

Castor wrinkled her nose. The tow ship smelled like something had died under the floorboards. It was pieced together with rotting, mismatched wood, and frankly, if not for the barnacles clinging to the side, acting as glue, she was sure the entire ship would fall to pieces.

"You're lucky I was in the area, lady. You probably wouldn't have lasted long in the water with that." The captain pointed to the pieces of her chariot, dragging behind the tow ship on a threadbare rope.

It could be worse, she thought. She could have drowned, or burned, or been eaten by a wolf shark. But any time she had gained as an advantage was lost, pummeled to pieces by volcanic ash.

"You going anywhere in particular on Ceryneia?" he asked.

"You can leave me at the docks. I'm meeting someone." That was assuming the thief who took the *Hind* hadn't already set sail for another isle.

"All right." He wiped sweat from the back of his neck. "Hold on." He pulled a lever on the side of the ship wheel and another sail dropped from the top of the mast. It made a terrifying creaking noise as splinters of wood rained down on the deck.

She hoped he would use the reward she intended to give him to clean his ship. Or at least buy some new parts for it. If she died on this ship, there would be no limit to her wrath. She would haunt this man for all eternity.

Water splashed over the railing and splattered on her clothes. Ahead, she spotted the island of Ceryneia, rising out of the water. The captain yanked another lever by his feet, and the mainsail spun around to slow them down.

"Interesting contraption," she said, and it was. He managed to sail a four-man ship by himself with all of these levers. She would have to borrow some of the concepts for the Arcadian fleet. It would mean fewer workers on their ships, less pay.

"Yeah, she's a beaut isn't she?" He patted the ship wheel as if it were a pet, or a lover. "Here we are." He yanked another lever and the anchor dropped into the water, sidling them up to an open dock on the north side of the island.

The ship bobbed in the port. The captain took off his greasy gloves and twined his fingers in his even greasier mustache.

"I think your little spirit said something about a reward." He held out his dirty hand.

"Four hundred."

"Your ghost said five."

"Yes, and if you'd gotten to me sooner, it could have been. Four hundred, take it or leave it." Castor put one hand on her belt of storm vials, the other on her coin purse.

"I guess I'll take it."

Castor gave him the four hundred coins and made for the dock.

"Wait, you forgot your chariot." The captain pulled another lever to release her chariot. It dropped into the shallows, sinking partway. "Have a nice day." He tipped his head to her. Castor kept walking.

She'd taken what she needed from the chariot, and eventually she could pay someone to dredge up the parts for her. It wasn't as if it would serve much purpose in its current state. If she didn't find the *Hind*, she would have to buy some other means of travel here at the market.

Castor pulled the hood of her cloak over her head. People would know her here. Her father operated an underground storm market in the burrows. They let people think they were buying stolen storms for cheap, when really, they were reused and rebottled storms—someone else's leftovers. Another one of Castor's ideas. She'd thought of it when they'd come here on a trip and found hustlers selling the used storms.

"Why don't we sell them ourselves?" Castor had suggested. "Why are we letting crooks profit from our power?"

The program made them thousands.

She always believed with enough good ideas she could convince her father that it was time to change the doctrine, but no. Instead, her father took her work, patted her on the head, and then gave it all to Pollux for the sake of that stupid law.

"Delia." Castor opened the box. "Do you see the *Hind* anywhere?"

"I never saw it before," she said. "I only came by some sailors who had seen it."

"You're a great help." Castor slammed the box closed and put it in her pocket.

She had to find this ship alone, with no idea of what it looked like, or if it was even here. The ship was a whisper, a rumor, a ghost. But it was real, and someone must have seen it.

Up ahead, a girl sat on the edge of a white ship, picking something out of the bottom of her boot with a knife. Her purple hair hung in tight curls around her browned cheeks. It matched the line of scales down her spine, readily exposed by her backless shirt.

Something was written in Borean on the front of her ship,

something about fire and destruction. Castor smiled. She liked how unassuming this girl was, as if she dared anyone to approach her.

Castor always enjoyed a challenge.

"I'm looking for a ship," she said to the girl.

"I'm not for hire." The girl continued to clean her boot, digging the knife deep into the treads. She wore several rings on her fingers, most of them worthless stones except the one in the center. Plutonian opal. Very expensive and very out of place on this hand with blackened fingernails.

"It's not your ship I want. It's one called the *Hind* I'm interested in."

The girl raised her eyes, purple as well, with a black pupil down the center. "You'll never get the *Hind*. Fastest ship in Olympia."

"Except when it docks," Castor said.

The girl snorted and closed her knife. She slid from the railing and dropped to the docks, falling inches shorter than Castor. Even so, she looked at her with another dare. "What makes you think it docked here?"

"I followed it here."

"And what's it worth to you, Lady Castor?"

Castor tugged at her hood. It hadn't hidden her from this girl. She saw everything. "What's it worth to you to keep it secret?" Castor tired of playing. She yanked a lightning vial from her belt, very conscious that this was all she had, these vials on her belt. The rest of her weather vials had fallen into the Aegean Sea.

"Six thousand coins and your best vial of lightning." The girl pointed to the jar in Castor's hand.

Who did this girl think she was? "Let me guess, I give you the coins and then you point me into some alley where your friends rob me of the rest."

"No." The girl twisted a curl around her finger. "I'm much more sophisticated than that. You give me the coins, the lightning, and I give you the ship."

Castor raised her brow. "You have the *Hind*?"

"Right here." She slapped her hand on the prow of the ship they stood beside. Castor took a step back to absorb it completely.

The bright white siding gleamed in the sun. The prow had been shaved into a point to cut through water like a knife. No barnacles dared to hang onto this hull. The main mast stretched high, high enough to hold a fairly large sail that could carry this little ship over the waves in record time.

Was this really the fastest ship in the sea?

"You mean to tell me, the very ship I want is sitting right here and you're willing to sell?"

The girl winked. "Exactly."

Castor tapped her fingers on her lightning vial. "If you know who I am, then you know I won't be cheated."

"I know." The girl paced in a small circle, eyeing Castor from toe to neck. "The problem is, you think this is coincidence. It's not. I've been sitting here for hours, waiting for you to arrive. My cousin Gus has been following you since we heard about the lottery. He dredged you right out of the water and dropped you here, about two ships from me so that when you went looking for the *Hind*, you'd find me." She pursed her lips. "Thanks for the bonus too. We weren't expecting that. We weren't expecting you to go over Typhon either. Real gutsy move. Too bad it didn't work."

Heat rose on Castor's neck. She hated being outmaneuvered. "You expect me to believe all this?"

"Yes. You see, when I heard about the contest, I knew it would only be a matter of time before one of you found me. I knew what happened with that Alcmen and didn't like the idea of the MindWorker finding me and working some of her blood magic. So I thought, why not turn a bad situation into a profit? If I was going to lose the *Hind* anyway, why not make it work for me?"

Not a bad plan. "You know I could strike you down and simply take the ship." Castor tapped her lightning.

"You could, but you wouldn't get far. My cousin Gus is pretty handy. He rigged this ship up with a lever only I know how to find. If you don't release it before you set sail, your rudder won't move."

The girl truly had thought of everything, and Castor could stand here and keep trying to find loopholes, or she could make a deal and get to the Mares before Genevieve resurrected.

"Six thousand coins," Castor said. "No lightning." She needed this one.

The girl shook her head. "No fire, no deal."

Castor shrugged. "Then I guess you can bargain with the Mazon. She's broke, though, and a monster, like her father."

"Sounds like you know that from experience."

"I do." Never again, though. She'd never let the MindWorker touch her again.

"Well, that won't be a problem with the fastest ship in the sea." The girl widened her grin, exposing a small space between her front teeth. "Six thousand coins and the lightning. My one and only offer."

"Fine," Castor said. She didn't have time for this. "But you get the lightning after you show me that secret lever."

"Fair."

Castor counted out six thousand in gold and handed it to the girl, her coin purse noticeably lighter. The girl whistled while she pocketed her coins, then climbed back into the ship. Castor walked up the gangplank.

The ship's deck shone bright white, recently washed. The chrome on the wheel sparkled like silver. This ship was about a quarter of the size of the tow ship that had hauled her here. She could manage it on her own. It wouldn't be easy, but she could do it.

"That switch is down here." The girl held up the hatch to get belowdecks.

"This better not be a trick."

"I don't have that lightning yet."

"Are you saying you'll trick me as soon as you have the lightning?"

"I'd never trick the future Duchess of Storms."

Castor smiled. "What's your name?"

"Adikia."

"Pretty."

"I know. Come on." Adikia led the way belowdecks into a small but comfortable room with a bed, a desk, and a washbasin. Everything had been emptied and cleaned. Adikia really had been waiting for her.

"It's right here." Adikia opened a panel on the wall and inside and to the left was a lever, hidden deep in the ship. "Flip it back when you leave, and no one can take it from you."

"It's a nice ship."

"The best," Adikia said, insulted. "That's why I stole it, and why I'm going to steal her back."

"What?"

"That's the best part." She grinned. "Your contest is going to be the greatest thing that ever happened to me. I get paid for giving the ship up, and then when this is all over, I steal it back. But don't worry. I won't do it until after you've won your game."

Castor's breath caught. Her heart pattered. Adikia's plan touched greatness, brushed against genius. She lost nothing from this apart from a few weeks without a ship.

"I guess I owe you a bottle of lightning." Castor handed the jar to Adikia. Cas twitched when their fingers brushed.

"Enjoy the ship." Adikia stuffed the vial into her pocket and climbed up the ship steps, whistling while she walked.

Castor followed her to the deck and watched her make her way along the pier, acting as if she had no worries at all. Castor envied that. She had the ship, her fourth task, but that wasn't a win. It wasn't enough. Next, she'd catch the Mares, and then have to kill the Hydra for the win.

She moved to pull up the anchor when she saw a man at the end of the dock, poking at her half-sunken chariot.

Her jaw twitched. The chariot was very clearly marked with the lightning bolt insignia of Arcadia, and no one stole from the Duke of Arcadia, not without being charred to ash in the process.

She needed to go. She needed to sail to her next task, but what happened when she let thieves get away with robbing them? It wasn't just their ability to tame the lightning that made Arcadia one of the most fearsome isles in Olympia; it was because they didn't hesitate to use it. If she lost that reputation, she'd be no better than Pollux.

"I'll be right back, Delia."

Castor ducked belowdecks to flip the lever and stash Delia's box under the mattress before she marched off the ship and took off toward the person poking at her chariot. She grabbed a vial of strong wind. That would be enough to knock him into the water and teach him a lesson.

She charged down the planks, unscrewing the top of the jar as she ran. She wanted him to hear her coming. She wanted him to lift his head and see her face right before she struck him in the chest with a blast of wind.

The man turned to her, and Castor skidded to a stop. This was no thief.

"Lady Castor!" The head of her father's security detail, Leto, held up his hand. They had found her. Four other Arcadian guards moved in from the marketplace, and Castor backed away.

It didn't matter how she lost, either to the disgusting Mazon, or because she became incapable of playing, or because her father's security tracked her down. If she didn't win, she lost. All ways back to Arcadia were shattered, except the way made by the Empresses.

Castor opened her jar of wind and knocked Leto from his feet into the water as planned. Then she turned to run and slammed into something else—a broad chest plated in rubber armor.

"We've been instructed by your father to hold you." Soter held her tight, clamping his hand on her arm. With his other hand, he ripped the belt of storm vials from her waist.

"You know you sound like one of those silly chatter squirrels, repeating every command Leto gives you." She twisted her arm, and he dug his fingers into her skin.

Soter hadn't been this large when they'd been children. Or this dutiful. They had all been friends once, Castor, Pollux, Soter, and his sister, Ariete. As they grew older, they split apart, four different directions. Pollux to his music, Castor to her ambitions, Soter to his service, and Ariete to husband hunting.

"Why?" he said between his teeth, while Leto climbed out of the water with the help of his guard.

"You want to follow Pollux when my father's gone?" she whispered.

Soter made no response apart from the fear written on his face. *If* he kept his job under Pollux, it would be unrecognizable. He would be stringing violins, or providing security for her brother's squealing fans.

He also used to believe, like she did, that Tyrus's Doctrine was a dried-up old piece of paper that had no place in Arcadia today. Or even a hundred years ago. It was centuries past its expiration date.

"Help me get out of this. I'll make sure you're rewarded," she said.

He parted his lips as Leto arrived. Too late. Leto and the others surrounded her.

"I apologize, Lady Castor, for the inconvenience," Leto said with mocking propriety.

She sneered at him. Leto always considered himself above her, being a member of the Arcadian guard for over sixty years. He too was past his expiration date, as old and wrinkled as the doctrine. He could use replacing too, and when she became Duchess, she would make sure he was.

"How dare you!" she spat. "You will return my belt this second and let me go."

He smiled at her, as if she were a child, something cute and innocuous. She wanted to rip the smile from his face and crush it under her boot.

"Come along, Lady Castor. Let us get you home. You have some things to discuss with your father." He steered her toward one of her father's ships, a fat bulbous thing made to carry his entire camp.

At least her father hadn't come himself. He had sent his servants, which gave her time to think of an escape or *something* before she faced the Duke. As they marched her to the ship, she eyed the vials clinging to Leto's frail waist. That might be the way. She knew how to use a jar of lightning better than anyone in her father's camp. All she had to do was wrestle it away from the old man, and if she couldn't manage that, then she had no right to call herself the Duchess of Storms.

CHAPTER 25
GEN

Gen couldn't sleep. It was too quiet here with the cocoon husks tucked tightly in her ears. It left her head empty for worrying and aching over her lost whale. She couldn't take it anymore. She crawled out of bed, tiptoed downstairs, and went outside for a walk, carefully stepping over caterpillars.

Overhead, the trees swayed with the breeze. Her head told her it should make a soft rustling sound, but from the other side of the cocoon husk, she heard nothing besides the sound of the breath in her lungs.

She kept thinking about what Flek had said about Pollux being untrustworthy. The worry nagged at her like an insect bite. She didn't want to believe it. It didn't fit Pollux's character. Throughout this competition, he'd done everything he could to keep her safe.

But why?

Every Arcadian she'd ever met only cared about money and power. He could be telling the truth. He might just want to keep his sister from leading the StormMakers. Or he could simply want to keep the island for himself.

Gen laughed. Pollux would make a terrible duke.

He was made for only one thing—his music.

She stepped out of the trees onto the beach. The moon shone down on the water, lighting up a school of glowfish swimming off the coast. Someone else walked the sand. Bale. He had his hands stuffed in his pockets and was kicking at seashells.

Gen made her way down to him, making heavy footsteps on her way. She didn't want to scare him, and it was easy to sneak up on someone when they couldn't hear. He turned before she reached him. She picked up a stick and wrote in the sand.

Couldn't sleep.

He picked up another stick. *Me neither.*

You want to talk about it?

No, do you?

No.

Bale quirked his eyebrow. Gen certainly wasn't going to tell him her worries about Pollux. Maybe he was out here worrying about *her* trustworthiness. Pollux was the only one of the three of them who seemed capable of trusting someone wholeheartedly. She envied that.

Silently, they both turned to the ocean and watched the waves roll into shore. The ocean made her think of the whale. She clutched her arms around her aching stomach and felt the phantom pain in her leg from when he had been gutted by Castor's friends. She could never forgive her for that. Never.

Bale tapped her on the arm and pointed to the water. "There's something there," he mouthed.

A shimmering pink tail came out of the water and sank down again.

Gen's heart stopped.

The whale. He'd come back to her. No . . . that wasn't her whale. It was another one. The second time it rose, she saw that this whale was smaller than her whale, and pinker.

Can you catch it? Bale wrote.

She swallowed. She wasn't sure. Whales were willful creatures. Even if she could catch it, she might not be able to keep it. She also didn't have the pocket crab that her father had used to catch his whale.

Some of the moths fluttered down to the beach. One landed on Gen's fingers and she spat on it. Thin wisps connected her to the little moth.

Can you fly that far?

She pointed to the whale, bobbing on the water.

The moth wasn't sure, but it was willing to try.

Gen plucked a sharp rock from the beach and sliced into her finger. Blood pooled on the tip. She splattered it on a handful of moths fluttering around her, dotting the pale pink and blue with red spots.

"That is disgusting," Bale mouthed.

"How did you think I would catch it?" she mouthed back. Spit or hair wouldn't be a strong enough link to lure the whale to her. She needed full connection, with blood.

With her blood on the moths' wings, she had complete control over them. They were simple creatures with very little will of their own. If she wanted, she could make them drown themselves or fly into a fire. This was the type of power people feared from her, even if it could only be applied to moths, which of course, she would never do. She would treat their offer to help with the utmost care.

She sent them flying over the water. Three of them blew away on the first gust of wind. Gen pulled them back to shore to keep them from drowning. Six more kept going.

Three more panicked when some of the whale spray hit their wings. They turned around, and Gen let them, knowing she only had three moths left to reach the whale.

The pink tail flipped upward, then disappeared under the water.

The last few moths floundered, not sure where to go. If the whale had swum off, she'd missed her chance.

"What's happening?" Bale mouthed.

"The whale might be gone."

Another wave rose up in the water. It would drown the moths if they had nowhere to land. Gen reached out to call them back when something pink and shimmering burst from the sea.

There! There!

Her three little months landed on the whale's back and clung there. Gen instructed them to shake the blood from their wings, and a few minuscule droplets soaked into the whale's skin.

She felt her.

This whale was female, as far as infinity whales conformed to gender. They could change at will.

If you could, please come closer to shore, Gen asked, and waited for a response, worrying this whale couldn't understand her.

Her old whale had been with the family for years. Gen hadn't even needed to make a fully formed thought for the whale to know what she wanted. What if this whale spoke differently? What if she simply didn't want to hear Gen?

If you could, she tried again. *The moths on your back are tired. Would you mind bringing them back to the land?*

The whale didn't answer.

Gen wrung her hands. It was foolish to think she could command a whale to shore. She wasn't her father. She'd only inherited the previous whale, and he'd only stayed because he knew her. If she couldn't capture an infinity whale, what business did she have chasing the Mares, or trying to kill the Hydra?

She couldn't do this.

What are moths?

The whale finally replied in scattered, broken thoughts.

Gen exhaled a breath. This whale wasn't stubborn. She was young.

Come here and I'll tell you.

The whale swam closer to shore, and Gen sensed her curiosity.

How are we speaking? the whale asked.

I'm a MindWorker. I can speak to whales and other things.

What other things?

Like the moths.

The whale came as close to the shore as she dared, and Gen waded out to meet her. She rose high over Gen's shoulder, near twice her height and still half the size of the old whale. She reminded Gen of an oversized Grouseberry pop, a large round ball of sweet pink cake. She was adorable.

The three moths fluttered from her back, and Gen pressed her bleeding palm to the whale's side. Their connection strengthened, making it easier to communicate. A shout instead of a whisper.

Where are these moths? How do you talk to animals? What is making that sound?

The whale had a lot of questions. She couldn't hear the caterpillars, but she felt their vibrations. That was what had drawn her to the island.

Gen couldn't take all the credit for bringing the whale to the shore. The whale had made part of the journey herself, and the moths had lured her here. But Gen had played a part. Before Alcmen, only two other MindWorkers had caught an infinity whale. It took a lot of luck and even more skill. This had been mostly luck.

I can show you other things if you let us ride with you.

The whale wanted to know *how* they would ride and who *they* were. *Are you heavy? Will it hurt? Where will we go? What other things are out there?*

It doesn't hurt. We're going to Thracia, and I will show you as much as I can.

Gen turned to Bale, who stood behind her in the sand. He tried not to look impressed, but she could see it in the quirk of his mouth, the wideness of his eyes. She had shown Bale something wonderful a MindWorker could do. Maybe this was a small step toward changing his opinion on them.

She waded back to shore and picked up a stick.

She'll take us, she wrote, then scrubbed the words out with her foot. *Get Pollux, Chomp, Argos, and our things and meet me back here. I have to stay with the whale.*

Bale nodded and made his way toward the village. Gen waded back to the water to stay close to the whale. If she strayed too far from her, she could lose the connection. She didn't have a lifelong bond with this whale like she'd had with her old whale.

A sharp pain jabbed in her stomach. As happy as she was to have found this new whale, it would never be a replacement for her old whale. If anything, this only made her miss him more. Because she knew, if she scoured the seas and met every infinity whale in them, they would never be family.

Bale returned with Chomp lumbering beside him and Argos riding on Chomp's back. Pollux and Flek jogged up behind him, carrying the meager possessions they had rescued from Pollux's chariot. Flek had her bag. He waded into the sea and handed it to her.

"Can't you wait for our ship tomorrow?" Flek mouthed.

"No, I can't." They'd already lost hours to this island. Castor could already have another labor or two done.

Flek ran his fingers under his chin before he drew one across his eyebrow and down the side of his cheek. She'd learned some of the language on her last visit here. This was a common phrase amongst Croecians. They used it in every parting.

Be mindful.

She nodded and instructed the whale to open her mouth. The whale stretched her jaws cautiously, watching as Gen stepped onto her tongue.

The whale shifted. Gen held her arms out to keep her balance.

It tickles, the whale said.

I promise it won't soon. She waved for Bale and Pollux to follow. When they stepped onto the whale's tongue, she shifted again. Pollux steadied himself on the whale's cheek and yanked his hand back, frowning at the glob of fish guts stuck to his fingers.

Gen shrugged. As much as she'd complained about sitting in fish bones and seaweed and inhaling that constant odor of low tide, she'd missed it.

They settled somewhere on the center of the whale's mouth. Before the whale clamped her jaw closed, Flek waved to them from the beach. The moonlight cast across his face, lighting up his pale skin. He shone almost as brightly as the whale. Gen waved back before the whale's mouth sealed closed.

She looked to Pollux on her right, Bale on her left. Could there be some truth to Flek's worries about Pollux? Yes. Did Pollux also deserve the benefit of her doubts? Yes.

This whale shimmied back into the water, and a few fish bones fell on Bale's leg. He grimaced and brushed them off, and Chomp licked the remains off Bale's pants. This was going to be an interesting ride.

Inside the round cavern of the whale's mouth, pink light cast down on their heads. Because of her smaller size, this whale would have to rise up from the water more frequently for air, especially with three people, a chaeri, a monkey, and a rat inside her mouth.

Gen took the cocoon husk out of her ears, then Chomp's and Argos's, and finally she plucked them from the little smoke rat. She directed Bale and Pollux to do the same. Pollux carefully removed his, one ear at a time.

"We're safe inside the whale," she said. Then she spoke to the whale. "Take us to Thracia, please."

In return, she received a large question mark. *What is Thracia?*

This was going to be more problematic. Her old whale had been close to three thousand years old. He'd known every island, every reef, every fish in all of Olympia.

"What's wrong?" Pollux asked.

"This whale doesn't know how to get there."

"I have a map of the islands." Bale took out a folded piece of paper from his bag and smoothed it on his lap. The other islands closest to Thracia were Eucleia and Gelos. Gen thought of Eucleia first, site of the annual Olympian chariot races. If the whale had been there, she would have heard the cheering and clattering hooves.

She had not.

Gen pictured Gelos then, most importantly, the thick coral reef surrounding it. Her old whale had always enjoyed snacking there.

This whale brightened when she imagined it. She knew it, and from there, it would only be another league or two to Thracia.

"Can you—"

Before Gen could finish the request, the whale dove under the water and shot forward. Fish bones slid across her tongue. Gen rolled backward, and Pollux caught her by the shoulders.

She turned and whispered, "Thanks." Pollux held on to her slightly longer than necessary. She stared hard into his pale blue eyes and forgot to breathe for a moment.

Then she remembered what Flek had said.

He released her, and she sat upright, catching the scars on the side of his neck. Gen brushed some of the fish guts from her pants.

"She's fast," Bale said.

Gen cleared her throat. "Faster than any ship."

Even the mysterious *Hind*. If she could catch the Mares and capture the *Hind*, she would have her six. She could win this without anyone facing the Hydra.

"We're lucky you caught her," Pollux said.

"We're lucky Castor didn't kill us."

"She wouldn't. She would only want to hold us back."

"Is that why she burned your face?" How could he still defend her after that? After knowing she had killed Gen's whale? He might not be like his sister, but if he still sided with her . . . that made him enough of a StormMaker to worry Gen.

"That was an accident."

"Shooting down your chariot wasn't. How do you know she didn't mean to kill us? Do you know what she's planning?"

"I never know what she plans."

"You only knew she wouldn't kill us."

"No, I hoped. I always hope she'll be better than she is!"

Why is it so loud? the whale asked.

Sorry. We'll stop. "You're upsetting the whale," Gen said.

"I think we're all tired," Bale said. "Why don't we get some sleep?"

"Wonderful idea." She scooted away from Pollux and leaned against the side of the whale, settling into the soft skin. Pollux hunched over his violin, his hair draping over the side of his face, and she watched him through the fringe of one eye.

Behind her other eye, she saw Flek's words.

He has secrets.

Pollux's secrets could be small or large, harmless or devastating, and she realized it didn't matter. Trust was something she needed to have in its entirety, and her trust in Pollux had cracks. It always would.

CHAPTER 26
GEN

The whale brought them to Thracia by dawn. Gen opened her eyes when the whale jerked upward, rising to the surface. Drool ran down her cheek, and she sat upright when she realized at some point on their ride, she had tipped over and fallen asleep on Pollux's leg.

"I'm so sorry."

"It's fine," he said, looking the complete opposite of fine. His jaw muscle tensed, his brow furrowed, and his breath came out in short gasps.

Gen wiped the drool from her cheek and prepared to stand as the whale yawned her mouth wide to the early morning sun.

What do I do now? The whale asked.

Go eat.

Where?

Around the island. I'll call you back when we need you . . . but if you see another ship, swim to safety, wherever that is. She wouldn't let another whale die in this game.

What will you call me?

I don't understand.

How will you speak Me?

Bale and Pollux stepped over fish guts and whale teeth to get to shore.

"Is something wrong?" Bale asked.

"I think she wants a name." Gen's old whale had never requested a name. He'd been fine being called *whale*.

"Call her Andromeda," Bale said.

That had been the name of Bale's girlfriend who had drowned. It felt like a precious gift to give her name to a whale. Gen couldn't deny it.

"Andromeda, then," she said, breaking all of her father's rules about naming creatures, but this was more than a name. It was an olive branch.

Gen dropped some of her rooted hairs into the whale's . . . Andromeda's mouth and stepped into the shallows. Andromeda flipped her tail and sank back into the sea. Bale and Pollux picked bits of seaweed off their shirts and pants. She smiled, watching the Lord of Storms rub fish scales from his expensive trousers.

In the harbor, the Thracian shipping fleet bobbed in the water. Gen stayed clear of the docks and climbed up the sand dunes on the other side. She had a plan. It wasn't a good plan, but it was something.

As soon as she had control of the horses, she would drive them down the beach and onto one of those ships. She'd have to steal the ship when she stole the horses or she would have no way to transport them. She hoped, when the dockworkers saw a herd of murderous horses coming toward them, they'd get out of the way. This was assuming she didn't get torn to shreds in the process of capturing and collecting them.

At the top of the dune, they stepped into tall stalks of wheat, taller than Pollux's shoulders. Thracia grew half of the Empire's grain in part because of these horses.

They didn't eat grass; they ate meat: the gophers, mice, and other vermin that would potentially destroy the wheat. None of the island residents would be pleased that she was taking their pest control. With the horses gone, they'd have to find another way to protect their crops, and it wouldn't be cheap.

The guilt simmered in her chest. She didn't want to take these horses, and she especially didn't want Thylox to have them. But there was nothing she could do about that. The Empresses had already made their decree, and if Gen didn't take the horses, Castor would, and she would likely char them, beat them, and frighten them to do it.

Remember, you promised to do anything to get Alcmen back.

Her definition of "anything" had been much smaller when she'd made that vow.

"Where are these horses?" Bale asked.

"Shh." Gen held her finger to her lips. "Please don't announce to the island we're looking for the horses."

"We should find higher ground. We'll have a better view," Pollux said.

"Good idea."

They walked through the maze of wheat. The spikes caught in Gen's hair, tangling it into knots. Their boots crunched on the fallen plants, and bugs hummed in their ears. When they found the edge of the field, they climbed onto a huge boulder. Gen carried Chomp up the side.

In the cove down below, a massive ship bobbed in the water. Gen's heart pounded. It was one of the Empresses' ships. The yellow flag waved from the top of the main mast, inked with four diamonds, the symbol of Olympia, the four oracles.

"'Bout time you got here."

Gen clutched her chest and swung around. Sitting on top of the next boulder was Thylox, wiping his metal leg with a greasy towel.

"The ship is yours," she said.

"The Empresses loaned it to me. Said it would make it easier to bring the horses back."

Well, that solved one problem. Gen wouldn't have to steal a ship.

"I thought you'd be the first to get here," he continued.

Thylox wore the same wrinkled clothes from the lottery. Or he had a trunk full of identical patchy gray jackets. Neither answer would have surprised her.

He wore a similar jacket the first time they met, years ago. He came hobbling up their ship with his new metal leg, freshly bought from a MetalBender. He'd wanted Alcmen to help him catch the Mares.

"I don't capture creatures for sport or profit," Alcmen had said.

"Not for profit?" Thylox sputtered. "What do you call this show of yours?"

As voices raised, they quickly took the conversation belowdecks. She'd only heard muffled shouts until Alcmen had pushed Thylox off their ship with the help of one of their stone wolves. Since then, she'd always had one question to ask him.

"Why do you want the horses so badly?"

"That's my business. For a year at least, it will be the Empresses'."

"Then what? You'll sell them to Eris?"

"No." Thylox spat in the dirt. "Don't you worry your pretty little head. These nags aren't going to market. I've got other plans for them. You want to tell me why you're traveling with one of the StormMakers?"

Gen glanced over her shoulder at Pollux. "No, not really."

"How about we end this stimulating conversation then and get to work?"

"Yes, why don't we do that? Where are the horses?"

"In about ten minutes, they'll break through that lower field, there."

He pointed to the east, where the field down below bled into this one. A wide dirt walkway wove between them, probably cleared by the horses.

She hoped Thylox suffered greatly, knowing he couldn't do this on his own.

"He's a MindWorker too, right?" Pollux whispered. "Why can't he get the horses himself?"

This was a complicated question to answer. "Different MindWorkers have different types of control. Some can only hold a few creatures at once. My father and I . . . we can connect to many animals at the same time. Thylox can't."

Pollux nodded. That seemed to satiate his curiosity. What she left out, what she didn't want to say, was that a MindWorker like Thylox had greater control. He might only be able to hold two or three horses, but he would hold them completely, with nothing more than a few of his hairs. A MindWorker like Thylox could probably control a person with his blood. But only one. Even he couldn't cause something like what happened with the Gargareans in the tavern. No one could.

As promised, in about ten minutes, the first of the Mares emerged from the stalks of wheat. The horse stood taller than the wheat stalks with her snow-white mane flowing behind her. She was beautiful. Another one followed, a sleek black Mare trailed by a dappled gray one and a chestnut brown one. Their manes swept behind them as they raced along the cleared path.

"They don't look so bad," Bale said as an unsuspecting groundhog emerged on the prairie.

The first Mare spotted the rodent, and she tore through the stalks of wheat to reach him. Her lip curled back, dust plumed in the air, and she snatched up the groundhog.

Another Mare chased after her and snapped at the groundhog in her mouth. She caught a piece of it and ripped it in two. The blood and fur that sprayed into the air sent the other horses into a frenzy. They all grabbed at whatever they could get, kicking and butting each other to reach it.

Gen's throat tightened.

"Gen, can we talk for a second?" Pollux took her arm and led her away from Thylox.

She counted twenty-six horses in the field below. Twenty-four full-size and two foals, not that it mattered if they were young or not. The foals stood almost as tall as the full-grown adults. At most, she could control eight or maybe ten of them. These weren't moths. They were large independent creatures.

That would leave sixteen of them loose. If they broke from the herd, Gen would be as dead as that groundhog.

"You can't go down there," Pollux whispered.

"What? I have to. I can't reach them from here."

"I'm with Pollux on this one," Bale said. "Is there a way you can capture them without going down there? What if Lux sends some of your hair down there on the wind?"

"No, my hair could go anywhere, land on anything, or hit too many horses. I can't control them all," she whispered.

"What do you mean you can't control them all?" Pollux practically shouted.

"My magic has limits. Can you hold twenty lightning storms?"

"No . . . which is why you can't go down there."

"Then what do you suggest I do?"

"Let us think for a minute."

"I don't have a minute. We don't have many tasks left. We can't find the *Hind* or your sister, and I have a better chance of capturing the horses than I do of killing the Hydra."

He pinched the bridge of his nose. "At least wait until we have a plan."

"I have a plan." She did not have a plan. Argos picked a beetle from her hair and shoved it into his mouth, and a small plan began to form.

She reached into her bag and removed some dried apricots, wrapping them with pieces of her hair. She handed one to Argos, and when he swallowed it, their connection strengthened.

I need your help.

His hundred eyes flicked to the murderous beasts below, as if he already knew what she would ask.

I promise you'll be safe. But I can't do this without you. Will you help me?

He remembered being in the cage and how she had released him, and he chattered at her gleefully.

Thank you.

"Argos is going to help," Gen said to Pollux and Bale. "He can blend into the dirt, get close to the horses, and throw my hair on a few of them."

"You think it's right to use your influence on him to send him into danger?" Bale asked.

"I will do everything in my power to keep him safe." She pulled the rat from her bag and stroked his back. "I can give him extra cover."

"What if *you* get hurt?" Pollux asked.

"What do you suggest I do?" she snapped. "If I don't do this, your sister will."

He sighed. "I don't like this."

"None of us do. This wasn't intended to be easy." She took a breath and steeled herself to walk down the hill.

"Is there a problem?" Thylox called.

"No." Gen took her first step.

Pollux picked up his violin case. "I'll be watching you."

"Don't use that," she warned. "If you scare the horses, I lose the task."

"If you're in trouble, I'm going to help you."

She held up her arm, and the bracelet winked from her wrist. "You promised you would do everything in your power to help me win these tasks."

"Are they worth your life?"

"Yes. My father's freedom is worth everything."

The crease between his eyes softened. "Gen, I'm . . . I won't scare the horses. But I won't let you die out there, either."

"Trust me," she said. "I'm trusting you."

"Come back, all right?" Bale said with the most concern for her safety she had ever heard from him.

Gen started down the hill and reassuringly scratched Argos behind the ears. The monkey was anxious. He sensed the horses, and he was prey. He had an innate sense to avoid things with sharp teeth and claws.

They won't hurt you. I promise.

Argos wasn't convinced.

"Stay with them," she called to Chomp when he moved to follow.

He raised his lip in a snarl and settled next to Bale, leaning against his leg.

Below, the Mares stomped across the fields. They had found another rodent. The last shrieks of its terror rang in her ears. Argos curled tight to her neck, trembling.

"Shh," she whispered. "Once I control them, they can't hurt us."

That wasn't entirely true.

The more MindWorker threads she threw out, the thinner each one became. If she, by chance, connected with eighteen of the horses, she would only be able to whisper down each thread. It would be like throwing eighteen lines in the air and catching eighteen gulls by the foot. With twelve, she would still have the power to keep them from flying away. With eighteen, they could pull her from the ground.

She had never attempted anything of this magnitude with such large and fierce animals. If things went wrong, she doubted even Pollux and his violin could save her.

She reached the center of the field, and Gen hid herself below the stalks. The closest horse stood twenty, maybe thirty feet in front of them. Gen fumbled in her bag for the tin of spare hairs and used the side of it to reopen the cut on her thumb. The blood pooled. She rubbed it onto the hairs and handed them to the monkey.

Blend into the wheat. Get as close as you can to the horses and throw this at them. One, six, get a few and hurry back.

Like the cattle, the Mares were herd animals. If she could control enough of them, she could use those to drive the rest to the ship.

Argos held the blood-stained hair in his tight little fist. Gen set the rat on her knee and asked him for a small stream of smoke, enough to cover the ground. It spewed from his open mouth, and

Gen nodded to the monkey. He blinked his many eyes in succession before shifting his fur color to the pale gold of the wheat.

He disappeared into the rat smoke and darted forward, leaving only small footprints behind. Gen followed him through the trail of fear he left in her thoughts. With each step closer to the sharp teeth and hooves, the more intense his panic became.

Keep going, Gen nudged him. She only needed one Mare. If she had one, she could use it to reach the rest.

Argos skittered toward the nearest horse, a black Mare gnawing on the last pieces of groundhog meat. She was a good pick. Not a leader, but not one of the older, weaker horses, either. A solid middle horse. She could sway the others.

The little monkey stopped a few feet before her, heart hammering.

Throw the hair, Gen said. *And run.*

Argos curled his fist back and readied to throw. The Mare raised her head and flared her nostrils. She smelled him.

Go!

Argos pitched the hairs and spun around in a flash of dust. The Mare lunged at the movement. Gen's blood-covered hairs struck the horse's side . . . and others. Four, no six different Mares. She couldn't tell. They were all of the same mind.

Meat.

They snarled and snapped and crashed into one another, trying to find the invisible prey.

Calm down, Gen pleaded, unsuccessfully. Their hunger held them with a tighter grip than she ever could.

Argos appeared from the wheat stalks, running directly for her.

"Go!"

She waved him past her, to Pollux and Bale. He raced up the hill, and the Mares had something bigger to devour—her.

She broke into a run. Heavy hooves shook the ground underneath her. Hungry cries echoed in her ears.

Fresh meat. Warm meat.

Slow down, Gen begged.

A handful of horses skidded across the dirt. Others smashed into them and kept up the chase. She gained a footstep, maybe two.

A high, shrill series of notes echoed from above—Pollux and his violin. Lightning cut across the sky. The younger horses whinnied and turned back for the lower field.

"No!" Gen shouted. "Stop!" She could do this.

Pollux changed his song. The clouds disappeared and a heavy wind blew across the field instead, sweeping over her shoulders to the lead Mares. It pushed them back enough to give her a few more steps.

She charged up the rocks. Pollux and Bale dove for safety. She needed to get the horses down the hill to Thylox's ship.

She knew what she needed to do.

She steeled herself and spun around, grabbing the first Mare by the mane. She flung herself onto the horse's back and nudged her in the sides.

To the sea.

The horse slid down the sandy hill, and the others followed. Not because of the horse, because they wanted to eat Gen, who was sitting on her back.

A Mare snatched at her leg. Gen jerked it away, feeling the hot breath on her calf. They reached the rocky beach, and Gen pulled on the horse to steer her into the open cargo hold. She balked at the door, and another horse snatched at a piece of Gen's elbow. Searing pain tore across her arm.

Get inside!

The horse charged inside. Gen slid off her back and hit the wooden floor. She scrambled to the edge as horses galloped into the ship. When the last two foals made their way inside, someone closed the cargo door, and everything went dark.

Through the thin lines of light breaking through cracks in the wood, she caught glimpses of teeth and flared nostrils.

Warm meat. Fresh meat.

The horse who ate a piece of her sang loudly in her head. She screamed back at it.

"Stop!"

The horse froze in place. The other Mares crashed into its side. Gen ran her fingers across the wood, hoping for a weak spot. Her fingers fell into a deep groove, and she called on her Mazon strength, ripping some of the wood loose.

Not enough, though.

Sharp whinnies and clattering hooves echoed in her ears. The horses she'd connected with pelted her with hunger and desperation.

Stay back! Stay back!

The horses spat back with their own cries.

No light. Need meat. Trapped!

Their panic fed each other.

Some of the Mares threw their bodies against the wall, fighting for an escape. Others decided to enjoy a last meal. One snapped at her foot. She yanked it back and flung out with two fists. She caught three horses and one caught her on the arm, slicing through her skin.

She wouldn't survive in here indefinitely. She pulled at the side of the ship and ripped out another piece of wood. She tried to squeeze her shoulder through. The torn wood scraped against her arm.

A horse lunged at her, and she stepped aside. It crashed into the side of the ship, widening her hole. Gen shoved the dappled Mare aside and ripped another piece of wood free. She pushed through the opening, arms first. Pollux grabbed her by the wrists and pulled. She gripped hard to his hands and held his gaze.

"Don't let me go," she said.

Another horse bit into her ankle from behind. She cried out and Pollux pulled. She tumbled out of the ship, and they collapsed onto the rocks together. Her entire body pulsed with the fervor of her heartbeat and the agony of her wounds. In the corners of her mind, she could also hear the horses.

No light. Need meat. Trapped!

"I'm so sorry," she whispered. This was the chatter squirrels all over again. What had she done?

Thylox stood over her and Pollux, a gloomy shadow on her broken soul. "You damaged my ship," he said.

Gen sat upright, appalled. "You shut me in there with them!"

"I knew you'd find a way out." He picked at the grease under his nails, and Gen stood up to face him. Before he could flinch, she unceremoniously pulled her fist back and slammed it into his jaw. Her knuckles drove into his stubbled chin with a crack, and he lifted up and into the air, landing in the sand. His body flipped over twice before he finally settled at the edge of the water.

"You have your horses. Fix your own damn ship," she snapped.

"Wait." Thylox brushed sand off his jacket. "For your trouble."

He reached into his pocket and tossed her a jar. She caught whatever it was, ready to fling it back, until she noticed the green goo inside. It was stink lizard pus, an insult from one MindWorker to another. The lizards were so common and docile, anyone who could stand the smell could collect the pus.

But she kept it. She had used every last drop of hers, and from the sting in her arm, and her head, her knees, her side, and her wrist, she would need something.

"Let's go," she said to Pollux and Bale. She plucked Chomp from the ground and pressed him to her chest.

Trapped. No way out. No food. No air.

The horses kept screaming at her. She had done a terrible thing. A terrible, awful thing, and she couldn't take it back. This game cost more than her life; she was paying for Alcmen's freedom with her soul. She had lost her whale. She had almost become a murderer to kill Castor, and now she had handed over the beautiful Mares to Thylox of all people.

At the top of the rise, she opened the jar of stink lizard pus and smeared some of it on her skin, wincing at the burn and horrific odor.

"Are you all right?" Pollux asked.

"No."

Capturing the Mares was supposed to be grand, a heroic act that would dredge her reputation from the depths of despair and launch her to greatness. With the horses trapped in Thylox's ship, she felt uglier than before.

"We should have waited," Pollux said.

"For what?" she snapped. "Your sister to try and kill us again?" She sucked in a breath when she spotted Argos, sitting on Bale's shoulder.

The little monkey shifted color quickly, from red, to green, to brown and yellow. He couldn't settle on one, and his thin voice called to her in broken shouts of terror.

They're going to eat me. Eat me. Eat me. Die. Die. Die.

Oh no. Not only had she sent the Mares to their doom, she had also traumatized Argos.

She called him to her. "Come here. Let me take a look at you."

"What's wrong with him?" Bale asked.

Argos quickly leapt from his shoulder to hers, continually changing color. Yellow, blue, red, green with purple spots, pink stripes, blue starbursts.

Gen had only seen this once before in a chameleon monkey Eris had sold to someone as a pet. The owner brought the monkey to Alcmen for healing when it seemed to have trouble changing, and thankfully, that chameleon monkey had known how to heal itself.

"Portokali," Gen said.

"The fruit?" Bale asked.

"Argos won't be able to settle on a color without it. He'll keep shifting back and forth like this . . ." *Until the strain of it kills him*, she didn't say.

She clutched Argos to her chest and buried her nose in his changing fur. First the whale, now this. She wasn't a great MindWorker like her father, and she wasn't as strong as her mother. She wasn't as driven as Castor. She was just a girl who could talk to animals. She couldn't kill the Hydra. Trapping the Mares had nearly destroyed her, body and soul. Tears streamed down her cheeks.

"Gen." Pollux gently touched her shoulder.

"I can't do it." She shook her head. "I can't be the kind of person I need to be to win."

"It's okay." He squeezed her shoulder.

She raised her chin to face him. His expression wore no judgment. No disappointment. He didn't look at her like she was a failure. He looked at her like she had won already, had saved her father from prison and kept Castor away from the Arcadian throne. No one ever looked at her like that, and she didn't want to lose that.

She wiped the tears from her chin. "We need to take Argos to Lerna. Immediately."

Gen didn't know what other tasks remained. She did know, however, the Hydra was still alive. She felt it in her soul. She had five tasks. No matter what happened, she had secured the tie. But if they went to Lerna to save the monkey, she wouldn't have time to find another task for the win. She would either have to accept the tie, or hope Castor would refuse to face the Hydra and let Gen have the win with five.

That, she knew, would never happen. It was more likely Castor would choose to face the Hydra, die, and Gen could win that way. Except then Pollux would be devastated. She could not win this game. Not without someone else getting crushed.

"Let's go then." Pollux held out his hand to help her up and smiled reassuringly. Gen took his hand, lacing her fingers around his. As he picked her up, she noticed the red mark on his wrist, where the bonding bracelet had cut into his skin.

She yanked her hand back. "What happened?"

He held up his arm. "I broke my promise when I played the lightning."

She nodded, imagining him trying to save her life while the bracelet tightened with every stroke of his bow.

"You don't need to wear that anymore. I release you from that promise. You've done more than enough." She touched her fingers to the bracelet, and when she did, it glowed red, opening to release his wrist. Her bracelet opened too.

It dropped off her wrist, and she handed them both back to Bale.

"I would have worn it to the end," Pollux said.

"I know that."

Pollux had done more than enough to prove himself. It was time she did the same. Whatever secrets he had, she was certain they didn't have anything to do with her. Or this contest.

She clutched an ever-changing Argos to her chest and called the whale. While they waited for Andromeda to return, they found the rat, grazing through the trampled wheat fields.

Gen ran her finger across his back. Even as Thylox's ship set sail, Gen heard the panicked horses calling to her. It sent a shudder through her spine.

The rat gazed up at her, cheeks filled with seeds, and she scratched behind his ear. "Why don't you stay here? You'll be safe. Now." Without vermin-eating murder-horses, this would be the safest place for a rat she could imagine.

He sent her thoughts of approval. She wouldn't sacrifice any more creatures to this game. Whatever dangers she faced next, she would face alone.

CHAPTER 27

CASTOR

Castor tried not to laugh as her father's guard wandered the deck of the ship, trying to figure out how they had lost a two-hundred-pound mainsail.

"Who was watching the ship?" Leto shouted.

"We were, sir," Damon said. "Melitta and I."

"Then how did we lose our mainsail?" Leto thrust a wrinkled hand at the empty mast.

"I don't know." Damon bowed his head. "I accept whatever punishment you deem fit."

"I don't want to punish you. I want a mainsail. Where are they?" He leaned on the rails and searched the busy marketplace for Nikias and Philo, the other two guard members he had sent into the market hours ago to secure a new mainsail.

Leto was blind to leave Melitta and Damon on the ship alone. Everyone on Arcadia knew they were dating. They had probably been belowdecks, testing the firmness of his cot mattress when someone helped themselves to the expensive linen sail. Leto was an even bigger fool to think Nikias and Philo would find a replacement. They would probably end up buying back their own mainsail at twice the price.

"Maybe you can stitch a sail together with the shirts on your backs," Castor said, and Leto shot her a glare.

"Don't push him," Soter warned.

He leaned across her chair, always hovering. He smelled like Arcadia, like fresh rain and fallen leaves. If she couldn't get off this ship and back to the labors, she might never breathe that scent again. Her father would have her removed from his sight, sent to the Tegean mines or married off to some odious groom.

"You think I'm afraid of an old man?" she snapped.

She didn't fear him. She *hated* him. This was exactly why she was fighting. She was one of the most powerful women on Arcadia, second only to her mother, and they had her sat in this chair like a child in a crib.

"You don't have to be afraid of someone to be respectful," Soter said.

"He's a servant. Easily hired, easily fired."

She would fire everyone on this ship once she won her prize. She couldn't have traditionalists in employ, and Soter had clearly become one of those since taking his service. She knew, once she won this, the Empresses' decree would put her in her rightful place, but she would still have work to do, molding that place to fit her. And it would start with an entirely new staff, soldiers that were hers. Not her father's.

"What happened to you?" Soter's broad arms crossed his chest, muscles rippling. Earlier this year, he'd won the StormTrials, a competition for the guard to prove who was the fastest and strongest. They'd had to capture the flag at the peak of the Ice Mountain, surviving chilling temperatures and the attacks from other competitors. Soter reached the flag forty minutes before the second-place contender.

Soter had always been the epitome of Arcadia, with pale-snow skin and even whiter hair. Ice blue eyes. But since he had gained a foot and a half of height and rolls of muscle, he'd become idyllic. Two years ago, before he joined the service, Castor had kissed him as an experiment. It had been lackluster. Lips and saliva. No lightning. She had much preferred kissing his sister, Ariete.

"I could ask the same of you," Castor said. "We used to tease Leto endlessly, shoot him in the back with lightning sparks, and laugh as the old man fumbled to find us. Now you're practically licking his boots."

"I grew up, Castor. We all did. We moved on, except here you are, still acting like a spoiled brat."

If she had her vials, she would have expressed her rage in lightning. "How dare you!"

"Is there a problem?" Leto walked across the deck toward them. The vein on his forehead throbbed in an erratic rhythm.

"No problem." Soter stepped aside, shoulders back, head high.

"You should kneel, Soter," Castor said to him. "You'll be in a better position for bootlicking."

The muscle in his jaw flexed.

"My apologies, Lady Castor." Leto gave her a slight tilt of the head. "The replacement sail should be here soon."

She picked at her nails. "A competent guard wouldn't have lost his sail."

The vein in his head throbbed like an impending storm. She smiled at him and stood up. The three other guards on the ship reached for their vials.

"I'm only going to use the facilities," she said.

Leto waved to Eirene, one of the women on staff. She had been the second-place competitor at the StormTrials and stood as tall and nearly as broad as Soter.

"I don't need company," Castor said. What she needed was a moment to think, to find a way out of here before they scrounged up a sail. "I'm the Lady of Storms, not a child, not a prisoner. Or should I tell my father otherwise?"

"Go." Leto waved her away.

"Thank you."

She went belowdecks and looked inside the bunks and cabins for an unattended vial of wind or rain. Nothing.

Eirene came down the stairs. "I thought you were using the washroom."

"I am," she snapped, and went into the small compartment. She slid the latch to lock herself inside and went through the bottles of soap until she found what she needed—a single vial of rainwater someone had forgotten to remove.

She grabbed a towel and shoved it under the crack in the door and jammed another one into the drain cut into the boards. She opened the vial, and a rain cloud seeped out of the open jar, hovering above her. Patters of rain fell on her head. Under normal circumstances, this was all she would release, enough to wash with and disappear down the drain.

Castor kept the vial open, letting the entire dark cloud seep into the washroom. Rainwater pounded on her shoulders and soaked through her clothes. The water level rose quickly, coming to her calves, then her knees, thighs, and waist. When it reached her neck, she took a deep breath and sank underneath.

She heard a muffled cry from the other side.

"Lady Castor?"

The door to the washroom vibrated. Castor held her breath and pushed against the far wall. She would only have one chance at this. If she failed, Leto would throw her in the brig.

The door opened. The water rushed forward. Castor came out feet first, hitting Eirene in the chest. The two of them fell to the ground. Castor wildly snatched at Eirene's belt, grabbing a handful of jars.

One was filled with lightning. She felt it calling to her from the inside of the metal jar. She twisted that one open and pulled some of the lightning free, wrapping it into a ball that she left hovering over her palm.

"Don't move," she said to Eirene. "I will light up this whole ship, including you."

Eirene gently nodded.

"You chose the wrong side," Castor said.

"I'm sorry, my lady." Eirene didn't dare reach for one of the remaining vials on her belt. She knew, like everyone else, Castor was one of the best. She would char Eirene to ash before she could touch one of those jars.

"I'll give you a chance to redeem yourself. Give me your belt and stay down here no matter what you hear on deck."

"Whatever you say, my lady."

Eirene removed her belt of remaining storm vials and handed it to Castor, never shifting her gaze. Castor held the lightning while she fastened the new belt and replaced the jars in the slots.

Once they were all in place, she felt whole again, powerful, not like a child being watched.

"I will remember this once I have the Empresses' blessing." Castor turned to make her way up the stairs. "And I will not forget your sacrifice."

"Please, don't hurt them."

She hesitated. "I'll do my best."

Someone came down the stairs as she went up. Soter. Castor drew her lightning and pitched it at his chest. It exploded on his rubber armor. He flew back onto the deck and sparks sprayed into the air.

Castor reached for her next vial—wind. She opened it at the top of the steps and aimed it first for Melitta as she charged toward Castor with lightning in her hand. The wind swept across the deck, picked Melitta up by the ankles, and spun her around three times before dropping her into the sea.

Damon leapt in from the left armed with a lightning sword cracking in a sharp line toward the sky. Castor focused her wind into a tight spiral and pushed it hard outward. It slammed into his ribs with a crash, loud enough something cracked. He dropped his sword, clutched his chest, and stumbled backward. Castor gave him one last push that sent him over the railing.

"Stop this," Leto shouted. He held an unidentified vial in his hand.

Castor narrowed her eyes. Unlike Eirene, Leto would not give up so easily.

"You're acting like a child," he said.

"I am acting like a future Duchess who has been betrayed by her own servants." Castor plucked another wind vial from her belt. She would save the lightning for last.

"I don't serve you. I serve the Duke. I serve Arcadia."

She smiled. "Not for long."

She opened her vial of wind to strike him hard, to strike him first. She sent a tunnel of wind at his middle. He blocked it with his own vial of hail.

The icy shards flew at her fast. Her windstorm shaved them to points, and small daggers of sheer ice cut into her skin and clung to her arms. Her teeth chattered. The rainwater still on her clothes and hair turned to frost. She lost focus. Her windstorm flattened and became nothing more than a harmless gale.

Leto's hailstones rained down harder. They bounced off her forehead and boots, leaving bruises on her skin. He took a step closer and gave her a yellow grin.

"You are a child." He pelted her with more ice. "And I can't wait until the true Duke of Arcadia sends you to the mines."

Castor's teeth chattered. With shaking hands she fumbled for another vial. She would not lose this way, beaten by an old man. A large hailstone struck her knuckles, and she yanked her hand away, cursing.

"You are not fit to be Duchess," Leto nearly spat in her face, and all Castor could do was glare and chatter at him with frozen teeth.

He reached a hand out to grab her belt, to steal her storm vials from her once again, when an arrow fell from the sky and plunged through his shoulder.

Blood sprayed across Castor's sleeve. She gasped and took a step back as Leto and his hailstones fell at her feet.

Castor reached for a jar on her belt, whatever she could grab, and searched the sky for who had shot the arrow. A pair of boots hit the deck beside her. Castor spun and faced the girl from before, Adikia. She had a bow slung over her shoulder along with a quiver full of sharp-tipped arrows on her back.

"Come with me." Adikia held out her hand. At the prow of the ship, Soter picked himself up. Below her, Leto moaned, working to get another vial from his belt.

Could she trust the girl? No, but she had no choice.

She dropped her palm in Adikia's, and they thundered down the gangplank onto the crowded pier.

"Castor!" Soter shouted at her back, and she ignored him. *I will show you something about respect, Soter. Right after I win this contest.*

"I didn't need your help, you know," Castor said to Adikia as they raced to the *Hind*.

"That is such a lie," Adikia said. "You'd be halfway to Arcadia right now if I hadn't jacked your mainsail."

"You stole the sail?" Castor smiled. The girl was always one step ahead of everyone else.

"Well, my cousin and me. That thing was heavy! We're going to cut it up and sell it as bed sheets. We'll make a fortune."

"So you took it for the money." It made sense. Castor's father bought the finest linen. Any thief could make their weight in coin from it.

"Yeah, and for you." They stopped running. Adikia squeezed Castor's hand, then pressed her lips to Castor's mouth, hard and fast.

Castor closed her eyes as lightning raced through her veins. She leaned deeper into the kiss. This was what kisses were supposed to feel like. Like they were burning you up from the inside.

Adikia pulled back. Too soon. "Now get out of here, Lady Castor. I'll come see you later for my reward." The girl winked before she turned toward the market and disappeared into the crowd.

"What makes you think you get a reward?" Castor shouted to a ghost. Adikia was already gone.

Like the wind, Castor thought. With her lightning, she and the thief could make one unforgettable storm. Something for Cas to keep in mind once she finished this contest. Adikia was exactly the kind of person she wanted on her staff: cunning, clever, and attractive.

Castor raced up the *Hind* steps. She ran belowdecks to grab Delia and flipped the lever to release the ship wheel. She drew up the anchor and pulled the sheets. She turned the wheel hard port to get them out of the harbor. A breeze caught the sail, and they moved into the water.

Not very quickly yet. This didn't feel like the fastest ship in the sea.

She picked through her stolen storm vials for another gust of wind. Maybe a breeze would help. She opened the vial, and the wind pushed into the sail. It ballooned outward, the prow rose from the water, and Castor fell back.

She hit the deck and scrambled to hold the wind in place. She pushed and pulled the gust to keep it circling through the sail.

She picked herself up and pulled back her cold, wet hair. The wind slapped against her cheeks. The ship sliced through water like a sharpened blade. She could see why Adikia wanted this ship. It *was* fast. Castor licked her lips, tasting salt and a hint of something sweet the girl left behind.

"Delia," Castor shouted over the wind. "Find my brother. I need to know what he's been doing."

"Yes, Lady Castor." The bobbing light took off over the sea, and Castor steered the ship for Thracia. The horses weren't her first choice, but she knew they would be Gen's. She would have to steal them from her and then defeat the Hydra for the win. She could still do this. Leto and his crew hadn't cost her everything, and now she had the fastest ship in the sea to carry her forward.

While Castor waited for Delia to return, she got a feel for the ship, turning the wheel port and starboard to see how it bounced on the waves. She kept her wind gust rolling through the sails to give it a steady push southwest.

When Delia's box blinked with her return, Castor lifted the lid. "What did you discover?"

Delia's light fluttered. "Pollux has escaped Quisces intact."

Castor exhaled, relieved her brother was alive. Not as happy to hear he was on the move again. "Where is he?"

"He and the Mazon captured the horses, and they've been spotted en route to Lerna."

"Damn, damn, damn!" Castor slammed her hands on the ship wheel.

She'd been on Ceryneia too long, and the Mazon had regained her lead. Genevieve had the Mares, and only the Hydra remained. Even if Castor murdered the beast, she'd only gain the tie, and now she couldn't even murder Gen! Not while she was ahead. The Empresses would probably declare her the winner postmortem.

The tie was it. Her last chance. But a tie was not a loss.

She couldn't lose. Her father knew her plan, and he would keep sending Leto after her, his anger and resulting punishment increasing each time she defied him. If he didn't have her betrothed to some imbecile by mid-month, she'd spend the rest of her life deployed on Tegea, monitoring the mines while her youth and strength melted away. She would be less than second place. She would be less than her father's guard. She would be nothing.

She was at the northern tip of Olympia. Lerna was farthest to the south. The only way she could be further from her goal was if she sailed outside the Empire.

Should she give up? No. The Lady of Storms never gave up. She had to kill the Hydra before the MindWorker or lose.

"Delia, keep watch on my brother. I'll be there as soon as I can."

"Yes, Lady Castor." The little ball of light sailed off again, and Castor reached for a hurricane vial. "Let's see how fast this ship can really sail."

CHAPTER 28

POLLUX

Pollux rubbed his wrist where the bracelet had cut into his skin. Looking at Gen, perched on her whale's tongue with the ever-changing monkey clutched in her shaking hands, he wished he would have let the bracelet cut right through his arm versus standing helpless outside that ship while the horses tore her apart.

He hadn't known how to reach her. If he had shot through the side of the ship with his lightning, he could have hit her. Or set the ship on fire. He thought, for the longest minute of his life, he could lose her forever. By the time she tore apart the ship to escape, he had been about to do the same. With much weaker arms.

Now they were headed to Lerna, his sister was unaccounted for, and they had no idea what labors she had completed. The Hydra could be the last one. Castor could be on her way here right now, or already on the island. If she went for the Hydra, the tie, could he stop Gen from trying to kill it herself?

He rubbed his wrist over the red ring once more. Gen had released him from her promise. He no longer had to do everything in his power to help her win these tasks. Instead, he could do everything in his power to keep her alive.

The whale rose out of the water. He set his hand back to steady himself, and his fingers landed in something wet and slimy. In the rose-colored light of the whale's mouth, the gunk looked especially grotesque. He grimaced, flinging the muck from his hands. Watching the circus from the outside, riding inside a whale had seemed more magical from afar. How had Gen done this for so many years?

The whale slowly opened her mouth, and Gen stood up, resting her palm on the inside of the whale's cheek. Her chaeri followed her, and the monkey lay cradled in her arms. They all seemed to carry the same weight as Gen.

Before he rose, Bale leaned in close. "Are you going to let her go after the Hydra?" he whispered. It was the most concern he had ever shown for Gen's safety.

"She at least has the tie," was all Pollux said in return.

Castor couldn't win at this point. But she could try to kill the Hydra for the tie, which would only drag the game out longer. Most likely, the task would kill her, and he couldn't let that happen either. None of this was working out the way he had intended.

They stepped out of the whale's mouth onto the hot, sandy beach of Lerna. A bead of sweat rolled down the side of his cheek to his scarred neck. He moved to push away hair that was no longer there, remembering the flash of lightning that had burned it away.

"They'll have portokali in town. We need to get to the market." Gen led the way up the sandy walkway, and the whale sank back into the water, silently commanded by Gen's thoughts.

Pollux tugged on his already sweat-soaked shirt. Bale yanked a wide leaf off a tree and used it to fan himself. Pollux had been to Lerna many times. They were one of Arcadia's best customers. Not only did they buy excessive vials of rain, they kept a team of StormMakers on staff to help control them. To encourage tourism, the hired StormMakers pulled away the storms from dawn to dusk and rescheduled them for a more convenient nighttime rainfall. It allowed the rain forest to thrive, and the people to move about freely during the daytime.

Bale, Pollux, and Gen stepped into the market, a sorry sight with ripped and bloodied clothes stained with saltwater, seaweed, and now sweat. Tourists, vendors, and criers crowded the cobblestone square waving signs and baskets of flyers. Pollux sank into the collar of his shirt. This place was too crowded. Too noisy.

A crier launched herself in front of Pollux with a leaflet in hand. "Climb the Lernean Mountains with an experienced guide! Stop by Adventure Tours to book your outing today!"

"No, thank you." Pollux shrank away from the woman. She threw her feathered arms in the air and clicked her tongue behind her teeth, off to find her next victim.

"We need to find someone selling portokali." Gen waved them to the vendor booths while the monkey in her arms shifted from blue to green to something with red and white stripes.

"Pollux!" Someone called his name. "Lord Pollux!" Pollux ducked lower. Had Soter tracked him down again? Or maybe this was one of the Arcadians on staff here in Lerna. Either way, he didn't want to be seen.

"Who is it?" he whispered to Bale.

"It's Cristos," Bale said, and Pollux turned.

The tall, fair-haired man pushed his way toward them with his mustache twitching. Cristos was the only other person Pollux kept in his employ, and he kept him far more distant than Bale because Cristos was a loyalist. He believed with his whole heart that the Arcadian Doctrine should not be changed, which was why he had been eager to help Pollux keep an eye on Castor.

As Cristos shoved his way toward them, he looked pleased,

which meant something bad must have happened to Castor. Was she injured? Dead?

"Who is that?" Gen asked.

"Cristos," Bale said. "He's with us. Sort of. A bit of a misogynist but otherwise harmless."

A good assessment.

Cristos reached them out of breath, drenched in sweat. "I have been searching for you," he panted. "I had a feeling I would catch you here eventually."

"You have news then."

"Yes." He took several more gulps of air, and Pollux waited on the edge of frustration for him to tell them what he knew.

"I found Castor," he exhaled.

"Where?"

"Ceryneia. She went there for the *Hind*."

"What other tasks does she have?" Gen asked before he could.

"She killed the birds, stopped the Boar and the Bull, and found the *Hind*."

"That's four," Gen said.

Which meant she would definitely be coming here for her fifth.

"She was captured on Ceryneia," Cristos said.

"By whom?" Pollux asked.

"Leto. Your father has her. She's been contained." The smile on Cristos's lips returned. This was the reason for his joy. Castor was out of the game. Their father had won.

"She has four," Gen whispered. "I have five." She lifted her chin, and Pollux noticed tears in the corners of her eyes. "That means I've won, haven't I?"

"If five continues to be more than four," Bale said.

"I think so," Pollux added, trying to find the same happiness that spread across Gen's face.

He was happy. For her. And sorry for Cas. Their father would rage at her like he had never raged at anyone before. Cas would be dragged back to Arcadia like a howling cat, spitting and cursing the entire way. No remorse for what she had done. Only anger. Their father wouldn't take that well.

He would likely disown her, and without Castor, Pollux would be alone, the subject of all his father's attention and anger. Cas wouldn't be around to distract his father with business and strategy. Pollux wouldn't be able to sneak away and live his second life as Lux, Lord of Storms. He would only be Lord Pollux—Future Duke of Arcadia.

The end of this game would also mean the end of his time with Gen. Forever. The Sole Heir to Arcadia wouldn't be able to spend time with Genevieve the Circus Performer. All of his plans had depended on Castor being defeated in the game. Then she would have realized her options had run dry. Only with the Empresses' blessing could she take Arcadia. Without it, she would have had to appeal to their father. Then he would have let her stay.

She was supposed to lose. Not get caught. Cas never got caught. What happened?

He gripped the case of his violin.

"What do you want me to do, sir?" Cristos tilted his head.

"Return to Arcadia. I will meet you there shortly."

"Can I escort you there? I have horses."

"No," Pollux said. He couldn't leave Gen yet. He needed one more moment to think, to say goodbye, something.

"As you wish." Cristos made his way back through the market at a slower pace now that he had delivered his news.

"I can't believe it." Gen hugged Argos to her chest. "I've won the game. I can finally set my father free."

"I am happy for you," Pollux said with as much enthusiasm as he could manage. He was glad for some things. A world with Gen onstage with her father would always be a better world than one without.

"Oh, Argos." Gen bit into her lip. "We still have to take care of you. There!" She spotted a woman with green-feathered arms holding a basket of the round, orange portokali fruits. Gen pulled a coin from her bag, handed it to the woman, and gave the fruit to Argos.

The little monkey bit into the soft flesh, and in the middle of his fur turning from pink to gray, it slowly shifted from neck to tail to a smooth brown color over his blinking eyes. Gen returned to them, scratching the monkey behind the ears while he continued to eat the fruit.

"Once he's fully healed, I'll release him to the jungle. He can go home."

"That's great," Pollux said.

She shook her head. "It doesn't feel real. Something else must be waiting to burn me or eat me or something. I have won, haven't I?"

"The Empresses said whoever completed more tasks would get their wish," Pollux said.

"You don't think they'll be upset neither of us killed the Hydra?"

"Oh, I'm sure they'll be upset. But their word is true. They'll hold to it."

Gen released a long breath. A bead of sweat ran down her cheekbone, following the line of silver on her skin. He ached to follow that same line with the back of his fingers. Maybe he'd been mistaken, but when she'd removed the bonding bracelet from his wrist, he'd felt like something had changed. She hadn't looked at him like an enemy, or a means to an end; she'd looked at him like she really saw him for once, all the secrets he kept inside, and maybe with more time, that one look could have become something more.

But they were out of time.

"I couldn't have done it without you," Gen said. "Both of you," she added. "Pollux slightly more than you, Bale."

"Always glad to help." Bale rocked back on his boots.

"It was my pleasure," Pollux said. "I mean, not the actual completing of the tasks . . . it was a pleasure to be able to help you." *To spend time with you, to speak with you.*

Bale sighed and noticeably rolled his eyes.

"I am grateful you did," she said, "and despite Castor trying to kill us both, I hope, for your sake, she is okay."

Pollux had heard this before, apologies for Castor, not because they cared about her, but because they felt sorry for him for being related to her.

I'm sorry you have such a strong-willed sister. She's certainly tough to handle, isn't she?

In all fairness, his sister was not that difficult to handle, if you knew how to approach her. If their father had given her Arcadia instead of him, this would all be a very different story.

"Oh, she'll be all right." Pollux toyed with the clasp on his violin case. "A few years of exile might do her some good." If Cas spent a few months at the mines and came back cowed and subdued and begged their father for forgiveness, Pollux might be able to persuade the Duke to forgive her.

What was he thinking? That scenario would depend on both Cas and their father admitting wrongdoing. It was more likely that the Duke would let Pollux keep his violin, which was not very likely at all.

Gen frowned. "I lived in exile for a long time. I wouldn't wish that on anyone. Not even Castor."

"Then you are more forgiving than she will ever be."

"I take that as a compliment." She smiled at him, and Pollux had his chance to tell her everything. He could tell her about the many times he had gone to see her show, hidden in the back like a thief. Or how it had almost killed him to see her in the hands of the Mazon Queen. And how he would give away his entire inheritance if he could spend one more day with her, talking with her, holding her, being near her.

And what would all that accomplish? Only heartache and misery.

"We should probably go," Bale said, saving Pollux from saying something regrettable.

"Yes, in a minute." He turned to Gen. "Will you be all right here, on your own?"

"I'll be fine. I'm used to being on my own. The company these past few days was . . . nice." Gen wrapped her finger around the monkey's tail. "Pollux?"

"Yes?"

She hesitated for three long beats of his heart. "I'm sure we'll meet again on the stage. It will be good to hear you play again." She held out her hand, and he took her fingers, squeezing them tight.

"Until then," he said, because he couldn't tell her that he wouldn't be on the stage for a long time, apart from his promised concert to the Lion. As soon as he returned home, his father would sink his claws in deep and start molding him into a callous, coin-hungry duke. He might never be free again.

"I'll find us a ship," Bale said, and a loud bell rang through the market. At the clanging sound, vendors scrambled to fold up their signs and box up their goods.

"Rain's coming!" a crier shouted. "Everyone move inside!"

Pollux lifted his chin to the sky. Through the trees, the last threads of sunlight broke the leaves. It was almost dusk. Within the hour, this market square would be flooded with at least six inches of hard rain. The Oracles had gifted him with his one wish . . . more time with Gen.

"We can't leave," he exhaled. Saved by his own rain. The docks would be closed until morning, and Gen would never be able to make it into the jungle to return the monkey.

"What do we do?" Gen looked to the sky.

"We get inside, like the man said." Bale waved them toward the center of town. More bells rang out, echoing off the buildings.

Pollux waved them to the Eos, the largest and most expensive lodging on the island.

His father always stayed here when he came to Lerna for the sole reason of being noticed. The Duke of Storms didn't like nice things so much as he liked to be admired. He wanted everyone to see how profitable Arcadia was by wearing expensive clothes, staying in the best lodgings, and eating the finest meals, and if Pollux was going to take his place, he supposed he should start following in his father's footsteps by spending large amounts of coin.

They walked up a white stone path through the garden, past the massive Hydra-shaped fountain, molded by the famous MetalBender Chrysus. Water spewed from each of its nine heads into a pearl bowl below.

Gen kept her eyes on it as they passed, likely grateful she had been saved from seeing the beast in person. He was thankful too.

Neither Gen nor Cas would have to face the serpent. At least, whatever happened from here, they would all stay alive. That was something.

"Lord Pollux." One of the doormen tipped his head to Pollux when he approached. "How good to see you again."

"Yes, thank you."

"Did you say Pollux? As in Lux?" A young woman with blue-green hair pushed her way to them, and by the excited gleam in her eyes, he guessed she was a fan. This was something he would not miss about giving up his onstage persona—the attention.

He did his best to hide behind a potted plant. Not quickly enough.

"I love your music! I saw your show on Delos last month." She batted her eyelashes and grabbed for his arm. Bale sat off to the side, smiling conspiratorially. Pollux glared at him.

"Is this your violin?" The woman tugged on the case. "Will you play something for me? Please." More eyelash-batting as the bells rang out louder, warning of the storms. Pollux's cheeks flushed. His throat went dry. He couldn't speak. He couldn't move.

Then Gen stepped in front of them. "You think this is Lux? The violinist?"

The woman looked from Pollux to Gen, confused. He was too.

"You've made a mistake," Gen continued. "It happens all the time. You're the second person today."

"But the doorman called him Lord Pollux, and he has the violin," the woman pouted.

"The doorman was the first person to make the mix-up."

The aforementioned doorman ruffled his golden feathers as confused as everyone else.

"His name is Peter." Gen linked her arm though Pollux's. "He's a huge fan of Lux, like you. He's a little obsessed, actually, going so far as to grow his hair out and play a violin."

"Oh." The woman stepped back. "I'm sorry for my mistake."

"No problem," Gen called after her, and Pollux's muscles loosened.

"Thank you," he whispered to her.

"I owed you one," she said, sliding her arm from his as soon as the woman disappeared.

He touched his sleeve where her fingers had been, and they went into the hotel.

He booked them three rooms despite Gen arguing that he didn't need to pay for her room. He waved her off. As the future Duke of Storms it was to be expected he would live in excess, and he wanted his own room for some quiet time to think.

"We can clean up and meet down here for dinner in an hour," he suggested.

"As long as you're buying," Bale said as he snatched a glass of wine from a passing serving tray. He had no problem taking handouts.

Pollux sighed and went to his room. He took off his boots and sat at the corner of the bed on top of the crisp, white sheets. A vase of fresh flowers bloomed on the center table, making the room smell fresh and clean. He unclasped his violin and removed it from the case, running his finger along the strings.

For the longest time, this had been his only companion. He hated to let it go. The show he promised the Lion might be the last one he would ever play, at least as long as the Duke was alive, and by the time he wasn't, Pollux feared he wouldn't be the same person he was now. There were rumors his father had been more joyful once, and now . . . well, no one ever called the Duke of Storms a fun person.

Pollux pressed the end of the instrument into his chin and pulled the bow across the strings. He played an old funeral dirge from Arcadia, and while he played, a small raincloud formed inside the room, dropping mist onto his rug. He had always wanted to be someone else, someone without a title and expectations. He supposed Castor wanted the same. And Gen. All three of them wanted to change their destiny.

If only one of them could accomplish it, he was glad it had been Gen.

A loud crack of thunder interrupted his song, and on the other side of the paneled window, sheets of rain cascaded down from the sky. Pollux put his violin away and stood in front of the glass, watching the rain.

A few stragglers outside held their arms over their heads while they raced to the doors of the inn. He remembered his father sitting down with the Lernean council.

"Think about how much money you're losing when the rain cancels a week of activities. People come here to explore. They don't want to be shut indoors. With our help, you can plan for rain. You can thrive."

Pollux pictured himself saying those exact words and felt sick. Cas should be the one running the business. Not him. In his mind, they would always share Arcadia. Castor would do the sales pitches and handle shipments, and he could look after the people and keep Castor from destroying the Empire with crates of bottled lightning.

He wondered if their father already had Cas seated in his office chair while he jabbed his finger at her nose and shouted at the top of his lungs.

"Disgrace! Worthless! Embarrassment!"

Pollux had been there before. Many times. Cas wouldn't be able to talk her way out of this. Their father couldn't let a betrayal this deep go unpunished. He'd erase Castor from existence before he would admit he'd been challenged by his own daughter. It would damage his reputation as the infallible Storm Duke.

He sighed. If only Cas had talked to him before she ran off to the lottery. He would have listened to her. He would have helped. They could have fixed everything together instead of turning against one another. It was much too late for that, now.

He stepped away from the window. He should dress for dinner, except he had no clean clothes. He rang the bell for the valet and asked him to bring some fresh clothes for himself, Bale, and Gen. While he waited for something clean to wear, he stepped into the washroom, equipped with a small vial of gentle rain.

He unscrewed the cap and let the water roll down his neck and shoulders, stinging where it hit the pink scars on his neck.

When the new clothes arrived, he dressed in the light tunic and loose pants. They were clothes made to protect against the hot, humid weather and hung off Pollux like sheets. He supposed it was better than the stained and torn pants he'd been wearing.

Before he left the room, he looked back at his violin, propped against the bed. He never went anywhere without it, but he should get used to leaving it behind. He reached into the case, grabbed a vial of wind, and shut his violin in the room.

He met Gen in the hallway as she exited her room beside his. She had washed too, her dark and silver hair swept away from her face by a silver hair clip.

The valet had done a much better job picking her clothes than his. She wore a ruffled red dress with blue flowers on the hem. It drooped low on her shoulders, exposing the jut of her collarbone and the curves of her chest. She definitely had more silver skin than before. Washed clean, it gleamed in the lanterns. Even the monkey on her shoulder looked freshly cleaned, and her purple lapdog was nowhere in sight. She must have left him in the room.

Gen made a face. "Do I look all right? You're staring."

He shook his head to clean his mind.

"You look very nice." Nice seemed like a safe adjective, as opposed to beautiful, tempting, or perfect. Gen was not for him. Even if she did like him in the smallest amount, what would she do? Move to Arcadia? Become Duchess of Storms? She hated the StormMakers, and with good reason.

"You do too," Gen said.

Pollux pulled on the loose shirt. "I'm not sure this is my style."

"Of course." She linked her arm through his. "You are more of a crisp lines person, tailored suits and fine boots."

"Not exactly." He was more of a "cover as much skin as possible" person. This shirt exposed too much of himself, including the new scars.

They made their way downstairs. She kept her arm linked through his, and he savored the contact until she released him at the dining room. Bale was already seated at a table, drinking a glass of wine. He wore an almost identical outfit to Pollux.

"I took the liberty of ordering drinks," Bale said, and gestured to the half-empty carafe of wine on the table.

"How thoughtful of you." Pollux pulled the chair out for Gen and sat beside her. He wondered if Bale would continue working for him if there was no more traveling. No more wine. No more adventure.

He doubted it, and Pollux would miss him. Bale had always

brought with him a piece of reality that Pollux clung to. He liked the reminder of a world outside of his messed-up family.

The waiter came by, and they placed their food order. Argos skittered off Gen's shoulder and seemed fully healed as he changed to blend into the curtains and steal a piece of papaya from an unwatched plate. Bale drank the last of his wine and said, "Excuse me," before standing up and making his way across the restaurant. He found a place at the bar next to a young man with green skin and two curved horns on the sides of his head. Bale pulled a coin out of his pocket and slid it across the bar to buy the young man a drink.

"Can I ask you something?" Gen said.

Pollux turned back to her. "Anything."

"Why Bale? He doesn't seem to be very helpful. Couldn't you have found a better companion?"

"I suppose that depends on your perspective. He is very good at what I need him to do. He has a knack for lighting my performances, and he is excellent at annoying my family. He keeps my head from getting too big, and don't discount his other uses. He once dragged away a very overzealous fan who tried to cut off a piece of my hair."

She smiled wider. "You're really not like your family at all."

"I'll take that as a compliment."

She took the napkin from the table and set it in her lap. "I want you to know, I will pay you back for all of this . . . the food, the room, the dress . . ."

"I couldn't take your coin. Consider it a repayment, for all we've cost you." He swallowed. "I am sorry about the whale."

"I am too." She bit into her lower lip, her beautiful, plush lower lip. "I'm going to let Andromeda go as soon as I have my father. I don't want her to get hurt. Infinity whales weren't meant to be kept."

"It's not being kept if they choose to stay."

"That's what I said about my old whale."

Her dark eyes filled with tears; time to change the subject. "Where are you planning to go once you have Alcmen?"

"I don't know," she said. "Maybe we'll rent a place on Delos for a while, until we get ourselves situated. I think after where he's been, he might like to spend some time relaxing."

Delos, home to a series of warm springs. They bought vials of warm rain from the StormMakers to keep their springs fed.

"That sounds nice," Pollux said, already wondering when and how he could get to Delos to see her.

He shook his head. What would be the point? To torture himself more? He had to let her go, once and for all.

"You think he did it, don't you?" Gen said bluntly.

"What?"

"You think my father killed them."

"No . . . no I don't. Not at all."

This was not a lie. He had heard the stories about Alcmen like everyone else, but his father had trained him that lies were easy to sell. You could tell people their crops would dry up or the island would go broke if they didn't buy your rain, and they would believe it. Pollux had always believed Gen, and not entirely because he was in love with her.

"I saw the circus. More than once, actually," he continued. "The way your father loved it, loved the animals, loved you . . . people like him don't have the kind of violence in them that it takes to murder a roomful of people."

Castor did. His father did. Not Alcmen.

Maybe that had been, in part, what drew him to the circus, to people like Bale and Gen—they had their flaws, but they weren't pretending. Everything they were, they wore on the surface of their skin. He appreciated that.

"Thank you," Gen whispered, and he wondered if anyone had ever told her that. *I believe you.*

A group of musicians took to the stage while Bale had another glass of wine with the man at the bar. They would have to drag him back to his room if he drank much more. The violinist in the band removed his instrument from the case and held it awkwardly under his chin. He drew the bow across the strings, and it squealed. Pollux winced in agony.

"He's not nearly as good as you are," Gen said.

"Thank you."

She tapped her fingers on the table. "I'm sorry I told you to change your act. You really don't have to. I'm nervous, I suppose. I felt like we always needed so much glitz and glamour to put our show together and then you come along and make something wonderful without all that. What if all we had was the glitter?"

"That's not true. You could go out onto that stage naked and people would be impressed." He choked on his own words. What had he said? He stood up and set his napkin on the table. "Excuse me, I'm just going to go hang myself."

She grabbed his hand. "Sit down . . . and maybe stick with the violin. You're better with music than compliments."

"I can't argue with that."

The waiter returned with their food. Pollux directed him to deliver Bale's meal to the bar. He would be sick if he didn't eat something. As Gen picked at her seaweed pasta, Pollux absently stabbed at his shaved steak on toast. Argos returned from wherever he had been, carrying a fruit tart in one paw. Gen scratched him behind the ears as he gobbled it up.

"I think he's well enough to go home tomorrow."

"Good, I'm glad." The little monkey looked up at Pollux with frosting on his cheeks. Despite all the eyes, Pollux had grown accustomed to having Argos around. He would miss him too.

While they ate, the musicians played slightly out of tune to the beat of the rain outside. Pollux's fingers ached to play. It was like an itch he couldn't satisfy. But it was best if he got used to that itch. The days of Lux were over.

Gen set down her fork. "Let's dance." She held out a hand for him, and Pollux choked on his dinner.

"You want me to dance?" As much as he wanted to hold her in his arms and swing her around that dance floor, he wouldn't be able to let her go if he did. "I don't think so."

"Fine." She shrugged. "Argos, come with me." She curled her finger to the monkey, and he jumped on her shoulder with cream-covered paws.

Gen took him on the dance floor and spun in circles while Argos wove around her ankles. Pollux laughed. Until he noticed the other people on the dance floor moving away from her, pointing and whispering.

The woman at the table behind him said, "That's the daughter of the one who killed all those men."

The vein throbbed in his neck. Pollux should turn around and say something to her, and he couldn't force the words from his mouth. *Nonconfrontational* would be etched into the surface of his coffin. The only people he could stand up to were his father and sister, but he could never stand long enough, or go far enough.

It was as if an invisible wall always stood in front of him, and he couldn't break through.

Enough! He pushed his chair back and stood up. This time he was going to break it. He was going to have one dance with Gen before he became his father's protégé.

He moved to the dance floor and stopped when a pale light blinked against the window.

He narrowed his eyes. He knew that blink. It was his sister's indentured spirit. Pollux had told his father it was a mistake to get Cas her own personal ghost. Their father had bought it to soothe his guilt over cutting her out of their inheritance. Had she come to beg Pollux for help on Cas's behalf?

He went back to the table, picked up one of Bale's empty wine-glasses, and slammed it over the little spirit. The people at the table next to his glared when the silverware hit the floor.

Underneath the glass, the spirit blinked frantically. Because she had been bound by a SpiritWatcher, there was something corporeal about her, enough to be seen and heard and trapped. She couldn't escape.

Pollux tapped his finger on the side of the glass. "I'll let you out of there when you tell me why you're here."

The light blinked with less fervor.

"Will you answer me?"

She blinked twice, and he took that as a *yes*.

Leaning his ear to the table, he lifted the glass just enough to hear. "She escaped. She's on her way here to get the Hydra and the tie. She plans to defeat you."

Pollux slumped back into his chair and looked to Gen and Argos still making a scene on the dance floor. The light swept from under the glass and hovered in front of him.

"Why did she want me to know this?" he asked.

"She doesn't," Delia whispered. "I am telling you for myself. I knew you would want to know, and I want something in return."

"What?"

The spirit moved closer, hovering at the end of his nose. "If Lady Castor dies, you get my box. I want your promise you'll set me free when that happens, and I won't tell her we spoke."

He bit down on the inside of his cheek. "Done," he said. "You have my word." He didn't have any need for a personal ghost.

"Thank you." The blinking light soared through an open window into the rain. Pollux watched her leave, wondering if he could trust her at all. He could trust, though, that if Cas had escaped their father, she would be coming here. She would rather die than lose.

He looked to Gen, spinning around in her red dress. She looked so happy. Because she assumed she had already won, but she hadn't, not if Castor had a chance at the tie.

What would Gen do if she knew Cas was on her way here?

He knew the answer. She would try to kill the Hydra too, and both she and Cas would die in front of the immortal beast. He couldn't let that happen. This had gone far enough. Further than far enough. If Cas was on the isle, Pollux had one more chance to talk to her, one more chance to stop her. To end this. He could bring her home to Arcadia and they could solve this the way it should be solved. With reason.

"You are missing a lot of fun."

Pollux jerked around. Gen stood at the side of the table, the sleeve to the red dress slipping off her shoulder, her hair sticking to her flushed cheeks.

"Oh, I . . ."

"I insist you join us. I won't take 'no' for an answer."

Gen grabbed his arm and pulled him with a kind of strength he couldn't refuse, even if he'd wanted to. If he tried, she might walk away with his arm.

He took Gen's hands, ready to dance to the upbeat song when it abruptly changed to something much slower. She pulled into his chest and looked up at him. A thin sheen of sweat glistened off her silver skin. She practically glowed.

"I feel guilty," she said.

"You do?" His voice quaked.

"Dancing and eating while Father is still in prison. I know I had to tend to Argos immediately, and I couldn't get him home in the rain but I still feel . . . it was easier not to agonize over him when I was in misery too. Does that make sense?"

"It does."

She rested her head against his chest, and he pressed his palm into her back.

He wouldn't take this from her.

Tomorrow, when the rains stopped, he would find Castor. He would convince her to draw out of the contest versus getting killed by the Hydra, and he would give her half of everything: the StormMaker fortune, his title . . . whatever she wanted. They could change Arcadia together, and this would end the way it should have ended, without ever beginning.

Gen's finger slid across his shoulder, across the scars on his neck to the edge of his hairline. She tangled them through his hair. His breath caught. They stopped moving to the music, and Pollux went very still. He tightened his hand on her hip, to push her away, and instead she moved closer, tilting her chin upward. If he dipped his own chin, his lips would touch hers. He had envisioned this moment a thousand times, and here it was, begging him to grab it.

He couldn't do it.

He was essentially betraying her by not telling her that Cas was on the move. He couldn't kiss her and lie to her with the same mouth.

"I think we should—"

Gen pressed her lips to his before he could finish his thought, and then he forgot what he was going to say. Gen's lips were softer than he could have imagined. She tasted like salt from dinner and smelled like the floral soap from the washroom. Pollux slid his hand to the small of her back, and she parted her lips.

Then he felt something different, like a flash of lightning sparking between them. He was anxious, confused, sad, and incredibly lonely. He felt like every truth he'd thought he'd known had suddenly become a lie.

Pollux snapped back and looked down at Gen and her swollen red lips. Those were her thoughts, not his.

"I felt your feelings," he whispered.

She wrung her hands together. "It was an accident. I didn't know I could . . . I didn't mean to."

She had used her mind magic on him with their kiss.

"It's fine. It's getting late. I should probably go to bed."

"Pollux, I'm sorry."

"Don't be. It's just . . ." He paused for a long time, trying to find words that weren't there. "Goodnight," he finally said.

"Goodnight," she whispered.

Pollux paid the bill and went upstairs. He hadn't been thinking. He hadn't known that by kissing her she could . . . she could . . . *feel* him. If they'd kissed any longer, she might have discovered how he really felt about her, how long he'd pined for her. Or worse, she could have found out that Castor was free and on her way here. Then he would never keep her from the Hydra.

CHAPTER 29

GEN

Gen watched Pollux run from the room. Many people ran from her. She was used to the shrieks, the glares, the hushed whispers. She preferred the ones who outright called her a "monster" to everything else. It gave her something to hang on to, something to hate.

But never, in all her years of exile, had she been stung this hard. No one had ever lured her into trusting them, saved her life multiple times, kissed her, and then run away.

She ran her finger over her lips. Her father had never told her that she could connect to another person through kissing. Was that normal? Had that happened whenever he had kissed her mother?

It hadn't felt the same as connecting to another creature, though. Chomp's thoughts tended to come in at a burst. Her old whale had sent her long drones. Andromeda, the new whale, stayed quiet for lengths of time and then broke into rambling chatter.

Pollux had hit her with a wave, a flood, so many thoughts that tangled with her own. She'd had trouble separating them. Pollux had wanted to kiss her. He also *hadn't* wanted to kiss her. He was anxious about something and worried about something else. Or had those been her feelings? She wasn't sure. She only knew that as soon as he'd had the chance to get away from her, he had.

She went up the stairs and stopped at the door to his room. Faint violin music echoed into the hall, something long and low. A sad and wistful song. She pressed her ear to the door and listened to the mournful sounds. She raised her hand to knock. She wanted to know what had scared him. She wanted to know why he played this sad song. If they could just talk for a few minutes, she was sure they could figure everything out.

Or make it a thousand times worse. She lowered her hand. She and a StormMaker didn't make sense in any shape. Even if he wasn't like his family, he still belonged with them, and she belonged with hers. This was the end of their relationship, not the beginning. He would go back to Arcadia and she would have her circus, exactly as she'd planned.

Argos curled his tail around her neck in solace. She patted him on the back and returned to her own room, collapsing face-first onto the plush blankets where Chomp slept soundly. She buried her nose in his soft fur, and he roused and licked the top of her head.

"I guess it's just you and me." She ran her fingers through his fur and sighed.

Foul Arcadians. Even without their lightning, they found ways to hurt you.

She fell asleep on Chomp's fur and woke up with a slight headache, as if some of Pollux's worries still lingered there. She rolled onto her side and rubbed the sleep from her eyes. The rain had cooled to a gentle patter. She crawled out of bed, dressed in her old, stained pants, and tucked the red dress into the waistband because she had nothing else to wear. She had officially destroyed everything.

She couldn't depend on Pollux to fund her ventures any longer. She was back on her own, which meant wearing dirty clothes, stuffing the hotel's soaps into her bag, and taking the muffins and dried nuts from the snack basket.

She fed Chomp a few strips of dried meat while she ate the muffin. Argos picked at the dried nuts.

"We're going home today," she said to him. "Both of us." She wrapped a piece of hair around one of the nuts and fed it to him. They should stay connected until she had him safely returned to his own kind. As soon as he was settled with the other monkeys, she could call Andromeda to the beach and go directly to Olympia to collect her prize.

It was everything she had ever wanted, and still, something sour swirled in her stomach. She couldn't be settled until she had Alcmen in her hands.

Someone knocked on her door. Loudly.

"Who is it?"

"Bale. Is Pollux with you?"

"No, he's probably in his own room." Why would he be with her? He had shut her out.

Gen flung open her door to an unshaven, unkempt Bale. Dark blue hair sprouted on his pale blue chin and his mussed hair hung over his watery eyes. He smelled like last night's wine.

"I need some more coin. Do you know where he is?"

"No. Check his room."

"I did."

Gen's heart seized. She swept past Bale and made her way to the neighboring room. She knew something had felt wrong. She knocked on Pollux's door and heard no answer. She knocked harder and louder, and still nothing. Then she pushed on it with both hands and wrenched it from the hinges.

The door dropped to a white tile floor, kicking up a cloud of dust.

She waved it away and found the unmade bed in front of her and Pollux's old clothes wadded on the floor.

"Pollux!" she shouted, and rummaged through the closet and washroom.

He wasn't here, and neither was his violin.

"Maybe he's down in the lobby. Or the restaurant," Gen suggested.

"Already checked there. No one has seen him since last night," Bale said.

Gen closed her fist while Argos climbed the curtains and Chomp snarled at her feet. She'd felt it herself last night. Pollux had been worried about something, and Flek, Flek had warned her. *He has secrets.*

Castor hadn't been captured. The news of her capture had come from someone in Pollux's employ. This had all been a game to trick her, to keep her from winning.

She had taken the bonding bracelet from him herself, leaving him room to betray her. He had been playing her this entire time.

"He's with Castor. And the Hydra," Gen said through clenched teeth.

"Castor's been taken by the Duke," Bale argued.

"Who says?" Gen turned on him and tangled her fingers in his shirt. "Cristos? The man Pollux pays? Did you know? Did you?"

Bale shook his head. "You're wrong," he said, beginning to sober up.

She pulled at his shirt, tearing it at the edges. She drew her other fist back. She would knock the answers out of him.

Argos skittered down the curtains and let out a loud shriek before he tore from the room. Gen watched him leave, then tightened her fist. Bale stared back at her with the same unenthused expression he always wore.

"You can hit me. It won't change anything."

She made a move to strike him and heard something shatter downstairs. Followed by screams. She released Bale.

"Argos," she whispered, and left the room to chase after the wayward monkey.

Pulsing with heat, she found Argos in the lobby, swinging from the glass chandelier. A crowd gathered to watch, but they kept to the edges. Argos pulled crystals from the light fixture and tossed them down to the tiles where they shattered into pieces.

His anger was her anger. She had fed it to him in a massive dose. This had happened to her once before, when she'd been connected to Chomp. She'd been angry at her mother for making her clean the fireplaces. She'd fed Chomp that anger and he'd bit Zusma on Gen's behalf.

Argos didn't have sharp teeth like Chomp, but he had other ways to cause damage. He leapt from the chandelier to a tapestry on the wall and ripped through it.

"Come down here!" she shouted at him, and he ignored her. She tried to calm herself and couldn't. Pollux had betrayed her. Over and over again, and she had . . . she had been falling for him. How stupid. How foolish.

The hotel guards came onto the floor, brandishing vials of Arcadian lightning. The sight of them only made Gen more furious. Those foul StormMakers were always ruining her! Argos threw more crystals to the floor. She didn't know what to do. If she couldn't get Argos under control, they would kill him.

She pressed her hands to the side of her head. "Calm down. Calm down."

Chomp snarled by her ankle. Thankfully he wasn't under her control or he would be tearing through everyone in this lobby.

When she'd been a child, Alcmen had calmed Chomp by feeding him some of his own hairs to take control of him.

She didn't have Alcmen. She had no one.

"Oy! You little beast. Get down here!" Bale shouted at Argos from the floor and pitched something at him. A piece of fruit, it looked like.

Argos stopped plucking the chandelier apart and snatched the fruit. He shoved it into his mouth, at least giving Gen a temporary reprieve to do something. She took a deep breath, trying to calm herself, and then the monkey disappeared.

Not from sight. From her mind. She couldn't hear him in her thoughts anymore.

He skittered down from the chandelier, slid down the curtains, and landed on Bale's shoulder.

"Come on," he growled, and stomped out of the room.

"Who is going to pay for this?" The hotel manager ruffled his feathers at the broken glass, sparkling on the tile floor.

"Charge it to Lord Pollux," Gen said, and chased after Bale.

She caught him at the top of the stairs and grabbed him by the arm.

"You're a MindWorker. Like me." A very strong one, like Thylox, if he could wrench control of Argos away from her like that.

"Not like you," he snapped at her. "And don't call me that."

He reached his room and flung open the door. Gen caught it before he could slam it in her face.

"Why didn't you tell me?" she demanded.

"Because I don't want it. This power causes nothing but pain and trouble wherever it goes."

Gen crossed her arms over her stomach. A MindWorker had convinced Bale's girlfriend to swim out to sea. Where she drowned.

"It was you," she whispered. "You told her to swim out to the boat." No wonder Bale had never warmed to her. He hated her because he hated himself.

"I was young. Foolish. I did it with a kiss." He scratched the top of Argos's head, and Gen thought about her kiss with Pollux last night, how she had been able to feel his thoughts. Not enough, though. Not enough to know he would betray her. Not enough to control him.

She had to go. She had to stop him before he helped Castor kill the Hydra.

"Thank you for saving Argos, but I need to go."

Bale stood up. "He wouldn't betray you."

Gen snorted. "As if I would take your word for it. You work for him."

He bowed his head and pinched the bridge of his nose. "You are both such fools."

"I am not—"

"He likes you. He is doing all of this for you. Not Castor. Can't you see that?"

"No." Gen shook her head. Pollux had only been pretending to like her to help his family. Then she remembered how he had defended her against the Lion's men and swept them to safety when Castor blasted them out of the sky, how he was able to play a song for her about her whale, in perfect detail.

But that was all part of the ruse, wasn't it?

"Then where is he? Why did he leave us?"

"I don't know. But I know whatever he is doing is for you."

Gen's cheeks warmed. "I am still going to the Hydra."

"Then I'll come with you."

"I don't want you to come."

He shrugged. "You don't have a choice. Besides, I want to see the look on your face when you find out I'm right."

She narrowed her eyes at him, and they left the hotel together.

They went to the market, where vendors shook the excess rainwater from their awnings and the criers claimed their positions to begin advertising events and tours. She approached the first crier she found offering transport to the Hydra.

"I need to reach the Hydra," she said.

He eyed her up and down, the blue feathers on his neck shifting with the movement. When he caught sight of Chomp, snarling by her feet, he clicked his tongue. "The closest I can getcha is the viewing platform. It will be twenty silver. Each."

Gen didn't have the money. Neither did Bale. He had been in search of Pollux earlier for more coin. Then Bale pulled the bonding bracelets from his knapsack.

"How about these?"

The tour guide's eyes flared. "Done." He snatched the bracelets, worth far more than forty coins, and they followed him to his craft.

"I will pay you back. When I can," she said.

Bale smiled. "You can pay me back by groveling at my feet later to say, 'You were right, Bale. I am a total fool.'"

Gen frowned. "We'll see."

The Lernean tour guide stopped in front of a contraption strung with levers, cranks, and two patched-up wings over a small, wooden basket. They had definitely paid far too much for a ride through the jungle on this.

"Welcome aboard." The tour guide gestured with a feathered arm to the basket. "I'm Hermes. Make sure you strap in tight. This is going to be a bumpy ride."

Gen picked up Chomp and carried him into the carriage, where she sat on a splintered wooden bench. Bale sat across from her with Argos on his shoulder, still completely under Bale's control. "Get ready for take-off!" Hermes shouted as he pulled on a pair of goggles and pulled one of the cranks.

The wings overhead flapped up and down, creaking and groaning. The rush of wind ruffled Gen's hair. Hermes pulled another lever and slowly they lifted from the ground. The basket dangled precariously from the struts. Gen pulled Chomp onto her lap and held him tight.

The craft moved outward, toward the thick outcropping of jungle trees.

"What island are you all visiting from?" Hermes shouted at them.

"The isle of Not Your Business!" Bale shouted.

"I'm only trying to make conversation," Hermes argued.

"All we wanted was a ride," Bale shot back, and Gen was glad he could be grumpy and emotionally distant to everyone else too.

They lifted over the trees into the damp air. The rains hung heavy in the atmosphere, quickly heated by the morning sun. Gen leaned over the side of the basket, searching for the Hydra's swamp.

This wasn't a simple mission to track down Pollux. If Castor was here and they were going for the Hydra, she had to beat them to it. This contest wasn't over, and it would never be over until either she or Castor claimed six tasks.

Gen had to defeat the Hydra. It was the only way she could make sure no one would ever take Alcmen from her again. It was the only way she could stop Castor from rising out of the ashes to shoot her in the back. Gen had known it would have to be this way from the moment the Empresses added the Hydra to the list of tasks.

She knew what she had to do, but how? How do you kill an unkillable thing?

"What's that over there?" Bale pointed to a pile of rubble in the trees below, a circle of shattered wood and broken stone.

"That's the old viewing platform," Hermes said.

"What happened to it?" Gen asked.

"Hydra got to it. Ate three tourists too. We moved the new platform higher up, four miles out. Don't worry. You'll be safe from up there."

She took a breath. The Hydra needed a four-mile-wide berth for safety, and she was going to march right in there and face it.

"We're coming to the viewing platform. Hold on to your hats!"

The small flying craft dropped, and Gen, Bale, and the basket dragged behind it. Gen's stomach rose into her throat. Chomp dug into her thighs with his claws. Then they evened out, jerked upright, and slowly came down on a wooden landing.

Hermes pulled another lever and the door to the basket swung open.

"Pleasure doing business with you." He tipped his head to them.

"Thank you." She held Chomp and wobbled down the stairs.

Bale jumped down beside her, and Hermes and his craft lifted into the air to pick up another passenger. Over time, the Lerneans had lost the ability to fly with their own wings. It was said their ancestors had lost the use of their wings when their Chieftain made a bargain with Tartarus, the Sky Oracle, and the same Oracle who had gifted the StormMakers with their powers.

The Lernean Chieftain was to bring Tartarus one of the Hydra heads, and when he failed, he was banned from the skies. Their flying crafts were a way around that problem, and yet, in a thousand years, still no one had claimed a Hydra head because to take one made two more.

"Welcome to the Hydra's Lair." A Lernean tour guide approached them. Beautiful crimson feathers framed her sharp face and wide black eyes. "Is this your first time here?"

"Yes," Gen said.

"Well, here's an information sheet. Find me if you have any questions." The tour guide handed her a sheet of parchment.

The Hydra is one of the oldest and most interesting species on Lerna, first catalogued over one thousand years ago. It is the only serpent of its kind, featuring nine heads with the ability to regenerate two-fold. Another interesting feature of the Hydra is its poisonous blood. It's been discovered the only substance that can neutralize the acidic blood is the swamp water it resides in.

To kill it, she would have to kill it without removing the heads. Without letting its blood touch her. Without getting eaten in the process.

Simple. I'll have it dead and buried before lunch.

"I think I found Pollux." Bale leaned over the railing on the platform, pointing to a cluster of trees shaking in a violent wind. A crack of thunder followed, and one of those trees split down the center, collapsing in halves.

"That's toward the Hydra." Gen closed her fist.

She had been right. He had betrayed her. The pulse in her temple flared. She picked up Chomp, cradled him under her arm, and launched over the railing.

"You have my permission to tear him limb from limb," Gen whispered in Chomp's ear when they hit the muddy ground. He turned and licked her ear.

CHAPTER 30

POLLUX

Pollux ran down the jungle path. Mud splashed his boots from the wet ground, soaked by the rain. He had to get to Castor before she reached the Hydra. He'd barely slept last night, and before the rains had stopped, he'd gotten up, dressed, and paid for transport to the viewing platform. But Castor would be ahead of him. She always was.

He followed a set of smaller footsteps in the mud, unquestionably Castor's. He leapt over a fallen log and stopped. No more footsteps. Where was she?

"Go away, Lux," her voice called through the trees.

He searched the leaves for a glimpse of her white hair. "Cas?"

The scars on his neck prickled in warning, and he unlatched the case of his violin. He could lose the other half of his face today, and Gen wasn't here with her gentle hands and smelly cream to fix him.

"Stop following me." His sister emerged from the trees with a crackling ball of lightning in her palm. The sparks from it illuminated the solid set of her chin, the defiance in her eyes. She wasn't playing. Not that she ever was. Everything Cas did was done with intention, from entering this contest to burning his face.

He pulled his violin to his chin and touched the bow to the strings. This was it, the end of the song, the Symphony of Castor versus Pollux. They had been playing this tune for a while, two separate pieces that sometimes collided in a spray of sparks or burned flesh. But they'd finally reached the crescendo. No turning back.

"You can't defeat the Hydra," he said.

"Says who?"

"Cas . . . the beast has lived for a thousand years. You're going to lose, and you're going to die. I can't let that happen."

She heaved a breath. "You're only saying this because you want your circus girl to win."

"I want us all to win. Father is going to send you to the mines if you lose."

"Then I guess I can't lose."

Pollux pressed his fingers to the strings. "You're smarter than this. Leave. Come with me, and we'll tell Father you changed your mind. I'll split Arcadia with you. Equally. Cas, we can make our own doctrine. Father can't take it from both of us, and I guarantee, you're not going to get that kind of offer from the Hydra."

The lightning in Castor's hand burned with less fervor. This was what he should have done before. He should have been fighting *with* his sister, not against her. He only hoped he wasn't too late.

"How can I trust you?" Cas shouted. "You chose her over me."

"And you went to the lottery behind my back. You knocked my chariot out of the sky. We could have solved this at home if you'd only talked to me."

"He won't let us do what you're saying. He won't let us split it."

"We won't give him a choice, Cas. One day, Father won't be able to run our lives. We'll be in charge of them. Let's start now. We can have the documents drawn up today. Arcadia is ours. It always has been, it always will be."

"I don't know."

His sister had been clinging to this dream for years, of being in absolute control of the StormMakers. It would take more than a few choice words to push her from her plan.

He always knew what she wanted. He should have spoken to her long before the lottery, long before their father declared him the heir to Arcadia. Like Cas, though, he'd always thought their father would pick her. Not him. He should have known it would take more than that for their father to forgo tradition. Cas knew, which was why she was here. She thought she was on her own, and Pollux siding with Gen only proved her fears.

Even though he was partly to blame, he couldn't let Cas go through with this. He had to stop her one way or another. He ran his bow across the strings, and a thick fog poured through the trees. "I'm sorry, Cas, but I can't let you go to the Hydra."

The mist swallowed him, then her. He couldn't see anything, but he felt his bow and his strings. He didn't need his eyes, only his fingers. Cas wouldn't be able to hit him blind.

"Now we have nothing but time to talk," he said.

"Quit it, Lux."

"I will, when you say yes. Even if you kill the Hydra, it only gets you the tie."

"Then I'll win in the second round."

"What if you don't?"

"He won't forgive me, Lux. He won't let me come home."

"He will."

"He won't," she said. "I know him better than you do. While you were off playing your violin with Mother, I was the one by his side. He doesn't forgive."

A gust of wind swept across them, clearing away the fog.

Cas reappeared from the mist. Pollux readied to play another fog when he spotted a set of sharp, brown eyes watching them from the trees.

Gen.

Behind her stood Bale, shaking his head. He and Gen had found him. Pollux had wanted to finish this before they'd noticed he'd gone missing.

When he'd left, he'd considered leaving a note. But when he took the pen and paper, he didn't know what to write, and so he just left. He didn't think they'd track him so soon.

If Castor spotted them, this was the end of negotiations. She'd think this was all a trick, and she would never speak to him again.

"Cas, come with me now. You can't kill the Hydra." He reached his hand out to her, trying to keep her focus on him and not the trees behind her.

"You swear to me you'll share everything with me. The title, the fortune, the business?"

"I swear it." He tried not to sound desperate as he stretched his hand farther. "We won't sign anything unless we both agree to it."

"Maybe." She was breaking, but not fast enough.

Bale and Gen moved step by step into the trees. As soon as they crossed behind the next one, they would be out of view.

"We're going to keep selling lightning."

"We can talk about it."

"It has to be in the deal."

Bale and Gen were almost gone, and then he and Cas could start the true negotiations. Bale took one more step, and something snapped.

Castor spun around, and her anger rose, along with the ball of lightning in her hand.

"I knew it," she hissed. "This was all a distraction."

"It wasn't. I swear." He looked at Gen and screamed inside his head, *Go! Run!*

"You're a liar. You were always lying." Cas raised her arm.

Pollux pulled his bow across the strings, but Cas didn't fling the lightning at him. She sent it toward Gen.

His heart clenched. She knew exactly how to inflict the most pain on him.

He pulled on the strings and swept up the lightning as Gen moved to shield her face. His wind picked up the fireball and flung it into the sky. Before it escaped, it singed some of the trees. Thankfully, the ground was still wet or they would light this entire jungle on fire.

"Run!" he shouted to Gen. "I can't hold her indefinitely."

Gen made her way downhill to the Hydra's swamp, Bale close behind. Castor produced a second ball of lightning and tossed it toward his face.

He flinched before he played a small tornado, swept up the lightning, and sent it to the left. It struck a tree, scattering sparks on the ground.

"I see you can defend yourself. When you want to." Castor put her hand to her belt for a new vial.

Pollux held the bow to his violin, ready to deflect whatever she sent at him next. "I'd rather you didn't keep trying to cook me." The scars on his neck prickled.

"I didn't mean to hit you," she said.

"That might be more believable if you weren't trying to do it again."

"Good point." She conjured her own fog. Pollux shifted his bow to play a breeze, and when the fog parted, his sister was gone. Damn. At least he knew where she was going, to the Hydra and Gen, which worried him.

He kept his violin to his chin and took after her. Ahead, something crashed through the trees, something large and round—a ball of water.

It came fast. He couldn't avoid it. It struck him in the chest and knocked the air from his lungs, soaked through his skin. He slammed into a tree and clung to his violin. When he sank to the ground, he played her a frigid wind. He didn't want to hurt her, but he needed to keep her down. It was the only way she would stay still long enough to listen.

Snowflakes formed in the humid jungle, and the temperature dropped from sweltering to brisk. It was a song from his composition "The Long Winter." He could turn a temperate theater into a block of ice in under a minute. People came to the performance dressed in their thickest coats in preparation. He'd written the song when the circus died.

He sent a storm of hailstones after his sister. They struck her in the back, and she hit the ground.

"Your attacks have improved," Castor called.

"Did you ever stop to think that maybe I didn't hit you as hard as I could? That I didn't want to hurt you?" He picked himself up from the jungle floor, soaked through and coated in mud.

"Of course I did. That was why you always lost. You're too kind, Lux. You always have been. It's why you will make a terrible Duke."

"That's why I want you to help me." He kept playing "The Long

Winter." This would be his last chance to hold her, to try and reason with her.

The humid air in the jungle turned to snowflakes. Ice crept up around Castor's legs as she tried to right herself. Her lips turned blue, and icicles clung to her lashes.

"You know," her teeth chattered, "while you're here with me, she's down there with the Hydra."

His lip twitched. He knew that, which was why he needed to end this here.

"You've let the Empresses play you, Cas. Look at you. You're about to walk to your death for something I'm offering you for free."

"You're only offering me half. If I win, I get it all." The ice climbed up her legs to her thighs. Pollux kept playing, and the ice crawled across his shoulders, making his arms stiff.

"Why do you want me out of Arcadia? What are you afraid of?"

"Why do you want her to win so badly?" Castor retorted. "Is it because of your crush? She doesn't like you, Lux. She's only pretending to get what she wants."

He flinched. It wasn't true. Last night, when they'd kissed . . . it might have been confusing, but it had been real.

Castor flung a handful of lightning at him. He leapt to the side, and the lightning careened past him, close enough to warm his skin. Cas shattered the ice on her legs and broke into a run.

Pollux switched tunes, and a burst of cloud came from his strings, along with a subtle wind. It shaped the cloud into one of his first figures, an oversized representation of his father. He sent it into Castor's path, and she leapt back, terrified.

Their father had that effect, even in cloud form.

Pollux switched to a piece from "The Last Dance of the Circus

Man" before Castor could strike back. Heavy rains dropped through the trees, hard enough to pin her to the ground. He switched quickly to the winter song, and the puddle iced where she sat. He kept playing, letting the ice crawl over her belt of storm vials.

"Let it go, Cas," he said between his teeth. "All you get from this is a tiebreaker. The next phase will be harder. If these games don't kill you, Father might."

"Let him." She struggled to break free of the ice.

"I don't want you to die. I don't want you to be exiled. You're my sister."

She stopped struggling momentarily and flung wet hair from her face. "If it weren't for her, the Mazon," she said, "would you be against me?"

"Yes," he said without pause. "Arcadia can do so much more than weapons."

"People don't want those things. They want power. Control."

"That's what *you* want."

"*I* want it because *I* don't have it," she said. "Let me have it. When I'm Duchess, you can do whatever you want. You can *be* whatever you want. We can even help Genevieve get her murdering father back."

"I can't, Cas." That wasn't enough for Gen, and it wasn't enough for him, either.

"I know." She sighed. "And I'm sorry about this." She snapped her arm up. She had one vial tucked into her palm. She ripped it open, and the air heated with lightning. Pollux fumbled for his violin. The scars on his neck and shoulder tightened. He winced in anticipation of a second burn.

He pulled his bow to conjure a wind as the lightning shot toward him. It struck hard, true, against the base of his violin. The metal warped and splintered. The vials inside cracked open, and wind and fog and rain escaped into the air. He dropped the remaining shards to the ground and watched them smolder as his sister disappeared into the trees.

She had truly become their father then. The one to destroy violin number four.

CHAPTER 31

GEN

"Here." Gen handed Chomp to Bale. "Take him and Argos and go somewhere safe."

"I'm not letting you go alone," Bale said.

"All of a sudden you're going to play the hero? You've done almost nothing to help us this entire journey!"

He winced, and Gen softened. "All I mean to say is if you want to help, take care of them." She ruffled her fingers through Chomp's fur. "He's an old chaeri, Bale. He's too old to go back to the wild. If something happens . . . he'll need someone to take care of him. He'll need a MindWorker. And someone needs to make sure Argos goes home. Please. I don't want them to get hurt."

Chomp curled into her hand and licked her palm. She wouldn't have survived these last four years without him. She always thought he would be the one to go first. Now it could be her.

Gen choked back tears. "I have to go. Promise me you'll look after him."

"I will," he said softly, and she ran.

She ran before he could change his mind, or she could change hers.

Behind her, lightning crashed and trees cracked. Bale hadn't even demanded his apology. He had been right. They had both heard Pollux and Castor talking. Pollux had been begging Castor to give up. And he had almost succeeded. If Gen had trusted him and not followed him, he might have been able to do it. Bale had been right in so many ways. Pollux had done this all for her.

Now she had to do something for him. She had to kill the Hydra quickly, before Castor killed him. This only ended when the game ended, and the game only ended once the Hydra was dead.

The footpath came to an end. Gen made her own path, cutting through branches and trees. They scraped at her skin and pulled at her hair. As the ground sloped downward, it turned muddier, tugging at her boots. She slogged through it until she came to the edge of a green swamp.

She pushed her sweat-soaked hair from her face and caught her breath. Thick, green fog rolled off the water's surface, and above that, a hook dangled from the trees. Behind her, the sky crackled with distant lightning and thunder. Pollux and Castor were still fighting, which meant he was alive.

Gen came here wholly unprepared. No helpful creatures. No weapons. She reached for the nearest tree and wrenched a thick branch from the leaves. She pulled off the smaller shoots and twigs and fashioned something like a club.

Her mother had used a club like this in the circus.

Alcmen would throw Zusma rock hogs, curled into small stone balls. She would hit them with the club toward the crowd, and before they struck the audience, a red crane would sweep them up in a basket to the delighted and slightly terrified shrieks.

With the club in her hands, and this new expansion of Mazonness, maybe Gen could find some essence of her mother and actually kill the creature. Of all the people who had faced it, none of them had been Mazon. She would be the first.

And possibly the last.

She stepped to the edge of the water and touched it with her toe. Green ripples spread to the center of the pond. An eerie quiet lingered here. No bugs buzzing. No birds chirping. Only the distant crack of thunder and wind.

The other creatures either knew to avoid the Hydra's swamp, or they'd been eaten.

She tapped the water with the top of her club. Where was the thing? The water bubbled, and she took a step back. Something rose to the surface. Not a giant serpent, something small and orange, a piece of shell. Crab maybe? It must have been a remnant from one of the Hydra's meals.

Something jerked in the trees. A pulley. It dragged the hanging hook into the trees and returned it with a hunk of bleeding meat dripping off the end. Gen glanced over her shoulder, to the distant viewing platform. They had scopes up there for people to watch. They could likely see her and were luring the Hydra out of hiding for a show. They must have put coin on her head to see if she would live or die.

Gen held her club with both hands, breathing in and out. The meat dangled in the sky, dripping fat onto the water. She grabbed a fistful of hair and wrenched it from her scalp. It was foolish to assume she could control the Hydra, but it was worth a try. As far as she knew, no MindWorker had tried to fight the Hydra, either, and her current plan was to throw everything she had at the beast and hope it was enough.

The water stirred. She sank her fingers into the wood club, and her arm pulsed with strength. A black serpent head shot from the water, and Gen stumbled back.

Sharp teeth snatched and tore at the meat. Another blur of black cut through the air, and another. She could barely separate the heads. The meat was almost gone, and as soon as it was, the serpents would either sink back into the swamp or be looking for another meal. She had to move.

She pitched her handful of hair into the air. It landed on the hanging meat and one of the serpents swallowed it. The MindWorker string snapped back to her and she felt the snake in her head.

Meat. Hungry. Kill.

It screeched louder than any other creature that had spoken to her before and brought with it an enormous hunger, a desire to destroy everything in its line of sight.

Gen could use this to her advantage.

There's more meat for you if you destroy the others, she said to it.

Her snake wavered in the center and turned to one of the others. It snapped its jaw open and closed sharp teeth around a neighboring head.

The head snapped free, and black ichor sprayed across the water. A few drops landed on Gen's arm and sank into her flesh. Fire burned across her skin. She remembered the note about poisoned blood on the information sheet and dropped her arm in the swamp to douse the fire.

Her snake lunged at another, biting into its neck. That serpent snapped back. The one that had already been beheaded wriggled in the water, splitting into two.

Stop fighting, she called to her snake. This wouldn't work. If they kept attacking each other, they would only make more heads.

The water parted, and a white serpent emerged. The black heads separated to make way for it. Gen went still to avoid being caught by its red gaze. The white serpent instead turned its red eyes on the snake Gen controlled, and without hesitation, snapped the head free.

Gen's MindWorker strings broke, and she moved to avoid the blood spray. The white snake had known which of its heads had been poisoned.

The white serpent whipped its head to the shore, toward Gen. Gen clutched her club in sweaty hands and braced herself for an attack.

Kill this thing and end this, she told herself. *Kill this thing and you win the game. You never have to fight again.*

The white serpent flicked its tongue, and three of the black serpents flew at Gen in a flurry of teeth. Gen swung her club in one wide arc, striking all three of them. The last one she hit hard enough to knock the head loose. It flew across the swamp and smashed against the trees, thankfully taking the poison blood spill with it.

But another beheaded snake meant more coming her way. She was making the thing more, not less. She had to drive the serpents back without beheading them.

She knocked the fang off another snake and jabbed one in the neck, only partially beheading it. The third, she crushed the skull. Another came at her, and out of desperation, she whacked it as hard as she could.

Another head lost.

This was impossible.

She set aside the club and picked up a rock. As she lifted it over her head, she heard the sound of fabric ripping. Her pants, burst at the seam. Of course. She flung the boulder into the center of snapping snakes. The weight of it dragged three of them under the water.

She picked up her club and swung again. Another head free, a splash of blood on her leg. She stepped into the water to douse the fire. More serpents came for her, and from behind them, the white one watched with glinting red eyes, smiling, if snakes could smile.

The Hydra knew she couldn't kill it. It knew *nothing* could kill it.

Gen backed out of the water. She swung her club back and forth to keep the snakes at bay and turned over her shoulder to the trees. She would have to run and hope one of the serpents didn't snatch her by the foot before she ran far enough, fast enough.

She struck aside another head, readying herself to make for the trees when a cold wind pushed through the leaves.

"Pollux," she breathed.

Her heart lifted, and she stretched her ears for the sound of his violin. How could she have ever doubted him? He always came for her. Always.

But the music never came. Instead Castor emerged from the jungle with her hair crisp and white, sprinkled with snow. She lifted her arms, and dark clouds filled the sky, thunder rumbled, lightning flashed. The storm drew the attention of the giant serpent.

"Maybe I should wait for the thing to kill you," Castor said as she flipped a ball of lightning from palm to palm, grinning like the snake. "Then there will be no tiebreaker."

"Where's Pollux?" Gen demanded, her heart pounding. If she had hurt him, Gen would make Castor pay dearly.

"Why don't you let me worry about my brother?"

"Like you did at the stables? You nearly killed him."

Castor flinched. "You don't have to pretend with me. I know you're only using him for his money, his resources. You can stop acting like you care."

"I do care."

"You mean to tell me you actually like him?"

"Yes. Of course I do."

Gen's heart stopped. She had known she'd developed feelings for Pollux, but at this moment, she realized those feelings dug much deeper and with a far tighter hold than she could have imagined. She ached to see him. Now, tomorrow, and the day after that. She wanted to curl up next to him while he played his violin and see that look on his face when she came in wearing a new dress, like he had been slapped into a daze.

Oh no. She was in love with a StormMaker.

"Well, that's too bad," Castor said. "Because you can't have him. Or this win. I'm going to kill the snake."

She flung her ball of lightning toward the swamp in a spray of light, and the fire touched the water. The gray turned to bright, bright white, and Gen threw her arm over her face to shield her eyes. She fell back on the mud and curled into a ball.

Charred snake wafted on the air, and the swamp turned hot. The snake wailed and hissed, popping and crunching, crackling and burning. It shrieked like it was dying, and Gen wondered if it was.

When the shrieking stopped, and the light turned dim, Gen opened her eyes. Smoke pooled in the humid air. When it cleared, she saw the first Hydra head and instinctively reeled back. But this head was not moving. None of them were. They all lay perfectly still in the mud, burned and smoking. The heads fanned out from the center in a circle, charred husks of themselves. Only the white one remained, covered in ash with its tongue lolling from a stiff jaw.

Gen's shoulders dropped. Castor had done it. She had killed the unkillable Hydra.

Castor climbed down from her rock, smiling, and kicked the

white serpent with her boot. The massive head shifted to one side and rolled back.

She laughed. "The mighty serpent has fallen."

Gen stared at the dead serpent, willing it to move, hiss, bite . . . anything. Castor couldn't have won. Not that easily. The beast had survived for centuries, against hundreds of brave and foolish warriors. How could she waltz in here with her lightning and kill it in minutes?

But here it was, the still and charred body as undeniable proof. Castor had won. She'd defeated the Hydra, and it had only taken one blast of lightning.

Wait, no . . . this wasn't a win. She had only secured the tie. Gen would have another chance. Another chance to fight. Another chance to die.

"I've decided to be kind." Castor wiped the mud from her boots onto the dead serpent. "Despite you trying to kill me, and turning my brother against me, it doesn't suit either of us to keep this up any longer. Save us both the trouble of the tiebreaker. Give up, and I'll pay you a million in silver to step away."

"I can't." Gen shook her head. A million coins, two million coins . . . even though that number made her head spin, it wouldn't save her. Money couldn't clear Alcmen's name.

"What is it? You think you can keep up this charade with my brother and take it all the way to Arcadia? You think you can marry him, become the Duchess of Arcadia? Take my place?"

"No." Gen cared for Pollux, yes. She wasn't near ready to discuss marriage. She also had no desire to be Duchess of the StormMakers. She'd rather wade through piles of manure again than be known as Gen, Duchess of Storms.

Castor sighed. "Well, I can't say that I like it, but something can be arranged. If you really do care for Lux, Lady of Storms is a commanding title. There isn't much the StormMakers can't gain, especially for themselves." She paced in front of her. "You give this up, let me have my claim to Arcadia, and we will do everything in our power to get your father out of prison. We always protect our own. Let me handle the business, and you and Lux can do whatever you want. Play violin, have dogs jump through flaming hoops . . . I don't really care."

Two days ago, Castor had tried to kill her. Today she was inviting her to join the family.

"I don't want to marry Pollux," Gen said.

"Then what do you want?"

"I want my father. My reputation. I want our circus. I want my mother back. I want everything how it was four years ago."

Castor snorted. "That's impossible."

"I know that. But if I win this, it will be as close as I can get." She wiped the mud from her face and started up the hill. "I will see you at the tiebreaker."

She needed to find Bale, Chomp, and Pollux, get something substantial to eat, and change into clothes without tears or stains. No, the contest wasn't over. She would have to fight again, harder, possibly longer, but at least she wouldn't have to do it today.

"You're making a mistake," Castor called.

"Maybe," Gen said over her shoulder, and stopped. Something shifted in the water. Gen's muscles tightened. "Castor, I think you should step away from the water."

"Why?" Castor balled her hands on her hips. "There's nothing to be afraid of." She kicked one of the dead Hydra heads as proof, and the white serpent head blinked one red eye.

"Castor, move!" Gen shouted.

Castor spun as the white serpent shot up from the water, very much alive. She managed to fire off a crack of lightning before it struck.

"It's still alive!" Castor shouted.

Worse than alive. All of the black heads that had been charred and broken wriggled in the water, splitting into two.

Gen picked up her club. "We need to go. Before they re-form."

"You're welcome to leave." Castor's hands crackled with lightning. "I'm not going anywhere."

The first of the regrown snakes launched at Castor. She drove it back with a shot of lightning. The serpent burst into flames and dropped to the water, charred and black. Her lightning sealed the wound and saved them from the blood spray. But it didn't save them from the doubling heads.

One of the other snake heads lunged at Gen. She whacked it in the neck and moved away from the swamp.

"We can't kill it. We have to go."

Gen hadn't been able to defeat it before, when it had fewer heads, and this proved Castor's lightning couldn't kill it either. It truly was immortal.

"I'm not going anywhere." Castor raised her hands to the sky, and the dark clouds rumbled with thunder.

Gen should leave her here. A part of her wanted to. A greater part knew Pollux would never forgive her if she did. She would never forgive herself. She beat away another snake head and moved to Castor. She would carry her out of here over her shoulder if she had to.

She made a move to do that when something else rose from the depths of the swamp.

"What is that?" Castor shouted.

"I don't know."

The water already teemed with snake heads, sixteen maybe, thirty-two—they didn't stay still long enough to count them. But this was no snake. A piece of orange shell emerged from the murk: a giant claw, followed by another claw and a hard-shelled body. A massive crab stood on the bank of the swamp, blinking at Gen with two beady black eyes.

This had not been on the pamphlet.

CHAPTER 32

CASTOR

Castor scorched another serpent head with lightning. Beside her, Genevieve struck at the massive crab that had appeared. She smashed it with her club, and her tree branch shattered. Oh well.

The massive crab wasn't on their list of required tasks. As long as it remained focused on Gen and not her, Castor didn't really care.

She pitched another ball of lightning, and six more serpent heads went down in ash. Another group came at her. She reached for a vial of wind and pushed them into the water. She was very aware that even after capturing several vials of lightning from the storm she passed through on her way here, the storms on her belt were disappearing quickly—thanks to her brother's interfering.

The thing had been unmistakably dead before, and now it slithered across the water in uncountable heads. They grew faster than before while the white one hovered behind the mass. That was the one Castor needed to reach. It seemed to be the key to regenerating the others, and this time, when the serpent fell, she would char it to ash before it could rise.

She hit two more black snakes with wind and reached for another vial. Before she could, seven more serpents lunged at her.

Beside her, something splashed. She flicked her eyes to the Mazon. Gen stood under the crab with her muscles tensed and her hair dripping with mud. The crab snapped, and she grabbed it by the claw. One twist of her body, and the claw snapped free.

Castor winced. The Mazon had vastly improved her skill since the statue smashing on Athenia. If Castor didn't kill the Hydra soon, Gen might, and steal the win.

Castor grabbed another wind vial and sent it at the center of the Hydra. It pushed the writhing black heads aside and opened up a direct path to the white head of the Hydra. Castor flung lightning between the snake's venomous eyes. It dodged quickly to the left, and her lightning exploded on a rock. One of the serpents lunged at her, and Castor flattened to the mud.

She lifted her head, reminded of how she had eaten mouthfuls of manure at the stables. She had vowed then she wouldn't lose again. Looking at the swamp, the mass of black snakes moved in from the sides to defend their leader. Castor reached for another vial when something wrapped around her ankle.

A scaly appendage grabbed her foot and dragged her toward the water. Three of the snakes lunged at her, fangs bared.

"Let me go." She ripped open a vial of lightning.

Lines of fire struck each snake in turn, but she didn't hit the one that held her. It yanked her into the swamp up to her chin. She swallowed a mouthful of brackish water and slammed the heel of her boot into the serpent.

The serpent yanked on her foot, and green water poured down her throat. She scrambled for another vial on her belt and felt only empty spaces. She looked to Gen. The Mazon slammed the severed crab claw into the crab's shell.

"Hel—"

She went under. She couldn't see anything. The water was so

murky. She fumbled for her belt and kicked her legs, trying to break free. The serpent tightened its grasp, painfully. She sucked in another mouthful of water and choked. There was no air.

She twisted her body back and forth, frantically trying to escape its hold or reach a vial, and the snake kept pulling her deeper, farther away from the air and light. She was going to die here. A loser. That was what struck her the hardest.

Dying a winner was acceptable. Dying a loser was impossible.

She clawed at the water, thinking of Adikia, the girl with the purple hair, and how she would never know what other devious plans the girl had made.

The tight hold on her ankle suddenly loosened. Castor pulled free and swam her way to the surface. She broke through and spat out filthy swamp water before she collapsed on the mud. Her heart pounded, her vision blurred, but above her, she made out the outline of her brother, bouncing a rock in his hand.

"Get up, Cas. Get out of here."

He flung his rock at the Hydra, striking one measly head between the eyes. It only succeeded in pissing the thing off.

"Don't," she choked, and fumbled for her waist.

She snatched one more vial as the black snake heads circled around them, slowly. There were too many. The snakes couldn't move without running into one another.

She ripped open the vial and blasted a hole through the center of them, trying to reach the white head and end this. The smell of charred snake filled the air, and a handful of heads dropped, making way for more to strike.

They launched themselves at Pollux this time.

"Pollux, go!" she shouted.

Pollux flung another rock that bounced harmlessly off a serpent skull. All he had were rocks. She had taken away his violin, his means of defense, and he came to her anyway.

She struck one of the snakes with lightning. Three more came at Pollux in a spray of teeth. He held up an arm as if that would stop them.

"No!" Castor screamed.

She had never wanted Pollux to die in all of this. She had only wanted what was rightfully hers. She should have taken his offer. She should have tried harder with him. She readied herself for the agony of losing him forever when a massive crab claw came down from the sky.

It crushed all three serpents in one strike, in a crunch of bones, and buried them in the mud. Castor spun to face the Mazon.

Behind her, the crab sat in the water, all six legs in the air. Gen had killed it. Her skin shone bright silver in the sunlight, and over her shoulder, she brandished the massive crab claw. Castor's breath caught. For a moment, she saw someone else. Not her competitor, not some washed-up circus girl, or a murderer's daughter. She saw a warrior.

"Don't touch him!" Genevieve shouted at the snake.

She swung the crab claw back and forth in front of her, knocking Hydra heads out of her way as if they were blades of grass. Some of the blood sprayed onto her skin. She washed it in the water and kept going until she reached the center, the white serpent.

It was fully exposed.

This was Castor's chance. She had one vial of lightning left and a clear and undeniable shot to kill the thing. She reached for the vial as Genevieve stood thigh high in the water with her severed crab claw.

Gen had the snake distracted. Castor could hit it this time, and it wouldn't run. She opened the vial, ready to char the snake for good. The Hydra lunged for Genevieve, teeth bared, and Gen swung her crab claw with both hands.

The crab claw plunged into the center of the Hydra's chest, spraying blood everywhere. The Hydra shrieked in agony, and Castor's lightning flew right over its head. Genevieve twisted the crab claw back and forth while poisoned blood sizzled on her skin.

The Hydra hissed and screamed, a sound that pierced the air.

Castor covered her ears. Her brother ran into the water. He grabbed Genevieve and pushed her into the swamp water to wash off the blood. The Hydra blinked its red eyes two more times before it dropped.

The swamp went still, a kind of stillness that could only be found in the darkest part of night, or when someone or something takes its last breath. This time the Hydra wouldn't rise. Castor didn't need to kick it to know. She felt it in every one of her panting breaths and the splash of water as Lux plucked Gen out of it.

He held Genevieve in his arms and buried his nose in her neck, and the Mazon clutched him with the same desperation.

They really cared for each other.

Enough that the Gen had killed the Hydra, not to win, but to save him.

Castor didn't know whether to hate her or thank her. She loved Lux too. But he would never love her as much. No one would. Her father didn't. Her mother didn't, and now Pollux had left her behind too.

Castor had lost everything. This marked Genevieve's sixth task. There would be no tiebreaker. There would be no Duchess of Arcadia. She would be banished, sent to the mines. Nothing.

"Cas, are you all right?"

Lux finally acknowledged her, still holding tight to Gen's hand.

"Don't speak to me," she snapped. Lightning burned in her veins. "You betrayed me. You betrayed Arcadia. I never want to see you again." She stumbled away from the water to hide in the trees. She was the Lady of Arcadia. If she lost that . . . who was she?

She wiped her face with the cleanest part of her shirt and tasted sour swamp water. She spat it out. She had lost. She. Had. Lost. As much as she'd feared it, she never thought it could happen. She had pinned everything on this win. *Everything.*

The Boar would be looking for payment soon, and she had nothing to give. She couldn't go home. As soon as people learned she had been disgraced by her father, no one else would take her. Everyone on her side had only been there because of her money and influence, and now those were gone.

She needed a plan, and coin. As much as she could get before her father closed her accounts. Marriage, that awful word, moved back into her vocabulary. The easiest way to maintain her position would be with a partner, someone of fortune and power. Memnon was her first thought, the leering and paunchy heir to the mining colony on Tegea, where her father would coincidentally have her sent.

He'd had a crush on her for years. He might take her even with a stained reputation and nothing to offer. But he was barely one step above toiling in the mines he owned.

She had been so close to having everything, and it all slipped through her fingers with one dead snake.

She'd thought she would be the one to change Arcadia. She would be the next Tyrus, forever altering the face and government of the

StormMakers. Hundreds of years from now, people would follow her doctrine, thank her for their prosperity and renowned success.

Instead, their empire would sink, and that bitch Mazon would be at the helm. If she stayed with Lux—and why wouldn't she now that he was to be Duke of Storms?—*she* would be the Duchess, and no one would remember the failed Lady Castor.

Genevieve hadn't just won the contest, she'd taken Castor's dreams, her life.

She tripped over a rock and hit the dirt on her knees. The hot, angry tears behind her eyes spilled free. She buried her face in her hands and wept for everything that had been stolen from her. She would never forget this. Never.

CHAPTER 33

GEN

That was six. The dead Hydra in front of her was the sixth task, completed. Gen hadn't even been trying to kill it. She hadn't dreamed it possible. Her only goal had been to save Pollux from its grasp. When she'd seen it poised to devour him, something had risen up inside of her. It had been like a fire, built on rage and necessity. She could have torn apart the Hydra with her bare hands.

No one would ever hurt him again. Not while she had breath in her lungs and strength in her arms.

She nudged the white Hydra head with the toe of her boot and held her breath, waiting for it to twitch or hiss or flicker. The serpent stayed limp, unmoving, unhissing. How had she killed it? The unkillable beast?

Gen pressed her arm where blisters formed from the Hydra's blood. Nothing a little stink lizard pus wouldn't fix. She'd not only come out of this a winner, but nearly unscathed.

Well, not unscathed. She would forever be marked by scars from hoof prints and orthus bites and a vengeful Mazon Queen.

"She's gone." Pollux came jogging back from the jungle. He'd chased after Castor. "I don't know where she's going."

"You said it before. If Castor doesn't want to be found, she won't be found." Castor needed time to lick her wounds. Had Gen been the loser, she would be doing the same. Then, after she'd come to terms with her loss, she'd start devising a new plan to save her father. Gen worried that Castor would eventually do the same, concoct a plan to get rid of Pollux so she could claim the StormMakers.

He shook his head. "I tried to reason with her, Gen. I really did."

"I know. I heard."

He took her hand. "I should have told you she was coming here."

"It's all right. I think I know why you didn't."

If he had told her that Castor planned to come here, Gen would have run straight for the Hydra. He had been trying to save them both, the best way he knew how. By staying out of the fight.

"I should have told you a lot of things." He blew out a breath. "I didn't want to help you purely for Cas."

"Bale told me."

"He what?" Pollux's jaw dropped. "I am going to kill him."

"Don't." She pressed her hand to his cheek, right above Castor's burn scars. "I'm glad he told me. I was so used to assuming everyone despised me. I couldn't see anything else."

How quick she had been to believe Flek's assessment of Pollux. The big secret Pollux hid was that he liked her. She had spent four years alone with Chomp and her whale thinking everyone in the Empire despised her, and of all people to secretly admire her, it had been the Lord of Storms. She never would have guessed that one.

"You have been everything to me." He laced his fingers through her hair. "I've seen your circus fourteen times, on eight different islands. The reason I play my violin is because of you. I have wanted to talk to you so many times, and after what my family did . . . I knew you wouldn't want to look at me. I'm sorry, in so many ways I can't even begin to describe. I never imagined you would actually return my feelings, which is why I never told you. I'm a coward—"

Gen grabbed him by the collar and pulled him to her. She pressed her lips to his. A rush of feelings swam through her thoughts: relief, gratitude, desire, worry, and anxiousness. Like before, she couldn't pick through each feeling to make sense of it. She only knew that her defeat of the Hydra hadn't settled everything. Not for Pollux. Not for her.

She broke their kiss before she learned too much. She remembered what had happened with Bale and his girlfriend. She needed to get a handle on this before it went too far.

Pollux ran his tongue over his lips. "There is something else I have to say. Being the Duke of Storms is a demanding job. I won't be as free as I was before." He looked to the fallen Hydra. "I have to be the Duke, but I have a choice in how I do it. I'm not going to let him bully me anymore. When Arcadia is mine, I'm going to run it the way I see fit, and I'm going to get my sister back." He stroked his fingers through her swamp-coated hair. "I'm going to see you again, Gen. Whenever I can."

"I hope so." She nodded. Everything would change with this. Some of it good. Some of it not so good. She would take that as it came. Nothing could be worse than wading through mounds of cow manure.

Someone came skidding down the path. Bale appeared with both Chomp and Argos in tow.

"Chomp!" Gen shrieked, and knelt down to scoop him up from the mud. She pressed him to her chest and nuzzled deep into his fur.

"You both look terrible," Bale said.

"How kind of you to notice." Gen set Chomp on the ground, and he sniffed at the fallen Hydra. "I did just defeat an immortal beast, you know."

Bale looked down at the mass of serpent heads, wrinkling his nose. "It doesn't look so dangerous."

"Because it's dead. You should have seen it ten minutes ago."

"You told me not to help," he argued.

Gen sighed.

Bale threw his thumb over his shoulder. "I saw Lady Castor heading back up to the platform, and there are some other people coming down here."

"What other people?" Pollux asked as a crowd burst through the trees.

"Genevieve Drivas." A woman with blue feathers poked her nose toward Gen's. "I'm Iris Mendosa, Lernean Councilwoman. We watched the entire show from the top of the viewing platform, and I have to say, it was magnificent. It looked like you were going to lose there for a moment. You must have been terrified."

Gen blinked, trying to find her words. "I was."

"I'd never seen such a thing," another man said. "What made you think to use the crab claw?"

"I don't know."

"Can I get your autograph?" Someone else shoved a parchment and pen at her.

"I guess so." She took the pen and stared at the faces around her, the first time she had looked upon smiling faces in a while. No one sneered. No one picked up their children and ran.

They *wanted* to speak to her. They wanted to know her.

They liked her.

The Empresses had been right. She had done something grand, something bright enough to blind the people from what had happened in that tavern years ago. She had made her own reputation, and everyone had seen it.

"What was it like fighting the crab?" a boy asked her.

Gen picked up the discarded crab claw and swung it across the air. "Something like this," she said while they ducked and gasped, exactly as they had when Zusma would spin a sailboat over her head in the middle of the circus tent.

She slapped the claw into her other palm. "You see, I noticed right away the crab shell was strong, but brittle. If I twisted it just so . . . it would snap free." She slung the claw over her shoulder, and everyone gasped.

The Lernean councilwoman touched Gen on the shoulder. "Would you be willing to repeat that performance?" she asked.

"Right now?"

"No, but soon, and for a larger audience. Our problem with showing the Hydra was how far we had to keep it from people. Now that it's no longer a danger, I think we can offer a closer viewing experience, and you might be able to help us with that. What do you say?"

"You want me to do a show?"

"Yes, I suppose you could call it that."

Gen's mouth spread into a grin. By the end of the week, she would be known as *Gen, the Hydra-Slayer. Gen, the Giant Crab-Killer.*

Behind her, Pollux watched with a faint smile on his lips, nodding for her to enjoy her moment. She smiled back, vowing not to forget that when everyone else had despised her, he hadn't. He had loved the monster.

EPILOGUE

GEN

The whale burst out of the water in the shallows of the isle of Athenia. Gen rolled back on her heels and landed in a pile of seaweed. She sat up, plucked the seagrass out of her hair, and reached for her hat.

Andromeda opened her mouth, and Gen picked up her bag. She called for Chomp, who was conveniently awake after being rattled around in Andromeda's mouth. Traveling inside a young and eager whale had some benefits; Gen didn't have to wake up her sleepy chaeri on her own, as the bumpy ride did that.

The young whale also shortened every trip by minutes if not hours, she complained much less, and she was eager to go anywhere Gen asked. And still, every time Gen called for Andromeda, and the small, pink whale answered with a pleasant *I'm coming!,* Gen wished for the long, droning complaints of the old whale.

She hoped, wherever infinity whales went when they died, he had an endless supply of fish to eat and no reason to complain. Soon, she would be able to give him eternal peace by answering his last wish. She would reunite their family.

Gen stepped off the whale's tongue onto the white sands of Athenia. "I might be a while," she said. "You can wander, but stay safe."

Andromeda whistled at her in response and wriggled back into the water. She splashed Gen with a flip of her tail before she sank under the surface.

Gen had planned to free the whale after the competition, but Andromeda wanted to stay. Without Castor trying to hunt her down, she would be as safe with Gen as she would any other place. Maybe even safer. Only a fool would try to kill the whale that belonged to the Hydra-Slayer.

Gen smiled and tugged on her jacket. The white Hydra scales glimmered in the afternoon sun. A tailor on Lerna had made the jacket for her. After her wardrobe had been completely decimated, Gen had had nothing else to wear. The Lernean Council had given her some prepayment in exchange for a contract to do twelve performances on the island with the stuffed corpse of the Hydra. A reenactment of sorts.

She'd agreed for an upfront payment and a few Hydra pieces to improve her wardrobe.

They had given her enough of an advance she could buy a new ship too—as soon as she collected her father. They could start rebuilding immediately.

She approached the palace bridge. The two Gargarean guards standing at attention on either side whispered to one another, not quietly enough. She heard every insult. She smiled as she passed and tilted her hat a touch lower. "Good morning."

They glared at her shoulders, too cowardly to say anything to her face. She was the Hydra-Slayer. No Gargarean had ever slain a Hydra. They had only been able to defeat the Mazons with the help of the Arcadians, and soon, when Hippolyta crawled from her pit with her new children, they would all be running for their lives.

She would enjoy that day.

At the palace entrance, the same little gray-faced man met her at the door, slightly grayer, slightly rounder.

"Mistress Genevieve." He bent his head. "So good to see you again. Right this way. The Empresses are expecting you."

He tottered into the castle, and Gen followed him over the polished floors toward the solarium. Chomp's nails clicked on the floor beside her, echoing in the silence. Without all the guests and servants rushing around for last-minute preparations, an eerie quiet hung in the halls, like the Hydra's swamp before the serpent rose.

The man spread open the atrium doors, and among the poisonous plants and vines stood Pollux.

"What are you doing here?" Her insides sparked. She hadn't seen Pollux since they'd left Lerna. He had led her to believe it would be a while before he could get away. With Castor missing and the gossip surrounding the Empresses' lottery, he would be needed by his family.

He held up a piece of paper with the royal seal, the four diamonds of the Oracles. "I was ordered to be here."

Gen laced her fingers through his. "Why?"

"I don't know."

That worried her. What if the Empresses thought he had helped her too much? What if they decided she didn't win?

He leaned down and kissed her forehead. "Don't worry. I'm sure it will be fine. You defeated the tasks. We can all count. You won this, Gen. They can't take that away."

Yes, six was more than four, but the Empresses had the power to change the numbers. They could make six less. They could do whatever they wanted. She couldn't count on having this won until she had her father in her hands.

The doors to the solarium opened again, and the gray attendant led in another guest, a sullen and glittering Lady Castor.

"Right in here, madam."

He closed the doors behind her, and Castor hung in the corner with her arms crossed, sparkling from head to toe. She wore a star-dust gown, worth the cost of at least three water silk gowns, and she looked beautiful, especially considering when they'd last seen her, she'd been covered in swamp.

"Cas." Pollux released Gen's hand and made for his sister. "Where have you been? We've been sweeping the seas to find you."

"Maybe I didn't want to be found." On her shoulder, a pale light bobbed up and down. A spirit. The way it hovered so close to her, it had to have been bound by a SpiritWatcher. No wonder Castor had been able to find the *Hind*. She'd had ghostly assistance.

"We need to talk," Pollux said to his sister.

"I don't want to talk. I'm only here because the Empresses summoned me, and as the future heiress of Tegea, I need to make sure we maintain our bonds with the Empire."

Pollux furrowed his brow. "Future heiress of Tegea . . . you're marrying Memnon?"

"The wedding is next month. I'll send you an invite." Her voice cracked on the words. She clearly didn't want to be marrying this person. Why was she? From what Gen knew of Lady Castor, she didn't do anything that didn't please her.

"You could at least send a message to Mother," Pollux said.

"Why? Has she convinced Father to forgive me? If my letter is penitent enough, will I be welcomed home?"

Pollux frowned. "I'm still working on Father. He'll come around."

"I'm sure he will. Tell him in the meantime, Memnon and I will be scheduling a meeting to discuss an increase in metal prices."

"Does everything have to be business with you?"

"Yes," she said simply, and tilted her head to the side to whisper something to her spirit.

Before the small light drifted from the room, it swept in front of Pollux's nose. He shook his head and mouthed, "Sorry," and the spirit flitted away. Gen would have to ask him about that later.

The tension curling in the air clung to Gen like a film. The game was over, but the pain it left behind would linger for ages. Gen felt sorry for Castor. She had been a victim as much as Gen, another pawn in the Empresses' game. She had only landed on the other side of it.

"Castor," Gen started, intending to apologize for nearly drowning her in manure when the gray man appeared on the dais and cleared his throat.

"If you'll please show your attention. Their Royal Highnesses are ready to see you." He reached for the dais doors, and they all turned to face the gilded throne. Gen's silver skin prickled in warning as it had the moments before she'd stepped into Hippolyta's secret den.

The two Empresses emerged through the curtain once more, dressed in another custom-made glittering gown, half red, half white, the only gown in here worth more than Castor's. In her hand, Red held a long chain. At the other end of it, a young man with pale blue hair kneeled at their feet. He reminded Gen of a younger and fitter Mr. Percy. This had to be his son.

"Mistress Genevieve." The Red Empress sat down and pointed for the man to sit beside her. He did, squatting like Chomp at Gen's feet. Gen's throat tightened. *She* had done this. She had sold him to them by defeating the Lion.

"Lord Pollux and Lady Castor," Crystal added demurely. "Thank you for joining us."

"Our pleasure," Pollux said while Castor picked at one of the crystals on her cape.

"Lord Pollux, it's been so long since we've had you in our company. But I don't see your violin. I hope you didn't stop playing."

"No, Your Majesties. I'm working on a new violin. My last one suffered some damage." His pale eyes flicked to Castor, the one who had damaged it.

"A shame," Red said, "but I'm sure you'll have it ready for your next performance at the Lion's Den." She dug her sharp nails into the throne.

Gen knew they must have been watching her, but they'd kept a closer eye on her than she could have guessed, sneaking spies all the way into the Lion's own rooms.

"Lovely suit," Crystal said to Gen. "Is that pure Hydra skin?"

"Yes." Gen tugged on the sleeve. "I bring you a prize from the creature as well." She reached into her bag and removed the belt of Hippolyta along with a custom-made knife carved from one of the Hydra's sharp fangs. Bribery never hurt.

She left the gifts at the foot of the dais and backed away, trying not to look at the young man on the chain.

"How did you manage to pry that from Hippolyta's waist?" Crystal ran a finger across her lips.

"You knew she was alive?" As soon as Gen asked the question, she realized how stupid it was. Of course they knew. She had underestimated them.

"There is little that happens on the islands that we don't know about," Red said, and twisted her long neck toward Castor. "We're delighted to see you looking so well. How is Master Memnon?"

"As delightful as always," Castor said through her teeth.

"Oh good. We're looking forward to the wedding."

"As am I," Castor said in a tone that suggested she would rather murder her fiancé than marry him.

"Isn't it funny how these things turn out?" Crystal said. "Days ago you left us two young women in need of something, and you return a bride-to-be and a Mazon warrior."

"That should be gift enough," Red said, and Gen's stomach twisted. No, no, they couldn't do this. Not after she gave them Percy's son and Thylox his horses.

"Now, now," Crystal said, "a promise is a promise. Let us declare our winner."

Gen closed her eyes and held her breath. It would all be worth it when she had her father. She had to remember that. This was the only way.

"Congratulations, Lady Castor," Crystal said.

The three words cut like knives into Gen's chest. "What? No! I completed six of the labors. The Lion, Livia Kine, the belt, the stables, the Mares, and the Hydra. It's six."

"It's true," Pollux said. "I was there."

"Well, then you know that Lady Castor had already cleaned a good portion of the stables by the time you arrived. So in part, that task belongs to her," Crystal said.

"She also destroyed much more of the Hydra," Red added. "Fifty-six heads to fourteen."

They were counting heads? "But there was the crab, and I killed the Hydra," Gen's words came out choked and garbled. "I took its life."

"I don't recall there being a crab on the list," Crystal said. "Do you?"

"No," Red said, "and with the delivery of the *Hind* by Lady

Castor, the future Storm Duchess is our winner. Congratulations."
She clapped her hand on the armrest, and Castor's lips spread into
a smile.

"I won," Castor said in a whisper. "I won," she said louder, and
her eyes sparkled with fire. "Arcadia is mine. You lose." She jabbed
Pollux in the chest. "I'll see you at home. Father and I have some
things to discuss." She spun around, striking Gen with the bottom
of her cape. "Thank you, Your Highnesses. Your wisdom and mag-
nanimity is boundless."

"We'll contact your father immediately with the news," Red said.

"Arcadia is blessed to have such a strong leader," Crystal added.

"You are making a mistake," Pollux said.

"No." Castor turned on him, teeth bared. "You made the mistake.
You chose her, and if you want to maintain your current position
with the StormMakers, I would suggest you think of the many ways
you will begin groveling. Farewell."

She swept from the room in a trail of sparkles. Gen clutched her
chest, trying to count the Hydra heads she had crushed, the amount
of manure she had cleared. She thought of her whale, who had died
for nothing, and the horses, trapped in Thylox's ship, screaming to
escape. Percy's son sitting next to the Empresses' throne like a pet
with a chain around his neck. They had all paid the price for nothing.

"Do you think we're cruel?" the Red Empress asked.

Yes, Gen wanted to spit at them. Yes. She wanted to scream it
a thousand times, but if this proved anything, things could always
get worse. The Empresses could make things worse.

"My father did not kill those Gargareans," she said instead.

"We always did like Alcmen," Crystal said. "We would like to
offer you a second chance for his freedom."

She raised her chin. "A second chance?"

"Don't," Pollux warned, rightfully. She had been a fool to take the first chance. She would be a bigger fool to do it again.

But what was her other option? Walk away empty-handed? Leave her father in prison?

"The rules will be much less complex this time," Crystal said. "You complete two final labors for us, you have your father."

It was never that simple. "What are the labors?"

"Oh, nothing too difficult." Red ran her finger across her lips. "We only want a couple of trinkets. The golden apples of Hesperides."

"And the Cerberus," Crystal added.

The blood drained from Gen's body. The Cerberus was the most coveted item in the Elysium Empire, leagues away, through foreign territory. Taking it would be a declaration of war. It would also win the war. The Cerberus was the Elysium Emperor's most-feared guardian, a monster with as many heads as the Hydra that could spit flames and burn down islands faster than lightning.

And that was the easier task because the golden apples were a legend. No one even knew where they were. They were part of Elysium lore.

"Why?" Gen asked. They had been at tentative peace with the Elysium Empire for centuries. Why did the Empresses want her to start a war? Why did they want apples that might not even exist?

"That is our business. Not yours. All we need to know is if you will do it or not."

"Don't do it, Gen," Pollux begged. "Please. We can find another way to get Alcmen."

"I don't think so," Crystal said. "The only way Alcmen leaves his cell is with our say."

"So what do you say, Mistress Genevieve?" Red inquired. "The apples and the Cerberus for your father. Otherwise, he stays in our prison, slowly losing his shimmer until he eventually withers and dies, always to be remembered as a murderer."

Gen flinched at the last part. She might be able to resurrect herself with these valiant acts, but she could never do enough to resurrect him. And as long as he was caged, she would be too.

"I want something from you first, a sign of good faith," she said.

Crystal leaned across her knee. "Ooh, this is interesting. The subject making demands. Please, go on. I'm curious."

Gen took a breath. "I want my father. I want him here. I want to see him before I go, and I want you to keep him here while I'm completing your tasks. You can hold him in the palace."

Red raised an eyebrow. "The Amazing Alcmen as part of our household? That could be entertaining."

"Not in chains either," Gen added.

Crystal smiled. "I think we can arrange that. Do we have a bargain then?"

Gen raised her chin and looked between the two venomous Empresses. This was the monster she truly had to defeat to win, and despite Pollux pleading with her to refuse them, she had to accept. Regardless of the number of heads Castor had charred, Gen was the Hydra-Slayer. She had defeated six nearly impossible tasks. She could do two more.

"I accept."

"Wonderful," Red said. "We'll have Gregor make the arrangements. You are more than welcome to stay in the palace until you start your journey."

"Thank you, Your Highnesses." Gen bowed her head and snapped her fingers to call Chomp to her side.

She spun on her heel and hurried from the solarium. She couldn't stand here another second. Chomp's nails clicked on the tiles beside her, and Pollux huffed behind her. They slipped through the doors, and as soon as they slammed closed, Pollux took her by the shoulders.

"What are you doing?" He looked as angry and terrified as he had when he'd dredged her out of Hippolyta's lair.

"I have to save him," she whispered.

"This won't save him. You will never find the apples. They don't exist. They're a children's story. You will spend your life searching for them, and your father will never be free."

"He'll be here. They promised."

"And this will be better than where he is? Did you see that man in chains?"

"Yes, I did." Gen twisted out of his grasp and marched out of the palace, past the Gargarean guards and onto the well-manicured grounds. She had done it again, agreed to the Empresses' ridiculous demands without thinking things through.

Pollux followed her into the grass.

"I've made a mistake, haven't I?" she asked him.

Pollux, who could never hold his anger for long, took a breath and loosened his shoulders. "No, not necessarily." He rubbed the faint scars on the underside of his chin. "We can all count to six, Gen. They changed the outcome of the lottery for a reason. They assigned you these last two labors for a reason."

"I think their reason is to toy with me."

"No, it's too calculated. They have a purpose in all of this, and if we can figure that out, we might not have to play their game."

"I don't expect you to help me, Pollux."

"Of course I'm going to help you. It's not like I have anything else to do. I have recently been relieved of my position on Arcadia." He slid his arm around her waist to the small of her back and pulled her close.

"That's right. I'm so sorry. None of this turned out the way we wanted." She ran her finger down the collar of his very fine silk jacket.

"Don't be. I was never fit to be Duke, and now I have more time to spend with you." He pressed his lips to her temple.

"What do we do about the Empresses?"

He ran a finger through her hair. "We consult an expert on extortion and plotting."

"Who?"

"My sister."

Gen coughed. "Castor? She hates us." And more importantly, Gen wasn't fond of her, either.

"She did hate us, right up until she was declared winner of the lottery. Cas is a very different person when she gets her way."

"I think I'd rather chase after the Cerberus."

He snorted. "We always have that as a backup plan."

Acknowledgments

My path to publication has been something like the road Frodo and Sam took to Mordor. I started writing seriously twelve years ago with the dream of one day seeing my book on shelves. It took much longer than I thought to reach that day, but here we are. With such a long journey, I never would have made it on my own. Thankfully I had my own fellowship to carry me through.

To start, I have to thank my Sam—my husband, Barry. Even though I had plenty of chances to turn back, you wouldn't let me. You were always there to share the load when I couldn't bear it alone. I couldn't ask for a better friend or partner. I also have to thank my agent, Valerie Noble. When I started to lose hope in finding a home for Gen and Castor, you never did.

To my editors, Mari Kesselring and Meg Gaertner, for being that home, and what a wonderful place for us to land. Thank you both for helping me bring out the best (and worst) in Castor and Gen to shape *Game of Strength and Storm* into the best possible version of itself. Your unwavering enthusiasm for this book is contagious, and I hope it continues to spread.

To my friend Jill Pierce, who has read most of my manuscripts throughout the years and always responds with a genuine "This is the best!" I really needed to hear that every time you said it. Thank you. To my cheerleading squad, John and Laura LaTour. You were the raft that kept me from drowning some days. I couldn't have stayed afloat without you.

To my early readers: Parker Goodreau, Rebecca Kenney, Aya Rothwell, Ivy Moser, Rachel Kenyon, Marie Ventura, Harlan Dechamps, and Lydia Weltmann. All of your notes, support, and feedback helped mold this story into something special. Thank you for your time, input, and friendship. I truly cherish it.

To Arleen York. It breaks my heart that you will not be able to see this book on the shelves at our local Barnes & Noble, and we won't get to talk about it over coffee. I hope you are looking down from above knowing how much you helped to inspire this and shape my language into something meaningful. I miss you.

To my mom and dad, thank you for gifting me with the tenacity and confidence to stick with my writing even when it didn't work out the first time, or the second, third, fourth, and so on. You taught me if I want something to keep at it until I get it, and I did.

To my sister Jenny Lee, thank you for your excitement over this book. You are one of my most vocal supporters, and it means a lot to me that you are so proud. To my sister Melissa, thank you for inspiring me with your own work. You pushed open a lot of closed doors, which made it much easier to follow behind you.

To the entire team at Flux, Emily, Meredith, Karli, Jake, S. Charlton at Beehive, and everyone else, thank you for pulling together to create such an amazing cover and getting the word out about *Game of Strength and Storm*. It really took a village to make this happen.

I also need to give a shout-out to the Twitter writing community: Vera, Alexis, Dennis, Kat, Katherine, Addy, Amanda, Rhian, Tova, Charlie . . . and ack! There are so many of you and I love you all. You definitely make it feel like there's a mob of us against the world, and it's so empowering to be part of that mob.

To my fellow #22Debuts: We all took different roads to be here but we made the last stage of the journey together. I hope we all continue to publish many more stories in the future. And finally, to you, the reader. A book is just a song unsung if no one is around to read it. So thank you for reading my words and listening to my song. I hope you enjoyed it as much as I enjoyed creating it.